PRAISE FOR THE WILD DARK

"An inventive, thoughtfully-constructed, chilling fantasy." - *Kirkus Reviews*

"A darkly imaginative world combines with a story of love beyond death to keep the pages turning." ~ Wendy N. Wagner, author of *The Deer Kings* and *An Oath of Dogs*

"The Wild Dark is a wild ride! Kat[herine] Silva has written a page turner with echoes of King and Barker. […] Curl up with this one on a cold autumn or winter night." ~ Morgan Sylvia, author of *Abode*

"THE WILD DARK kept me wandering the woods of Katherine's dark fantasy long into the night, relentlessly pursued by her soul-eating wolves. A perfect fall haunting!" ~ Cat Scully, author of *Jennifer Strange*

"… a page-turning apocalyptic thriller that kept me up way past by bedtime." ~ E.J, Fechenda, author of *End of the Road*

"Beautifully written, THE WILD DARK certainly lives up to its title." ~ John McIlveen, bestselling author of *Hannahwhere* and *A Variable Darkness*

"Katherine Silva perfectly blends police procedural thriller with dark and haunting horror and left me wanting more." ~ Janine Pipe, Splatterpunk Award nominated author of TWISTED: TAINTED TALES

The Wild Dark

Other Books by Katherine Silva

The Collection: A Novella

Night Time, Dotted Line

The Monstrum Chronicles

Vox: Book One

Aequitas: Book two

Memento Mori: Book Three

The Wild Oblivion

Orchards

THE WILD DARK

BOOK ONE OF THE WILD OBLIVION

BY
KATHERINE SILVA

Strange Wilds Press

Paperback ISBN-13: 978-0-578-95370-0
E-Book ISBN-13: 978-0-578-95371-7

This book is a work of fiction. Anything that bears resemblance to real people, places, or events is coincidental and unintentional.

Content warning: This book contains death, violence, physical abuse, substance abuse, cancer, suicide and needles.

Published by Strange Wilds Press

Kindle first edition: October 12th, 2021
Paperback first edition: October 12th, 2021

Cover photos by Clément M., Sasha Freemind, and Gauravdeep Singh Bansal courtesy of Unsplash

Cover design by Katherine Silva
www.katherinesilvaauthor.com

Life is a balance of holding on and letting go.

-Rumi

NE

Dreams cocooned me, wrapping me in their silky embrace like a thousand scarves. I didn't care if I never woke. In them, I wasn't guilty. I wasn't alone. All was as it should be. But something yanked me out before I was ready to leave.

I opened my eyes to the darkened room. Rain poured outside, its white noise a strange comfort outside my bedroom window. I pulled the thick wool blanket closer. The small room had put me on edge at first, before I knew where everything was. As the days passed, I recognized the outline of the chair next to the door, the trunk full of blankets at the end of the bed, the small flickers from the fire in the woodstove outside my bedroom door. This place had become more than a temporary retreat. I turned onto my side and looked out at the rain.

Why did I wake up?

A board creaked on the porch.

I stilled. It wasn't the old cabin making its usual sounds: the structure groaning in the wind, pipes rattling, treads loosening on the stairs out front… This was something heavy walking across the floor of my front porch toward my door.

No one lived within several miles of this camp. I was in the middle of the woods.

I slipped my legs out from under the covers; goosebumps instantly growing on my skin. Quietly reaching behind the side table, I curled my fingers around the baseball bat there. An inch of safety nudged me as I tiptoed to the window and peered out. The bushes blocked most of my view and the downpour made it hard to make out any shapes in the night.

It could be anything, I told myself as I slid my sweat pants from the top of the chest and pulled them on. I crept toward the main living area. Another window looked out on the deck next to the front door. I steeled myself as I looked out.

The deck was cloaked in shadows. To my left was an upright shape: a person walking in an ungainly way. They shifted back and forth as though they couldn't get their balance.

Must be some drunk hunter looking for a place to sleep it off, I thought. I kept a firm hold on the baseball bat and moved to the front door. The memory of my days as a cop rushed back to me like an old friend. It had been months since I'd carried a badge. But more than anything, I wanted to see the look on the guy's face when I ripped open the door and shouted for him to get down on the ground with his hands behind his back. He'd probably pee his pants. He'd probably stumble off the deck and run back into the rain from wherever he'd come from. Then, I could get some sleep.

The creaks stopped in front of the door. I braced myself, my hand on the doorknob. As I readied myself to jerk open the door, cowardice got the better of me.

"Who's there?" I called.

There was no answer. Not even the sound of another footstep.

"Hello? Do you need help? Are you lost?"

Nothing.

The rain was pretty loud. Maybe they hadn't heard me.

I turned the knob. Drowned by the deluge and wind, a faint voice blended with the static ambient.

"Liz."

My name. They'd said my name. As quickly as I could manage, I jerked the door open and swung my bat up. "Who the hell is—"

My voice echoed into the empty night. I frowned and stepped out onto the deck, looking from left to right. There was nobody. I stopped at the end of the deck, staring into the bushes. Water splashed against my bare toes as I tried to find some shape hiding within. I couldn't have been hearing things. There had been a shape out here. The creaking was loud. I checked the other side of the deck. No one. There weren't even any wet shoe prints on the wood.

A twig snapped in the trees. I trained my sights on them, squinting through the deluge and the dark. Something stood there, staring straight at me. The eyes were golden, barely catching the licks of the firelight from within the house. A low growl rose up. I took a step back, a board squealing under me. I glanced down for only a moment. The brush rustled as something dashed off into the thicket.

I backed into the cabin and locked the door behind me. The crackle of the woodstove seemed loud in the quiet space. I added another log to the fire, and stirred the embers with my poker. I wasn't going crazy. Someone had been here: a human someone.

Grabbing a fleece blanket from the chest in the other room, I curled up in the chair in front of the fire and stared through the glass window into the stove at the flames. I listened for anything out of the ordinary.

I had to have imagined it all.

I waited for sleep to take me but I was too wired, the voice on playback in my mind. I forced my eyes to close and lay my head against the soft upholstery. The sounds of the rain merged with the crackling of the fire, washing in and out of my ears. The heat warmed my chilled skin and the blanket suddenly became a netherworld of comfort.

Even in sleep, that voice called to me from the darkness. I knew that voice. It knew me, too. No amount of sleep could change the impossibility of that voice's owner being here now.

He was gone.

He was dead and gone.

THEN

"I'm calling it: we're heading back, Liz!"

My partner's voice echoed through the trees. If I squinted, I could make out the beam of his flashlight and the outline of his body.

I trudged toward him, my boots snapping on twigs and squelching in the mud. My rain poncho was sopping inside, and the cold had penetrated me to my core. The storm was still hours from being over.

"Liz!"

"No!" I broke into a clearing.

Brody Aritza emerged seconds later from the opposite side, a soaked black rain jacket covering his shoulders, his slacks splashed with mud above his boots. His always dark and searching eyes were on fire. "What do you mean, 'no'? The next team is here. It's time for us to pack up and go home."

I took a couple steps away from him. "We should check down by the river again."

"What?" he shouted. The pounding of the rain nearly drowned out his voice.

I turned back. "The river!"

"Lennox's guys cleared the river; you know that."

"There's always a chance they missed something."

"Liz."

I headed back in the direction I'd come from. "We need to check again."

Brody ran after me, boots splashing and sucking in the wet earth. "They've been thorough. It's a missing girl and they know the risks. The next team will check again. We've been out here for over eighteen hours."

A balloon of defeat rose in my chest. I slowed to a stop. "She's only eight. She couldn't have made it too far."

"They'll do their best to find her, but I'm beat and I can tell you are, too."

"I'm okay."

He scoffed. "You've got circles the size of Frisbees under your eyes." I heard a wet slap behind me and turned to the sight of Brody on his knees in the mud. I stepped back and helped him up.

"Fuckin' hell…" He wiped his hands on his pants. "It's Thanksgiving. Go home and eat some turkey."

I stared off in the direction of the river. I could almost imagine it through the trees: a churning mass of black water and the stone bridge that crossed it. Little Chloe Clark could be crouched with one of her Barbie dolls, pretending they were hunting lost treasure.

"Her imagination gets away with her," her mother had said as she feebly held a glass of water and took small sips. "She wanders sometimes. A couple days ago, she said she saw big dogs in the woods. She went looking for them, I'm sure of it."

We didn't have wolves in mid-coast Maine and no one in the Mottershill area owned big dogs. It could have been a black bear…but there was no evidence of one having been near the Clark residence. No paw prints, no scat, no scraped trees or carcasses.

"Hey." Brody came around in front of me. "Did you hear me?"

I sighed. "She has to be out here somewhere."

His eyes softened. "It's two o'clock in the morning. The next team has hotter coffee and fresher eyes than we do. They'll find her." He put his hand around my shoulder and turned me back around. We walked through the woods, slopping through puddles, climbing gnarled roots and slippery hillsides until we reached Brody's black Dodge Charger. Stripping our rain shells and blasting the heat, we drove back to the station.

The city of Flintland was cloaked in wooly blackness. The frosted glows of streetlamps were our only guide along the roads. Each avenue of darkness was spotted with signs of New England architecture. Main Street was lined with brick-and-mortar businesses in Georgian buildings, River Road with old-world white saltboxes, Flintland Greens with crisp Federal stone rows, and the occasional Victorians, all punctuated by silent sidewalks. The sound of rain and Brody humming Neil Young's "Harvest Moon" made me feel like I was inside a warm dream.

We stopped at the only twenty-four-hour convenience store in Flintland for coffee and day-old breakfast pastries. I hadn't realized how hungry I was with the adrenaline fueling my every move. I practically devoured my stale apple turnover before we left the lot.

"I didn't even buy a turkey," I said, wiping the crumbs from my blazer. They stuck to the wet fabric regardless.

Brody frowned. "Seriously?" He opened the glove box in front of me. A wad of napkins rested inside.

I grabbed one and dabbed at my blazer. "I was going to get Chinese."

Brody scoffed. "What are you: nineteen?"

"Last time I tried to cook a turkey, I turned it into jerky." Josh had insisted on cooking the turkey since then.

"Fine, then. You're coming to our house." He popped the rest of his blueberry doughnut in his mouth.

I glanced at him. "You've got family coming in. I don't want to mess up your plans."

Brody rolled his eyes. "It's Carmen's mom and her sister, Carey: the annoying one. I told you about her, right?"

"Yeah: she has a new boyfriend every six months."

"Besides, I'm pretty sure Carmen bought a turkey the size of a water buffalo. Probably won't even fit in the oven."

"All right, all right. You've made your point."

Back at the station, we changed into a couple of too large cotton shirts left over from when the station sponsored a fourth of July community marathon. As I stuffed all of my wet garments into a gym bag and left the locker room, Brody approached from his desk, his own bag slung on his shoulder. "They're gonna find her, Liz."

I locked eyes. "I wish I was back out there."

He blinked slowly and walked by me, resting a hand on my shoulder. "Go home," he repeated. "You've got to spend some time there eventually."

The door squeaked shut behind me.

After a sleepless couple of hours and a breakfast of peanut granola, I found myself at Brody's house, an aged Georgian Colonial in the Upper Vale neighborhood on the north side of Flintland.

"You missed the dog show," Carmen called from the kitchen. She was peeling potatoes. Occasionally, I'd hear the thump of one as it was placed aside.

"Who won?" I asked from the living room sofa, taking a sip of my wine. It was only noon but Thanksgiving was always one of those holidays where I believed day-drinking was half the point. I was hypnotized by the swirling of flames in the fireplace. Exhaustion tugged at me, its claws sinking deeper.

Before Carmen could answer, Brody stuck his head out from the bathroom, fiddling with his tie. "Lemme guess? It was that damn poodle again, wasn't it?"

"They *are* one of the smartest dogs, you know," Carmen said, coming to the kitchen door. Carmen was Brody's fire-cracker, a brilliant spark of energy that lit up his life and kept him going through the thickest and darkest of our cases together. She was always ready with hot coffee, a listening ear, and a warm embrace.

Nearly ten years Brody's junior, Carmen had wavy dark hair that flowed down over the shoulders of her white sleeveless top. Her newly painted nails glimmered under the firelight, matching her deep maroon lipstick. Carmen was the kind of woman who always knew the right amount of makeup to wear no matter the occasion. I don't think I'd worn mascara since college, and it had been even longer since I'd worn lipstick.

The first time we met, I'd been invited over to their house for lunch. Carmen had asked me my drink of choice and when I'd responded with a whisky and soda, she'd smirked and poured all of us a round. "Finally." She turned to Brody. "Now I have someone reliable to keep an eye on you."

I knew then that Carmen wasn't just Brody's wife. She was his equal in every sense of the word.

Brody shook his head from the bathroom. "Why do they make them get those stupid haircuts anyway?" he commented.

Carmen laughed. "Actually, the poodle didn't win."

"What?" Brody let go of his tie and all of the knot work unraveled. "Are you telling me the one year I don't get to watch, one of the others wins? Which one?"

The front door opened.

Carmen shrugged. "That Mexican dog. The one with the really long name that no one can say."

"The Xoloitzcuintle?" Josh exclaimed from the door, as he

hefted a carrier full of chopped wood toward the bin by the fireplace. It collapsed inside with a thunderous boom.

Brody stared at him and chuckled. "Of course, the globetrotter would know it."

I smiled as Josh returned to the entryway to brush off his brown wool coat by the doormat. Wood chips, bark, and lichen tinkled down onto the rubber. He joined me on the couch. I breathed in the aroma of pine that clung to his clothes and sandalwood from his shampoo. "He only knows it because he wants one," I said.

When I'd driven home hours ago in the dark early morning, I'd expected an empty house to greet me, a hot shower, and a cold bed. Josh's black Land Rover was in the driveway and inside, I'd found his six-foot frame wrapped in flannel blankets, passed out on the couch. His bags were left scattered nearby.

Josh wasn't supposed to be home for another week. He'd told me before he'd left on assignment. But Thanksgiving wasn't another holiday to us. It was the first holiday we had spent together as a couple, the holiday where I told my mother I never wanted to see her again and he'd held me for an hour while I cried. It was the holiday where he took me out to his parent's lake house on Erie and I remembered the warmth of a connected family. It was the holiday that we made five different kinds of pie for last year and danced to Feist and Hozier for hours.

He came home because Thanksgiving was important for us to spend together.

The frostbitten depression at not finding Chloe Clark in the forest slid to the back of my mind. I'd kicked on the heat, ran a hand through his hair to wake him, and took him up to bed with me.

"Damn right, I want a dog." Josh smiled. "Someday, I'll convince you."

I laughed. "And I'll take care of it while you're off gallivanting in Argentina or Russia."

"You don't really "gallivant" in Argentina. You tango." Josh put an arm around my shoulders. I closed my eyes and relaxed into his embrace. He swayed me softly side to side. "And in Russia, any form of enjoyment besides drinking is strictly prohibited."

"Good thing we're not in Russia," I said.

"Get a room, you two," Brody murmured through a smile as he joined his wife in the kitchen.

"Josh, you'll have to tell us all about your latest trip," Carmen said from around the corner. *Plonk*. Another potato dropped into the pot. "Where were you photographing this time?"

"Swimming with sharks again?" Brody asked.

We got up from the couch and walked to the kitchen. Josh leaned on the wall next to the hot water radiator while I poured him some cabernet.

"Scuba-diving in Belize's Barrier Reef," Josh answered. "This was for Earth Exploits Magazine. Five days in Dangriga riding back and forth out to the reef, a couple days in Billy Barquedier National Park reserve taking photos of the waterfall, and finished up the trip with a little stand-up paddle-boarding on the coast. All in all, pretty routine."

Carmen clicked her tongue. "Looks like you burned. Poor, poor thing."

Josh had a red stripe caressing his upper cheeks and the bridge of his nose. Unbeknownst to our hosts, his chest and back were the worst, cherry colored and hot to the touch.

"I'll take it," he said. "Coming back here was like returning to Ice Station Zebra."

"But damn it if you don't look good in that flannel shirt." I leaned over and kissed his cheek. The prickles of his stubble poked against my lips. I tried not to cringe when I pulled away, but he laughed regardless.

"Come on, you know this is the stage before a sprawling mountain man beard." He brushed his fingers over his jaw.

I sipped my wine. "I'm not used to you with a beard."

He put a hand to his heart. "How else will I survive the wintery climes of the North East?"

"I agree with Liz; I've never been much for kissing men with beards." Carmen gave Brody a sidelong glance. "Not that this one would ever grow out a beard."

Brody frowned. "Not a good look for me." He opened the oven door to peek at the turkey. The scent made my mouth water.

"No?" Josh said. "I think you should grow it all out or maybe do a soul patch… It would make you look…"

"Like a Puerto Rican Howie Mandel?" Brody prompted.

I nearly choked on my wine, while Josh giggled to himself like a nine-year-old.

"Give yourself some credit," I said. "You've got more hair than Howie."

"Fine. Frank Zappa, then."

"Don't you think you're a little short to be comparing yourself to ole Frank?" Josh said after he'd caught his breath.

Brody, who'd picked up a knife to cut carrots, wagged it at him.

"Excuse me if I didn't eat steroids for breakfast when I was a kid like you did."

Josh shrugged. "They tasted good in the Lucky Charms."

Another knock at the door brought Carmen's mom and sister, who brought along an unexpected and uninvited surprise boyfriend. Needless to say, Carmen kept her annoyance well-disguised while Brody's squeaked out every now and again with a sarcastic comment.

Dinner was an impressive array of indulgences: an oven-roasted turkey rubbed with thyme and topped with slices of pear, velvety mashed potatoes, garlic green beans, a belly-warming butternut squash apple soup, a carrot and beet salad mixed with oranges, and fluffy biscuits slathered with butter.

After our meal with over-full stomachs, everyone retired to the living room to sip coffee and listen as Josh regaled them with stories of his latest photography adventures. I stepped outside onto the deck in hopes that the fresh air would help me digest better. The view from Carmen and Brody's house looked down across yellow fields toward the forest. Mist seemed to rise out of the trees like smoke.

Brody's words from earlier were an unwanted weight on my mind. I'd been out too long in the wet and cold. There was a feeling like cotton was stuffed in my ears and nose. In spite of that, I'd been alive there. Being safe and secure in my friend's home while that little girl was lost only made me more uneasy.

I took a sip of my wine, hoping my sinuses would clear. They didn't. I was going to get *so* sick.

"Hey," Brody appeared behind me holding a cup of coffee. He offered it to me. "Kind of nippy out here, huh."

I shook my head and held up the glass of wine. "Needed the fresh air."

After a moment, he added, "Things seem better between you and Josh."

I stared at Josh who pretended to paddle a SUP board using his beer bottle as a prop. Everyone laughed around him. "The distance makes it hard sometimes."

"The distance sums up his career."

"I know." I twisted the engagement ring on my finger.

Brody's eyes dropped on it. "Look at me, Liz."

I did.

"This job's been there when you've needed it. When you guys tie the knot, it'll still be there."

"I know what you're going to say: I should take a break." As if on cue, I sneezed.

"Yeah, well, something tells me you'll be taking one sooner rather than later." He chuckled.

I smiled but it faded within seconds. "It's not that the job won't still be there. It's that…I'm worried my priorities will change and I won't know what to do with myself."

He took a gulp of his coffee. "Pre-wedding jitters are something everyone can identify with. Take it from me."

"You two turned out well." I glanced at Carmen, whose cheeks were red from laughing so hard.

"We have our fights. It's not perfect; no marriage is." He put a hand on my shoulder. "You're going to be fine. Understand?"

"And you're not saying that to make me feel better, right?"

"If I wanted to bullshit you, you'd know the moment the words left my mouth."

I pursed my lips. "You *are* pretty obvious when you lie." Then, I sneezed again.

He held his coffee out for me. "Here, take the rest of mine and come inside. You're going to give yourself pneumonia if you stay out here any longer."

"But that'll give me the oh-so-needed break from work," I answered, reaching out to take his coffee. The mug fumbled out of Brody's grip. Both of us bent down to catch it at the same time.

Two

My head was like a pound of feathers when I woke the next morning; scattered and heavy. I'd slept in the chair by the fire, my neck cricked in an awkward position. I stretched, filled the kettle with water, and put it on the woodstove. The fire had gone out completely. My breath puffed in the chilly air of the cabin. *Lucky the pipes didn't freeze*, I thought as I rebuilt the fire. Once the satisfying snaps and pops started and red glow built, I returned my attention to breakfast.

I tried not to think about last night's disturbance, instead choosing to distract myself with what needed to get packed up and sorted for my trip home. I'd been out in the New Hampshire wilderness over a month. I wanted to stay longer. The changing season, however, was going to drive me out. The cabin wasn't winter-proof. If I stayed any longer, I was liable to get snowed in and as much as I liked the isolation, freezing to death wasn't how I wanted to die. I had to go home. I had to figure out what the hell I was going to do with my life now.

Last night's visitor crept into my thoughts regardless of how busy I made myself. It wasn't Brody. It *couldn't* be him. I must have imagined his voice in my head because I wanted him here, that's all. Maybe it was just my nightmares.

Memories of my life before had haunted my sleep for a year now. As real as the taste of wine on my tongue or the warmth of a hand on my cheek, I was back in time again. I was back in those places where Brody and I were together. Sometimes they were unaltered, like last night, and the nostalgia of certain memories was enough to carve me open.

The high-pitched whistle of the kettle broke me from my thoughts. I poured the water into my prepared French press and inhaled the potent steam as the coffee steeped. I brought it out onto the front porch along with a cup and sat in one of the large wicker chairs. The rain had stopped and there was an unsettling silence. A thin mist clung to the bare birch branches and evergreen needles. The sun warmed the haze and burned everything in gold. I poured and sipped my coffee.

I'd loved to adventure outdoors as a kid. I'd imagined there were wild woods for me to conquer and undiscovered kingdoms to be claimed. As I grew older, the world outside grew less entrancing and more sinister. I couldn't relax in the woods. There was always something I had to watch out for. Nothing needed discovering anymore; it was about protecting others from it. I had to make sure the dark corners didn't grow larger or blacker.

The only reason I came out here after everything was because I was tired of thinking of the woods that way. I was tired of focusing on the shadows and never the light. It had been a long time since I'd gone for a therapeutic run in Flintland's many park trails or had relaxed at the campground near Lake Storm. After spending a whole month out here, I thought this place was different. Last night had brought back the anxiety full force.

Tires crunched through dirt. I recoiled at the sound and coffee spilled onto my pant leg. I hissed and practically slammed the mug down on the coffee table.

A green Jeep emerged from the trees. I noted the lights on top and the forest ranger decal on the side. It parked next to my grey sedan and out stepped a man in a dark brown coat and green pants. A beige cap hid his short dark hair. He walked to the porch stairs and stopped there, looking up at me. The sun cast eerie shadows against the side of his face. "Good morning, ma'am," he said with a slight drawl in his voice.

I wiped at the wet spot on my jeans with the cuff of my sleeve. "Morning."

"My name is Ranger Feld. I work with the New Hampshire Forest Protection Bureau."

"Yeah, your Jeep gave you away," I said. "Can I help you with something?"

Feld cleared his throat, and rubbed the back of his head. "We're assisting the Cardend Police Department with a missing person's report. I wondered if I could have a few moments of your time to ask you some questions."

A series of memories blindsided me: trudging through wet leaves and softened earth in the cold, flashlights wagging back and forth in thick fog. Brody and I huddled over a map with thermoses of coffee, steam pouring into the cold air.

"That is, unless I've caught you at a bad time?"

I blinked. Feld was staring at me. "Ask away," I said.

Feld climbed the stairs and handed me a flyer. "You haven't seen this guy around, have you?"

I took the sheet but I stared right through it. I was struck by the sound of the ranger's boots on my deck. It was the same sound from last night. I was positive I wasn't imagining it.

Ranger Feld stared at me patiently, so I forced myself to focus on the photo. The man pictured had white hair, a long thin face, many lines in his forehead, and an elastic smile. Large glasses framed his studious eyes. He seemed happy and yet discerning. He reminded me of what my dad could have looked like if he'd lived past my tenth birthday. I'd seen him a million times and never since.

I handed the paper back. "No. I haven't."

Feld took the flyer awkwardly. He had several of them in his hands. He hadn't expected me to return it.

I picked up my coffee cup, the ceramic in my fingers tethering me to the present. "Who is he? Where did he go missing?"

"Local guy, Gerald Castle. He owns a cabin not too far from yours. He was closing it up for the winter. Usually, he comes at the end of October to do it, but he got waylaid. His wife called the police when she couldn't get ahold of him." Feld leaned against the railing opposite me. "I'm surprised *you're* still out here this late."

I took a large gulp of coffee. "I'm heading home tomorrow."

"Where is home?"

"Maine."

"Portland? I have a cousin there."

"No." I looked away at the trees. "Flintland."

Flintland didn't have as glittery a reputation as Portland. The town of around fifty thousand citizens was between Portland and the mid-coast, large enough to have a cornucopia of issues like an opioid crisis, a blooming homeless community, and a growing crime rate.

Feld cleared his throat. "I guess you wouldn't get much relief from this cold weather if you went home anyway."

"I'd miss the quiet."

The sunlight dimmed behind some clouds and a cold breeze rushed over us. Feld shoved one hand in his pocket and his shoulders scrunched up toward his neck. I thought about offering him coffee but that meant he'd stay longer.

"I'm sorry I wasted your time." He turned away. "Have a nice day."

"I..." I'd let the word slip out even though I hadn't meant for it to. Damn it all.

Feld stopped and looked at me expectedly.

"I think someone was walking around on my porch early this morning. There was a silhouette that looked like a person. I asked for them to identify themselves and they never answered."

I'd left out an important detail: they'd said my name.

Feld frowned. "But you didn't know who it was?"

"By the time I opened the door, there was no one there."

"You're sure it was a person and not an animal?"

I frowned. *So, now you don't believe me?* "I told you I saw a silhouette."

"We do have a lot of bears around here. They stand pretty tall and probably could have looked human-like in the rain last night."

"Walking around on its hind legs?"

He cleared his throat. "Some do that."

I leaned forward in my seat. "Do you actually want to find this Castle guy or not? I'm confused."

Feld put up his hands. "I'm only trying to eliminate the possibility that it wasn't him. If you called out to him, why didn't he answer? Why would he come to your cabin door and then leave in the middle of the night?"

"I don't know." I was starting to wish I hadn't said anything. Worst of all, I already doubted my own senses. The late hour, the darkness, the rain…and I'd dreamed of things that made my skin cold.

A blue jay squawked somewhere far off. I sat up a little straighter in my chair, my fingers clutching the coffee cup harder.

"Listen, I'm not trying to alarm you," Feld said, taking a step toward me. "People come out here to get away. They come for the peace and quiet and forget there are plenty of things out here that go bump in the night. We have bears, coyotes, moose, fisher cats… They make weird noises; they can spook people."

I tried to ignore the heat rising in my face. "I understand that."

"I was…." He trailed off and stood in front of me for a moment as if he wasn't sure what to say. "If it *was* someone else, do you have someone you can call or…."

"I keep a baseball bat in the bedroom."

His eyes widened. "That's not exactly what I meant."

"I'm ten miles from the nearest road and nearly thirty miles from town. By the time anyone got here to help, it would be too late." A twitch in my shoulder gave me pause. "I've seen it."

He shifted his feet back and forth and squinted at me. "When you say that, what do you mean?"

The familiar ache in my shoulder radiated further up. It took everything I had not to put my hand on it. "I'm former Flintland PD."

"But not anymore?"

So stiff, it was frozen. I massaged my shoulder. "Is there anything else I can help you with, Ranger Feld?"

He shook his head slowly before putting one of the flyers on the table, weighing it down with my French press. "If Castle shows up here, call the number at the bottom of the sheet." He tipped his hat. "Thanks for your time." He clomped down the deck and shuffled through the dry leaves to his car.

I went inside, not wanting to watch him leave. I found myself at the window regardless. The taillights of Feld's Jeep vanished around a bend in the road.

Silence surrounded me in full. The brief interaction with Feld had left me angry and a smaller part of me hungered for more. It had been over a week since I'd gone down into town below for supplies, nearly a month since I'd spoken to my family or anyone back home. My sister had promised she wouldn't call. Dana knew I needed the time to myself, even if she'd thought I shouldn't be alone.

"You call me if anything happens," she'd said, over the phone, before I'd left. I assured her I would promptly and hung up.

At the department, others stared at me when I'd turned in my badge and gun: a pitying stare that I'd come to loathe. While they didn't ask straight out why I was leaving, they all knew. Maybe it was worse that it had gone unsaid by the rest of the force. Probably because they knew it was better for me to leave than keep withering in place.

The mist never lifted as the day progressed. It rained again around noon, the storm resuming last night's fury in little than a half an hour. I spent much of the day packing up my belongings, draining water from the camp's pipes, and trying to finish up reading a book my sister had recommended a long time ago. It was a Gothic romance, or at least, that's how Dana had described it. It was full of pain and sickness and night and it made my stomach twist and turn as I tried to focus on the words. I slapped the book shut, still several chapters from the end and stuffed it into my packed suitcase at the end of the bed.

I needed to get gas in town and a few other essentials for the trip back home. I didn't want to have to stop tomorrow and be tempted by the promise of remaining in town where no one knew about my past — no one but Ranger Feld anyway. I wouldn't have been surprised if he'd tried to look me up the minute he got back to a computer. Not that it mattered anyway; I was never going to run into him again.

I snatched my keys from the hook by the door, locked the cabin, and climbed into my car. Flipping on my wipers, I drove down the pot-hole riddled dirt driveway toward the main road. The path slinked through the woods, down steep hills, switch-backing until the reflective paint brightened the highway ahead.

The mountains rose around me like chopped waves in a sea of trees. I could easily be lost in them, knowing that miles and miles of wilderness and its cracks and crevices separated me from the doldrums of my every day routines. This place had yawned open, allowing me inside its dark mouth to escape all else. I was grateful —and terrified. What Feld had said stuck with me the entire ride down into town. It *was* dangerous out here and someone as desperate for refuge as I was could easily mistake isolation for tranquility. That was why I needed to leave.

I passed the rain-soaked forests and the turbulent rivers along the roadside as I drove further down into town. Buildings slowly appeared until I finally reached an intersection with a gas station directly across the road. I rolled in, pumped my gas beneath the cover of the forecourt, and went inside to grab some road snacks. The halogen lights blinded me as I scoured for things to take with me the next day. *Pringles for the win,* I decided grabbing a couple cans. Snagging a bottle of water from a fridge, I went to the coffee station. I was craving another cup and I'd used the last of my grounds that morning. Coffee dribbled into my paper cup as I glanced around the convenience store.

The teller was a wiry college-age kid with blue hair and several tattoos showing beneath his black uniform. A couple of girls his age poked through snacks in the aisle two rows behind me, their dialogue a plethora of "Oh my god" and "Shut up".

The bell dinged on the door as a hunter in a heavy wool coat and blaze orange hat walked in and went to the counter, paying for some cigarettes. He'd left his chipped light blue truck running near the door. A dead deer glared at me from the pickup bed, a pair of small antlers meekly jutting from its head.

I pulled the full cup away from the machine and fitted the plastic lid over it, my thoughts still in another place.

Deer used to frequent Josh's camp near Storm Lake in Northern Maine. I remembered sitting on the porch with him in the early morning, watching them tentatively edge out of the trees.

I hadn't told Josh I was leaving. We barely spoke anymore anyway.

"You hear anything about that missing guy?" the kid behind the counter said to the hunter with the cigarettes.

"They're still looking. But word is they found his car this morning up on the notch road." the man answered, dropping a crinkled ten-dollar bill on the counter.

I looked up. That's near where I was staying.

"They did?"

"Yup. Driver's side door torn off. Had to have been a bear. The idiot probably left food in his car."

The kid nodded and handed him his change. "Did they find anything else?"

"Yeah." The man scooped the coins into his hand. "Blood."

I turned to bring the coffee, the water and snacks to the counter. I didn't want to listen anymore and I had errands to run. I wanted to get back to the cabin before nightfall. I walked up the aisle and wondered what time I should head out in the morning. When I looked out the big windows to the gas pumps, I froze.

There was a man standing next to my car. I couldn't make out his face but the posture, the outline I recognized. The coffee cup slipped out of my hand and splattered at my feet.

"Uh oh," one of the girls said nearby. They laughed.

I grabbed some napkins from behind me and dropped them onto the spilt coffee. As they bled through, my gaze wandered back to my car. The man was gone.

"I'll get it," the clerk mumbled from behind the counter. He shuffled to the maintenance closet to collect a bucket and mop. The irritation in his voice wasn't hard to miss. The hunter stared at me as if I'd grown an extra arm.

I tossed the napkins and the empty coffee cup in the trash. "I'm sorry." I moved to grab another paper cup but whispering behind me made me turn.

The girls murmured to one another, their eyes shifting to me every now and again. I stared at them until they finally turned and left without buying anything. I watched them climb into their Mini Cooper from the safety of the store, waiting for the silhouette to appear. They pulled out, and left. No one else appeared. No other shapes were suddenly visible in the parking lot.

The clerk plunked the bucket down on the tile and with a squish, the mop hit the floor. My thoughts turned fleetingly toward getting another cup of coffee, but I didn't want to break my eye contact from the window, just in case....

"Hey," the attendant said. "You're standing in it."

That broke my gaze. I stepped back and let him sweep the mop over the place I'd been standing.

"I thought someone was standing by my car," I said by way of explanation. I owed him at least that.

He craned his head to stare out the window. "There's no one out there now."

"It was only for a second. But I could have sworn…"

"Did you want another coffee?" he asked, one of his eyebrows suspiciously perked.

I shook my head.

At the counter, he rang me out with an irritated frown on his face.

The hunter stood nearby, flipping through a magazine. His eyes bored holes into the back of my head.

The attendant tore my receipt from a long stream of paper, and handed it to me. "Have a nice afternoon."

I snatched my bag of food from the counter and pushed out the glass doors into the parking lot. I was sure the hunter and the attendant were already hypothesizing which mental hospital I'd escaped from. I made my way toward my car, listening for any noises out of the ordinary. The rain was coming down hard now and traffic on the road nearby made it hard to differentiate any strange noises apart from it. I reached my car under the cover of the forecourt and set everything down on the hood. I circled the vehicle, peering in at the backseat; no one inside. I crouched down onto the cement and peered under the car. Again, there was nothing.

I got in and locked the doors, an inch of safety calming me. It was nearly three. I'd slept only a few hours last night and the pouring rain only made my eyelids heavier. *It's your imagination,* I thought. A sudden yawn reinforced the idea more. *You're still obsessing over last year.*

I pulled out of the gas station, confident I wouldn't be visiting that particular one again, and drove down the road further into town.

THREE

THEN

My shift ended as the purple in the sky was beginning to blacken. Brody and I had finished up the day filing paperwork on a perp we'd arrested the day before for breaking and entering. While he was desperate to get home if only to immediately crash on his own couch, I'd made plans to get a drink with Josh that evening at Rainey's.

It was not necessarily the place I'd expected my fiancé to pick. While Rainey's was a favorite of mine and Brody's merely because of its reputation as a cop bar, Josh had more of an affinity for See No Evil, a bar in Olympia Junction that served a wider array of craft beers and had a darker, more intimate atmosphere. Rainey's was often loud, packed, and was three blocks from the station and across from Flintland Greens, well away from our home on the common.

Christmas lights speckled in the darkness, twisted around the ornate metal lamp posts that ran down the main drag and zigzagged overhead between the buildings. A fresh coat of snow had fallen earlier that dusted awnings and gave the city that quintessential holiday touch we'd all been anticipating. Each winter had seemed warmer than the last and while it wasn't uncommon for Maine to get snow as early as the end of October, we hadn't seen hide or hair of it until then: the last day in November.

I parallel parked behind a van with one too many political stickers and climbed out into the blustery evening. People wandered the sidewalks, winter coats pulled close, the general murmur like a hum beneath the wind's musical gusts. As I approached the bar, the door opened in front of me and Josh came through, staring down at his phone. When he looked up, his eyes rounded. "Hey!"

"Did you come out looking for me?" I gave him a small hug and a quick kiss.

"Actually, no." I couldn't tell if it was from the cold or not, but I noticed his cheeks redden a little. "I missed a call. Couldn't take it inside with all the noise. Why don't you head on in and order? I'll be right in."

"Large nachos? Narragansett?"

"Yes, please!" His attention was already focused on redialing the number.

I opened the heavy wooden door, embellished with Celtic knots into Rainey's. A long, polished bar ran down the left side of the room, the glass shelves behind it lined with every kind of Irish whisky one could dream of. A stained and tattered green carpet stretched between the bar and four black vinyl-seated booths. All the seats at the bar were taken, occupants watching a tied college football game, but one of the booths stood empty and I recognized Josh's coat tossed across one of the seats.

Joan Rainey, the owner's daughter, was running orders that night and was quick to take mine (a Sazerac and onion rings) along with Josh's. I pulled my hair out of its ponytail and shook it out, the tell-tale bump from having it up all day remaining. I examined the split ends. I couldn't remember the last time I'd cut it. It was getting long again, past my shoulders. I'd probably hack it off myself when I got frustrated…and then Carmen would fix it because that was her calling.

Brody's wife always joked about wanting to become a hairstylist, but she'd said her mother would have disowned her on the spot. Carmen's mother had emigrated to the United States from Brazil and had warned both Carmen and her sister that if they didn't take every advantage, they could get out of their new life, she'd go to her grave in complete anguish. Carmen served on Flintland's city planning board, but I knew she sometimes longed for a less stressful trade, perhaps one where the worst thing that could happen was giving someone a bad haircut.

Joan delivered my Sazerac and I took a drink before realizing Josh still wasn't back from his phone call. As the dry whiskey coated my throat, I looked back over my shoulder to the entrance where Josh paced back and forth between the two big windows, still on the phone. At least he was smiling. Maybe it was his best friend, Dan, calling about plans for the bachelor party. Or his mother, wondering about what song they'd dance to at the wedding.

As busy as we'd been lately with work, our wedding had sadly fallen into the background. We had already picked a date, put a down payment on the woodland retreat for the reception, and asked Josh's friend from his men's ultimate Frisbee league if he wouldn't mind DJing for us. But all of the small details between the actual date and now weren't at the top of our priorities. I wondered if maybe we should postpone it, get our ducks in a row before any more concrete plans were settled. My job could have me chasing a perp all over the Reef the night before I wed and Josh could get a job to photograph canoeing in the Iguazu River the same week of our honeymoon that he'd *have* to take.

This was going to be an expensive endeavor and once in a lifetime. I wanted to do this right.

As I was putting the Sazerac to my lips once more, the door to the bar banged shut. Moments later, Josh slumped down in his seat across from me.

"Should have brought your coat out," I said, nodding to it crumpled up on the seat.

He cracked open his beer. "It's a wee bit nippy out there," he kidded, putting on an Irish accent.

We sat for a few moments enjoying one another's company in silence. At the end of a long day, I longed to be with Josh. It was as simple as sitting on the couch together, his arm around me, my hand holding his knee or even cooking a meal together in the kitchen and ranting about each other's days.

As curious as I was about the phone call, we ended up spending our time at Rainey's catching up, pouring over current events, completely devouring our food. We didn't get to go out together often so this was a rare night where we could enjoy each other completely and not worry about small, stupid things. I offered to drive us both home and we'd pick up Josh's car in the morning but he seemed eager not to leave it in town and I conceded. Josh didn't have many possessions he truly cared about but his Land Rover might as well have been the Arc of the Covenant. It was often packed with clothing and camping equipment in the event that he needed to leave on assignment right away. Lots of the stuff in there was pricey and high quality; things he couldn't afford to lose, especially where we were trying to be budget conscious.

I pulled into our driveway shortly after he did and the lights over the garage popped on as we both edged in. The night had turned bitterly cold between getting to the bar and leaving. We climbed the garage stairs up into the kitchen and closed out the cold. The furnace had kicked on, the pleasant hum lulling me toward the couch and Josh's warm embrace. We kicked off our boots and tumbled on top of one another on the green sofa, laughing about something stupid we'd overheard in Rainey's.

These were the few and far between nights, the nights we both savored even though we still got spans of uninterrupted time with one another. Some nights I'd come home and couldn't let the job go. I'd go out to the garage and run on the treadmill until I exhausted myself, pour myself a nightcap and fall asleep, while he stayed up. Other nights, I'd come home and Josh would be in full photo editing mode, making headway on pieces he'd taken on recent excursions. He needed space and inspiration to cut through the thousands of photos on his memory cards. I'd turn on reruns of Community in the bedroom and eventually black out.

By the time both of us were naked and sweating, the temperature had cooled to the high fifties in the house and the wind outside was buffeting the windows. They rattled around us as we lay panting.

We both went up to bed, snuggling into the comforter and sheets. He put an arm around my chest and I nuzzled back into him as much as I could. "Who was the call from?" I finally asked.

Josh's breath paused behind me. "It was Earth Exploits Magazine."

Another job. It wasn't often that Josh got a repeat call from the same client so quickly. Usually, private parties would hire him for a distinct trip and that would be the end of it. But Earth Exploits was rapidly growing as a premier outdoor adventure subscription. While their magazine was the bread and butter of their business for the first few years, their online presence had exploded in the spring and they'd had Josh on call for most of the fall once he'd made it onto their radar. So far, he'd done three jobs with them.

Of course, it meant that he'd be leaving again: probably tomorrow. They were never in the habit of notifying people ahead of time it seemed.

"Where do they want you to go this time?"

"Solomon Islands."

"Is that…Southeast Asia?"

"Close to Australia."

That was the furthest away he'd ever been. "Wow."

"Yeah, they want me to leave Tuesday."

Three days from now. At least we had a little more time together.

"They also offered me a job."

I flipped over. "A *job* job?"

He nodded; his eyes electric. Had he been able to produce his own light, Josh's smile would have blinded us both. My lips curled into a smile as I realized how good this was. He would have job security and a salary. More than that, it was something he loved to do.

"Did you accept?"

His smile thinned. "I told them I'd need to talk to you first."

"The hell you'd need to talk to me for? This is your dream job!" I gave him a small push. "I can't think of a reason why you wouldn't take it."

Josh held my hand to his chest and chuckled. "I know, right?"

"So, why didn't you say 'yes'?"

"Because if I take the job, I'd need to move out there."

My euphoria withered with his words. "To Los Angeles?"

Josh frowned. "Yeah."

I cleared my throat and reached over to turn on my bedside lamp. The warm bloom ushered the darkness away but didn't make me any less cold. "Why couldn't you do the job from here like you've always done?"

"It wouldn't be the same job, Liz." Josh sat up, propping his pillow so he could lean back against it. "They want me to take photos, yes. They also want me in charge of magazine layout and choosing photos for their web features."

"Why can't they send you the files to look at?"

"Because it would be easier if I was there. A lot of those discussions need to happen with Hugh and Marcy. They want their new deputy photography director in the same building while making creative decisions that affect their investments."

I didn't know who Hugh and Marcy were. Josh had mentioned the names once or twice before but it didn't matter. What did matter was their opinions were more important than mine and that made my blood boil. I didn't say anything, instead choosing to stare down at the sheets between the two of us.

"There's smoke coming out of your ears right now," he said.

I looked up at him and the heat in me was suddenly doused in cold shame. "I want you to be able to do what you want to do, Josh. You know that. But that would mean we'd both have to move out there."

"I know. Which is why I wanted to talk to you first." He turned in bed and took hold of my hand again. "I'd really like this job, but if they are happy with having me as a freelance photographer, I can take that, too."

I could tell that it hurt him to say that. Josh wasn't only passionate about his photography: it was what he lived and breathed for. When he came home from trips, he itched to show me hundreds of photos of the places he went, the people he met, and the things he did. He would proudly spend hours tweaking a handful of photos and walk me through each and every edit he performed. He'd tell me how he wished he could take me with him every time, and I'd say I wished I could go.

Maybe this was what our relationship needed? Maybe I'd become too static here, too lost in the job to be able to recognize the benefit of it anymore. There were probably departments all over Los Angeles that needed officers. I could transfer. I could learn to love the heat, earthquakes, smog, and city life.

Maybe.

At the same time, I knew myself. I knew I struggled to handle change. It was why when I'd found this house and bought it and spent years renovating it, I treated it like an extension of myself. This house wasn't only some place to fix up and sell someday. It was safe, and it was mine. It was a home. When I'd found the job with Flintland PD and Brody, I knew deep down that this was where I belonged, that again, I'd found someone who I felt safe with and understood. And falling in love with Josh here? It had been the same. Or so I'd thought. I thought Flintland, even with all of its imperfections, was ours.

I touched his face. "Let me think, okay?" I had to compromise. I couldn't say "no" and watch my fiancé molder in a job that was sub-par to what he truly loved.

I turned out my light and we held each other in the dark, though maybe not as closely as we had before.

FOUR

The Laundromat in Cardend, New Hampshire was decently occupied when I got there. I found a washer to quickly dump my laundry into and settled into one of the plastic orange seats nearby to wait. Amidst the thumping of tumbling clothing, the scraping of buttons and zippers, and the flipping of magazine pages as others lingered, I buried my head in my hands and thought about what I'd seen at the gas station. There could very well have been someone standing there. It could have *looked* like Brody. I'd been fooled before.

There were many times I'd gone to the grocery store, or been out for a walk around town and thought I'd heard his gruff voice nearby. I'd always snap my head up as if expecting him to be there. Every time, I forgot for a split second that he was dead, enough to make me ashamed.

I combed my fingers through my hair and rubbed my skull. It had been seven months since his funeral. My partner, Brody, lying in the dark mahogany casket as he was lowered six feet into the earth… That moment stained my memory. The sky was eerily silver though not raining. He'd died in January, but the service had to be held months later when the ground had finally thawed.

My boots were too small and I'd shifted my weight from one foot to the other. I kept noticing a small stain on the minister's white collar. A plow was clearing mountainous piles of snow in a vacant lot down the road. The sound of the metal scoop scraping on the pavement was like nails on a chalkboard.

Josh was clean shaved for the first time in months. He'd done little but grasp my fingers lightly through "Amazing Grace", neither one of us really able to look the other in the eye.

Carmen looked like a shadow of the woman I'd once known. Her pallor was practically the same shade of white as the flowers on Brody's casket. She wore no makeup, and every time her eyes moved in my direction, a hot stone pushed at my insides. I watched her foot tap the ground in a tremor that overtook her body the further into the service we went.

All of this pain and it was all my fault.

The bell on the Laundromat door jingled and I turned my head, that sensation that he could still be here returning in an instant. But it wasn't Brody's face. Ranger Feld was closing the door behind him, a load of laundry balanced precariously under his arm. He was still wearing his uniform. A little girl with a mess of tousled brown curls tugged at his jacket and skipped around him. He turned and our eyes met.

I looked away. *So much for never running into him again.* I wondered how much he knew. All it took was one sensationalist news article and he would have an opinion of me like everyone else back home.

Feld came around the row of chairs and dropped the basket into a seat a few spaces down from me. He and the girl loaded up a washer, a second uniform tumbling in along with jeans, t-shirts, some pink pajama pants with little giraffes on them…maybe they were horses. He closed the window and set the washer, then handed the girl a picture book that was tucked under his arm. She sat diligently in one of the seats and flipped it open. Then he came over to me.

I stiffened in my seat with expectation. *Here it comes.*

"Hi." His mouth twitched like it had done at the cabin.

"Hi."

"I wanted to apologize for this morning," he said, glancing around at the other patrons, as if he thought they might eavesdrop. "I was a little distracted when we talked—"

"It's all right, Ranger Feld," I interrupted. "I was running on fumes. Didn't get much sleep last night. I shouldn't have been such an ass."

A slight smile warmed his cheeks. "So, should we start over?"

No questions. No judgements. He still didn't know about me. "Sure."

He nodded and returned to sit beside the girl.

I sat there for another ten minutes, and thumbed through a house decorating magazine, feigning interest in it. I turned my head to observe Feld and his daughter. She held the book open on her lap and read the sentences aloud, but not loud enough to obscure R.E.M. playing on the radio.

The girl coughed, the kind of wet cough that makes you automatically cringe when you hear it.

"Evie, remember to cover your mouth, okay?" Feld said, reaching into his pocket for a pad of paper. He scribbled down a note.

"Can't believe your mom didn't get you any cough medicine."

Evie kept reading from the book in her lap. "Suzie smiled and stared at the chicken—"

"Kitchen," Feld corrected.

"That's what I said." She looked up at him deftly. "Is it called the Chicken because that's where you make chicken?"

He grinned and shook his head. "It isn't called the Chicken, honey."

Several minutes later, they flipped back to the front of the book to start again and I returned my attention to the magazine. There was a rustic dining table set up in a house that looked like it belonged in Beverly Hills. The old-fashioned charm they were trying to manufacture made all the hairs on my arms stand. I stared at it for the longest time. All I could think of was Thanksgiving last year, Brody's house, that authenticity in contrast to the shiny pages beneath my fingers.

"Hi!"

I looked up. Feld's daughter stood in front of me, her eyes big. "My daddy and I are getting pie. Do you want to come?"

I glanced around for Feld. He was completely oblivious, talking to an older couple as they scooped their clothes from a dryer.

An instinctual "no" popped onto my tongue but for some reason, I couldn't say it.

"Well?" She swung her picture book back and forth.

"Evie!"

Feld came up to her and put his hands on her shoulders, trying to guide her away. "Honey, what are you doing?" He glanced at me. "Sorry, she—"

"It's fine," I said, forcing a smile.

"I asked her if she wanted to get pie with us," Evie said, still staring at me expectantly.

"Well, that was nice of you, Hun, but I'm sure she's got other things she needs to do." He stared at me for a moment and said, "Unless you *wanted* some pie. It would be my treat."

Spending time with anyone when I was going to leave the next day was pointless. I couldn't let any attachments form. But the girl had this look in her eye, like a puppy staring up at you with a toy in its mouth, not desperate but silently hoping. Worse, my stomach betrayed me by growling. I hadn't eaten anything since that morning.

"She *is* hungry!"

Fuck. I missed talking with someone; anyone.

"Sure."

The rain had lightened to sprinkles and the sun was peeking out. We crossed the street, a brisk autumn wind nipping at our backs. Feld's daughter skipped down the block to the brick-fronted Annie's Diner, pausing to cough every now and again. We sat in one of the booths with the plush red seats surrounded by low lights and walls that glowed bronze in the strips of afternoon sunlight. Feld ordered cherry pie for the three of us, orange juice for his daughter, and coffee for us. I didn't bother to protest despite the fact that I wasn't a fan of cherries.

"I didn't get your name before?" Feld asked.

I nodded. "It's Liz."

"Good to meet you, Liz. I'm Hank and this is Evie."

She gave me a happy wave and immediately burst into more coughs. Hank quickly pulled a handkerchief from his pocket and held it up in front of her mouth until the coughs dissipated.

"She's fighting a cold. I wish I'd known before bringing her into town," Hank explained, a slight guilt in his eyes.

"Your hair is pretty." Evie smiled at me toothily.

She reminded me of my sister when we were younger and the thought warmed my face. "I like yours better."

She plucked at a strand and pulled it out straight before releasing it. It shot back into a tight corkscrew curl. "It's too crazy," she said.

"Trust me: you have beautiful hair," I reinforced. "My sister has curls. I was always jealous."

She shook her head. "Even Mommy tells me it gets nuts sometimes."

Hank raised an eyebrow at her. "She meant *knots*, Hun. Not *nuts*."

The waitress brought our drinks. I immediately took a sip of my coffee, savoring the burst of caffeine. The cobwebs clouding my mind cleared.

"So, Liz," Hank said as he tore open a packet of sugar and dumped it in his coffee, "Is this your first time in the Whites?"

"No, I used to come here a lot as a kid."

"To Cardend?"

"No. Actually, Middlehitch. My dad's family owned a house there."

"Ah, Middlehitch is a fun little town. I take it you don't own the house anymore?"

I frowned. I remembered my mom carrying a cardboard box out the front door and loading it into our station wagon. Dana was already in her child seat in the back, crying and carrying on. She needed a nap. I remembered staring out at the view of the mountains from our front porch, across the field that led down to the fishing stream where Dad used to go spend his days.

"No. We sold it when I was a kid," I said, my voice cracking at the thought of that face on the flyer, my Not-Dad.

"Oh." He tipped the creamer pitcher toward his mug, letting the white liquid splash into the dark.

We were silent for a few moments before Hank spoke up again. "It's too bad you're heading home tomorrow. I was going to ask for your opinion on the case."

I scoffed. "I don't do that kind of work anymore."

"You wouldn't have to be officially involved. It's …we're not sure where else to look and if he did happen to be on your porch last night, you might be the last person who saw him." His eyes were hopeful. "His wife has had a hard, few years. They lost their son about a year ago in a drunk driving accident. I hate to think we might not find her husband."

For a split second, I felt bad that I couldn't stay.

No. That's how it starts. Don't. Get. Involved.

"I've really got to get back home."

"Are you a ranger like Daddy?" Evie asked suddenly. I'd almost forgotten she was there; she was being so quiet.

"Close. I was a police officer."

"So, you helped people, like my daddy helps people lost in the woods."

I took the opportunity to try and switch the conversation. I didn't want to talk about me anymore. "How long has your daddy been a Ranger?"

She sipped at her orange juice as her lip pouted in thought. "I don't know."

"Probably eighteen years now," Hank answered for her. "I got the job when I was fresh out of college. I guess at first it was a summer job. In the end, I kind of found myself out there and realized it was what I wanted to keep doing."

"You said that's what people come out here to do: find themselves."

"Isn't that what you came out here to do?"

I stared down at my coffee. Shit. He knew how to play this game, too.

When I didn't answer, he whispered, "Listen: whatever happened to make you leave Flintland isn't my business. Hell, you obviously came out here to get away from talking about it. I don't want to intrude on that."

I sighed. "Thanks."

Our pie came to the table. I had never liked cherries. Ever since I had cracked a tooth on the pit inside of one as a kid, I'd held a special vehemence toward them, one that only grew with time. Looking at them now made me sick to my stomach. I fished my fork around inside the gooey red innards, hoping to spread it out and make it look eaten. Hank and Evie scooped large spoonfuls out of theirs and ate them, although Hank's mind seemed to be in a far-off place.

The silence stretched and with it, the awkwardness. I decided to turn my thoughts toward what I'd learned in the gas station. "Someone said that they found Castle's car," I said after another sip of coffee. "Was that what distracted you this morning?"

"Yes and no," he said, taking another bite.

"That's cryptic."

"There *was* some troubling evidence at the scene." He gave a sidelong glance toward Evie, who was smacking her lips after a huge bite of pie. Some cherry filling dripped down her lip toward her chin. Hank dutifully wiped it away.

"They found blood," I answered for him.

He looked up, his eyes widening.

"Word's getting around."

He frowned.

It dawned on me that he was staring past me. I looked over my shoulder. There was a woman standing outside the diner window looking in, her expression agitated.

Hank stood up. "Evie, stay right there" He looked at me. "Would you stay with her a moment?" I didn't have time to answer before he stepped out of the booth and walked to the head of the restaurant. The woman came to the door to meet him. He pushed out and shook his head, his hands up defensively. Though I didn't know what they were saying, I knew the discussion was all but friendly. Both of them quickly progressed to shouting. Their body language was close. Wife? I hadn't noticed a ring on Feld's finger.

The woman pointed toward us and I turned around in my seat to face Evie who was licking the back of her spoon and looking at the striped wallpaper. *Ex-wife?*

Great, I thought. *Way to get involved in a domestic dispute on your last day here.* Everything in me wanted me to break free from the situation. But I couldn't leave Evie alone.

I closed my eyes. As soon as Hank was done having it out with this lady, I'd thank him for the sufficiently mashed cherry pie, if not just the coffee, and I'd return to the laundromat to collect my clothing. It wouldn't be dry, but it wouldn't matter. I'd officially stayed here too long. I needed to leave.

"Decide you weren't so hungry after all?" Hank asked from behind me. I turned to meet his questioning gaze. He was staring down at my pie. My efforts to hide my dislike of it had failed.

I stood up. "Whoever that was seemed pissed off. I shouldn't have come."

"Daddy, she said 'piss'!" Evie whispered accusingly.

"It really didn't have anything to do with you," he said. "Please, don't leave. I'll explain."

I found myself sitting back down. "My laundry is probably ready to switch over by now, so…tell me," I answered.

He opened up his wallet and handed a dollar to Evie. "Why don't you go ask the waitress if she'll give you a scoop of ice cream?"

Her eyes lit up. "Chocolate?"

"Sure." After she'd scampered away, he said under his breath, "I may regret that later."

I smirked but didn't say anything.

"That was Melissa, my ex," he explained, resuming the dissection of his pie. "We've been separated for a few months now and only recently started talking to lawyers."

I nodded to Evie who was balanced precariously on one of the leather stools at the bar. "I'm sure that makes things hard on her."

"The separation has been. I haven't told her about the divorce yet. I'm not sure how to. She's six. Her outlook on things is still wrapped up in fantasy. She loves fairies and dragons and says she wants to be a dinosaur hunter when she's older."

"She may be a few million years too late for that profession," I said.

"Since Melissa and I split up, we've been sharing time with Evie and that includes holidays. We've been fighting over which one of us will get to have her for Thanksgiving this year. She's been calling me at work about it, leaving messages at my apartment, and, as you witnessed, hunting me down in public to have her two cents spilled."

"She thought we were on a date," I said matter-of-factly.

He nodded. "I set her straight."

I took a sip from my coffee, now lukewarm. "Good. I don't need anyone else wandering around on my front porch the night before I leave."

"Maybe it *is* better off that you're leaving," Hank said, collecting the bill from the waitress. "We've got a major storm set to come in tomorrow afternoon. Those little cabins get snowed in pretty easily." He plucked a twenty-dollar bill from his wallet and dropped it on the table. "I hope we can find Castle before it starts spitting. If he's lost out there in that, he won't survive the night."

We walked back to the Laundromat. The air outside was frigid and another reminder that my time here was finite. I still had to get through one more night at the cabin before I went back home. I wasn't overly optimistic about tonight. What if that shadow returned to the cabin porch? Then again, I'd been here a whole month without anything strange happening.

By the time I'd dropped my heap of clothes into the dryer and pushed the button to start the spin cycle, I noticed a vaguely familiar song playing over the tinny speakers in the corners of the room. The soft strumming guitar accompanied by a soft harmonica suddenly brought me back to a crisp November day much like this one last year.

"I don't like Neil Young," I remembered telling Brody when we sat in his car once, enjoying our coffee. The grass in Laura Cole Park nearby was frosted over and the bare tree branches twisted toward the grey sky like thousands of fingers. It was days before Chloe Clark vanished, back when it seemed normal and our routine was the same every day; coffee in the morning, then everything else.

He'd turned his head a little to look at me. "How can you not like Neil Young? Everybody likes Neil Young."

"I don't know." I'd raised my shoulders. "I never got into him, that's all."

"Well, you can't say 'you don't like him' if you've never listened to him." Brody had tipped his Styrofoam coffee cup back to finish off the last of it.

"I've listened. I said I never got into it."

One of his eyebrows had perked. "What does that even mean? 'You didn't get into it?'"

I'd settled further into my seat. "Well, when I was thirteen, my mother sent me to summer camp. I didn't like it very much."

Brody had chuckled. "Why does that not surprise me?"

"The camp counselor in charge of our cabin would play 'Only Love Can Break Your Heart' on repeat from the turntable in the lounge whenever we were there. And by the time camp was over, suffice to say, I was done with that song and Neil Young."

"That's too bad. I openly weep whenever 'Harvest Moon' comes on. It's so beautiful."

I'd glared at him but couldn't hold it for long before laughing.

Smiling, he'd put his empty coffee cup aside and started the car's engine. It had rumbled to life beneath us.

"Trust me. Give Neil another try. You'll be swept away."

"Don't expect me to weep," I had muttered.

"There's hope for you yet."

The song on the radio ended and the DJ's voice sliced through my thoughts like a carving knife through fresh meat. It wasn't smooth. I was ripped out of that pleasant memory. I was forlorn, sitting in the Laundromat full of people.

"You okay?" Hank asked from a few seats down, his brow creased in worry.

"Fine," I managed. My mouth tasted stale and the yellow lights were beginning to bother my eyes. My laundry had only been in the dryer a few minutes but I found myself turning it off and scooping the sodden clothes out into a basket.

"What's wrong?" Hank asked again.

"I've got to go." I hefted the basket in my arms and moved toward the door. As I pushed out, I looked back over my shoulder at him and Evie, reading the same book. "Thanks for the pie."

After tossing my basket into the trunk, I took off back to my mountain refuge. The tiniest hint of color was breaking through the grey clouds on the horizon, a fusion of blue and orange that seemed more of a trick to my eyes than a reality. I scanned the small town of Cardend as I drove through it for, what I assumed, was the last time.

At roughly five o'clock, people were beginning to close up their shops on the main strip through town, waving glove-covered hands to their neighbors as they went home. The sociable kindness suddenly became a startling reminder for me of the town I'd grown up in; the place where everyone knows everyone else's names, a place I longed to escape from when I turned eighteen and could finally leave behind my mom and her new boyfriend. Flintland was still small by city standards, but it was enough of a change from the quaint "beautiful day in the neighborhood" town that I'd grown tired of since my dad's death.

I passed the Cardend fire station, a small brick building with a large warehouse built off of it. The bay doors were open and I noticed a small crew of men and women cleaning and sorting through equipment inside. That bitterness in my mouth returned in full force as I stepped harder on the gas pedal.

Wisps of snow had begun to fall by the time I followed the snaking road back to my cabin. I turned the car around in the driveway so that I could leave quickly in the morning, then went inside and added wood to the fire in the woodstove.

I wasn't hungry for dinner, especially not after remembering Brody so vividly. The song from the laundromat was stuck in my head, playing over and over. I went to the turntable in the other room and filed through the albums stacked nearby. The cabin owner I was renting from hadn't upgraded to the twenty-first century yet. I eventually plucked a classical album from the mix of sixties bands. I dropped the needle haphazardly into the record, not caring where I began, wanting "Harvest Moon" to stop playing in my mind. The music sprung up into the quiet cabin, drowning the familiar harmonica in my head with violins.

Crouching in front of the woodstove in the den, I prodded the logs inside with a poker and once again thought about the gas station. Then, I thought about the voice from outside my cabin.

I put the wire grate up over the woodstove opening and sat in the armchair, watching the flames grasping at each piece of kindling and the embers eating holes through the newspaper beneath. What if I went home and hallucinated Brody there? Had I made myself crazier coming all the way out here and shutting myself away for a month?

I sat for so long that by the time I realized it was finally dark outside, the record was playing an allegro, the notes rhythmically spiraling out of control in a way that matched my thoughts. I went to the turntable and picked up the arm, the scratch of the needle piercing my ears and making the thoughts stop. I flipped the player off and went to the window. Half an inch of snow covered my car and the ground. Flakes fell like large pieces of confetti. I could barely tell the outlines of the trees against the blue-black night. *I thought we weren't supposed to get this storm until tomorrow…*

Stoking the fire one last time, I shuffled into the bedroom, kicked off my shoes and pants, unhooked my bra and slithered in beneath the cool blankets, my eyes locked on the windows.

One more night, I told myself. *Then, I go home.*

I closed my eyes.

Home.

FIVE

THEN

The envelope on the top of the pile stared at me. It weaseled its way into my soul from the passenger seat as I drove to work that wet December morning. I tried throwing bills on top of it, anything to forget it was there. But I could still see it.

The PD parking garage was unusually packed, but my thoughts were elsewhere. The only parking was on the top level. Once I'd found my spot, I sat with the car idling and watched the rain bead on the windshield. On any normal day, I would have been out of the car in a heartbeat and on the way in. Procrastination had steeped in me all week. Dirty dishes sat in the sink at home. I'd done the bare minimum of shoveling in order to get the car out that morning after last night's storm. The number for the caterer's was tacked on the board by the phone. I had to go over the menu for the wedding with them. That *should* have been fun. I should have *wanted* to do that before everything else.

But ever since Josh's and my discussion about moving to Los Angeles two weeks ago, I didn't want to think about the wedding or the possibility of leaving Flintland. Everything was suspended in mid-air now. I longed for concreteness and certainty.

Snatching the mail from the seat, I stuffed it in my bag and stepped out of the car into a puddle.

"Fantastic," I muttered.

I found the stairs down into the garage and briefly waved my credentials to the attendant before pulling open the emblazoned glass doors to the Flintland Police Station. PD was housed in a six-story post-modern brick and glass beast flanked by the imposing neo-classical City Hall on one side and Justice Square on the other. The square housed the Flintland Mall and an international food court including the best Nigerian cuisine known to man. I'd vaguely pictured myself sitting at one of the picnic tables outside enjoying a Babatunde's beef suya earlier in the week. Brody had called it "crack on a stick" once and I agreed wholeheartedly.

I followed the drab carpet up the winding entry hall to the main foyer. The conference room and waiting area were abustle, with reporters checking their equipment and rehearsing, their garble of conversation like the draining of a full bath tub. A press conference? I didn't remember the captain mentioning it yesterday. Some shit was going down.

I waved to Officer Nico at the front desk and moved to the elevators. There was a lengthy queue. I opted for exercise and took the stairs to the offices. What reason did the chief have to call a conference for? There was only one I could think of immediately: the missing girl.

There was still no sign of Chloe Clark. The Flintland Police Department and several neighboring law enforcements had spent much of our time in the woods beyond the Clark family home. It was all we'd had to go on, the only place we knew she'd gone for sure. We had found her stuffed rabbit lying next to a large oak tree about a half a mile from the edge of the woods. But there were no other signs of her. Any boot prints she could have left behind were swallowed by a torrential downpour. We searched animal hollows, the old mill by the river, and interrogated neighbors. There was nothing. It was as if she'd vanished into thin air.

I'd almost reached the top of the stairs when Brody pushed through a glass door in front of me. When he reached me, he pulled my elbow to turn me around. "Where've ya been? They're getting ready to start."

I spun and followed, trying not to lose my balance on the stairs. "What's with the circus?"

"Police chief is making a statement about the Clark case," he answered.

We crossed the main foyer to the conference room and slid into the back of the room. I noted the line up at the front of the room. The Chief was talking to Captain Elijah Vance on the left. I nodded to the captain and he reciprocated. He was our direct supervisor, the one I'd thought would have explained this mess to us earlier. On the right side of the podium were city council members and the lieutenant of Brummel's police department in charge of the joint task force for Chloe Clark's case.

The press bounced in place, more edgy and rampant than when I'd first walked through. They were hungry. Everyone in Flintland worried about Chloe's and their own children's safety. They questioned us and our job. In disappearances and kidnappings, the first forty-eight hours were crucial. We were long past that. Chloe had been missing for nearly three weeks. In addition to all of that, Chloe had disappeared in one of Flintland's safest neighborhoods. Was there someone out there that had taken her? If so, would it happen again?

Captain Vance took the podium first. Old enough to be my grandfather, Vance still dressed and somehow looked twenty years younger, the thick frames on his glasses hiding the lines around his eyes. His hair had silvered only around the edges near his ears. Vance had a certain calm and collectedness when dealing with the media. That's probably why he decided to take the stand that day; to try and keep people calm.

"Ladies and gentlemen, I'm Captain Elijah Vance. I'm in charge of Flintland PD's taskforce working on the disappearance of Chloe Clark, age eight. She was last seen entering the woods that border her home on the eastern side of Flintland on November twenty-second, possibly following an unknown person or persons. Today marks nineteen days from when Chloe was originally reported missing. We've investigated all leads pertaining to her disappearance. Numerous volunteers have combed the woods along with our officers to search for her. We greatly appreciate the efforts of the community for this."

I glanced around at the faces in the audience. Disquiet hung like a mist over the room. The chief's preamble had done little if nothing to put people at ease. They were waiting for the bomb to drop.

"I'm now going to introduce you to Lieutenant Jack Lennox of the Brummel police department, who has worked in coordination with us on this investigation." Vance stepped out of the way and Lennox took the podium.

Jack Lennox had a ramrod posture, a long and hawk-like nose, and long gangly limbs. Everything about his appearance was perfection, from his pressed grey suit, to the clean part in his hair, down to the shine in his shoes.

With all of the doubles I'd pulled and hours spent exploring the woods, I'd barely put myself together this morning. My grey suit was wrinkled, my coffee weak, and my hair messily tied back, if only to hide that I hadn't had time for a shower, much less time to pull a comb through it.

Lennox appeared refreshed, even his green eyes had an energized shine to them.

"Must be nice not to lose sleep over this case," I muttered.

I felt Brody's eyes on me. "Wait for what the man has to say. It might surprise—"

Brody's phone suddenly chirped and he pulled it from his pocket to check the screen. When he looked back up at me, he had a glazed expression on his face. "I've got to take this."

I waved toward the stage. "But—"

"Fill me in." He maneuvered around some officers and stepped from the glass walled room into the hallway.

"Good evening."

I turned my attention back to the pulpit.

"I'm Lieutenant Jack Lennox of Brummel PD. On behalf of our agency, I'd like to extend our appreciation to the community and the Flintland police department for their countless hours spent in search of Chloe Clark."

I watched Lennox's face as he spoke, his lips and his eyes. Somehow, he managed to make it sound like he actually cared. I knew it was all a ruse. Over the last two weeks, I'd never come across him in the field nor canvasing the neighborhood. I think he spent more time ironing his suits than he did actually policing his officers. He reminded me of the officer who had spoken about my father's death to the local news station when I was a kid: every word that escaped his lips was calculated to evoke the right kind of response from reporters. Lennox was a silver-tongued mouthpiece and that was it.

My insides squirmed with the realization. Lennox was the chief's and probably city council's last-ditch effort to try and make the investigation seem like it was more successful than it actually was.

"It is my sad duty to announce that we must suspend our search for Chloe Clark pending further developments. In the last week, we have found no new leads in the case. The time that has elapsed concerns us and limits the efforts of our investigation. In addition, Brummel must return to making our own streets safe and secure. The Flintland Police Department will be continuing its investigation into her disappearance forthwith without our consultation."

Voices rose up and flashes reflected off the walls as the reporters and their cameras went wild. Turns out even someone with the gift of gab couldn't keep everyone's heads cool with that news.

My chest swelled as I thought about all that time spent searching for Chloe. The times her mother had let us use her home as a temporary base of operations, the tea and coffee provided by her at all hours, and all the stories she'd told us accompanied by photos in various albums….

But it wasn't all that. I was vaguely aware of a knot in my belly growing tighter and tighter with each passing moment. I remembered my father's death: the press conference held by our local police station in cooperation with our fire department said they were giving up. They didn't have the resources. The arsonist who had set the fire that my father had run into to save lives was never found because of them. Would it be the same for Chloe's kidnapper now?

Brody tensed beside me. I hadn't even realized he'd returned from his phone call. His eyes were locked on Lennox. "They're dropping out," he muttered.

"Why the fuck didn't we get a heads up?" I whispered. Each word was like a stone.

"Bet you Lennox sprung it on the chief this morning. City Council probably agreed the investigation was about due to close. That's why they rushed the press conference. He didn't want to waste any time."

I lost track of everything Lennox said from that point on.

"Wait? 'Due to close'?" What the hell does that mean?" I spat under my breath. "Do you want the case to end?"

Brody put his hand up. "Easy, Raging Bull. Let's talk about this outside."

We stepped out of the conference room, away from reporter's ever keen ears and crossed the foyer to an entranceway door. Brody sighed and said, "Look. You know as well as I do that in missing person's cases, we have a limited amount of time to find the victim alive. This little girl is a tragedy, and—"

"And they're throwing in the towel…at Christmas time," I said through gritted teeth.

Brody frowned. "We've got no leads, Lizzy. Where are we supposed to go next?"

My mind was like a scrambled egg. The frustration from the conference made me want to scream. "I don't know! But we had more of a chance of at least finding a body with help." I glanced at the waiting room where dozens of potential new victims and cases waited. "We can barely keep up as it is. Her case is going to get buried."

"You heard what I heard in there right?" Brody shrugged. "*Our* department is keeping the case open. We're not giving up yet."

Yet. We would eventually have to.

Brody turned toward the conference room. The session was over and I couldn't process what had happened. The press was still snapping photos as Lennox and Vance left the stage and exited the room.

My mind was awash with guilt, drowning me like the tide. We'd never find Chloe now. The image of her dead body was like having dust flung in my eyes. I remembered the anger I'd experienced so many years ago, learning my family would never have justice for my father's death. My gaze locked on Lennox, on his beady eyes.

Brody put his hand up and opened his mouth to say something.

I pushed past him and zeroed in on Lennox as he marched down the corridor toward the parking garage.

Brody muttered, "Mierda," behind me.

Captain Vance had veered off toward his office on the left leaving Lennox a sole target. He was moving into the curve beyond the opening under the stairs, the one place where you were completely out of sight from the press corps and the other offices.

"Hey," I said once I was close enough to Lennox.

Lennox turned. "Detective—"

"You son of a bitch!" I pushed Lennox, catching him off guard. He bumped into the bulletin board on the wall, knocking a few flyers down.

"The hell!" Lennox shouted.

"Liz, stop!" Brody called from behind me.

I glared. "You're going to run out on that poor mother, is that it?"

Lennox took a step toward me, a finger jamming into my face. "It wasn't my decision!" He took another step toward me and I subconsciously took one back. "Even if it was, how fucking dare you accuse me of not caring."

I lunged forward again but Brody slid in between us. "Don't. He isn't worth it," my partner said, putting my hands on my shoulders.

"Keep your partner on a leash, Aritza, before she does something she's going to regret."

Brody glanced over his shoulder at him, "Back off, pal, all right?"

"Not your pal," Lennox said under his breath.

"I'm sure your drycleaner needs your business right away," I said, staring Lennox up and down. "Probably couldn't survive without you."

Lennox's mouth went flat and he closed his eyes like he was trying to hold back. "Detective…." he breathed.

"That's enough." Another voice. Captain Vance stalked up the hall behind us, a quiet fury bristling in my direction.

I spun toward him. "Captain, we can't—"

"In my office, Raleigh, now," Vance commanded.

It was the equivalent of being told by my mom to go my room, except Vance actually inspired some level of impact when he said it. I stalked back up the corridor toward Vance's office.

"Aritza, get back to work."

"Yes, sir." Brody's footfalls echoed up the hall.

"Thank you, Captain," Lennox said.

"Get the hell out of here," Vance ordered. The disgust in his tone was palpable.

I left Vance's office twenty minutes later without much will to carry my own body around. The ream out was justified. I'd been an ass; let a case get to me again, and the only reason I hadn't been suspended was because Vance needed all men on deck. We couldn't afford a shortage of officers right now.

Upstairs at my desk, I glanced down at the envelope I'd been avoiding all morning. I rubbed my thumb over the address, Josh's name written in my best penmanship. Over everything was a large red stamp: RETURN TO SENDER.

The letter was short and sweet, nothing interesting. Questions about what kind of strange food he was eating, what kind of animals he'd photographed. An observation about our new neighbor who had a creepy affinity for lawn gnomes. How much I missed him but hoped he was having a good time. I didn't bring up moving or the wedding.

He'd never even got it. I stared at the address, checking the numbers and the words over and over. Nothing was wrong. It was the address he'd given me, where he was supposed to be on his latest trip. Why didn't he get it?

I'm not sure how long I stared at the letter but at some point, I noticed a shadow obscuring part of the envelope. Before I had a chance to look over my shoulder, Brody spoke.

"Did you transpose the numbers?"

I shook my head. "It's been a week and a half with no word."

He frowned. "I don't know if you know about this new thing called the Internet."

I scoffed. "He's in the Solomon Islands. There's limited internet access there and not much cell phone coverage. He might as well be on the moon."

"Well, that sucks," Brody said. He stepping over to his desk which abutted mine and slumped into his chair. "So, on a scale of ouch to I've-spontaneously-combusted, how bad was your talk with Vance?"

"Sprained ankle."

"You got off luck-y," he intoned, shaking his head.

"He knew Lennox deserved it."

"Of course, he deserved it. It was still a stupid thing to do."

I opened my laptop and logged onto the police database. "I must be getting dumber in my old age."

"How could I forget?" Brody snorted. "The hothead had a birthday yesterday, didn't she?"

"Mm-hmm." I stared into the mind-numbing neon screen and the endless files there.

"Did you get drunk with your girlfriends and dance the night away to ABBA?" he chuckled.

"It was Pet Shop Boys, but you guessed it," I said unemotionally, clicking on a folder.

I'd spent yesterday at the gym, then at home cleaning out the closet in the upstairs hall. Then the gym again. Then, chicken alfredo pizza from Topolino's, Then, gin. Then, a phone call from mom. Then, more gin. I woke up on the couch around one a.m.

I glanced up from the computer. A small rectangular present sat on Josh's envelope. I blinked at Brody. "What's this?"

"A little something, something. Thirty-five is a big year."

I picked it up and knew by the weight of it that it was a DVD. I yanked the gold ribbon off and neatly picked away at the paper grocery bag it was wrapped in. "Seriously? *Out of Africa*?"

He pointed. "I *helped* pick it out."

"And wrapped it from the looks of it."

He cocked his head. "Carmen mentioned you hadn't seen it. Guess you were talking about it recently?"

We had. She'd suggested a girl's night out last week and I'd jumped at it. I'd been at home alone every night for the last two weeks since Josh had left on assignment. The last time I'd had a quality girl's night out was…. I honestly couldn't remember. A topic of conversation had been Meryl Streep and our jealousy of her wit and talent. *Out of Africa*: not so witty.

"So, you picked out a film where the woman's husband is a philandering asshole and her love interest dies tragically in a plane crash?"

Brody's eyes widened. "*I* would have gotten you a box of Dunkin'."

I shook my head and set it aside. "Well, at least you tried." I glanced at the envelope from Josh again.

"You think he forgot, don't you?"

"Before he left, we talked about celebrating when he got back." I shrugged. "I guess I still hoped for a surprise or something."

"Maybe something happened to his phone." Brody said. "Maybe he's out on the ocean. Maybe both."

I didn't answer.

Brody's cell phone rang again. "Here we go."

"What's up?"

Brody's eyes shifted from the phone to me and he cleared his throat. "Nothing. It's…the water heater. Not working."

"Shit. That explains you ducking out of the press conference."

"Yeah, sure," he cut me off and picked up the phone. "Hey…. Yeah…. Okay." There was practically a minute of silence between each word. He hung up and returned to writing up a report.

The quiet that lingered between us was heavy and strange. "So?"

It took a moment for him to look up. "So, what?"

"The water heater?"

His eyes slid to look at the ceiling for a moment. Then, he got up from his chair and swung his black blazer on. "We've got a warrant to serve. We'll talk about it later, yeah?"

"Fine," I said, grabbing my own coat.

I had an inkling there was more going on than a busted water heater. Whatever that call was during the press conference had distracted Brody. Normally, he'd talk me down from being upset but he had appeared unfazed by the proceedings of the Chloe Clark case and now, didn't want to carry a perfectly benign conversation about a water heater any further.

I wish I'd pushed it then. Maybe it would have changed everything.

IX

NOW

I opened my eyes, my mind scrambling to detach myself from the world of sleep. I peeled back the covers and stood, backing against the wall as I tried to remember where I was. The pops and crackles of the fire in the den comforted my ears and my pounding heart slowed. The cabin. I was here and Brody was not.

A sound pierced the air.

Not any sound: a scream.

I reached for the baseball bat, leaning against the wall where I'd left it after last night's disturbance. I slunk to the window. Everything was black. The only shapes I could make out were the edges of the bushes and the tree tops, branches crossing one another in natural filigree.

The scream died off into the night. The tension in my shoulders subsided. That hadn't come from nearby. It was distant.

Then, like a warning siren, it rose up again through the trees, closer now. I couldn't tell if it was a man or a woman, only that it was primal and unnatural. Goosebumps rose all over my skin.

I grabbed a flashlight from a shelf by the door and flicked it on, a beam piercing the darkness. Throwing my clothes and a coat on, I hesitantly opened the door.

Bitter cold nipped at me within seconds of stepping out. Despite wanting to slip back inside, I closed the door behind me, then held the bat up defensively. The scream tore up into the air mere feet in front of me. Panic skittered across my brain. I scanned the snow-covered trees as I walked to the edge of the deck.

What the hell was I doing out here? *Go back inside!*

I couldn't. That scream uncoiled a thread of recklessness in me, something I hadn't sensed ever since I'd lost Brody. Something was out there. Who or whatever it was probably needed help.

Something crashed through the brush off to my far right. I swept the flashlight across the driveway into the trees, but moments too late to catch anything.

The wind whistled against the cabin and shook the trees. The sound of sticks and scrub crackling was still getting closer.

"Who's out there?" I called, my voice barely projecting.

The sounds in the underbrush suddenly ceased. My nerve wavered. What if this was the person who'd been walking on my deck last night?

The crashing in the thicket commenced again, still growing closer, louder, greater. It didn't sound like a person. It sounded much bigger.

I glanced over my shoulder at the cabin door. *Fuck this.* It wasn't worth losing my life thinking I was doing it for a good cause. If a bear lumbered out from those trees, I wasn't going to fight it. I turned on my heel for the door and wrenched the knob. But it stuck. I jiggled it, threw my shoulder into the wood hoping for it to give way. The door wouldn't budge.

Oh, shit. I'd locked myself out.

The car! I could still get there. I fished around in my coat pocket for the keys, my fingers swimming in warm empty wool. I'd left them inside. *Idiot!* I backed up against the door. *What do I do? What do I—*

The back door. There was a spare key back there. The owner of the cabin had mentioned it in his email. I slipped to the opposite end of the deck, staying focused on the woods. I was afraid to look away, knowing the owner of those terrifying screams could appear at any moment. Once I made it down the stairs onto the snow, I stole toward the back entrance. My breath was heavy in my ears. The squeal of my boots through the fresh snow was ear-piercing. I couldn't hear anything behind me. I didn't want to.

I rounded the corner of the cabin. A small staircase led up to the back door. In a box leaned up against the side of the building was a heap of rusted coffee cans, barely protected from the snow. I lifted the mat at the top of the steps but found no key there. The owner must have hidden the back door key in one of the cans.

A stick snapped toward the front of the house.

I picked up the first coffee can, groping inside. Nothing. I tossed it and moved onto the next. A crunch of snow froze me for a second. Masochistic curiosity begged for me to peek around the corner of the house. *Do you want to die?* I asked myself, checking another can. *Maybe. Maybe that's the answer.*

A few seconds later: *No. It's not.*

I searched another can: still nothing. Footsteps slinked along the side of the house.

Oh, please. Come on, come on.

Diving my hand into the next can, my fingernails curled around a key nestled in a soup of mud and slushy water at the bottom. I was at the backdoor in seconds, plunging the key in the lock, my breath rolling into the night air in anxious puffs. As the heavy footfalls reached the corner, I shouldered my way through the door and shoved it closed behind me.

The house was stifling and dark, the fire in the woodstove roaring. I rested my back against the door, listening through the wood. A coffee tin rattled against a few others and I held my breath. The boards on the stairs creaked slowly. Though I desperately wanted to move away from the door, I couldn't. Whoever was out there was right on the other side…as if they knew exactly where I was. For a few moments, I thought I heard breathing.

Lights suddenly flickered from the front windows of the house. *What the hell?* A Jeep climbed the hill into view, lights blitzing and sending revolving shadows soaring amongst the trees. I squinted, recognizing Hank through the windshield. What was he doing here? My relief sank into dread as he cut the engine. Someone was still outside, still at the back door. I ran to the front window, waving my arms. "Don't get out of the car!" I yelled.

Hank's eyes were wide as he leaned over into the passenger seat, digging into his glovebox. Then, he climbed out of the car.

I ran to the front door, my fingers tearing at the knob. "Don't!" I shouted as soon as the door was open.

Hank straightened, bumping back into the hood of the Jeep. "Are you okay?" he called.

"Something's out here! Get back in your car!"

He unholstered his pistol and held it up as he crossed the driveway.

"Stay there!"

Hank ignored me until he reached the porch and ascended the steps. I grabbed his arm and pulled him inside, slamming the door shut behind him.

"Did you see it?" I raced to one of the side windows. "It was out there. It was—"

His grip on my arm kept me in place. "Stop! Are you okay?"

I suddenly realized how much I was shaking. I pulled my arm out from his hand and said, "I don't know. Something was out there. I heard screaming."

"I got the call over the radio. There have been reports of screams all over the mountain."

I tried to listen through the door. Whatever it was had to still be out there, right?

The room bloomed with light. Hank had turned on a lamp. "Listen," he said, pulling his cap off and wiping his brow, "let's sit down and talk."

"I can't sit down." I stared out the window, unblinking. There! By a tree. Did something move? Damn, the wind was blowing harder than a few moments ago. How was I supposed to tell what it was with all of this—

The curtain whooshed shut in front of me. I turned and looked at Hank. "The fuck?"

"Tell me what happened."

I forced myself to sit in one of the rocking chairs. Hank sat opposite me and we went through everything I could think of; the scream that awoke me from my sleep, the sounds in the woods and my near escape after locking myself out like a moron.

He took a deep breath. "Well, I think it's safe to say that whatever was out there is most likely gone now."

He was probably right. But I couldn't get my thoughts to stop reeling, couldn't stop the anxiety of making it through one last night out here. I got up and snatched my keys from where I'd set them on the kitchen counter.

"What are you doing?"

"I'm not staying out here for the rest of the night. I'm going home."

"It's nearly midnight!" Hank said.

"Better late than never."

"You're shaking more than my aunt's miniature poodle and you expect me to let you drive?"

The cabin had closed in on me. Everything about it made me want for the familiarity of the home I'd left behind. I wanted my own couch, the water from my tap, my own bed.... I wanted to look out my window and view the other houses on the cul-de-sac where I lived.

Hank rubbed a hand over his mouth to his chin. Finally, he turned and opened the door, the rush of the trees practically deafening. "Okay," he said, "that settles it."

"What?"

"You'll stay up at the station tonight. We have a bed up there.

You can be on your way when the sun comes up."

"Was I not clear?" I spoke. "I don't want to be in these woods anymore."

"You're panicking!" he urged.

"So, what if I am? All I'm doing is leaving a few hours earlier than I'd meant to."

He took a deep breath. "I'm not going to let you drive out of here and get into an accident in the dark. We got a dumping of snow and all of the roads probably haven't been cleared yet. Hell, getting down to your cabin was difficult enough. It's only for the night. As soon as the sun hits that ridge, you can go. I won't stop you."

Now it was I who was standing still while Hank trembled. The frustration in his eyes belied the confidence that was in his voice a moment ago. From what little I knew of Hank, I reasoned it was out of character for him to make any kind of an outburst like that at all. I didn't fight him though. Instead, I nodded and said, "Okay."

Ensuring that all of my belongings were picked up and putting ash over the fire to put it out, I hesitantly left the cabin.

I wanted to drive my own car but Hank insisted that we both take his Jeep. He probably thought I was going to drive in the opposite direction the minute we hit the main road. The thought had crossed my mind. I grabbed my pack from my car, keeping on the lookout for anything out of the ordinary in the woods around us. He started the Jeep up and pulled us out from the driveway. I watched the cabin and my car in the side-view mirror, vanishing behind the hill as we descended toward the highway.

Morning will come soon.

Only a little longer before I could go home. It would probably take me the whole day in this snow but by nightfall, I'd be back within the comfort of my own sheets. I could leave all of this behind and begin again. I hoped.

"Fishing flies?" Hank was glancing at my bag.

I pulled it up into my lap, my mind taking me back. "A trip my fiancé and I took. Josh was determined to teach me fly-fishing. After about a million tries and lots of lost flies later, I finally caught a little brook trout with this; a disco midge." I pointed to the little hook with the burst of green fabric like a mane around the top.

"Little?"

"Seven inches. Not exactly Moby Dick."

"Well, my first one was only six." Hank turned his attention back to the road. He was trying to drive the Jeep through the snow that he'd packed down with his arrival, and every so often, would get stuck.

"You're engaged?" he said after getting us free from a small rut.

I shoved my bag down into the dark. "Not anymore."

Hank downshifted as we reached the bottom of the hill and turned the Jeep onto the highway. "Sorry."

A snowplow hadn't come through in a while. There was about two inches of snow built up on the roads, which made for slow-going. The further we drove from the cabin, the more my tension eased. Back there, the very thought of sleeping evaded me completely, but I knew the moment we reached the ranger station and I lay down; I'd be out cold. I didn't want to check out while we were still driving. It would only further illustrate Hank's point about me not being capable to drive. I didn't want him to have that satisfaction.

We ascended the mountain. The guitar strums and rich tones of Rufus Wainwright's Across the Universe were like background static in my ears. In a clearing atop one of the nearby hills, a small red light blinked.

"There it is," Hank said. "I'll have to check in with a couple people about those screams before we can get you situated."

"Did others check it out?"

He nodded. "I'll give him a call once we get—"

Static suddenly coursed over Hank's radio. He straightened. "Was there anybody talking now?"

I shook my head. "Only noise."

Picking up the receiver and clicking the button, Hank said, "Feld to Station 15, Feld to Station 15, did someone radio me? Over."

The white noise carried over the speakers. He tried once more. "Feld to Station 15. Can you hear me? Over."

"Maybe it was a mistake," I suggested.

"Feld to Whitmore. Andy? Did you call me?"

A hulking, black shape leapt from the culvert beside the road.

"Hank!" I shouted.

He dropped the radio, his foot slamming on the brake as he cut the wheel hard to the right. The scream of the tires lasted only a moment as the car slid to the edge of the road and rolled downhill. Wainwright's voice rang out in repetition as I screamed. Hank's shouting unloosed my terror again. I grabbed for him as my backpack flew past my head into the backseat.

The car crunched down a moment later then was tossed into the air again. I closed my eyes as we flipped between the earth and sky, tumbling downward. Somewhere amidst the screech of metal, and

Hank's cries, the music stopped. Shattering glass rang in my ears. I lost all sense of up or down and retreated into blackness.

Seven

Sharp pain stung across my middle. It pulled me back into reality with alarming haste. I stared down at the roof of the car, my arms dangling past my head. When I looked out the cracked passenger-side window, I recognized the gloom of night and swirls of falling snow.

I looked over at Hank. He hung limply, out cold. I couldn't tell in the darkness whether he was breathing or not.

"Shit," I muttered. The seat belt cut across my lap and held me in my seat. The shoulder strap dug into my scar. I fumbled to unbuckle the seatbelt, bracing myself with one hand against the roof.

Click.

I crashed down and cried as my shoulder caught the brunt of the impact. I flipped over onto my stomach and my head lolled to one side to peer out the driver-side window. It had shattered, leaving me a small escape route.

Leaning against the console, I put two fingers to Hank's neck and was thankful when I got a pulse. I touched his cheek. "Hank?"

He didn't stir. I patted his face. "Hank."

Still nothing. A thin river of blood ran down the side of his head. I followed it to its source and found a shallow cut beneath his dark hair. *I have to get him out of here.*

I tried to maneuver as close to the space between the steering wheel and the driver's seat but I couldn't reach Hank's belt buckle. I'd have to push his seat back. I reached under the seat, searching for the lever there. The seat glided forward and pushed me up against the dash. I struggled to force it back. Finally, the satisfying click of the seat told me it was stuck in place.

With more room, I moved in front of the steering wheel and positioned myself in a half crouch against the steering column. With Hank's upper body supported on my shoulders, I clicked the seatbelt.

Nothing happened.

Fuck. It was jammed. I'd need something to cut the belt.

As I wracked my brain trying to think of what I could use to cut the seatbelt, my sights dropped on the multi-tool case on Hank's hip. I wrestled out the hefty tool and opened the knife. Pulling the seatbelt tight for tension, I sawed at it. My right wrist throbbed with the effort. Every second was like an hour. The blade wasn't as sharp as I'd have liked.

When I only a half an inch left, the seatbelt snapped. Hank's weight crashed down on me unexpectedly, knocking me back against the steering wheel. The car's horn blared into the night, ringing in my ears. I pushed Hank off, cutting short the car horn. He groaned as he hit the roof of the car.

"Hank?"

He tried to sit up but immediately dropped again, hugging his arms against his chest.

"Are you okay?"

"We crashed?" he said, dazed.

"Something ran out in front of us on the road."

He breathed sharply. "My ribs." The dull pain in his eyes cleared some. "You busted your nose."

I touched it and pain radiated through my head. Blood was smeared on my fingers when I pulled them away. I licked my lips and tasted it. "We've got to get out of this car and find some help," I said, trying to push the pain to the background

He nodded. "The ranger station is only about a mile or so away. If we can get up there, they can take us to the hospital."

I nodded dumbly. Grabbing a t-shirt from my spilled bag in the back, I pressed it against the cut on his head. He seethed.

"Do you have first aid in the truck?"

He nodded toward the glovebox.

I tried pulling the handle but it wouldn't budge.

"I'm going to have to kick it open. Can you sit up over here?" I asked him.

He tried but, again, couldn't. "AH! Something's broken."

I unzipped his jacket and pushed up his shirt. Mottled purple and blue bruises covered his chest. I pressed on one rib carefully and he gnashed his teeth, the cry caught in his throat. I pulled his shirt back down and zipped his jacket again.

"Looks like it's the one rib. Don't move around too much; you could puncture a lung." I glanced out the car window. I hadn't noticed how cold it was until that moment. "You've got to stay here."

"Are you sure you can go alone?"

I stared at the woods outside the window. A sudden burst of

panic snarled and bucked in my head. I'd rather have waited until it was light to venture out. What if that thing that had made us go off the road was still around? The station was still a mile away and we were still surrounded by woods on all sides. But, if Hank had internal bleeding, morning could be too late. Not to mention the dropping temperature and the snow. I'd have to go by myself.

Hank must have read my expression because he patted his sidearm and shakily unholstered it. "Take this. Just in case."

Taking hold of the gun was like holding the hand of an old friend. It was like an extension of my arm locking into place the moment I got it.

"I'll be back as fast as I can."

I precariously army crawled toward the window, trying to avoid the shattered glass and metal debris. Once I'd cleared the opening, I stood in the heavy wet snow that bordered the woods and looked up toward the road.

Hank called my name from the car. I crouched down to look at him through the window. "Yeah?"

"Take this." He rolled a flashlight toward me and it bumped up against the window frame. I picked it up and clicked it on, gaining an inch of warmth in the darkness.

"Thanks."

"Be careful."

I turned toward the hill that led up the road and climbed. My boots slid on the slick snow but eventually, I made it to the asphalt. A plow truck had probably come through in the time we were off the road; there was only a thin layer of snow cover. Desolate, eerie quiet surrounded me. I didn't know how long I'd been out since the crash happened. It was still dark, no sign of the sun on the horizon. There was only one street light on this stretch of the highway. Anyone that might happen to speed by wouldn't notice a car flipped over in the ditch.

My shaking body was soon overrun by escalating pain. The ring finger on my left hand throbbed as if I'd punched a cement wall and my right knee like someone had taken a hammer to it. A coppery taste overwhelmed my senses. I spat out blood that had tricked into my mouth from my nose. I couldn't take stock of my other injuries in the blackness, nor could I do anything about them out here. I'd have to wait until I got to the ranger station. Gripping the gun and the flashlight as if my life depended on them, I ambled up the road.

There was something wrong with these woods. The further I traveled, the more a weight crushed down on me. *It's the shock from the crash*, I tried to tell myself. But I didn't believe it. At this abysmal hour in the morning, the world around me resembled a dark jungle. What's more was that the snow had melted away the further down the road I got, until I was staring into a plethora of lush foliage.

A dirt road branched off from the asphalt after about twenty minutes of walking. It snaked through the forest and up a slight hill toward the ranger station. Lights emanated a safe glow from its tiny windows. If I'd had the strength to run the whole way to it, I would have. The pain in my knee had grown worse and worse with every step. Adjusting my hold on the gun and the flashlight, I sloshed through the sodden bed of leaves that lined the road toward the station.

Sticks snapped in the darkness around me. It took everything I had not to lose the reign on my fear. I only had a little further to go and then everything would be fine. Brush shuffled in the woods to my left. I swung the gun toward it, my finger squeezing the trigger. Nothing happened. *Jesus*, I thought. *I didn't even turn off the safety*. Then, I thought about how stupid I was to even have my finger resting on the trigger. *Get your shit together, Raleigh.* I thought about Hank lying in the overturned Jeep. I needed to get back to him quickly. This was no time to shoot at shadows.

Nearly ten minutes later, I was hobbling alongside another Ranger Jeep parked next to the station. I leaned on it for a moment to rest before I climbed the stairs and looked inside. The desk up front was vacant. I pushed open the glass door.

Within moments of stepping inside, I doubled-over, my gut lurching. All of that exercise, the blood dripping from my nose into my mouth, the dizziness, the pain…it was finally getting to me. "Hello! Anybody here?" I called out.

A coffee mug stood precariously close to the edge of the main desk. I touched it; lukewarm. Radio static buzzed from one of the nearby rooms. I stood up, leaning on the counter and guided my way along to the first open door way. A tiny kitchen was inside with barely enough room to maneuver. The only window in the room was broken, the frame almost completely ripped out, and the surrounding plaster in the walls buckling.

I held my breath. What the fuck happened here?

Following the sounds of the static, I soon found myself in the doorway to one of the offices. The radio transmitter was on the floor, the back broken open and a mess of wires exposed. The computer was swiped from the desk also, the cracked screen glitching a tweaked picture of the station's website on and off every couple seconds. Papers and files littered the room in heaps. And amongst it all; blood was splashed in bursts over it. There were no bodies.

I moved further into the room and went for a phone on one of the desks, dialing 911.

The phone rang.

And rang.

And rang.

I stared at it. There must have been something wrong with the line. Someone would have picked up by now. This didn't make any sense.

Wind whistled through the opening in the kitchen wall. I explored the rest of the rooms on the ground floor, passing by a set of stairs that led up to a darkened second floor. More chaos awaited me in all the rooms: over-turned furniture, broken glass, lines of blood climbing the walls like ivy…but there was no sign of anyone else.

Arterial spurting. I'd learned enough from our crime scene geeks in Flintland to know that the owner of this blood was likely dead. A major artery was severed. Without help, they'd probably have bled out in minutes. From the quantity of it, I knew there should have been a body here.

Or bodies.

Somehow creepier than all of these findings were the enormous scratches on the floors and walls, blood caked inside of them. Could a blade of some kind have done this damage? But the slashes were in sets of two, sometimes three. They were more like animal scratches.

Overhead, the floorboards groaned.

I froze.

After another minute, the floor creaked again.

It wasn't the wind and it wasn't the building groaning like they sometimes do. For all I knew, someone could have been upstairs in trouble. But wouldn't they have answered me when I'd called out the first time? Maybe they couldn't? I stood at the foot of the stairs like a petrified child and slowly raised one foot to the first step.

The gun slowly came up as I chambered a round. If somebody came at me from the top of the stairs, I could put them down. I hoped I could. It was like trying to hold a fifty-pound barbell with my right hand. I switched over to the left and immediately regretted it when my finger raged in pain.

The ceiling groaned twice more. Whoever was up there was moving toward the staircase.

Not as confident about my aim as I had, I backed out into the room with the front desk. Rounding it, I rifled through the items on it for the keys to the Jeep out front.

The top step on the staircase groaned.

I yanked open some drawers. In one, I found three sets of spare keys with a tag for each vehicle's license numbers. I backed out into the frigid night again and limped down the stairs toward the Jeep parked out front. After checking through the keys, I plucked the correct key out and plunged it into the door lock. The door popped open. At the same moment, glass broke inside the station.

Slamming the door, my eyes shot to the rearview mirror. A shadow moved in the front window. I turned over the engine, put the car in gear and stomped on the gas pedal. The car lurched forward, bumping along the pot holes in the dirt drive. I eased my foot off the gas, determined not to crash again. After a minute, I carefully turned it onto the road.

Hold on, Hank.

The shape I'd glimpsed in the window hid at the edge of my mind like a monster. In the thick darkness, I swore that it leered beyond my headlights at every turn. It was something that not even the comforting thought of sleep and blankets could silence.

I'm losing my mind.

EIGHT

It wasn't too long before I recognized my own footprints in the snow from where I'd climbed up from the culvert. My heart still hammering from what had happened at the station, I pulled the Jeep off to the side of the road and climbed out, leaving the engine running. The air was strangely warmer than before. I limped to the top of the culvert and looked down at the totaled car. "Hank!" I called.

No answer.

Scuttling down the side of the hill, my heels dug into the snow to try and keep my traction. I ended up sliding most of the way down to the car. I peered in the broken window and nearly lost my balance.

Hank was gone.

I stood up, spinning around as I searched the tree line. "Hank!" I could barely make out anything past the thousands of trunks and bushes in the darkness.

"Liz!"

It was faint but I whipped toward a drainage pipe a little further down the culvert. "Hank?"

"I'm here." His voice was exhausted.

I shambled over to the pipe trying to avoid the slushy patches beneath me. Hank was curled up inside, shivering. His eyes were a strange hue against the whiteness of his face.

I crouched down in front of him. "What happened? Why did you leave the car?"

"I couldn't stay there. Something was shuffling around in the bushes." He slid toward the opening. "Did you find the station okay? How long until the ambulance gets here?"

I thought back to the bloody rooms I'd walked into at the station and the noises coming from the second floor. "There wasn't anyone at the station."

He looked at me with wide eyes. "There are three other rangers on call right now. You must have gotten the wrong place."

"The whole station was torn apart."

Hank stopped moving. "What do you mean 'torn apart'?"

"There was blood, Hank." I hesitated, helping him to his feet. "I took one of the Jeeps from the lot."

His weight suddenly dropped against me and I struggled to hold him up. He groaned, holding his side. His silence was somehow even heavier.

"I can get us to the hospital if you give me directions." I continued.

"How much blood?" he asked.

"Enough."

It took us nearly half an hour to climb the hill. Hank struggled to keep his footing, his hand glued to his side and an eternal wince on his face. I finally managed to pull him up and get him situated in the Jeep. By the time I was in the driver's seat, he was wheezing and drifting in and out of consciousness. I put a hand to his forehead. He was burning up.

The Jeep blazed down the mountainside toward town, its white colored hills and picturesque views still wrapped in darkness. The car clock read four-thirty. It was hard to believe that all of this had happened in a mere couple of hours.

Drawing closer to town, I noted a haze of light smoldering beyond the tops of the frosted trees. Then, closer: the black wisps that rose up weren't fog but smoke. When the house came into view, I slammed on the brakes. Hank folded against the dash and woke, howling in pain. "What the hell?" he exclaimed before he quieted.

A plastic jungle gym melted on the front lawn in front of a fully engulfed home, the neon yellow slide oozing into the purple swing set. My fingers were numb as I clicked the car door open and slid out of my seat. The heat was intense, singing against my skin even from the road. The insides of the house were blackened and much of the roof had already burned away. The crackling wood creaked and groaned. It would probably come down any moment.

I climbed back in the car and drove, trying to keep my eyes on the road. Hank continued to watch the house as it soon became a match-light in the rearview mirror. "What the hell is going on?" he murmured.

The smoke hung in the air like a wool blanket the closer we grew to town. The nearer I drove, the more I considered turning us around. Burning plastic, wood, and metal tinged the air, the stench growing thicker. We turned left at the gas station, which was packed with cars. We breached the outer edges of town.

The grocery store parking lot on my left was in chaos. Cars, campers, and vans were parked haphazardly across the pavement as if a child had left his toys scattered. The store was bright and thrived with silhouettes inside. People rushed out with carts piled high with grocery bags.

"Stop, stop, stop!" Hank ushered, grabbing the wheel right out of my hands.

I pumped the brakes and pulled us toward the curbside. We stared at the scene, immobile.

A woman ushered her children into her station wagon closest to our end of the parking lot. Behind her she dragged a shopping cart full of canned food and cereal boxes. A man ran up and hooked his arm in the handle, yanking it out of her grasp. She screamed and pulled a bottle of mace on him, spraying it at his face. The man collapsed, screaming as she shoved the cart back to her car and threw things in.

"Hank…" I whispered, beginning to lose control over my voice.

He took his hand off the wheel and sucked in a deep breath. "I need to get to Melissa's. Evie is there."

My eyes were glued to the scene in front of me. "Where are the police? What the fuck is happening?"

"Drive!" Hank ordered; his voice desperate.

The Jeep shot down the road toward the center of town, a route I'd taken yesterday. It was foreign to me now, the road littered with smashed vehicle debris and discarded possessions.

The town center of Cardend was a throbbing heart of anarchy. Mothers and fathers sprinted down the road toward us, cradling their children. Others yanked them behind like rag dolls. A man in an oily jumpsuit smashed a car window with a crowbar on our left. I slowed the Jeep, trying to make my way through the human thicket. "Where do we go?" I asked.

Hank pointed to a corner up ahead. "There." As a group of teenagers ran by us, I accelerated the Jeep around the turn and hit the brakes in time.

What had looked like an empty road was crammed with cars, most left abandoned. A few people were still pulling their belongings from them. An overturned passenger bus blocked the road ahead of them.

I looked into the rearview mirror. "What now?"

Fists suddenly hammered on my window. A man with a camo jacket was trying to wrench open the car door. Hank swung the gun up from where it rested on the center console and aimed it at the window.

The man stumbled away from the Jeep, tripped backward over the curb, and scrambled away into the darkness.

"Back up! There's another road we can take!" Hank said, setting the gun aside, his hands shaking.

Reversing back out onto the main street, I turned up onto a hill that cut around the main drag. Hank said it would put us a couple miles from his ex's house but it was the only way that looked clear. I gunned the Jeep's engine and shot up the hill. The screeches and shouts from town faded behind us as uneasy silence filled the car.

"Is the country being attacked?" I asked, not expecting an answer.

Hank flicked on the radio, cycling through static until he found a voice. He cranked the volume.

"—are erratic and violent. Officials are telling people to lock your doors and stay in your homes. If someone you know is or if you, yourself, are showing signs of psychological trauma or violent behavior, isolate them or yourself immediately and contact local authorities."

"Psychological trauma?" I shook my head. "What is this?"

Hank didn't say anything. We continued listening to the radio.

"Sources say people are succumbing to a magnitude of delusions: from seeing their dead family members to bizarre and bloodthirsty creatures. Reports have flooded in over the past hour from Paris, Brisbane, New York, and London, to name a few. The CDC is at a loss to explain a virus able to spread globally in such a short amount of time as this. So far, there has been no response from the White House on this developing pandemonium. We will update you with more news as it becomes available to us."

"It's a virus?" Hank whispered.

I thought about everything I'd seen: the black shape that had caused us to crash, the person walking on my porch the previous night, the eyes glowing in the woods, Brody at the gas station.... It had to be a delusion. It wasn't real. But instead of acknowledging it, I answered, "I don't know."

Around several more twists and curves in the landscape, we hit an intersection and swerved onto another side road. Cars backed out of driveways on both sides of us. One almost caught the left fender. If I hadn't been driving so fast, it probably would have. We passed another house, the front door wide open, but no movement about.

Hank told me to go left and I jerked the steering wheel that way. Beneath the hazy glow of a streetlight, I recognized bright red spatter on snow. I kept my eyes on the road until Hank pointed to a yellow duplex with black shutters.

An abandoned sedan with all four doors open was blocking the driveway. I swerved the Jeep up onto the front lawn past it and we climbed out. Hank ran for the front door while I tailed behind him. This small collection of houses was already deserted, every car gone save for the one blocking the driveway to Melissa's house.

I hadn't grabbed my bag back at the crash site. My phone was inside. I had begun to worry about my sister, Carmen, Josh, and my former colleagues back in Flintland… If things were as bad as they were here, I could only imagine the turmoil there.

"Melissa!" Hank shouted, trying the knob. It was locked. He pounded on the door. "Evie! Evie!"

"You have a key?" I asked.

"It was on my keychain in the Jeep," he said despondently. "Oh!" He leapt off the welcome mat and tore it up; no spare key. He shouldered the door and doubled over in pain. The door remained firm.

My eyes darted to the nearest window. Picking up a brick from the garden, I hurled it through. The noise stung the quiet around us. I'd expected a scream of surprise from inside but there was only silence. I knocked the rest of the glass out with the brick.

Hank nudged me aside. "I've got to make sure Evie's okay."

"You can barely stand right now." I forced the gun into his hands. "Keep watch out here. I'll find her."

I planted both hands on the window sill and jumped. Slithering into the opening, I rolled into a table, knocking a potted plant over. My wrist and knee were on fire.

"You okay?" he asked.

"Fine, but I killed the Christmas cactus." I glanced around. I was in a living room, flanked by a couch and television on either side. The light in the hallway was on.

"Evie!" I called. "Melissa?"

Silence.

"I'm here with Hank. He's right outside. But he's hurt."

I found my way into an adjoining room; a kitchen. A butcher block sat at the edge of the counter, a chef's knife missing from it. A quick search determined it was nowhere nearby. There was a lot of blood at the ranger station, and lots of people acting violently out on the street in town. What if Melissa was acting out, too? "I'm not going to hurt you," I said, projecting as much composure as I could muster.

A scream rang out from upstairs. I ran toward it, crossing into the dining room. As I rounded the table, a body tumbled down the stairs, crashing into the wall.

"Oh my god!" I rushed to the base of the stairs. Melissa lay there, one of her arms up over her head. Beneath it, the chef's knife stuck out. Inky blood smeared her white sweater. I quickly assessed the top of the steps. No one in sight.

"You." Her red-rimmed eyes focused on me. Tears streaked her face. "You were at the diner?"

I crouched down by her. The knife wound was deep, and from the amount of blood, had likely punctured a lung. Blood bubbled up from her lips. "Don't move. Don't talk. I'm going to call someone for help. Is Evie upstairs?"

Melissa grabbed the back of my head, her bloody fingers digging into my hair. "They took her. My Evie," she croaked. "They took her." I tried to unlatch her hand, but she drew me closer. "I don't want to die." She degenerated into sobs. "Please."

"Who has Evie?"

She let out a high-pitched yelp and squeezed her eyes shut.

"Melissa, who has Evie?"

"My step-dad." Her breath came in short bursts. "Shane."

"Is he upstairs?" I glanced up. No sounds coming from the darkness above and no movements.

When I noticed she hadn't answered, I looked down again. Her eyes were closed.

"Melissa!"

Hank ran in from behind me. He crashed to his knees beside me and snatched Melissa's hand into his. "What happened? Who did this?"

Hank's voice made Melissa's eyes reopen. She let go of me to grasp Hank and I stood, taking my gun back from him and turned off the safety. "Stay with her. I'm going to check upstairs." If I was right, the attack had just happened. Someone was still up there.

I quietly climbed the stairs, keeping my back to the wall. A nightlight was the only source of illumination in the hallway. As my vision adjusted to the new level of darkness, I recognized the shapes of several doors, some open and some closed. A streak of blood ran along the white wall and stopped at the door furthest down the hall. A stuffed animal zebra lay on its side, propping the door open. I crept over carefully, and nudged the door open the rest of the way with my foot.

I was looking into a girl's bedroom, the walls painted pale pink. The hot pink and orange covers were thrown off the bed and tangled on the floor. A small wooden table with painted flowers had collapsed on one side. Holding the gun out in front of me, I stepped over to the closet where the doors were pulled shut. Someone could have been hiding inside…

A shout came from the hall outside. “Liz! Watch out!”

I spun around. A dark figure was rushing at me, a crowbar hefted high over his head. My gun swept up and the shot rang out in my ears.

The man staggered back and collapsed into the hall. I swallowed and tried to catch myself as my knees wobbled. Good thing Hank had noticed him or this guy could have killed me. I moved forward toward the hall to make sure the assailant was dead.

“Thanks, Hank. I wouldn’t have—”

Before I was even in the hallway, Hank yelled my name up the stairs. “Liz, are you okay? What happened?”

He wasn’t in the hall. That wasn’t his voice that had warned me. But I had recognized it.

“I’m fine,” I lied, exiting the room into the hall. It was empty, no one else in sight. “There was a man up here. He attacked me. I shot him.”

Hank climbed the stairs, panting heavily. As he joined me, I noticed he now had an icepack and was holding it to his ribs. “Are you sure you’re okay?” he asked.

I nodded. “He’s dead though.”

Hank swallowed hard. “So, is Melissa.”

The revelation sunk in like oil, heavy and thick. Her injury was too severe; we wouldn’t have had a chance to get her out to our Jeep, let alone out the door.

“I’m so sorry,” I answered instead, touching his shoulder.

He cocked his head as he examined the man I’d shot.

I couldn’t look, my thoughts drifting to the voice that had warned me. “Do you know who this guy is?”

“He looks familiar, but I can’t place him.”

I finally made myself look. He was about six feet tall. Mud caked the bottoms of his Timberland boots, mud that I should have noticed on the carpet downstairs if I had been paying better attention. His glassy eyes were fixed on a random spot down the hall from us. Blood was still flowing from the gunshot in his chest.

I crouched down and checked his jean pockets. I found a wallet in the back left one. Flipping it open revealed a worn driver’s license. I told Hank the name and he shook his head. The jacket pocket, however, held a set of keys and a keycard. “Cardend Hydroelectric?”

Hank straightened suddenly. “That’s where I know him from. He always used to hang around with a group of guys at the bar in town.

I think he hit on Melissa a few times when she waited tables there."

I sighed. "That explains what he might have been doing here but it doesn't explain where your daughter is."

"I searched the rest of the downstairs," he continued, his eyes glistening. "Evie's gone."

"Melissa said that her step-father took her. Shane?"

Hank's face dropped. "You must have heard her wrong."

"I didn't. She said the name "Shane" clear as day."

"Son of a bitch," Hank snarled, his hands balling into fists.

"Sounds like a real piece of work."

"He was."

The floor was no longer solid underneath me. "Was?"

"He died about five months ago. Cancer." He moved beside me and leaned over to pick up the stuffed Zebra, wheezing as he did so.

"What made him so terrible?"

"He was manipulative, narcissistic…but incredibly smart. He was pushing for Melissa to get sole custody of Evie, even though he didn't think Melissa was capable enough. I knew his aim. He was going to deem Melissa an insufficient mother right after she did the same to me."

"Why go to all that trouble? Why did he even want sole custody?"

"Shane never did like Melissa. Having a step-daughter with a drug addiction was one of the worst things he could have on his record, especially in his bid to become a state senator. He employed everyone he could to try and sort out the mess of Melissa's collapsing life. He even had a guy inside DHS that would have lobbied for him to have custody when the time came."

"What a bonafide asshole."

"Yeah."

"Where is Melissa's mother in all of this?"

Hank sighed. "She died when Melissa was a kid. I think all of Shane's restrictions and rules made Melissa act out even more as a teenager. I thought I could make her happy when we married, thought we could get out from under his umbrella. Even after ten years, Melissa was too deep though. Depression and anxiety gave away to drug abuse and I lost her." I noticed a tear fall from the end of Hank's nose.

"I'm sure you did all you could," I said. I didn't know that. I wanted to think that Hank was as genuine and as good of a person as I'd come to believe, but I also knew marriages didn't always self-destruct because of one person. Maybe he'd gotten fed up with her. Maybe he couldn't handle her self-abuse anymore because it hurt too much to watch.

He straightened, his gaze growing hard. "It still doesn't explain what happened to Evie."

"Well, let's think outside the box. Did Shane have any other living relatives; anyone who might have wanted to pursue the custody battle after his death?"

"God…" Hank muttered, his arms suddenly growing tense. "Damn! I should have known."

"What?"

"It's Edith; Edith Alanko. She was Melissa's sponsor and Shane's girlfriend."

"So, she had access to the house? Access to Evie?"

Hank nodded. "Edith was by Shane's side until the end, worked from his home. She has as many connections as he did; everywhere in town and across the state. In addition to being Melissa's sponsor, Edith worked for the county administration office, had her hands in education, utility companies, budgeting committees… Hell, even judges at the Goddamn fair. Edith's influence is everywhere."

I frowned. "Why would she want Evie? A career woman like that doesn't seem like the kind of person who would want responsibility of a child."

"It was Shane's last wish." Hank said as he absentmindedly kneaded the zebra with his fingers. "Edith would probably have tossed a virgin into a volcano if Shane had asked it. She was obsessed."

"To go so far as to have Melissa murdered?"

"There was a rumor going around that Edith hired some guys to injure an incumbent on the town select board, so that a vote in favor of Shane's candidacy would go through."

"A rumor isn't enough to say concretely that it was her."

"There's no one else!" Hank growled. "If Melissa said it was Shane, she must have meant Edith. It's the only thing that makes sense."

I took a deep breath. He was getting upset and, in his condition, that wasn't the direction I needed to be sending him. As much as my instincts told me this was a leap, I knew we had no other direction to go in. Then, I remembered the radio. People were hallucinating dead relatives. What if Edith was one of those people? Could she have done this under "Shane's" influence?

"Could we track Edith down at her home?" I asked.

"She won't be there." Hank said. "Shane left his house to Edith and it was back near the middle of town. It was a mess there. She'll be trying to get somewhere safe and away from all this mayhem."

"What about Edith's family? Could she have gone to stay with one of them?"

Hank's eyes dropped back on the keys in my hand. "The hydroelectric plant. Edith's brother manages that plant and lives in the office above. It explains why this piece of shit is here. I bet that's where Edith's taken Evie."

"Wait," I said, stepping over the man. "We need to think first. We're both beaten to hell. We should think about trying to get some medical assistance first."

"Are you fucking kidding?" Hank said, shooting daggers at me. "Evie needs me. She's sick, remember?"

I did. The little girl coughing up a storm at the café yesterday was enough to make me more concerned. From the state of Evie's room, it looked as though the cold had gotten worse. Tissues filled the little wastebasket next to her bedside table but there was no sign of any cough syrup or decongestant. Not only was the girl getting sicker by the minute, she was in the hands of someone who likely didn't care.

I sighed. "I need a minute. One minute, Hank. Please."

He leaned on the banister, clenching his teeth as he held his side. "Don't take too long," he finally said, and hobbled down out of sight.

I waited until I heard him leave by way of the front door. Wanting to ease my mind, I stalked to the room at the other end of the hall. I elbowed the door open and swept into the room. My own image stared back at me from a bathroom mirror. I exhaled.

Easy, Raleigh, I told myself. *First, get the girl back. Then, figure out what's going on.*

I flipped on the small orange light in the bathroom and took stock of my injuries. The bridge of my nose had swollen to the size of a shooter marble and blood was splashed all over my right cheek. I had a decent-sized welt on my right temple and in addition to several small cuts and scrapes, my left ring finger had turned completely purple around the knuckle. It could have been worse. It could have been *a lot* worse.

I carefully cleaned the blood from my face, and taped my ring and middle fingers together. A quick glance through the cabinets revealed no pain killers. I needed something to calm my thundering headache and throbbing knee, but I'd have to settle for this for now. Lastly, I packed a handful of cotton balls, bandages, and antiseptic into a unicorn backpack from Evie's room. I didn't find anything in the way of cold or fever medicine. I suppose it made sense, given that Melissa was a former addict. Couldn't have anything in the house that might lead to a relapse. We'd need to find something for Evie when we found her.

I descended the stairs and stared at the wall, not wanting to look at Melissa's lifeless form. The jeep's engine idled outside the cracked front door. Even if I could clean up some of Hank's milder injuries, I wasn't going to be able to fix his ribs. That would take time and rest, neither of which he was willing to give me right now.

As I stepped over Melissa's body, I lifted my head and froze.

The air in my lungs vanished. My fingers, my arms, my face.... All of them were numb. My chest heaved, trying to find oxygen.

The light bleeding in from the kitchen cast half of Brody's face in a strange shadow. His near black eyes watched me knowingly, his mouth pinched and the veins in his forehead popped as they did when he was trying to hold back emotion. Everything from his crew-cut black hair, to his tri-blend black suit, pale blue suit-shirt, black Oxfords, and red tie was the same as the day he died. Clean. No blood. As if it had never happened.

He took a small step forward.

"D-Don't." I forced the gun up between us. "Stay right there."

"Liz," he said. The hairs on the back of my neck stood. I couldn't stop myself from shivering. His voice sounded exactly like I remembered; gravelly and low. It was the same as I'd heard upstairs. He was the one who had warned me about the attacker.

"Who the hell are you?" I demanded.

He cocked his head slightly. "You know."

"Bullshit." I ground my teeth. "Brody's dead."

"Yeah, you might be right about that."

I swallowed; my jaw clenched so tight that I thought I was going to break it. We stood for several more seconds before he tried to take another step toward me.

"I said, 'Don't'."

He put his hands up. "Would this make you feel better?"

"What are you doing here?"

"I wish I had an answer for that, but I don't."

I gripped the gun tighter. "You were at the gas station yesterday, weren't you?"

He nodded.

"And my cabin? Were you the one on my deck that night?"

He pursed his lips. "Which night? Liz, I've been there multiple nights."

A chill zipped back and forth between my shoulders. "Why?

How?"

"I told you; I don't know." His eyes warmed slightly. "It's so good to see you though."

I didn't know what to say to that. I'd thrown up a wall between me and my grief fragile enough that it could come crumbling down at any second. My lip juddered. "*What* are you?"

Brody's smile faded. "Shit, that hurts."

"Answer the question."

"Hell, I don't know. A spirit? A fucking bodiless soul?" He shrugged. "If I can't answer, are you going to shoot me?"

"You know that I can."

"Sure, I know you can. You've got one of the tightest shot groupings in the department."

My grip on the gun faltered slightly. *How could he know that? Unless he was…*

He continued. "It would be pointless for you to try."

"Why is that?"

"Because, to you, I'm a hallucination or a ghost: neither of which can get shot."

"I'm ready to test that theory."

"Say you do. Your buddy comes running in and asks why you're blowing holes in his walls. What then? Do you tell him you saw me, your dead partner? What'll he think then?"

I would have to tell Hank that I was as delusional as everyone else. But then, I'd be a liability. He was only concerned with his daughter's safety at this point and if anyone got in the way of that, including me, it wouldn't take him more than a moment to decide what to do. At least, that's how I assumed he would act. I'd seen the strength of a parent's love for their child and what they could be capable of on the job a number of times. Recklessness was an afterthought.

I got dizzy all of a sudden. My grip on the gun was clammy and my finger killed with how I was holding it. As much as I desperately wanted to believe that this thing in front of me, whatever it was, wasn't Brody, I couldn't deny the things it knew. Even its twisted way of talking me down was like Brody.

"What do you want from me?" I asked.

Brody's hands lowered slightly. "I want you to put down the gun and listen to me."

"Why? You can't get shot."

"You're either going to misfire or drop it. I don't want you getting hurt."

"I'm not putting down my gun."

"Then, at least sit down before you fall down."

My hand was shaking harder than ever now. I needed rest but I wasn't ready to lower my guard completely. I sat on the landing step, and put the other hand up to steady the gun. He never moved.

"What's happening out there?" I asked him.

"I told you I don't know. But we can't stay here much longer."

I shook my head. "I need answers; now."

"I don't have 'em and now's not the time to get into it." Brody stared down the hall toward the front door. "Your friend is going to leave you high and dry unless you get out there right now."

I followed his gaze. It had been five minutes now. I was surprised Hank wasn't dragging me out to the Jeep.

"Don't worry," Brody's voice brought my eyes back to him. "I'll be there."

The front door creaked open. "Liz, *come on!*" Hank called.

I turned back to Brody but there was only an empty doorframe. A part of me buckled with the revelation. He was gone again.

I stood, wiped a hand over my face, and followed Hank back out to the Jeep. "What were you doing in there?" he asked, shifting the icepack.

"Trying to get a grip," I said, placing the gun uneasily in the cup holder between us.

"How's that going for you?" he asked and I detected cynicism in his tone.

I stared at the house as I shifted the Jeep into gear. "Not well."

"I can't say I'm doing much better," he agreed.

I backed the Jeep out onto the road and drove back the way we came, trying not to look in the rearview mirror. Brody's countenance haunted me every time I did.

INE

THEN

I opened the passenger door before Brody had fully stopped the car. The apartment building was on the corner of East Lake and Walnut, catching the last rays of the setting sun before it dipped below the buildings. The dingy white siding buckled on the front face from where a car had struck it weeks before and a black garbage bag was taped over one of the windows.

I'd answered plenty of calls in this part of Flintland before as a rookie. Our unit called it "The Reef" because of how rough the neighborhood used to be. The Reef had the highest concentration of domestic assaults, thefts, and drug-related crimes in Flintland. City Council had tried to spiff up the Reef a few years back by fixing up the low-income housing. Even after all of the upkeep, the place had sunk back into its previous state. They'd also installed CCTV at all the traffic lights, but that didn't keep the dealings and muggings to a minimum; it meant not as much crime happened out in the open now.

The call dispatch had received ten minutes ago, however, was different from the norm. Patrol generally would have answered this one but missing persons had become a hot button topic for Flintland PD ever since Chloe Clark's disappearance. Captain Vance wanted criminal investigations detectives involved on any potentially related incident, especially if it involved minors.

I'd climbed only the first step to the two front doors before the engine to Brody's Dodge Charger cut and his car door opened. "You weren't even going to wait for me?" he called.

I scoffed and scanned the list of names on the apartment call list next to the door. "Moving a little slow today, are we?"

"So, that's how it's going to be," he said as he joined me at the top of the steps. We locked eyes and I noted the hint of sarcasm in his. We resumed checking the apartment list. I pointed to the name we needed; Jessica West. Brody punched the call button.

"I had a long night," he added, clearing his throat.

"Too many things going bump?"

He chuckled. "Too many thoughts rolling around in my head. Couldn't switch 'em off, you know?"

I knew. Josh had been back only a few days from his latest trip and already, I could tell that something was different. I'd asked him about the returned letter, about why he hadn't contacted me at all during the time he was gone. He told me he had no idea that I'd even sent a letter, that it must have been returned by the hotel. He told me that he'd been on the go constantly and when he did have moments to take a breath, he usually spent them drinking with the others on the trip to form connections and to sleep. I felt excluded and forgotten about, but tried not to show it. After all, this was what he did. I couldn't get upset every time he failed to check in, every time he left me here....

There was more though. Now that he was back, it was like there was an itch about him that I couldn't seem to scratch, one where he couldn't sit still for long periods of time. When he used to be contented sitting for hours on the computer fixing photos, he now stared at them. I knew he was still waiting for an answer from me. The job would have been everything for him and yet, I still couldn't bear the thought of leaving Flintland behind. I'd begun wondering more and more if a long-distance relationship could work between the two of us but every time I dared imagine what it would be like, melancholy chewed at me. Was I really going to put my job over him? Was he really going to put his over me? Was there no compromise?

That morning, instead of following the normal ritual of working out before Josh got up and then enjoying a quick cup of coffee or tea together, I drove out to the woods beyond Mottershill, the same woods that lined the edge of the development where Chloe Clark had gone missing. I climbed over knotted roots and slid down steep leaf-coated embankments, not really sure what I was searching for but unfettered all the same. I could breathe out here. I could focus on something else besides me.

I was out there for several hours. By the time I got home, Josh had gone out and it was time for me to go in for my afternoon shift.

Instead of mentioning any of this to Brody though, I answered, "So, what you're saying is that you need me to watch your ass more than usual today?"

I couldn't tell him yet. I still wasn't ready.

"Maybe," he grumbled, thumbing down the button again.

I gave the street a glance. There were a couple kids riding down the sidewalk on their BMX's and a woman down the block was toting a bag of groceries into the front door of a house. Surprisingly empty for a Friday evening.

This time, a voice responded in the apartment speaker. "Yeah?" It was tremulous and high, like the sound of someone who'd been caught naked.

"Jessica West? We're with Flintland PD," Brody answered. "You called us?"

The front door buzzed and the lock clunked open.

"I've got your back," I said, waving Brody on.

The main hall was pungent with the scent of thousands of cigarettes smoked and several burned into the faded green carpet. The faded floral wallpaper was permeated by the stench and it made both Brody and me gag as we ascended the stairs to the next level.

The bleary afternoon light barely penetrated blinds at the end of the second-floor hall. The overhead lights appeared to be burnt out and one test of the light switch proved it. A man and a woman screamed at each other behind one of the many shoddy doors we passed. A baby cried from somewhere down the hall and heavy bass thumped and vibrated the floor. As we passed a door, a loud BOOM echoed from behind it. Both of us ducked against the walls, hands on our holsters. The first boom was followed by laughter and the sound of engines revving and two voices conversing.

"Video game," I said, letting my hand drop from my holster.

Brody rolled his eyes as we both straightened. "Fucking hell."

We stopped at the third door down on the left. I knocked, while Brody sized up the corridor.

"Remind me to mention to the landlord that his lights need fixing," he muttered.

"Among other things," I added before the door opened.

A woman peered through the crack in the door, her frame dwarfed by an oversized hoodie with one of the local high school teams names on the front. Her eyes were red. She'd been crying recently but after a quick survey, she didn't appear to have been harmed. My hackles eased a little. "Jessica West?"

She nodded and let the door swing wider to allow us inside.

Jessica's apartment was neat, spotted with rustic furniture. A cabinet in the living room showed off kitschy snow globes and glass angels, the kind you'd often found in collections at the thrift store. Hell, maybe that's where she'd found them. I took a quick scan of the photos on the wall. Most were of Jessica and a teenage boy; probably her son.

Jessica sat in a cat-scratched wingback chair in the living room, stuffing exploding from the bedraggled blue threads. I spotted the cat on further inspection of the room, curled up behind a plant on the table next to the window, drinking in the last banking rays of sun.

Brody and I sat ourselves down on the couch opposite her and promptly sank in further than I think either of us expected. Brody straightened his posture and tried scooting to the outside of the cushion. It didn't help.

"Ms. West, we're here because you filed a missing person's report with the department." Brody flipped open his notepad and squinted to read his own chicken scratch. "A William West is missing. Relation?"

"Will: he's my son," she said, sniffling.

"When was the last time you saw Will?" I asked.

"Yesterday morning. He said he was going to visit Nana after school. When he didn't come home for dinner, I called his cell phone but it rang and rang." Jessica's eyes welled up with tears once more.

"Did you check in with your mother to make sure he made it there?"

She balked at me. "My mother's dead. I already told the cops that. He went to visit her grave. Do you people even talk to one another?"

Apparently not, I thought as I glanced at Brody out of the corner of my eye. "Did he say anything before he left?" I continued. "Anything that might have seemed off or unusual for him?"

Jessica straightened in the chair and crossed her arms. "My son didn't run away."

"So, everything is fine at home?"

As if to accentuate my point, the screaming from down the hall intensified.

Jessica's eyes narrowed. "Listen, I work two jobs. This is the best I can do. Will still has two years left of school. When he's not there, he's volunteering for Big Brothers Big Sisters and playing point guard for his basketball team. He doesn't have time to fuck around nor does he want to."

"There's no husband in the picture?" Brody asked.

"The man who fathered Will walked out when he was six months old. My mom helped raise my baby. Damn near did it for sixteen years. She died last May and it's been hard." Jessica nodded as if reaffirming the statement to herself.

I glanced at a photo in the cabinet of curiosities. It was dated but clearly a photo of an older woman and a young kid at a birthday party.

"Does Will go visit your mom's grave often?" I asked.

Something banged into the shared wall from the neighboring apartment.

Brody jumped to his feet and I jerked from the sudden movement.

"All right, I'll be right back," he said as he wove around the furniture and seconds later, the apartment door opened and closed.

I glanced at Jessica. "Are your neighbors always this…loud?"

"Mmm-hmm," she hummed. "Sometimes louder."

Brody raised his voice on the other side of the wall. I couldn't tell exactly what he was saying but I could tell by the tone of his voice he'd had enough.

I repeated my last question to Jessica about visiting the grave.

"Usually once a week although it's been hard with basketball practice. He's missed a couple weeks. I could tell he really wanted to go yesterday. It's like he's trying to make it up to her or something." Jessica scoffed but her expression quickly soured. "I never liked him walking to that cemetery all by himself. There's a lot of crazy people between here and there."

The noise next door had quieted. Moments after I noticed it, Brody returned, though didn't sit. I could tell he was more wired than when he'd entered and made a mental note to check in with him once we got back to the car.

We wrapped up the questioning by asking which cemetery Jessica's mother was buried in. Then, both of us offered our cards and told Jessica if she could think of anything else helpful, she should give us a call. Before leaving the apartment building, Brody banged on the door of the arguing couple again (as they had begun yelling again) and warned them he'd be back if there were any noise complaints. Such a threat usually didn't do much in the way of domestic disturbances, which both of us knew. I swore by the time we got back to Brody's car; they had probably started up again.

Brody clicked his seatbelt on and turned his key in the ignition. We sat in park for a moment, he checking his notes while I thought over our interview.

"That arguing couple really got you, huh?" I finally said.

His mouth formed a grim line and his glare told me I should let it go.

I wanted to poke the bear though. "Anything you want to talk about?"

Brody stared straight through the windshield; his arms propped up on the wheel. After a moment, he turned and said, "Right. Here's the thing: that couch was swallowing me whole; I needed an excuse to get up."

"And you left me behind to die?" I put my hand to my heart. "Ouch. What happened to looking out for your partner?"

"The couch wouldn't have eaten you, you're all bone."

I chuckled. "Wow. I work out *every* day."

"You work out in the woods today?" He said this without humor which pulled a cord in my chest. He suddenly reached over and tugged something gently from my hair. A dried leaf, half disintegrated and brittle to the touch.

I didn't know what to say at first. *Fuck.*

Brody flicked the leaf out his window and turned back to the wheel, carefully pulling out away from the curb and into traffic.

"I went for a hike this morning," I said, staring down at the buttons on my blazer.

"Sure," he said, an earnestness in his voice that I immediately knew wasn't real.

My shoulders tensed as I glanced over at him. "Go on and say what you're thinking."

"I think you're holding onto something that needs letting go," he said, his voice measured and his eyes remaining on the road ahead. "You're too stubborn to do it."

At the time, an infinitesimal part of me wondered if, somehow, he'd guessed my trouble with Josh, if he had somehow gotten wind of the promotion and had known I was thinking about leaving the entire time. I knew he was more likely alluding to the Chloe Clark case. No matter which one he meant, it still made heat rise in my face.

"I'm the stubborn one?"

"Yes, in this partnership, you are typically the one who has a hard time letting cases go. Don't think I can't tell what it's doing to you." His tone took on a harsh edge and made me lean away. "Someday, before you know it, it's going to eat you alive."

"And as always you deflect the conversation from being about you to being about me."

He took his eyes off the road for a moment and in that quick glance, I detected something I had only seen in his eyes a handful of times: fear. "What the hell is that supposed to mean?"

"You're not telling *me* something, you secretive son of a bitch." I added the last bit under my breath.

He shook his head. "It's nothing for you to worry about."

"Then, *my* shit is nothing for *you* to worry about." I yelled back.

Brody's grip on the wheel tightened. "Fine."

Neither of us said anything for a while but the whole rest of the ride, a pile of stones sat in the base of my stomach.

St. Gabriel's Cemetery was only three blocks from the apartment complex. Brody drove slowly. The car stereo was off, which wasn't unusual, but made the ride feel three times as long. I tried not to think about our argument, instead focusing on the town around us.

After taking our first right at the end of the road onto Giroux Street, we rolled past a slush pile of businesses, all in a state of foreclosure or decay. A bustling corner store and pawn shop appeared to be the only places thriving, their red neon lights glaring in the early dusk.

We stopped at our first red light. In the distance, St. Gabriel's Church rose up over the traffic. The neo-gothic building was at a T intersection a few more lights ahead on the aptly named Church St., named for the six houses of worship that lined it: Catholic, Presbyterian, Methodist, Lutheran, Jewish, and Baptist. It was one of the busiest and most diverse places in Flintland on a Sunday. There was a line of people in raggedy clothing, some pushing shopping carts, others rolling bags toward the Catholic church entrance. A sandwich board out front displayed SOUP KITCHEN: All Souls Welcome! FREE.

"This is your church, isn't it?" I asked Brody, as we rolled up to the T intersection before it.

"Yeah." He turned the car left and we headed away from the line of people.

The cemetery was directly next door, enclosed within black iron gates, stone walls, and backed by woods. It was small, about five acres in the center of Flintland, elevated and neatly kept in spite of the neighborhood we'd left. Somehow, it existed in its own quiet realm. With the unusually warm weather in the last few days, most of the snow had melted and left the cemetery a surprisingly green swath, framed by bare oak trees and tangled hedges.

Brody parked on the street and we got out. The sun had dropped down below the horizon, the sky cooling into frosted purple hues. We climbed a set of stairs through the main gates and took a cursory sweep of the land. Brody explained that the cemetery was split into three different sections. The far left was lined with a number of elaborate granite sculptures and contained more of Flintland's upper-class plots. The middle contained several older graves and a few mausoleums, while the right side was the most open and reserved for deaths over the last fifty years.

"Did you learn this at Graveyards 101?"

"It's a cemetery. Graveyards aren't attached to the church." He raised his brows. "There endeth the lesson."

We traversed toward the right side of the cemetery, our shoes squishing in the soft grass. The light was waning and it was getting harder to see. Lines of mossy headstone silhouettes stretched on and on, arching over hills.

At first, Brody seemed to know where we were going and I followed him without question. But the further into the cemetery we went, I noticed his pace slow and a confusion cross his expression.

"So, do we have any idea where this grandmother is even buried?" I asked.

"Probably down here," Brody said, leading me through a couple rows toward the far corner of the cemetery. After a moment, he changed direction and said, "Never mind."

"I thought you knew this place pretty well."

"I thought I did, too," he said.

A lone crow cawed from a branch in the brush to our left. Brody stopped and stared at it a moment.

"What?"

"I don't remember this being so thick through here." He nodded toward the woods. "Thought they'd cleared a lot of the underbrush out this summer."

I followed his gaze into the trees. With the night coming on, it looked pitch black inside, like looking into a well. "Maybe it grew back?"

Brody hummed but didn't say anything. We continued in the direction Brody had chosen. Eventually we came across an emblem that pointed us toward a newer plot of graves. As if bolstered by the signage, Brody confidently led the way into the lot.

"How do you know she's here?"

"A few members of the congregation have been buried here in the last few months. Good spot for families who don't have enough money. The church fronts as much as they can to help out."

"You've been to congregation member's funerals?"

Brody glanced over his shoulder at me. "You *do* understand the meaning of the word 'congregation' right?"

"Hey, I'll admit that my interest in organized religion is less than stellar. I didn't think you were that close to people you hang out with once a week, that's all."

"Once a week for fifteen years, Liz. Some of these people have been over my house to help with the roof. I've been over to theirs to install ramps for wheelchairs. You'd probably recognize a few of them from our summer barbecues. Carmen and I usually volunteer twice a month to work the soup kitchen. It's more than standing in a room reciting Bible verses. Some of these people are like family."

The statement made me shrink inside. No, I'd never gone to church as a kid. No, I'd never joined any clubs or extra-curricular activities in college. My friend circle had always been tight and if thrown into a crowded room where I knew less than half of the occupants, I'd slither away as quickly as I could. There were very few people in my life I'd willingly dedicate my time, money, and energy for. If Brody hadn't been so welcoming when I'd joined Flintland PD, I might always have been a wildcard, prone to anger and solitary confinement.

I opened my mouth to say something and instead, caught site of a figure crouched by one of the graves. "Brody," I said, nodding toward the person.

We drew closer. A young man was cowering in front of a gravestone, his hands curled around his head, moaning. Brody carefully edged toward him. I stayed back, my hand hovering over my holster.

"Hey," Brody murmured, edging closer. "Will? Will West?"

The young man's head jerked up; eyes wide. "No! My sweet boy, my sweet boy…." he cried. It was him, the same kid from those pictures at the apartment. What was wrong with him though?

"Liz, call an ambulance," Brody said, crouching down by Will. "Hey, Will, I need you to calm down. Paramedics are on their way. I need you to talk to me though, okay?"

I stepped away, making the call to dispatch. I wound my way through the darkness, the crows caw retreating as it took flight against the blackening sky. I primed the unlock button on Brody's key fob and the car lights blinked on and off in the darkness nearby. Once there, I climbed inside and drove the car deeper into the cemetery, following the overgrown paths until I found Brody and Will in the headlights. In the trunk, I found a space blanket in our emergency kit and handed it over to Brody.

Brody knowingly draped it around Will's shoulders and whispered to Will before standing up. He motioned me to step over to the side. "How long on the bus?"

"ETA fifteen minutes. It's rush hour." I glanced over his shoulder at Will. "Is he on drugs?"

"Not sure. He's not responding to his name. Keeps saying the same thing."

I frowned. "My sweet boy?"

Brody shrugged. "Hell, if I know."

I rounded my partner and stepped over to Will. With the headlights on him, I noticed his hands and knees were coated in dirt. The grave he was standing by looked to have been dug out a little. Was he trying to dig to his grandmother's coffin with his hands?

"Hey," I said gently. "I'm Detective Raleigh. We're here to help you, okay. There's nothing to be scared of."

Will's eyes flickered to me for only a brief moment before he resumed his chanting.

"Will, your mother called us. She's worried about you."

"Jessica?" He perked up.

I frowned. He called his mom by her first name? Some kids did this, I guess…

Will shook his head, slowly at first then more madly. "No, no, no, no, no! I'm not supposed to be here! This is the devil's work!"

"Easy, easy," Brody said from behind me. "What's the devil's work? Why aren't you supposed to be here?"

"Because I'm already dead!" he shouted. "I've condemned my grandson to Hell!"

EN

NOW

It wasn't long after leaving the house that my right knee locked up. Pushing on the gas pedal hurt more than I could bear. Hank took over driving despite my initial fear to let him. There was a quiet rage on his face that didn't belong. I thought back to when he'd been in my cabin last night, a time that seemed forever ago. He'd stumbled over his words trying to convince me that my panic was getting the best of me. The roles had swapped now and I hadn't said much to try and talk him out of his plans to get Evie back.

They weren't really plans, per say. He was going to confront Edith at the hydroelectric power plant and give her an ultimatum…using his gun as a threat. He hadn't stated that, but he kept occasionally reaching down to touch it during our drive, as if to make sure it was still there. What was worse was that I knew he'd carry through with pulling the trigger if he had to. This was his daughter at stake. Plus, she was sick. He'd do whatever he had to do to get her back.

We'd cut around the town center again, shooting straight across to another road. My heart sank into my stomach as I noticed a few people still actively running around. The group of teens that had passed us in the alleyway was looting the hardware store. The café where we'd enjoyed our cherry pie the day before was dark, its glass front smashed in.

The vision of the road ahead suddenly tilted and the Jeep veered toward the store fronts.

"Hank, what are you—Hank!"

He was slumped against the window. I grabbed the wheel and jerked it back toward the road. The jolt awoke him and he regained control of the car. He'd paled considerably, his lips blue and he tried to hide a violent shiver as he readjusted his posture in his seat.

"We need to go to the hospital," I said.

He didn't answer.

"Hank—"

"We can't afford to stop," he said under his breath. "Not when Evie is sick."

"And how are you going to get her back when you can barely keep the Jeep going in a straight line?" I countered. "If we don't stop, you're going to run yourself into the ground and then what help will you be to her? None!"

He coughed and glanced at me out of the corner of his eyes.

Without saying a word, he took a left up ahead, following road signs for Cardend Memorial. We were barely a quarter mile down the road when the red taillights of cars blurred the darkness in front of us. Hank slowed the Jeep to a stop and we both stared in awe. The entrance to Cardend Memorial was packed with vehicles of all shapes and sizes. Several were left abandoned, while others waited, impatiently honking horns. Beyond the throng of cars, the emergency doors were guarded by a swarm of police vehicles and hospital staff, all trying to funnel people through for care.

"This is insane," Hank whispered, looking in the rearview mirror. "There's no way we're getting in here any time soon."

"What about a family physician of some kind?" I asked. "Anyone else in town who could take a look at you?"

"Doctor Calhoun is on vacation. He goes down to Florida to visit with his daughter's family every November."

"He can't be the only fucking doctor in this whole town!" I shouted.

"Most people go to a physician through the hospital. They cover more types of insurance and have better hours. Doc Calhoun has been getting ready to retire since last spring. He barely took patients anymore."

"Jesus Christ," I grumbled. "Think. Otherwise, we'll *have* to wait." I wasn't making this a choice.

Hank exhaled a shaky breath. "There's a treatment center in Pineberry, a little town south of here. They deal with substance abuse…"

I didn't even need him to explain. He must have taken Melissa there for her drug problem. "I can imagine they have their hands full right now," I said.

"They have a staff of nurses, physicians, and counselors usually. I don't know how they'd do with setting broken bones and I know they aren't equipped for surgery…"

"What if we get over there and they are as swamped as this place?"

"It's either Pineberry or we wait here all night."

I sighed. "I don't know…"

Hank shifted to look at me more directly and winced with the slight movement. "At the rate they're letting people in here, we'll be lucky if we can even get inside in a few hours. The resources here are strained. They aren't going to be able to help the number of people waiting out here all at once. It's a rural hospital."

"What about triage?"

He scoffed. "What about it? This is madness right now."

I glanced at the scene before us. As much as I didn't want to agree with Hank, I knew he was right. Over the last few minutes, we'd been there, more and more people had left the comfort of their vehicles and tried to gain entry to the hospital on foot. A crowd had gathered at the doors. The police lights sprung to life and officers were motioning for people to get back in their cars.

"It's now or never, Liz," Hank said.

I followed his gaze. Headlights from more cars were coming into view on the road behind us.

"Fine. Let's go."

Hank shifted into reverse and whipped the Jeep around. Gunning the engine, we flew down the road away from the lights.

The drive to Pineberry was silent. I watched Hank like a hawk, determined not to let him fall asleep at the wheel again. At the same time, my own mind was clouded by the thought of Brody appearing to me again. The Alice in Wonderland-ish conversation we'd had back at Melissa's house left me more confused than ever. *I must have a concussion*, I decided. *The car accident was bad. It's fucking with me.* I was also acutely aware that panic was taking its toll on me, too. I'd never been much for hypochondria but if there was a global pandemic, it was easy to assume that I could have been mistaking the symptoms of my concussion for whatever else was going on.

Even if I had seen and heard Brody days before the accident.

I couldn't believe it.

I didn't want to believe it.

As we entered the town of Pineberry, I noticed it was barely a town at all, more a collection of shabby buildings buried in the woods between Cardend and Middlehitch. It reminded me vaguely of an old western, with a stream of shops on each side of a road that cut through the center of town. As soon as we were through it, we were surrounded by trees again.

Hank muttered something and I barely caught it. "What?"

"I was saying that I thought Pineberry was bigger than that. Of course, nothing seems the same right now as it once did."

About a half mile from town, Hank pulled the Jeep onto a dirt road that led us even further into the woods. A brick facility appeared from the darkness in front of us, the words "Pineberry Treatment Center" emblazoned on the glass front doors. There were only a few cars in the lot. *Good*, I breathed. *Fewer people to deal with.*

I looked at Hank again and knew it would be a struggle to get him inside under my own power. He was struggling to keep his eyes open. I reached over him and adjusted his seat so that it lay back.

"What are you doing?" he said warily.

"You'd barely make it to the front door. I'll be back with someone soon."

He nodded and I got out of the Jeep.

I stepped onto the sidewalk, up to the glass front doors and gave them a pull. They didn't budge. Locked from inside, though the lights were on. There was a front desk with a computer in the main lobby but no one was there. They must have locked the doors in order to protect the patients. I banged on the door a few times and yelled in frustration.

"Hey!" Hank called weakly.

I glanced back over my shoulder at him in the Jeep.

"There's a back entrance."

Nodding, I made my way around the side of the building. There was a set of automatic doors labeled EMERGENCY under a porte-cochere. There was an abandoned silver Honda Civic nearby with the drivers' side door thrown open. The automatic doors to the clinic were smashed clean through, glass teeth rimming the metal around the top and sides. The entrance way was dark. I carefully moved inside.

Phones rang out from distant places but no one ever picked up. Intercoms echoed into the empty halls. From the number of cars outside, I assumed that the night crew was much smaller than the day staff. Judging from that shattered emergency door and the abandoned car, someone had gotten in, probably someone who didn't belong.

The news was saying people under the influence of this virus were exhibiting symptoms similar to patients with psychosis: delusions, behavioral changes, disorganized thinking.... While my experience with mental health patients was far less considerable than with heroin and crack users, I did recognize that the behavior of everyone until now seemed like too large a scope to be caused by a psychotic break. Thousands of people all at once? Millions even? It didn't make any sense.

The people we'd come across were frantic and afraid. They'd

torn Cardend apart looking for supplies and a way to escape or maybe a way to hide. I wasn't sure. All I knew were the kernels of info from the news broadcast on the radio earlier. I wasn't sure how this had affected the patients in this clinic either, but I knew something wasn't right here already.

I followed a corridor until I came across some closed heavy doors. The metal plate on the wall indicated that there were offices that way and the pharmacy. Maybe there was someone there that could help. I braced myself as I pushed open one of the doors.

"Don't open it yet."

I whipped around, putting my back to the wall.

Brody's form flickering in and out of existence.

"What the hell," I muttered under my breath, my heart fluttering in my chest. "Why are you following me?"

"You're the only one who sees me," he said, rolling his shoulders out. "I've walked in front of countless others and no one notices. It's only you."

I turned my attention back to the doors behind me, though I was afraid to let him out of my sight completely.

"What the hell are you doing here anyway?" he asked.

"I'm trying to find someone that can help Hank."

"Good luck with that. From the looks of this place, I'd say they can barely handle what's happening here."

"I don't know what the fuck to do!" I said, exasperated. "Hank needs help, at least something for the pain. He's not going to last much longer if I don't do something."

"The pharmacy could have basic pain meds there. It would have to, a clinic as isolated as this. Of course, it's probably locked up tight right now."

My fingernails bit into my palms as I balled my hands into fists. "You're supposed to be a ghost, right? You can walk through walls and shit?"

He walked closer. The scent of his cologne was faint but still made me nostalgic. He held out his hand and said, "Go on."

I reached out to him. The air crackled and his fingers turned to dust, the air around them warping. My own were plunged into icy cold. He cringed, closing his eyes. I swirled my fingers in the space where his hand would be. No texture, no substance…only air; cold air.

"How is this possible?" My voice wasn't my own.

He looked me in the eye. "I don't know. But now isn't the time to try and explain it."

"I have to be hallucinating," I said under my breath. "It's the only explanation."

"In the hallway to your right, there's a guy curled up on the couch begging for a hit and two nurses trying to get through to the cops. One's got a Johnny Cash t-shirt on; the other's sitting on the windowsill chain-smoking like nobody's business."

I stared at him and followed his gaze down the hallway. "Bullshit."

"Go see for yourself."

Turning from the stairway door, I maneuvered down the hall, moving as slowly as I could to avoid making noise. Before I even reached the first open door, the wavering high-pitched voice of a woman broke through. "What do you mean you don't have enough support? Christ, I have seventeen patients and two staff members here exhibiting the symptoms. One of the patients is even missing. High risk. Opioids. She's only been here a week, and she's easily triggered."

I cautiously peered into the room.

It was a large gathering room with a kitchen built on. Several couches and tables with chairs dotted the area. My eyes dropped immediately on a rail-like man cowering on the sofa furthest away, his hands over his eyes as he sobbed uncontrollably.

The stench of cigarette smoke hit me squarely in the face. It didn't take long to find the owner of it, perched in the kitchen window, shaking her head. She looked like she was talking to herself.

A larger woman in a t-shirt was clutching at a receiver for a wall phone, her back turned to me. "You need to send us help! Who knows where she's gotten to…? She could get herself and someone else killed if she gets a hold of anything. We're only a staff of six. No one on day shift is answering their phones. We can't do this by ourselves." She spun around and I ducked back out of sight, but not before I noticed the words "Folsom Prison Blues" on her shirt.

I pulled away from the scene. No one had the time to look at Hank or me for that matter. They were overwhelmed as it was.

I returned to Brody who had remained by the entrance. I put my hand on the wall nearby, desperate to touch something concrete again. No matter how much I wanted to believe I was imagining him, there was no way I could have known who was in that room and what they were wearing ahead of time. Which only meant one thing…

"Trust me now?" he said, cocking his head.

I bit my lip to hold back an unexpected sob.

This was real. *He* was real. I covered my mouth.

Brody got closer again and put his hands up. "Hey, hey. It's okay. Let's get what you need and get out of here, huh?"

I cleared my throat, forcing myself to concentrate on the mission in front of me. "There's no one here that can deal with cracked ribs or busted fingers right now. They're under duress. If you can scout ahead and let me know what the hall to the pharmacy looks like, that will make getting in and out a hell of a lot easier."

Without another word, Brody walked by me and passed through the door as if it wasn't there. Wisps of his body trailed behind him like smoke.

I stood for nearly a minute, listening for anything beyond the doors. Finally, Brody said, "You can come in."

Sucking in a deep breath, I gently pushed on the door and peered through. No one was in sight. I crept down the length of corridor, my footsteps muted by the sterile grey carpet. Most of the offices I passed were shut with no lights on.

Ahead, a grey push door with a side plate labeled STAIRS loomed. As I moved toward it, a door behind me suddenly opened. I quickly pushed into the nearest room, a supply closet, and closed the door. Crouched in the dark, I waited for the strained voices to pass, and they did, quickly. When I was sure they were gone, I cracked the door open a little. Brody was standing outside.

"They were talking about a missing patient, Liz. No one's seen her in hours; not since all this shit started apparently."

"I heard," I said, coming out into the hall and closing the closet door behind me. The destroyed emergency doors could have been from someone desperate to get out. But it didn't explain the empty car with the door open in the lot.

Brody sighed. "Maybe she went to the one place where she knew she could get a dose."

I followed Brody's eyes to the stairwell for the pharmacy. I gave him a look. "Don't they usually guard the pharmacies in places like this? She'd have to be suicidal."

"Who says she isn't?"

The gravity of his words struck me.

"All I'm saying is you should be careful," he added.

Nodding, I squeaked open the door and carefully made my way down the steps.

"Why the hell aren't you at home, Liz?" Brody asked from behind me.

I stared at each step as I descended. "Vacation," I said shortly.

"Well, that sounds like a lie," he muttered.

"Yeah?"

"You and vacation aren't exactly synonymous with one another. How many times did Vance ask you to take time off?"

"Well, I finally took it," I answered shortly, coming to the first landing and turning.

"How come Josh isn't with you?"

I stopped briefly, the question stinging. "What do you mean? You don't remember?"

"Remember what?"

I turned to him. "We broke up."

He looked lost. After a second, he murmured, "I'm sorry."

"Me, too." I kept going.

At the bottom of the stairs, I crept to the door and listened. Nothing. I let Brody go ahead. After a few moments, he gave me the go ahead and I snuck in. The halls were much darker down here. The lack of noise had me holding my breath.

I rounded a corner and shrank back out of sight. There were two people slumped against the wall, both no more than eighteen. Their skin was nearly the color of the walls, deep purple circles beneath their eyes and track marks jabbed into their arms. The first was a girl with short black hair. Her eyes were rolled up into the back of her head; her breathing was shallow and erratic. She was still wearing a nametag from whatever therapy session they'd been doing upstairs: Chelsea. The other was a boy, off in a complete trip with a smile broadening his lips. He didn't have a nametag but wore a jacket. Probably the one who came in the car. Broke her out of her room maybe?

I looked to Brody and he gave a nudge. I strode into the hall, carefully stepping over outstretched legs and prone bodies. As I approached Chelsea, she stirred suddenly, rolling a little to her right. I kept to the opposite wall, my grip on Evie's pack tightening in spite of myself.

They're kids, I reminded myself. *Worse for the wear, too. Victims of whatever the hell is happening.* It was only then I noticed a smear of something on her chin. Not only her chin, though. It was on her hands and shirt, too. I leaned closer and then as if struck by lightning, yanked myself back. "God, it stinks…"

Finding the door to the pharmacy ajar, I pushed inside.

The shelves were ransacked, pill bottles scattered over the floor and papers in disarray. I turned the corner and nearly choked on my breath. A bald man with a cracked set of glasses lay in a puddle of vomit on the floor. A needle was stuck in his neck, another one broken off and lying on the floor nearby. The stench was bodily fluids, the same ones on Chelsea outside. Had she done this?

Brody moved around me and stood in front of the body. "They pumped him full of drugs. Probably because he got in their way. Grandpa didn't stand a chance down here without an orderly."

I let out as even a breath as I could.

"There's no telling how long those two out there will be on their trip to Never Neverland," Brody continued. "Get what you need so we can high-tail it out of here."

I set Evie's bag on the counter and went to the nearest cabinet. I grabbed a bunch of bottles that I recognized names for, most of which were for pneumonia and pain-killers. If Hank developed an infection, those would be the best things to have. In a cabinet toward the back, I scraped some tiny bottles of morphine, antibiotics, and penicillin down into the backpack. There were bottles of Tylenol and packages of Nyquil that I instantly threw in, knowing that we'd need something to treat Evie's cold when we eventually got her back.

Evie's backpack was small and it filled up quicker than I'd have liked. I noticed a soft lunch tote sitting nearby, probably belonging to the body at my feet. I emptied it of the sandwich and pudding. Bottles of disinfectant lined the bottom shelf. I stuffed a couple into the lunch tote, zipped it closed, and turned for the door.

"Get down!" Brody hissed.

I let myself drop to the floor and scooted under the counter, pulling the tote close to me.

The door creaked open and a pair of knee-high converse lazily tromped in. I recognized them and the torn jeans above them: Chelsea was awake.

Evie's backpack, I realized. I'd left it sitting on the medicine cabinet across the room. Next to me on the floor, the pharmacist's empty gaze bore into me.

Chelsea stumbled against the counter above me. I pulled my legs up tighter against my chest. She was carrying a needle in her hand, a smidge of medication still in it. No doubt, she was looking for more.

Brody stood directly in front of her. He sidestepped her as she stumbled by him.

"Just wait for it," he said. "She'll juice herself again and then she'll be down for the count."

As much as I hated the idea of letting this girl continue to abuse her body this way, I was more worried about her noticing me. If she was willing to kill the pharmacist for a fix, it meant she'd be ready to take me down, too. As much as the cop in me knew the procedure to talk a drug abuser down, try to get the meds away from them, and immobilize them, my body was in no shape to take that on if she refused. I didn't know how I was even still standing.

Chelsea shuffled right into the pharmacist's body and slammed down against the floor, barely catching herself.

I braced myself, my eyes drifting to the needle in the pharmacist's neck.

"Don't make a sound," Brody said.

Chelsea pushed her knees up under her and half curled up, still moaning. Then, her eyes locked on me. She whipped around like an animal, the syringe in her hand swiping through the air. I ducked, the needle slicing the air in front of me. I threw myself toward the dead pharmacist. I wrenched the syringe from his throat and rammed it straight into Chelsea's cheek.

She screamed, swinging at me blindly.

I rolled out of the way, her needle snapping as it hit the linoleum. I jumped to my feet and snatched Evie's backpack from the cabinet. Chelsea was climbing to her feet when I shoved out the door.

"Hurry!" Brody yelled from somewhere behind me. I ran to the stairwell door, my lungs burning, my knee threatening to drop out beneath me. The two bags flip-flopped in my hands with each stride. Throwing the backpack on, I tore open the stairwell door and slammed it behind me, then bolted up the stairs. My legs throbbed as I climbed higher and higher. The one time I dared look over my shoulder, I stumbled over myself on the steps.

Brody was suddenly at the top of the stairs, his voice desperate and filling my ears. "Get up! Get up! Go, girl, go!"

I yanked open the door to the offices and launched myself through. My footfalls drummed against the carpet as I neared the doors to the main hall. Chelsea's scream echoed up the stairwell behind me, a sound so inhuman that I imagined was being chased by a monster instead.

I pummeled through the doors and out of the emergency entrance. A pink sky welcomed me back to the world outside. My feet slapped on the pavement as I raced toward the front lot. I looked over my shoulder again. I was alone.

I collapsed against the side of the building, struggling to breathe. The edges of my vision were hazy and I knew exhaustion was itching to pull me down into its dark embrace. I forced myself to stand and continue to where I'd parked the Jeep.

But as I neared, my steps slowed and soon stopped. The spot where I'd left the Jeep was vacant. No one would have stolen the Jeep with Hank still inside. It meant only one thing: Hank had left to go to the hydroelectric plant without me.

I slumped onto the ground, the tote sliding from my hand.

I noticed Brody on the edge of my vision.

"He's gone," I said.

"Maybe you're better off not getting involved. He's going to get himself and whoever he's with killed," Brody answered.

I grabbed the tote from the ground and, against my better judgement, returned to the back lot. I climbed into the abandoned silver sedan, tossing the packs into the backseat first. The keys still jingled in the ignition. "I don't think he's fully aware of what he's doing," I answered. Hank's forehead was burning when I'd last checked it. A fever would make him confused and potentially heedless of his own actions.

"Seemed pretty determined to me. He's a father who will do anything to get his daughter back. He's reckless and it's not going to end well."

I swallowed and looked back at Brody. "Wouldn't you do the same if it was your daughter?"

He didn't say anything.

The car started up after a few twists of the key and coughs from the engine.

"You know, I never said I wouldn't do the same," he said from outside.

I put the car in reverse and maneuvered the car so that I had a clear shot to the driveway.

"But then again, I'll never know what that's like," he added, suddenly from the passenger seat beside me.

I spun toward him; my teeth gritted. "Why me?"

He cocked his head. "What?"

"Why can I only see you? Why not Carmen? Why aren't you with her?"

For a moment, a shock came onto his face, as if he hadn't even thought about her; his own wife. "I don't know."

"I don't believe it."

"I can't." He put a hand to his temple. "I don't remember."

"What's the last thing you *do* remember?" I wasn't sure I really wanted to know.

"I thought about her. I was in that place. It was cosmic and dark and surrounded by these eerie sounds. I thought of her, but I ended up here instead."

I shifted into DRIVE, my throat panging with the angst of what he was telling me. I didn't understand what he meant by "that place", but I did get that he hadn't meant to show up here with me. I wordlessly steered toward the dirt drive that led to the main road.

"Are you sure you want to do this?" he asked.

"Hank came for me when he thought I was in trouble. I owe him the same."

He shook his head. "Okay."

We drove back toward Cardend.

ELEVEN

The outside temperature had risen as the sun gradually lightened the sky. I turned up the air in the car, trying to keep the windshield clear. The warmth from it made me sleepier. Pain and exhaustion would take me down soon. I knew I needed to rest. Fear poked a hole in my tiredness though, made my eyes sweep the surrounding forest and the blackened roads, searching for the Jeep or Hank. He'd nearly crashed earlier trying to stay awake. What if he'd done so again and injured himself even more?

"You look like you're about to keel over," Brody said, his voice clear and unhampered by fatigue.

"You suggesting I stop?" I answered.

"If you keep driving, you're going to end up in another car accident." His eyes widened. "Hmm? Don't you think?"

I'd told him what had happened earlier. I'd stopped at one point to reapply bandages and tape my fingers. Most of it had torn and fallen off during my encounter in the clinic with Chelsea. My nose was throbbing and every time I looked in the rearview mirror, I thought I'd stolen someone else's skin. I barely recognized my own bruised face.

Despite Brody's point, I kept driving. "I can't stop until I know Hank is okay."

Brody sighed. "This guy…. Are you two…?"

"No," I snapped.

"Okay, okay. Easy. You seemed close."

"It's amazing how chaos brings people together," I answered, not looking at him.

Brody cleared his throat. "You're putting yourself in harm's way for a guy you met a day ago."

Tempted to stop and reem him out, I kept driving, kept my eyes on the road. I couldn't get distracted. "Taking off and leaving him is not the answer. What about his daughter? She's in serious danger unless we find her."

"You said it yourself: the world's gone to the pits. You got attacked by a drug-fueled kid in a clinic basement and barely survived a car wreck. You've been going all night without any sleep or food and you're asking me why you should stop?" He shifted in the seat. "We watched out for one another every day for almost ten years. I'll be damned if I'm going to let you do this to yourself now."

The brakes came on softer than I wanted. We slowed to a stop in the middle of the road. "It was my fault," I said, clutching the steering wheel so hard, my knuckles turned white. "Because I didn't pay close enough attention, you died. It was my fault. I have to live with that."

He frowned.

"I can't let that happen again." I put my foot to the accelerator and continued down the road.

The car ride was quiet for the next ten minutes. Brody stared down at his feet, but I could tell he was locked in some kind of mental battle. I didn't want to say anything else and tried to keep the torrent of tears from releasing. I didn't want to remember that day. I'd done everything I could think of to forget it. Yet, it was now seeping into my brain like vile black ooze that never stopped gushing.

A fork in the road banished the thoughts temporarily and I veered the car onto a dirt path that vanished further into the gnarled forest, following the signs for the hydroelectric plant.

"I don't remember how I died," Brody said finally.

My vision shifted to him. "You don't?"

"The last thing I remember was the taste of some coffee, rolling around in bed not wanting to wake up, the taste of cherries, and kissing Carmen. Then, boom: blackness."

I inhaled. I didn't know how long ago he could remember. For all I knew, that could have been any morning. "What's the last case you remember us working on together?"

His brows furrowed. The veins in his forehead appeared again. After a moment he said, "Was it a girl?"

A girl. I took a stab at who he could be thinking of. "She went missing in the woods."

He nodded.

"The Brummel police department suspended the search. I was really upset; nearly took off Lennox's head over it." I chuckled a little. "The day before was my birthday."

His lips straightened. "Nope."

The memory was snatched through my fingertips like a ribbon. I cleared my throat and said, "Never mind."

He sighed. "It's hard to think back to what came before The Woods."

I looked at the trees to my left as the car bumped over potholes in the frost-heaved road. "You mean the woods near my cabin?"

"No, the—" Brody tried to grab me and a shot of cold raced through my arm. "Liz, stop!"

I jammed on the brakes and stared at the road up ahead. The Ranger Jeep was parked askew in the center of the dirt lane. Unbuckling myself, I threw open the door and jumped out of the car. I forced my sore legs into a sprint as I splashed through mud and slush. The driver's side door was wide open and the Jeep vacant.

"Where is he?" I muttered to myself. "Where is he?"

I rounded the front of the Jeep and gasped. Hank was lying in the middle of the road, face down.

Falling to my knees next to him, I flipped him over and put my fingers to his throat. Blood pumped faintly beneath my touch. "He's alive," I said as Brody jogged up beside me.

"Hurry and get him back to the car. It's not safe out here."

Hooking my arms under Hank's, I whipped my head from side to side, scanning the woods. "What do you mean?"

"I'll tell you once we get somewhere else. Let's go!"

Nearly an hour after I'd gotten Hank in the Jeep and backtracked to the main road, I brought Hank back to Melissa's house in town. It was the only safe place I could think of. Hank was lucid enough to help me get him inside and onto the living room couch, but it took the last of my strength to get him there. My finger and knee had swollen to the point that moving them even slightly sent pain shooting through me. *Don't fall asleep yet,* I told myself, trying to keep my mind from plummeting into the mire of fatigue that ground at me for hours.

Hank's clothes were sopping wet, soaked through by sweat and snow. I searched the wardrobe in the master bedroom and found some flannel pajamas to change him into. After bandaging his superficial cuts, I grabbed a heap of blankets from the bedroom closet and lay them across him. He shivered beneath them. His pallor was nearly white.

For the first time, I admitted the possibility that Hank might not make it.

In the kitchen, I boiled some water and cracked open the refrigerator in search of food. There were several left-overs in the fridge, including a casserole dish with homemade lasagna. I grabbed a fork from the dish drainer, carved out some onto a plate and tossed it in the microwave. I sat there for a minute like a zombie, watching it spin under the yellow light, listening to the popping and crackling as it heated up. Once it was out, I wasted no time in digging in. Hot food: I wouldn't have believed I was so hungry if I hadn't cleaned that plate as quick as I did.

The kettle on the stove whistled and I abandoned the thought of a second helping to take it off the burner. A container of chicken bouillon was nestled toward the back of one of the top cabinets. I spooned a little bit of it into a mug with the hot water and took it with a spoon into Hank. He was barely awake, mumbling things I couldn't understand. I spoon-fed him some of the broth and managed to talk him into a couple Ibuprofen before he lost consciousness again.

I plunked the mug down on the side table and my stomach turned.

I hobbled to the bathroom, barely collapsing at the toilet before I vomited. A minute later, I finally managed to stand up and rinsed my mouth out with water.

"You need to get some rest," Brody said, standing in the doorway.

"Not going to happen."

"Liz—"

"He could die."

"I'll watch him," he offered, glancing back into the living room at Hank. "I'll wake you up if anything happens."

As much as I wanted to keep an eye on Hank, my body longed for sleep more. I nodded and stumbled into the master bedroom down the hall. Searching the closet granted me with one of Melissa's wool sweaters and pair of sweat pants. I took off my shirt before I realized that the bedroom door was still wide open. I closed the door. I closed the curtains on the windows. Then, stripping down, I redressed in the dry clothes and crawled under the covers. I didn't even remember falling asleep.

A plate filled with steaming spaghetti and meat sauce was set down on the table in front of me. Carmen's hand had slid out from beneath. I'd picked up my wine and took a long sip, its dry, jammy flavor sinking me further into the memory: the first time Josh and I were invited to dinner in Brody and Carmen's new house. It was years ago but every detail was still so fresh.

"New being a technical term. Squeaky boards, a leaky roof, a chimney that Santa's anorexic cousin couldn't squeeze down if he wanted to… Home sweet home," Brody had said ten minutes into dinner.

"All it needs is a little work," Carmen had added, giving Brody a peck on the cheek before she got up for more wine.

"And who will be doing that work?" He'd stuck up his thumbs and jabbed both of them at his chest.

"We'll hire a team for some of it." Carmen had returned with a bottle of Malbec and poured more into my glass. "Besides, I wouldn't trust you to fix a clogged toilet." She'd winked.

"I was going to ask if I could use the bathroom but now, I'm not so sure I want to," Josh had said.

"Hey, hey," Brody had objected. "I may not be Mr. Fix-it, but I make up for that in the spider-killing department."

Carmen had giggled. "That you do."

I'd glanced down at my plate and frowned. I was staring down at a toilet bowl, the taste of the vomit still sour in my mouth. When I looked up, everyone was staring at me.

My eyes snapped open. I'd left the bedside table lamp on; the comforting glow eased my heartbeat. The rustling of trees outside was like an ocean in my ears. My head pounded and my muscles screamed whenever I moved. I forced the covers off me and stood. My leg nearly gave under me. I let the bed catch me as I dropped down onto it. My knee was fucked.

Once I was steady on my feet, I opened the bedroom door and limped down the hall to the living room. Hank was still sleeping. Brody stood near the television. He perked up as I stepped further into the room. "Hey."

"How is he?" I asked.

"Sleeping like the dead. I think he needs another dose of pain-killers though."

I picked up the mug of cold bullion from the side table and went to the bathroom to dump it out. As I watched the broth swirl and disappear down the drain, I thought about my dream and the safety of how it had begun. I suspected I'd never know normalcy like that again, not with everything that had happened yesterday.

"How'd you sleep?" Brody asked.

"Fine. What time is it?"

"Seven-thirty."

A whole day gone, I thought. "Earlier in the car, you were talking about how you woke up in the woods."

He nodded.

"What do you remember?"

"A boom and blackness. Next thing, I woke up somewhere I'd never been before. It was a forest, but the trees were taller than any I've ever seen. They vanished into the sky and this strange fog clung to my skin. I remember having this realization like I'd been hollowed out inside."

I sat in the armchair nearby and let my sore muscles relax. "You didn't remember dying?"

"At the time, no. I still can't remember what had happened before. The longer I spent wandering in these woods, the more I realized that I couldn't be alive. This was like no place on Earth."

"Was it Heaven?" I ventured a guess, feeling silly for it.

A chill ran through me as he shook his head again. "I didn't sense peace. This place wasn't bright or beautiful. I didn't feel God's presence."

"Were there others there?"

Brody glanced out the window to his left. "There was no one else for a long time. Or at least it felt like a long time. I don't really know how long I was there. I know that at some point, I noticed someone in the distance who looked as lost as I did. I tried shouting to them. But they never heard me; I don't think they even noticed me. They turned and walked back into the fog like some kind of figment of my imagination.

"Eventually, there were more of them. Again, none of them saw me." He stopped and frowned. "Or maybe some did. Maybe some of them were shouting at me like I'd done to them and I hadn't seen or heard them either."

I tried to picture the place Brody described. I thought I understood the fear of being alone. But this was different. I wrung my hands in my lap. "Then, what?" I prompted.

"People started vanishing. Behind the trees in the grey, there were buildings. I moved toward them, thinking if I could make it there, maybe this whole nightmare would end." His face scrunched up. "But they were weird, you know? Not like any kind of structures around here. They shouldn't have been able to stand. The architecture was all crooked and confused."

I thought about Antonio Gaudi's architecture in Spain. The first time I'd seen the Sagrada Familia, I'd thought I'd crossed into Tolkien's Middle Earth. It was like a giant sandcastle, jutting into the sky. Its enormity and appearance didn't fit with the rest of the Barcelona that I'd experienced. I could only imagine Brody might have thought similarly about whatever buildings he had seen.

"That's when the wolves appeared."

My memories of Spain washed away like watercolors with his words. Brody's mouth was cracked, his eyebrows tugged downward.

Though I desperately didn't want to ask, I knew that I had to. "The wolves?"

"They were shadows of things that looked like dogs in the distance. The difference between them and the people was that they knew I was there. As they got closer, their shapes got bigger and hairier. Worst thing was their smell, like bad decomp. They shrieked in the distance and I knew they were hunting."

I thought back to the bloodied ranger station and the sounds on the floor above me. Was that what had killed everyone?

"That day when I appeared on your porch, I realized that somehow, I'd left that place, whatever it was. Purgatory, maybe? But I didn't come alone."

I exhaled, loudly and without meaning. Goosebumps stippled my skin and I was suddenly extremely aware at how cold the room had become. I grabbed a blanket from the back of the chair and swung it over my shoulders, as if trying to escape inside of it.

"Other people came with me. So did the wolves. I heard people screaming in the distance as these things caught up with them. I ran. The one time I looked back…" He closed his eyes and shuddered. "Of all my years on the force, it was the worst thing I've ever seen." His voice lowered. "Like what I'd imagine Hell is like."

I backtracked to the moment when we'd found Hank and Brody's fearful gaze at the trees around us. "Earlier, when you said the woods weren't safe, you meant because of the wolves, didn't you?"

Brody stared at the floor. When he looked at me, it became harder to breathe. "They followed us here so they could drag us back."

Over the next twenty minutes, everything I'd once known and recognized collapsed beneath Brody's words. Brody reasoned the wolves were guardians of his forest purgatory and that they were meant to keep him and the others trapped there. Something had happened though, something that had allowed him and the others to cross over. He'd called it a "wall dissolving" or "the fog clearing". Those creatures had followed Brody and thousands…maybe millions of other specters back to the world of the living with the sole purpose of hauling them back to the forest realm.

I sat in the armchair with my hands clasped together as I listened to him theorize what was happening. None of it made any sense: ghosts, monsters… As much as I didn't want to believe that the world had succumbed to some type of psychotic break, it made even less sense to believe that Brody had escaped a kind of hell along with the souls of countless others. It forced the belief that there was a place that people went after they died and that it wasn't necessarily a heaven or a hell. Worst was the idea that there was something far more horrific that had also crossed over.

The realization that I was looking into my dead partner's face, animated and the way I remembered made me brush off any ideas of my own madness. I desperately wanted to hug him, smell a hint of his smoky cologne, and…. I stopped myself short, taking a deep breath.

Brody's image flickered across from me, like a distorted image on an old television screen.

"Why does that keep happening?" I finally asked, having not said anything for a long time.

He looked down at himself. "I don't know."

There was something in his voice though and I recognized it in his eyes as well. He was holding something back from me. He knew.

Hank stirred next to me.

"Hank," I said as his eyes finally opened.

Sweat covered his brow and his breath was shallow. The longer he lay there, and looked around the room, the more I realized he probably had no memory of taking the Jeep and no memory of stumbling out of it either.

"What happened?" he finally asked. "Where's Evie?"

"I found you unconscious on the road. You've been out for a day."

He shifted slightly and winced. "I don't remember leaving the treatment center…"

"It's okay. I won't take it personally," I commented with a smirk.

"I would," Brody remarked under his breath. I resisted the urge to glare at him.

Hank braced his hands on either side of him and pushed up.

I put a hand to his chest. "Hang on. You've got a fever, possibly pneumonia. You can't."

He swiped my wrist off of him gently and swung around to let his feet touch the floor. He looked down at the pajamas. "Did I put these on?"

"Your clothes were sopping wet."

Hank stood up and shuffled to the bathroom. The faucet squeaked on and water splashed. "I'm going to get Evie."

"The hell you are," I answered, jumping up from my seat. "Look what happened to you the first time."

"All I need is a little to eat and to take a hot shower." He came to the door of the bathroom and sighed. "After that, I'll be fine." He closed the door before I could say anything.

I rubbed my hands through my hair. The spray of water from a showerhead fuzzed on in the background.

"Stubborn," Brody observed.

"But he's got a point."

"And what's that?"

"We're both sitting on our hands here while his daughter is out there with some deranged bitch."

"The man is sick, Liz, and you're not much better."

I opened my mouth to retaliate and a large bang from the bathroom silenced me. I ran to the door and ripped it open. Hank had collapsed in the shower. "Shit!" I yelled, rushing in.

"I told you," Brody said.

Quickly grabbing Hank's arms, I dragged him out. It took me another ten minutes to get him back onto the couch by which time, he awoke again.

I glared. "Don't make me handcuff you to the coffee table."

He weakly nodded and muttered, "Sorry." A few moments more and he was out cold again.

I stood up and strode down the hall toward Melissa's bedroom.

"Liz?" Brody tentatively called after me.

I closed the door behind me, despite knowing it wouldn't stop him. I went to the closet and filed through the clothes there. Eventually, I found a pair of jeans and a shirt, both a tad small but dry at least. Throwing on a pair of warm wool socks, I retrieved my wet boots from the corner of the room and opened the door.

Brody was standing outside. "What are you doing?" he asked.

"I'm going to get Hank's daughter from Edith."

"You know that's not a good idea."

I side-stepped him and headed toward the front door.

"Liz, you said it yourself: you have no idea what to expect. Besides, your buddy shouldn't be left alone." Brody thumbed over his shoulder at Hank.

I grabbed my coat from the hanger by the door and swung it on. "He's got to fight that fever on his own. I can't reset his rib: therefore, there's nothing more I can do. I'm not going to wait here when I could be getting his girl back."

"You can barely walk straight," he said. I blinked and he'd shifted in front of me to block the front door.

"I'll rest when she's safe." I raised my eyebrows.

"Liz—"

"I can do this without you, Brody, or you could help me out. Do what you did for me at the treatment center. Be my eyes. It'll make things go a lot quicker."

For a moment, I thought he was going to blow his top. His form fizzed and grew hazy for a few moments and I took a cautionary step back, not wanting to get too close. Finally, he became clearer and glanced back at my bedroom. "Don't forget the gun."

TWELVE

THEN

The second week of December, my nights were filled a cocktail of felonies: an armed robbery at Ace's Pawn Shop; a DB in an apartment off of Abeline Park; a domestic disturbance in a cape at the end of Montroy Circle.

Another missing person.

Another robbery.

An assault.

I didn't lose control often; I couldn't afford to. But sometimes, the triggers on the job were impossible to avoid. At the end of a long week, it was hard to carry on, to keep professional. A perp would say something, a spark to lite the fuse and it would take every speck of reason in my brain not to lose myself into the void of rage.

In the beginning, honing the apathy hadn't been easy. I was passionate about every case, every wrong someone did to someone else, all for the stupidest, littlest reasons. In ten years of defending the public and protecting the innocent, my moral compass had swung and pitched and ultimately evened out with a twitch here or a twitch there. But every now and again, I wasn't strong enough to keep it from bubbling up.

The assault; that was what put me over the edge that week. Two roommates had gotten into a fight over money. One hadn't been paying his share of the rent and was overcharging the other. What had begun as a small disagreement ended in a bottle broken over the lazy renter's head and a fractured eye socket in the other one. We weren't even the first two on the scene, but we had more than our share of trouble keeping the two renters apart. I ended up getting punched in the cheek. Apparently, neither of them cared about hitting a woman, but hell, those old sensibilities our parents believed in were rarely practiced now adays. Brody eventually pulled his sidearm and forced the two to separate long enough to get cuffs on them.

I refused medical, threw ice on my jaw at the station, and at home the next morning, took it out on my punching bag in the garage.

Even when I'd tired myself out and retired to a nice long shower, I still needed to even things out in my head, flush the week's shitty happenstances down the proverbial toilet.

It was never as easy as sitting in my living room chair alone. If Josh was around, I could talk it out and be somewhat human again. But when he was away on assignment, the quiet ate at me and lately, that was happening more and more. I wanted company, but to also submerge myself in the privacy of my own thoughts. If I was working a double shift, it meant finding a secluded spot in the station's lunchroom. But often, I'd choose one of the corner tables in the Lofty Grounds coffee shop. I'd fill a mug with whatever the blend of the day was, plug myself into my phone, and play music. Usually ambient classical; nothing fluty and frilly, but often piano with a beat and often something repetitive where I could get lost in the rhythm and the replication. Even on a busy day at the shop, I could dig in.

I'd sat with my eyes closed and thought about my family cabin in Middlehitch, the one that was no longer ours. I thought about the way the warm afternoon sun ignited our fields of goldenrod, the distant sounds of the creek gurgling, the rough boards on our wrap around deck as I lay on my stomach, drawing. My pencils would hiccup over the uneven surface, dip into knots, the lines imprinting the grooves and swirls of each board into the paper.

I imagined the sound of my mother stirring something in a pot on the kitchen stove, that cyclic swirling of the spoon scraping on the metal, and the waft of a mouthwatering dinner reaching out to me through the screen door. My sister's voice lilted from the open window on the second story, singing to her dolls. My dad's silhouette emerged from the edge of the woods, the tall fly-fishing rod in one hand and his tacklebox in the other, his long legs striding toward our cabin with a lengthening shadow between them. That memory: that perfect moment in time was all I had left of all of us together, mostly of my dad. I meditated on it, so I'd never lose it. This was my coping mechanism, a meditation that never ceased to bring me back from the edge of anger.

This time, when I opened my eyes, the chair across from me wasn't empty. Brody was there with a mug of his own coffee. The steam hazed over his face. I wished he hadn't seen me. Normally, if you recognize a friend in a shop, you go greet them. Normally. What happens when you want to be where people can observe you but you don't want to engage? It makes things difficult. Something about staying alone in my own house and doing this same ritual was emptier, as if opening my eyes to no one reinforced losing my dad, not talking to my mom. With other people around, I was reminded of what I do, the good in it. It helped bury the lingering loss, if only for a little while.

Brody talked but I couldn't hear him through the piano. I paused the music and yanked the buds from my ears. "Sorry?"

"I saw you through the window," he repeated. As if I hadn't deduced that myself.

I nodded, not sure what I could add to the statement. Brody knew why I came here. He knew what this routine meant for me. So, why hadn't he kept walking?

"Anyway, um…." He scratched the back of his head and took a long sip from his coffee. "I thought you could use the company."

I chuckled. "No, you didn't." All I wanted was to vanish back into that memory. The wind through the grass called to me. The setting sun. My father's shadow.

He mirrored my smile. "You're right. I'm the one that actually needs the company."

Even through the smirk, I could tell that sentence was delivered with hesitance. I took a sip of my coffee; bitter, dark, but only warm now. I'd been sitting here longer than I'd thought.

"What's up, buttercup?" I asked. Part of me was confused by his sudden desire to open up, especially after our last discussion about it had ended so heatedly.

For a moment, Brody stared at my coffee cup, his face dowsed in this weird uncertainty that seemed completely foreign for him. Maybe he was going to tell me the real reason for all of his distractions the last couple weeks. But instead, he leaned back in his chair and cleared his throat. "This case. This case has me confused."

I let out a breath I hadn't realized I'd been holding. We were working a number of cases right now. But only one of them had completely turned on its head and left us without any understanding of what had transpired. "Will West?"

Brody nodded. "Vance had me close it. Missing person who isn't missing anymore. No crime committed. He wants us to move on."

I knew that was the only logical next step, even if things didn't add up with how we'd found Will. "Did the hospital do a tox screen to find out if he was on any drugs?"

"Reports came back negative. The hospital held him for a couple nights in the psych ward but after they agreed he wasn't a danger to himself or anyone else, they let his mother take him home. The on-call nurse told me his delusion hadn't changed: he thinks he's Will's grandmother."

I shook my head. "It has to be a mental break. That's the only explanation. The stress of losing a loved one, the low income, the pressures of high school…. Maybe it all climaxed into this?"

"That's the way the hospital is spinning it, too," Brody muttered. "Something called a 'Cotard delusion'. They said it was 'something like that' but not exactly that. Who knows?"

"Do we know what the mom is going to do?"

"She's barely scraping by. I don't think she can afford psychological treatment for her son, even if he does need it."

I grew cold despite the sun cutting through the bay windows to our table. Unfortunately, state Medicare for low-income citizens was a priority that hadn't been realized everywhere in our beloved state. Flintland's resources were strained as it was. A lot of people who needed the help couldn't afford it and the penalty for not having medical insurance was a mere slap on the wrist compared to the monthly cost people had to shell out. Jessica and Will were only another lost pair in a system designed to let people fall through the cracks.

"You know the strangest thing though," Brody said. "That Will had in-depth knowledge of his grandmother's childhood, her upbringing, details that most grandkids glaze over. He also knew things that Jessica had spoken with her mother about in confidence."

"When did you find that out?"

Once again, Brody cleared his throat. "I went by her apartment to check in on her after I found out the hospital had released her son. I also gave her the number for Father Stephens."

"Your priest?"

"I figured any kind of comfort would help. Her mother was part of our congregation. At least its someone that knew her."

I pursed my lips. "You think there's more to this, don't you?"

"It's like we're missing something." He spun the mug slowly on the table between his thumb and index finger. "But I don't know how to explain it."

It would have been backward telling my partner that he needed to let this go. Brody had become emotionally invested in few cases during our time together. If anything, it made his resolve to finish things that much more intense. This case wasn't solved. It didn't feel finished. I knew that; but I also knew there was little we could do at this point for follow-through. There were other people and other things that needed our attention.

We sat there for several minutes drinking our coffee and not making eye contact. I eventually refilled my cup and savored in a hot

Sumatran blend.

"There's something else," Brody said as soon as I'd settled back into my chair. By the look on his face, I knew I wasn't going to return to my meditation.

When he didn't elaborate, I nudged my head. "Okay."

"I've got to take a couple days next week. The captain is temporarily assigning Sargent Dalbord with you until I get back."

I squinted. "Everything all right?"

"Yeah, no. It's nothing." He didn't even make eye contact as he stood up.

"A couple days?" I asked.

Brody slugged down the rest of his coffee. "Maybe a few more than that."

Sure, he's taken time off from work before. Not often, but it happened. And usually, Brody was dying to tell me what little stay-cation project he and Carmen were working on. But this statement was closeted and weird.

"Brody, tell me what's going on."

He looked at the ceiling, that uncomfortable smirk reemerging. "It's…uh…"

All of my muscles were tense. "Tell me."

Brody took a deep breath and slid back down into his seat. "It's Carmen and me. We're having some problems. I'm moving into a new place next week."

My lip fell. The words were like splinters. "What?"

"Yeah."

"How long has this been going on?" I already knew the answer.

"A while."

"And you weren't going to tell me?"

His breath hitched. He tore at a napkin on the table, picking little pieces away. "Listen, I don't want to get into this right now."

"Bullshit." I put my mug down, maybe a little too hard. The sound of it smacking the table made a few people nearby lift their heads.

He frowned. "It's my fucking marriage," he growled under his breath. "I didn't think this was going to happen."

"Is it over?" I asked, holding my breath.

Brody raised his eyebrows and shrugged his shoulders. "I have no frickin' idea."

I couldn't think of anything to say. A few weeks ago, we'd all sat together for Thanksgiving dinner and there wasn't an inkling of friction between Brody or Carmen. I suppose that was the whole point though, to try and prove to their family and friends that everything was okay.

Brody stood up again. "I'm gonna go."

I didn't try to get him to come back. I watched him take his mug to the counter and then leave, his steps quick and his body stiff as he disappeared down the sidewalk.

Meditation was impossible now. All I could do was think about Brody and Carmen and about what had happened to cause this sudden discord. As I thought about it, I realized it probably wasn't sudden. Brody had said this was going on "a while". More than the two weeks that I'd only started to notice.

So much for being a good cop. I'd missed a dissolution of two people I cared about going on right in front of my eyes.

That wasn't all. My own relationship with Josh was going down the drain as quickly. I hadn't talked to anyone about it, not even Brody. It was as if I was standing back and watching it happen; a self-sabotage of happiness.

NOW

I followed the long-distance electric lines back to the road that led to the hydroelectric plant. The road was completely surrounded by dark tangled woods. After Brody's story, I kept my eyes vigilant on the wilderness for any signs of life. The high winds still hadn't let up. With the trees and brush thrashing from the gale, it was hard to identify anything. After twenty minutes, I rolled the Jeep into a clearing. The rushing of water was now thunderous and blocked out the sounds of the storm. I killed the headlights and sat perfectly still, the engine rumbling beneath me.

About fifty yards ahead, I recognized the long brick powerhouse edging out of the darkness. High tension line outlets bristled across the roof like barbed wire and golden lights shone through the frosted windows. This building housed the generator which hooked up to the turbines underground. I glanced further off to my right and noticed the reservoir. I let the roar of the river on the other side pull me back into the here and now.

Cars filled the lot, several packed to the brim with supplies. People had rushed here in a panic, probably thinking it was a good place to hide from whatever was going on. Maybe Edith had swayed loyal constituents of Shane's to come; or her brother who managed the plant had told his workers they should come. If Edith was as connected as Hank had intimated, she probably had muscle inside, too.

I pulled the car around and parked it further down the road out of site. Then, I crept back to the building, Brody shadowing me.

"What now?" he asked as I hesitated outside the main entrance.

"You go through, make sure no one is in sight and tell me when it's all clear."

Brody frowned and leaned close to me. The temperature around him was so cold, I felt it beneath my heavy coat. "I'm not going to ask you again: are you sure you want to do this?"

"You know when I've made up my mind." I nodded to the door.

Brody passed through the solid wood and I was suddenly alone with the wind.

Minutes passed by. The time grew agonizing with each second that passed. When Brody's form came through the door, I practically jumped backward with the tension I'd been holding in.

"The door's unlocked and you've got a window. Come on." He gestured with a nudge of his head.

"Where do I go once I'm inside?"

"There's an empty room directly across the hall."

I quietly turned the knob, pushed in, and ducked into the room opposite me. Most of the lights were off, disorienting me immediately. I peered out from the doorway, taking in the long corridor ahead of me. Far off voices yelled. Children wailed. My throat dried out in seconds.

"Where now?" I asked, trying to focus.

"At the end of the hall, there's a staircase that leads up to the top mezzanine where the control panels are. There were a bunch of kids down in the main chamber but only one up in an office on the mezzanine by herself. That's probably your girl."

"Was she okay?"

"A little banged up and scared."

"Anyone else up there?"

"There wasn't when I looked."

I nodded and stepped out from the doorway. I slinked along the hall, paying attention to each footstep and every ambient noise. The river's current blocked these sounds out the closer I got to the staircase. Brody stayed ten steps in front of me and was at the top of the stairs by the time I'd reached the bottom of them. I put my foot on the first step.

"Stop!" he hissed.

I froze in place.

"We've got one up here. He must have come up a staircase on the other side."

"Is he armed?" I whispered.

"Looks like a pistol."

I need to distract him somehow. Bring him down to my level so I can knock him out.

The idea of knocking out a total stranger hit me like a rock slide. Less than twenty-four hours ago, I'd killed a man in self-defense. Now, I was going out of my way to possibly do the same to more.

"Hey," Brody said, catching my attention. "Come up with something quick."

I glanced around. I couldn't use Hank's gun. A gunshot would put the entire place on high alert. I finally noticed an open toolbox. I slid a hammer from the pile, positioned myself at the foot of the stairs, and struck the bottom step as hard as I could. CLANG!

Brody's eyes went wide. "What the hell are you d—"

I slammed the hammer down again. BANG! This kind of sound was intriguing but not immediately recognizable like a gunshot.

He turned toward the top of the stairs. "He's coming. Get back!"

I left the hammer sitting on the floor and flattened myself back against the wall. Brody stepped down into view, keeping his gaze toward the top of the steps. "Give him a few more seconds."

My heart throbbed. I balled my hands into fists, and kept my eyes on the opening to my left.

Brody took a step back. "Right…now!"

The man stepped into view, greasy hair beneath a stained ball-cap and the gun out in front of him like an inexperienced schmuck. I grabbed his wrist, throwing him off balance. With a foot out to trip him, he went down fast and hard. I slammed the hammer into his jaw before he had a chance to retaliate and he was out.

I got up and took a deep breath.

"You still got it, kid," Brody said, with an approving nod.

"Not the time." I heaved the man's body into the shadows. Every part of me was on fire with the effort. When I was sure he was out of sight, I climbed the stairs.

From the top, I could look down on the largest room in the plant. A row of turbines rose up along the middle of the room. Frosted windows looked out over the dam and the river it fed into, streaks of white moonlight bleeding eerily across it. Five other men were positioned down below, several guarding what appeared to be their families. Women huddled close to their children, who wailed and stared up at the great machines in more fear than wonderment. The lack of light up here kept them from noticing us, something I was suddenly grateful for.

I bent low and made my way along the catwalk toward the control room at the other end, the lighted buttons inside my only guide in the darkness.

A few more steps. Almost there—

"Eric!" A loud voice bellowed from below. I flattened myself against the floor and carefully glanced over the edge of the catwalk.

A stocky man lumbered in from one of the back doors down below, toting a rifle over his shoulder. "Eric! You up there?" he yelled again turning in my direction. I got a glimpse of his big cheeks, thick mustache, and small dark eyes before I pulled my head down.

"Anyone seen Eric? I need his help," he addressed some of the people on the floor.

The realization hit me. Eric was the one I'd knocked out at the bottom of the stairs.

"You've got to move, Liz," Brody said from behind me, making all the hairs on my arms stand. "Get the girl and get out."

Cautiously, I picked myself up and kept as close to the wall as I could as I made my way to the control room door. My heartbeat drowned out the sounds of the others down below. At the door, I carefully stuck my head in. A single desk lamp brightened the cramped space. A roller chair was stranded in the middle of the room, a sweater hanging off of it and trailing on the floor. A couple of weak coughs made me round the desk. Two small pajama clothed legs stuck out with two raggedy puppy dog slippers at the ends.

"Evie?" I asked.

Within moments, Evie's head poked out from behind the side of the desk. Her eyes were red and rimmed with tears. "Liz!" she whined through a stuffed nose, scrambling over to me.

I caught her, her force nearly bowling me over. "Hey, hey. Shh! Calm down. I'm here."

Her small, warm body shivering against mine brought back what little strength I had left. I'd become a dried husk, even after the day of rest.

But she was safe. That was all that mattered. Now, I needed to get her back to Hank.

She pulled away. "Where's Daddy? Why isn't he here?"

"He's safe. We're going to take you to him."

Evie frowned and looked over my shoulder expectantly. "Who's *we*?"

I looked up at Brody who cocked his head.

I focused on the girl, smiling to hide the stab of pain that came with his expression. "I will. I meant 'I will'." I stood up and hoisted the girl up into my arms. She was heavier than she looked and the weight against my worn-out muscles nearly brought me back down to my knees. "Come on. We need to leave now."

Brody went through the door we'd entered through and I followed. Within seconds, he rushed back through. "Quick, someone's coming!"

I backed into the room. There was another exit from the control room and I blindly wrenched the handle open, not knowing who or what would be on the other side. A short stairwell led to another metal catwalk. We followed it as it coursed through the innards of the building like an intestine, the walls blared yellow-orange from lanterns placed intermittently. The murmur of voices made my pulse quicken.

Evie was ten times heavier with every step. We closed in on a door at the end of the next hall, a door that hopefully could bring us back around to the parking lot in front.

A door opened behind us. By the time I'd bent to put Evie down, Brody was shouting at me. "Head's up!"

I pointed my gun down the hall as a man emerged from a room. Our eyes locked. As his hands went for his sidearm, I pulled the trigger.

The explosion erupted through the hall. Evie screamed behind me.

The man jerked and collapsed hard onto the catwalk.

My injured finger throbbed with agony. I turned back to Evie. "Run, go!"

We pushed through the next heavy door, me hobbling, Evie several steps ahead of me. I didn't know if I'd killed him or not, but the gunshot was loud and would attract more attention. A set of stairs and one door later and we were suddenly out beneath the moonlight once more. Cold winter air settled across my face. Heavy winds buffeted us and the trees shook as if trembling in fury across the bridge before us. The water churned below as if it were being boiled. We'd somehow ended up on the top of the dam. The access gate at the other end would put us across the river and back to the parking lot.

Evie shivered. I picked her up once again, feeling my knee buckle slightly under her weight. "Wrap your legs and arms around me. We're going to run."

She did as she was told, coughing the whole time. I adjusted the gun in my hand, though doing so made my finger go rigid with pain. I snuck across the cement walkway, the railings a godsend. The wind tossed me toward the falls more than once and if they hadn't been there, we'd have gone over. About midway, the door opened behind us. I swung around.

It was the same man again, staggering through the door.

I brought up my gun, finger taut on the trigger.

He threw up his hand and shouted my name.

I let the gun drop. *How? How could he know?*

It occurred to me that Brody hadn't followed us out onto the catwalk.

"It's me, Liz," he said, panting.

"Brody?" I cried.

The man lifted his head and nodded, trying to get to his feet.

My feet were iron weights. I looked back at the foreign face. If it was Brody, I couldn't leave him. But I couldn't take Evie across and get back in time before more people showed up.

I set Evie down and pointed to the other side of the bridge. "I need you to run to the other side. Stay there until I get there."

"No!" she cried, tears streaking her face. "I'm scared!"

"I'll be right behind you. I have to help him. Now, go!"

She spun around and ran. Listening to her fading sobs, I limped back to Brody. He was beginning to straighten up when I reached him. He leaned on me, nearly bringing me down with him. I looked into the man's face. A shock of blue eyes, brown hair with a clean-cut beard, and chiseled cheeks. It wasn't my partner. Yet, the longer I looked at him, it was. "What the hell did you do?" I asked him, helping him to his feet.

He breathed erratically. "You shot him and there was a chasm inside him telling me to jump in."

"We're almost there," I said. I looked up toward the other end of the bridge and gasped.

Evie had frozen a quarter way from the end of the bridge and sat hugging her legs, weeping uncontrollably. A refraction of headlights cutting across trees sent my heart into a flurry. Someone else had arrived in the parking lot. "Evie!" I yelled, trying to pull Brody along with me.

The door opened behind us again.

Brody grabbed my gun from my hand and spun to take the shot.

Two gunshots rang out. Brody's shoulder split open and he sank to his knees out of my grasp. Before I could help him, he turned to me, his face scrunched up in pain. "Get the girl."

I rushed toward Evie and picked her up in a fireman's carry without losing momentum. My body burned with the effort.

More gunfire crackled behind me and I couldn't help but turn when we reached the other end of the bridge. The man was lying where

I'd left him, unmoving while others approached him. A stab of guilt sliced up through me until I noticed a suited figure among the others. Brody was suddenly standing there, looking himself over.

He's a ghost again, I realized.

"Go! Liz, go!" he shouted.

I heaved Evie to the end of the walkway and descended a couple metal stairs at the end, my boots slamming against the cement landing. The bushes around the corner rustled and I stopped short. Without a gun on me, I no longer had anyway to protect Evie. I put her down next to another door that led inside and slowly backed against the wall, watching as a shadow neared.

A body came into view. I grabbed the person's neck, forcing them down into a headlock.

"Liz! Liz, stop!" Hank cried, thrashing to get free.

I let go, and he scrambled away, huffing.

"What are you doing here? How did you…?"

"Melissa's SUV." He coughed. "It had enough gas to get me here. When I woke up, I knew you'd come here." His eyes focused on Evie and she practically jumped into his arms. "Evie? Baby, are you okay?"

I glanced back across the bridge. The rest of the men had finished examining their dead friend and were tromping toward us. They were all armed, one with a crowbar, another with a tire iron…

"Hank," I said, tossing the keys to the Jeep to him. "Get her to the car. Go!"

Hank whisked Evie away, running down the next flight of stairs. Their footfalls crunched in the dirt as I followed. When I looked back to find Brody, I noticed he was gone.

The doorway in front of me suddenly opened, catching me in the face. I dropped against the cement, barely catching myself.

"Well, here's a question?" someone said suddenly. A woman with short blonde hair stood over me, a gun in her hand. "Who the fuck are you?"

Edith.

I wildly searched for some way out. I was trapped. Edith completely barred me from getting by her and her goons with blunt weapons had reached the middle of the bridge. There was nowhere to go. I gazed over the railing toward the mist rising from the bottom of the falls. Nowhere to go but down.

"Liz!"

Brody had reappeared closer to me, his voice desperate. "You don't know how long of a drop that is."

Edith glanced up. She looked over her shoulder as if seeing something I couldn't. "What's that, Shane? She's got someone helping her, too? Someone like you?" She turned back to me. "Isn't that interesting?"

I froze. Edith was talking to a ghost, her ghost. When Melissa had died, she'd been right. Shane had come back to take Evie away from her with Edith's help.

"Shane says your friend is telling you not to jump. That's about a sixty-foot drop, darlin'. Unless you want to wash up on shore dead, you'd best follow his advice."

The men were almost to me. I got to my feet. "It couldn't be any worse than what you would do to me if I stayed," I answered.

"You're right," Edith answered, her expression dead serious. "Except your death might be quicker here." She aimed the gun at me. "Either way, I will get Evie back from that deadbeat and you'll be out of the picture."

As Edith's arm straightened and the gun met my gaze, I frowned. Edith had never fired a gun before. She didn't have the safety off and her grip was tenuous, as if the thing might bite her.

I cocked my head. "Well, come on then. Do it."

Edith pulled the trigger. Nothing happened.

I rushed her, slamming my shoulder into her. We both collapsed on the concrete, Edith screaming as I landed on top of her. Before I had a moment to get my bearings, something hot slashed across my arm. I winced and fell back, noticing a fresh slice through my sweater sleeve.

Edith held a knife in her gloved hand and a satisfied grin on her face. It must have been in a pocket; it hadn't been there a moment ago. I got to my feet as she went for another strike. I dodged, and swung my leg up, my boot connecting with her stomach. Edith dropped again.

I grabbed the rail, using her as a step to vault over her. The path to the car was open.

I ran for it. My boot was suddenly yanked out from under me and I crashed down against the concrete. My knee twinged as I landed awkwardly on top of it. Before I could get up, two meaty hands cramped down on my jacket and hauled me to my feet. One of Edith's thugs had grabbed me. He slammed me against the railing, bending me back over the churning water. His hands slipped around my throat and squeezed.

Air thinned as I struggled to gain purchase with my feet. I gasped, my fingers scraping at his hands.

"Time to join your friend in death," Edith called from over his shoulder.

I grabbed the man's shirt collar and pulled, arcing my back to pull him off balance. He lifted off the concrete unexpectedly, hands releasing me to grab hold of something. He didn't have the time.

I clutched at him as we soared over the edge. As his body soared past mine, I hooked my legs around the railing and released him. Screaming, he tumbled down into the falls. His form was soon lost in the mist and the roar of water below.

I hung there with a mixture of revulsion and relief pouring into me simultaneously. I grabbed at the bar above me and pulled myself up. The moisture on the rail was slick and I slipped off, swinging down.

I couldn't tell where Edith was. As the thought hit me, she screamed, "John! NO! You killed my brother!" Any moment, she could be on her feet. Any moment, she could be here, helping me follow after John.

"Brody!" I shouted.

His face came into view above me. "Liz! Hang on!"

I strained to reach the railing again but I couldn't. "Help me!"

"There's nothing I can do," he cried, his hands sliding through the railing as he tried to reach for me. "You're going to have to climb up yourself."

I grimaced, my legs straining with the effort to hold on. My knee felt as though someone was wrenching my leg bones out from it on either side. I made for the railing again but my fingers slipped once more and I thudded back against the cement, nearly banging my head in the process. Little by little, my legs gave.

Come on, come on! I swung up again, using all the energy I had to crunch my abs. I slapped my palm over the rail and held on.

"Good girl," Brody murmured. "Now, pull yourself up."

My shoulder screamed at me. My injured finger sent barbs of pain up my arm. My fingers slid over the metal. The force was too great. I was going to come down hard and I was going to fall.

A vice-like grip locked around my hand. I stared up at Hank, who struggled with all of his might. His face creased up in agony and he lurched forward, holding his ribs with one hand. My legs slid from the railing and I sailed down, Hank's grip on my arm stopping me short of falling into the cascade at the bottom.

"Hank!" I yelled.

"I've got you!" he yelled. "I've got you."

"Pull!" Brody hollered at him, though he knew he couldn't be heard. "Pull, God damn it!"

I read it in Hank's face before he could. He was too weak. His ribs were broken and he was still fighting the fever. Before, his fingers slipped, I met Brody's eyes and caught the point of shock when he realized I was going to fall.

Then, I was suddenly airborne, the twin shouts from Brody and Hank like high-pitched whistles in my ears against the current below. The cold mist hugged me and then the water hit me like a cold punch to the head. I sank beneath the surface and everything turned black around me.

THIRTEEN

I dreamt I was hovering so close to the ground that I could smell the earth. Moldering wood and pine needles and the wet dog smell of my cotton sweatshirt. The sopping moisture against my chest. I moved slowly, like I had no control over it, but inside my heart squelched with the idea that something was coming after me. I needed to move. I needed to get out of here. As I imagined teeth and jaws sinking into the flesh of my arm, I rolled over and fell out of a bed.

It was my childhood bed. I remembered the creamy yellow walls of my room, the lacy curtains on the dark windows, the grey headboard with pinstriped orange design my mother had painted. The rug was course under my skin as I lay there, dazed. Then the door opened in front of me. My dad stepped through and carefully lifted my body, cradling me as he tucked me back into the plush blue blankets on my bed. He sat for a moment, his hand resting on my arm, and I drank in the sight of his lean face, his plaid shirt, his tousled brown hair. I was safe.

"Go back to sleep, bean," he said. As I closed my eyes, his lips touched my forehead.

There was a rushing sound then, as though my ears were about to pop. I waited and waited and waited for them to. The longer I waited, a chill bloomed across my body, even beneath all of the blankets. I opened my eyes again.

Reeds and dirt and wet smooth stones gazed at me. One was pressing into my cheek like a finger. Beyond, I recognized a grey sky against a blur of green and amber and brown. Trees, gusting in the wind and tall reeds rustling nearby. Water lapped at my feet gently, warm and cold at the same time.

The movement of the grass gave way to curling flames. I sat in my dad's armchair, nestled into a thick red and green blanket decorated with fish and I watched the news. My sister was already asleep on the couch next to me. My mom was on the phone in the hall. She was quietly berating someone. Something was wrong. I think I must have known. I don't know if the fireman the cameraman filmed going into the building was my father or not. I was transfixed by the inferno, by its scope and power. This was filmed hours ago. It was filmed when there was still hope that the fire department could manage the blaze, before the second floor collapsed. My dad was probably still alive in the shot I was watching.

The fire roiled on the television screen, devouring and growing. Sweat beaded on my skin as the heat intensified all around me. I imagined the conflagration as it consumed my house night after night, the fire ignited by a dark figure tossing a Molotov cocktail through the open window. I screamed for my dad and he never came.

Hotter now. So hot.

As the ceiling crashed down, I jerked into consciousness and my eyes snapped open. Bleary streaks swirled around me as my head moved from side to side. A warm hand rested against my forehead and gently pushed me back down into the darkness of sleep.

When I opened my eyes again, the shapes of things were more defined. I recognized a lamp, its light too bright for me. I rolled away from it and took in the other side of the room. A window overlooking evergreens, a baseboard heater humming, hardwood floors the color of maple syrup, someone's boots. A bedroom.

Then, I became aware that I was naked. I cautiously touched myself. Not completely naked. Underwear and a nightgown. I didn't own a nightgown.

I patted through the bed, searching for some evidence of my own clothes. Nothing. There were rice bags surrounding me, warm but no longer hot. There was a dresser across the room from me. The only door to the room was mostly closed, only a crack leading out toward darkness.

I peeled back the covers on the bed slowly, making as little noise as I could and lowered my feet to the floor. Pain was like a mist around me, there but not important enough for my mind to concentrate on.

As I carefully moved to the dresser, the floor squeaked beneath me. *Fuck*. Sliding open one of the drawers, I found a yellow t-shirt. I flung the nightgown off, and yanked the shirt over my head.

Time was jumbled, like someone had broken up a put together puzzle and sifted their hands through the pieces to separate them. One moment I was lying in a riverbed, the next reliving the night my father died, and now I was here…wherever *here* was. Was I still dreaming?

"Hello?" I called out, my voice loud and sudden in the room. I had expected someone to respond. Nothing but eerie silence followed.

I looked around, searching for some sign of familiarity. There were two windows, one looking out on the side yard, the other out to the street front. An old Buick Roadmaster was parked in the driveway. The wind howled around the corners of the house and a tree branch scraped at the nearest window.

Someone had to be home. Lights were on and a car was in the driveway. Why hadn't they answered?

I quickly checked the next drawer down and slid on a pair of sweatpants. Then, I looked for a weapon. While it seemed as though whoever lived here had saved my life, I didn't want to leave anything to chance. I couldn't after everything that had happened. I found a pistol in the sock drawer, but it wasn't loaded. I picked up a candle stand from the night table. It looked as though it would break easily but it was the only thing I had.

Moving to the door, I carefully peeked into the dark hallway. No one in sight. The bleak light from my room illuminated the corridor enough so that I could make out the staircase. There was a light on downstairs and the bitter smell of coffee wafted up to reach me.

"Liz?"

I swung around, ready to bring the candle stand down on someone's head.

Brody stood by the dresser; his eyes wide. "Easy! Easy!"

I gasped and set the candle stand down, my lungs heaving.

"You're okay," he said softly.

I tried to speak but a cluster of prickles suddenly forced me into a fit of coughing.

Brody stepped closer. "Sit down: you're still pretty beat up."

I did as told, slumping down onto the bed. Once the fit passed, I wiped the saliva from my lips and inhaled deeply through my nose. "Where am I?"

"A little way off of Route two."

Every breath was a chore. "What happened?"

He cocked his head. "You went into the river at the mill. Traveled a good distance before you washed up on shore. Thank God Edith's brother went in before you or you wouldn't have had anything to hold onto going down river."

The thought made me gag.

"The guy downstairs found you. Brought you to his home. There were moments I wasn't sure you were going to make it."

The fever must have broken, I thought. "How long have I been out of it?"

"Three days."

"So, that's why I could eat a cow." I stood up once more. "Who is this guy? Why didn't he answer me when I called?"

Brody's face darkened and my gut pinched with worry. "What?"

Brody stared at the floor. "I think he might have lost his wife some time ago. There's a little shrine to her in the living room."

I frowned, realizing what he was getting at. "Has he been *seeing* her?"

He shook his head. "I think that made it worse."

The sudden prickle returned to my chest but I resisted the urge to cough. "What do you mean '*made* it worse'?"

Brody didn't say anything.

I left the candle stand behind and exited the room into the dark hall. My feet padded on the chilly floorboards as I rounded the banister to the staircase and glanced down. It led straight to the front door in a small entrance way with two doors on either side. The light was coming from the right, behind a partially opened door. I recognized the crackling of radio static from inside and the pleasant strums of a guitar against it.

I cautiously made my way down the steps, each one creaking under my weight. I hesitated on the first one, but after I realized there was no one coming up, I kept going. I pushed through the door and poked my head through.

A lone man sat at the kitchen table; his head leaned back at an odd angle from his body. A chunk of the back of his skull was blown out, the gore speckling the honey-colored boards beneath and the white walls. Still dripping. His glasses had fallen into it.

I stepped back until I made contact with the buffet, with anything solid and forced myself to close my eyes if only for a moment of reprieve. The image was stained in my memory though. When I opened my eyes again, I made myself look at anything but the man and stepped around the devastating tableau into the kitchen on the other side.

Brody was waiting there for me.

I glared at him. "You could have told me upstairs."

He gaped at me. "Maybe I wanted to give you a chance to catch your breath first before walking into *this*."

"Could have said, "Dead guy downstairs at the kitchen table. Take a moment before you go down.""

He cleared his throat. "He left you a note."

I edged toward the dining table until I noticed a small piece of stationary paper poking out from his hand. I carefully slid it free. His hand was still warm. I read the note quietly.

After a moment, Brody said, "Well?"

I pushed the paper away. "Clearly, you already know what it says."

"I watched him write it. Did you even read it?"

I frowned. "He apologized. Said '*she* never came back'."

"His wife. He was expecting her to appear like ghosts have been appearing to people all over the world. But not to him. Not this guy." Brody shook his head.

"Then he's unlucky," I said, stepping away into the kitchen. Another room. A separation from the body of the stranger who had saved my life. The stench of blood was so strong in the dining room, it was making my stomach do flips. "And he couldn't cope."

"Wow," Brody growled. "Where's your compassion?"

I glanced at the key hook next to the coffee maker in the kitchen. The note had mentioned I could take the car and whatever supplies I wanted…if I survived.

"I'm talking to you."

My shoulders tensed and despite the heat in my face, I cautiously said, "You wanted to give me a minute? Let me have it."

The smell of blood was clogging my nose. I needed to cover it with something, anything.

I unhooked a mug from a hanger under the cabinets and poured myself a cup of coffee. It was still hot, steam flowing from the rim. I pulled out a stool at the counter that separated the kitchen and the dining room and plopped onto it. The first sip tasted bitter and I practically burned my tongue. The next was better.

Brody patiently stood with his arms crossed waiting in the kitchen door.

Finally, I asked him, "Did Hank make it out of the hydroelectric plant with Evie?"

"I don't know."

"What do you mean, 'you don't know'?"

"I'm not connected to *him*. I followed *you*. One minute I was there, the next I was on the riverbank knowing you were somewhere in the river."

I exhaled. I didn't understand how this ghost connection thing worked but apparently, it meant Brody could always find me. I briefly wondered if it could work the other way around.

Then, I remembered what else happened, what didn't make any

sense. "I don't understand what happened back there…with you and that guy that I shot."

Brody didn't say anything.

"Did you…." I closed my eyes a moment. "God, I can't believe I'm going to even say this… Did you possess him?"

"I don't know," he said. "But when you shot that guy, I got wrenched toward him like I was being sucked in."

"Into his body?"

He slowly nodded.

I didn't know what to say. Thankfully, the silence didn't last for long.

"I knew he was dying. One moment, I was yelling at you to run and the next…" He scoffed, not humorously but in that confused way I remembered. "I was stumbling out the door and the pain…"

The memory of the gunshot tore through me in an instant. Brody's body falling. The blood. The panic.

I jumped up from the stool, my hand sweeping the coffee mug from the counter. It shattered on the stone tile beneath me.

"Hey, you okay?" Brody had taken a half step toward me, arm out as if he could catch me.

He didn't remember. *He didn't remember.* I took a slow deep breath through my nose and exhaled through my mouth. "So, if you took the guy's body, where did *he* go?"

Brody frowned. "Somewhere else. It's like the moment I got inside him, this other presence, this guy, evaporated."

"What does that mean?" I asked, tapping my palm on the counter in confusion.

"When I…he got shot again by Edith's guys, I went somewhere. For a moment, it was like being back in those woods again. Maybe that's where he went, too. Then, I was back on the platform as this." He gently gestured to his flittering form.

My head swam with the desire to go back to sleep, but after everything I'd heard, I wasn't sure I could. I leaned on the counter. "So, you can jump into anybody?"

"I don't think that's how it works. For instance, I don't think I can go inside you." He put up his hands. "Nor would I, so you know."

"I appreciate that," I said emptily.

"I think they need to be on the verge of death." He shrugged. "But hell, if I know. This has only happened to me once after all."

My stomach growled. The last time I'd eaten something, it was the lasagna from Melissa's fridge, which I'd then puked back up. The hunger was a cavern opening up inside. I slid from the stool and quickly took stock of the kitchen cabinets. I filed through boxes of rice and beans, crackers, and some cans of tuna fish. "Do you have any idea where we are?" I asked.

"About five miles downriver."

I found a jar of peanut butter, unscrewed the lid, grabbed a spoon from the dish drainer, and dug in.

Brody chuckled. "That's all you could find?"

"Reminds me of college," I said in between licking the peanut butter from the spoon. The small thumping at the base of my skull had gotten stronger. "Now, if only there were Oreos."

As I spooned another glob of peanut butter out, I cautiously wandered the house. A stack of bills on the kitchen counter led me to a name: Maynard Crane. There was a living room off to the right of the kitchen with a stone fireplace, plush leather couch, and rocking chair. I noticed a collection of photos above the fireplace as well as a white urn, no doubt containing the ashes of Maynard's deceased wife. A small plaque next to it read "Forever in the arms of love, Linda Crane."

The entire house was an ode to their marriage now that I paid attention. Most rooms were spotted with photos of them together, and several of Linda, walking on a sandy beach or planting flowers in the garden. They had seemed genuinely happy. The number of insurance and hospital bills piled on the kitchen counter and the amount of alcohol in the cabinets was enough to discern how things were for Maynard after Linda's death.

The two of them had been outdoor enthusiasts for which I was glad. I found a pair of Outdoor Research water-repellant pants in the bottom drawer of the room I'd woken up in as well as a Patagonia Capilene base layer long sleeve shirt. Being in warm clothes again, a modicum of ease returned to me.

Downstairs, I glanced out the small window in the kitchen door to the driveway. Next to the aged station wagon was a canoe resting upside down between two saw horses. It was in a photograph in the living room with Maynard rowing toward a brilliant pink sunset.

"At least he left you a couple methods of transportation," Brody said.

"I think I've spent enough time on the river," I mused.

I returned to the kitchen. That thumping in my head had gotten a hell of a lot worse in the few moments that had passed. I wearily leaned on the counter, the muscles in my shoulders locking up. The peanut butter tumbled into the empty abyss of my stomach.

Brody frowned. "You're not looking too hot."

I stood up and the whole room pitched. "Fuck, I need to lie down again."

As I stumbled toward the stairs, I realized I wasn't going to make it. The bedroom was too far. I crawled on all fours to the couch in the living room and rolled up onto it. The beating in my head was rhythmic, the pain blinding.

Suddenly, I was fifteen, my mom driving me back from summer camp. She didn't even ask me if I liked it. I made sure to tell her how much fun I'd had, even though I'd spent most of the time by myself. I wasn't the sort of kid who automatically made friends with others over the course of a week. Maybe it was that I knew none of them would ever really understand my boredom, my lack of finding depth in the humdrum of every day monotony. But I lied for my mom. I wanted her to think I preferred being away from home, that I preferred being away from her.

The station wagon was stifling. We had the windows rolled down but the air was stale outside on a ninety-degree day and there was no wind to speak of. I poked at my mosquito bites, while my mom told me about my sister's dance classes. My mother had signed Dana up for ballet, and Dana had accepted because she was a girly girl who wanted to make her mom happy. I'd rebelled from the idea of putting on anything that might show my figure off. I'd rebelled from the idea of standing at attention on my tippy toes so that some old long-necked ex-dancer could chastise my posture and poise. I was happier in the dirt. I was happier being lost in the wild.

Maynard's living room had taken on the qualities of my childhood home. Lying on the couch was like being on the knit tri-colored sofa that used to be in our den, reading a Goosebumps book and eating cookies. My mom leered at me from the kitchen, her face fraught with disapproval. I didn't care. Dad wasn't here anymore.

The memory dissolved into a white ceiling. I desperately tried to remember where I was and when it all came back to me, it didn't bring me any comfort. I flipped over, looking for Brody, but he wasn't there.

The room was vacant. The sound of the furnace kicking on below me made me realize how quiet the house was. I pushed myself up from the marshmallowy cushions and stood. "Brody?" I called softly. The wind outside howled in response.

Memories flipped through like snapshots in my mind: the house, Maynard's body in the kitchen, the conversation with Brody, the peanut butter, the photographs…

I peeked into the kitchen. "Brody?"

Still no one.

A rustling.

My skin prickled. What had that been? It had sounded so close, like it had come from the living room. *Hell, maybe Brody is possessing Maynard's corpse and is giving it a test drive.* I shook my head. No one was in the living room. I glanced back down the hall toward the dining room. Yup, Maynard was still there. Still dead.

Twigs snapped outside. I moved toward the glass patio doors and squinted. Clouds twisted throughout the night sky, preventing much moonlight from cutting through.

Wait.

There; I had almost missed it. Something crept along the edge of the woods, still in shadow. I couldn't make out a shape. Then, the clouds unveiled the moon and light struck the forest. The insides of my mouth dried out within moments.

A creature stood in the underbrush, the lunar glow shining off its black figure and smooth back. Its sinewy legs were long, claws like white serrated knives. A shaggy tail whipped the air as it swung back and forth. The head was slender and long-snouted. A reptilian neck swiveled toward me, golden eyes searching before I ducked out of sight.

My body quaked as I cowered behind a chair. Brody's story immediately leapt into my brain about the wolves scouring the woods in search of human souls. Is that what this *thing* was?

I crept into the kitchen. Every step I took, my brain seized with panic.

Where had Brody gone? It was weird that he'd vanished after we'd had a conversation about how he could always find me. No matter how many times I hissed his name, he didn't appear.

I had to focus. I had no idea where my boots were, but my guess was that Maynard tried to dry them somewhere. On the mat near the front door, there were two pairs of hiking boots. The ones I assumed had belonged to Linda were too small. I shoved my feet into Maynard's. A hair too big, but they'd have to do. Having boots too small in the winter would freeze my feet.

The station wagon was my best way out of here. I needed supplies before I set out into the unknown though. As I opened cupboards and pulled out food in the kitchen, I began to change my mind. *Maybe I should stay concealed.* This house was warm, had food and supplies.... Just because that creature was outside, didn't mean it knew I was here. *If I stay really quiet, maybe I can—*

BANG!

I turned toward the living room. There was movement on the patio.

BANG! The glass doors reverberated with the strike.

It was trying to get in.

I lowered myself toward the floor. *The car keys. Where are the fucking keys?* I remembered the hook by the kitchen light and carefully snagged the keyring there before crouching next to the stove.

Another bang from the living room jolted me. Then, the sound of cracked glass.

Did it actually see me? It doesn't make sense why this thing is so Hell bound on finding me…

I stopped and glanced at the body in the dining room. The blood. I bet that thing could smell it like a shark in the ocean from miles away.

Glass shattered in the living room.

There was no more time. I had to get out of here now.

A snort made me glance back toward the living room. The creature towered over the sofa, head bobbing with each sniff of the stale air.

The head snapped up and I pulled myself back into cover.

I glanced around, trying to find some place I could hide. The room was wide open, nothing to cower under. The creature was going to instinctively head straight for the dead body in the dining room. It would need to pass through the kitchen to get there and would find me inevitably. My only chance was to go for the bathroom on the opposite side of the hall and hide behind the door.

Claws clicked on tile and I realized it had already gotten closer, too close. It would catch me if I darted into the bathroom. I scrambled for the cabinet under the sink and cracked it open. I squeezed myself in around the sink pipes, moving a bucket and some drain cleaner out of the way before I could get the door mostly closed. My knees couldn't quite tuck in and the door bumped against them, leaving them open a crack.

Through the sliver, a shadow entered the kitchen. I forced myself to start breathing through my nose.

The creature slowly came into view. Closer now, I noticed its thick, bristling fur, like stalks of grass. Strange that it had looked so smooth under the moonlight outside. Its claws were the size of my fingers, and scraped on the red tile as it moved further into the room.

I didn't dare move, my knees cramping against my chest as I

tried to stay as still as possible.

The creature barely paid the kitchen any attention, instead moving straight through into the dining room toward Maynard's body. I stayed where I was, the sound of a Neil Young song on the radio like a terrible omen. I remembered the last time I'd listened to it. Josh and I had fought about his job while I cooked dinner. I suddenly wanted to be back there, back when all I had to worry about was an argument and burned ground beef.

The sound of tearing flesh immediately made my stomach bottom out. I cautiously pushed the cabinet door open and climbed out, hands first. The sudden exposure made all the hairs on my arms stand at attention. I forced myself to hold my breath, my fingers clutching the keys to the station wagon like my life depended on it.

Finally able to get to my feet, I crept into the hall, eyeing the kitchen door. This was my chance to go while it was distracted. Maybe it was some form of grotesque curiosity that made me turn back. But when I did, the wolf's pin-like teeth shredded the skin on Maynard's arm. The blood spilled from its mouth as it snapped the muscles and tendons down.

I gasped as its golden eyes met mine.

I bolted. Every movement was slow. I wrenched the kitchen door open and slammed it closed as something barreled into it at full force. I fell backward, landing in the dirt inches from the car.

Move! My brain fired as I struggled to get back up on my feet. I scrambled to the driver's side door of the station wagon and tugged on the handle. Locked. My hands shuddered as I separated the car key from the mass, the metal clattering wildly. I dropped them into the gravel below the car door.

The door buckled, the frame cracking. It wasn't going to hold. I needed to hide.

The canoe. I ran to it and climbed up inside. I grabbed hold of the first thwart and hoisted my feet up onto the second as the front door buckled.

A long, thin shadow stretched out onto the dirt.

I held my breath and gripped the wooden thwart in front of me. Stretched out, vulnerable, there was no way I could make an escape if this thing found me.

The shadow grew larger as it approached the car. Each talon on each paw dug into the earth. The creature's head dipped down, sniffing the ground where I'd stood. The shadow turned and closed in on the boat. The smell was awful, like a body left in the sun. Its jaws lowered toward the space near my feet. I fought the urge to cry, the terror exploding in my gut. The steam from its nostrils clouded the opening below me.

Fuck. I was *fucked.*

From across the driveway, a small skittering like a mouse or a chipmunk dashed through some dry leaves.

The shadow vanished from beside the boat. In an instant, the creature barreled across the driveway.

I let go of the thwart and lowered myself back to the ground. Creeping to the car, I got down on hands and knees and recovered the keys. I plunged the car key into the lock. The monster turned. Horror consumed me. Knowing I only had seconds, I ripped open the door and threw myself inside. The creature was already to the front of the car by the time I pulled the driver's door shut.

I stuck the key in the ignition and turned it, the engine roaring to the life. The creature backed away from the car, glittering eyes focused on mine through the cracked glass. I couldn't look away, transfixed by the sight of something so unearthly and terrifying. Somehow, I had the wherewithal to blindly search for the shifter. Once my clammy palm had cupped over it, I pulled it back into drive. My foot pumped the gas pedal and the car rocketed out from beneath me.

The creature lunged at the car. Claws screeched against the metal as I ducked away. One quick look in the rearview mirror showed the monster bracing itself in the driveway, shaking its head. As the car reached the street, I pulled the steering wheel hard to the right. The wheels slid before finally gripping the asphalt. I stomped harder on the gas pedal and the aging station wagon picked up speed. My eyes darted to the rearview mirror. A black blob at the edge of the driveway grew smaller and smaller, eventually blending with the darkness

All the air rushed out of me that I'd been holding in. I kept my sights on the dark road as it coiled through the night, the only light coming from my headlights.

Where do I go? What do I do? I wasn't even sure exactly where I was.

I looked up into the rearview mirror in time for Brody's face to materialize out of the darkness in the backseat. He leaned toward me, his brown eyes nearly black and whispered, "That was a close one. Good thing you're okay."

FOURTEEN

I stamped on the gas pedal, charging the station wagon through the darkness until the faintest trace of light glared through the trees ahead of me. I'd watched the miles pass on the odometer, unable to ease my foot off the accelerator for fear that what I'd escaped back in that house would appear from the woods nearby.

Brody hadn't said a word since he'd appeared in the backseat. He'd since phased in to the front, a movement that took only a moment to happen but still left me wondering if I'd imagined it. Every few minutes, I'd shift my eyes over to study him, and I'd catch him scrutinizing me, a look I didn't particularly like.

"Stop looking at me like that," I finally said, gritting my teeth.

"You should take a break."

I raised my eyebrows. "You think I'm going to stop after that fucking thing nearly killed me?"

He shrugged. "You're going to have to at some point."

"Not yet. Not 'til we get back to Cardend, find Hank and Evie—"

Brody exhaled.

"What?"

He leaned closer. "Listen, I know you and this guy really connected but—"

I curled my lip at him. "Jesus, Brody! This has nothing to do with feelings! Hank has a daughter who is still too young to look out for herself and both of them are sick. They need my help."

"So, you say."

"God damn it, what is your problem?"

"You," he said, wearily. "You keep looking for trouble."

My grip on the steering wheel somehow got tighter. "Not on purpose."

"Listen."

I glanced at Brody and sighed. "What?"

His eyes softened. "I don't know why I'm here. But the only thing I can think of is that I need to keep you safe. You were my partner for ten years. Watching you keep throwing yourself into danger and not being able to do a damn thing about it is…." He closed his eyes.

"Frustrating?" I finished.

"…agonizing."

A part of me unclenched. I had spent so long trying to convince myself that I could handle what was coming at me alone, that I hadn't stopped to think about Brody himself, a man I'd trusted and loved, who should have been laid to rest. He should have been in whatever blissful afterlife he believed; not here in this hellish whatever world.

But I also knew there was something he wasn't telling me and that made the fist inside tighten again. "You know I'm a cop; not a damsel in distress." I said, "Besides, I handled that wolf thing without you."

He sat up straighter. "I'm sorry I wasn't there."

"Where *were* you exactly?" I gave a sarcastic chuckle. "Boca Raton?"

"Sometimes, I get pulled away. I'm back in the woods, in that purgatory again. I'm not really sure why it keeps happening but I have to concentrate really hard to emerge back here."

"It's that static thing that keeps happening to you, isn't it?"

He nodded.

"Is that where you're supposed to be?"

Brody frowned. "I hope the hell not."

"This seems to all be happening because that wall you were talking about, the one that separates your purgatory and our world dissolved. Maybe the ghosts are supposed to be in purgatory. The wolves go back, everyone is better off…"

"Everyone except the dead," Brody growled. "I didn't devote myself to God for thirty years to be tossed in some Hell with monsters hunting me down. This *isn't* right. I'm not supposed to be *there*."

"You're not supposed to be *here* either."

He cleared his throat. "Why are you so eager to get back to Cardend when you have no idea what's happened to your own family, to Josh…," he paused "…to Carmen."

I sudden pang stuck in my throat. I couldn't believe that Brody had barely mentioned Carmen up until this moment. What's worse was that I couldn't believe *I* hadn't thought of her. What had happened in Cardend had happened in Flintland, I was assured. The radio several nights ago had said it was worldwide. I'd tried to find a station in the car earlier, but all that came through the speakers was static as I spun the tuner knob through all of the numbers. There was no telling how bad things were in some of the bigger cities. But if Cardend, a tiny New England town, had been this horrible, I didn't want to imagine.

"I'm going to bring Hank and Evie to Flintland. They shouldn't be alone. It's too dangerous," I answered.

"And what exactly are you going to tell them when they catch you talking to me? Huh?"

"They won't."

"How?" he grilled me; his voice hard. "How are you going to manage that?"

"Because I don't plan on talking to you once they're in the car."

He reared back. "Well, how do you like that?"

"After what Edith did under Shane's influence, if Hank finds out I'm seeing things, he'd probably kill me."

"Then why risk it?" Brody asked. Something in his face changed suddenly and he scoffed. "You wish I wasn't here, don't you?"

"You know that's not true," I said, each word sticking in my mouth before it was released.

"Oh, yeah. I'm really getting that. Most people I know would sacrifice an arm and a leg for an extra day with someone they lost. But not you. I've gathered that much."

I stomped my foot on the brakes, the tires squealing to a stop. I spun at him, the temperature in the car soaring. "I'd give anything to see my dad again." When he didn't say anything, I shook my head. "You don't have a damn clue about what I've lost, Brody. I've lost everything."

"Enlighten me, Liz. I'm *dead.* How haven't I already lost everything?" he barked.

His words hit me like bullets. I huffed in air, trying to think of something that would make me sound less like the selfish asshole I'd made myself out to me. I came up empty.

Brody exhaled and leaned back into the seat, pinching his nose. "I'm here. I can't touch anything or anyone. Every hour I'm around you, it makes it hard not to want to hug you, push you, shake you…just so you'll know that I'm different from the air around you. I don't know why I'm here and I'm sick and tired of you blaming me for your shitty life now."

I stared down at my lap, my throat tightening. "I'm not blaming you," I whispered.

"Then why are you so eager to act like I'm not here?"

"You don't remember what happened before you died! I envy

that. I wish I could forget. I want to look someone in the eye and not have all of that past baggage pile up. I want someone not to recognize me or what I did. Or what you did. Or the whole shit storm that came after."

He stared at me for so long that I had to look away and wipe my runny nose. "Why can't you tell me what happened?"

I stared ahead at the road. "Honestly, I hope you never remember." I shifted the car back into gear and drove us down the road again.

The sun had come up, burning the sky in bright fiery red streaks. As the minutes dragged, a haze fell over the color. The air was so dry in the car, my lips felt like they would crack from whispering. As snowflakes fell, I stopped the car and stared in shock at the road ahead.

Evergreens had burst through the pavement as if they'd sprouted overnight. Dirt and chunks of asphalt littered the road. The trees barred the route ahead, grown so thick together that I wasn't even sure the road still continued that way.

Brody's jaw hung open next to me.

"Did we take a wrong turn somewhere?" I asked, searching the foliage ahead of us.

"No. This is the route." Brody answered. I didn't like how sure he sounded.

I spotted a misshapen white speed limit sign inside the edge of the woods. "But I don't understand. Where did these trees come from? It doesn't make any sense."

"Sure, because everything else was making perfect sense," he answered.

I opened the car door and climbed out to take the sight in without the windshield's barrier, as if it would magically clear the trees away. No such luck.

It's impossible. This can't be happening. It doesn't make any sense.

No matter how many times I tried to deny it, the forest was there and it wasn't moving. I walked up to the edge of the trees and touched the scarred grey bark on the closest one. Beyond was like looking into a slowly blooming underworld, the light and greenery alien against the snow-coated crumbling tar and wreckage of telephone poles that had fallen like dominos alongside the road.

I turned and looked at Brody who had spawned a few feet behind me. "What *the shit* is this?"

"We should get back in the car," Brody answered instead, never taking his eyes off the trees.

"Not until you answer my question."

"Think about it," he said under his breath. "We crossed over first. Then the wolves came after us. It was a matter of time before purgatory came, too."

I turned back to the tall jungle realm. It was a land with an agenda, a land seeking its lost souls. This awful place was going to get them back and would destroy our world to do it. "A fucking haunted forest," I murmured.

"We've got to turn back the way we came."

"There's got to be some way around," I reasoned. "Or maybe through."

"You *don't* want to go in there." Brody was suddenly in front of me, his gaze locked on mine. "I've been trying to break out of that place for so long. If you go in, you won't come out."

The sounds of crickets were like a symphony from inside, a noise that suddenly seemed surreal and dangerous. My mind flashed back to that monstrous creature in Maynard's house, its hideous face and razor teeth that I'd nearly succumbed to. There would be more of them in these woods no doubt. And if Brody was right and there was no way out, I could have been signing my own death sentence trying to get through to Hank and Evie.

"Come on, the storm's picking up," Brody called, on his way back toward the station wagon.

The longer I stared, the more I thought of Cardend, of Hank lying immovable on the couch, of his hand feebly grasping at mine over the dam. I thought about our lunch in the diner the day before, his stammering when he ordered me to come with him to the ranger station. I thought about Evie's puppy dog slippers and her large sad eyes.

But I couldn't go to them.

Brody's words from earlier sunk into my consciousness. It was time for me to worry about the people closest to me. Dana. Carmen. Josh. Were they okay? Had they managed to get out of Flintland before everything completely collapsed?

"Liz! We've got to get going, now!" Brody called.

I backed away from the forest, as if looking away would dissolve Cardend from my memory.

Goodbye, Evie. Goodbye, Hank.

I finally turned away and climbed into the station wagon. Neither of us said a word as I pulled the car around and headed back the way we came, back toward uncertain dread and waiting disaster.

THEN

I tilted the glass back and let more of the poison pour across my tongue and down my throat. It wasn't the best whiskey. It was hardly what I'd describe as good. But it was cheap and made the memories fade and the pain sting a little less. That was all that mattered. As long as the next few hours dragged on and tomorrow took a little longer to get here, I'd be fine. I could have stayed in those moments forever.

I didn't even think to question why Rainey, the bartender, disappeared for so long. I only noticed it when it was too late, after the little bell above the door jingled and the familiar waft of Brody's cologne settled over me.

"Mind if I join you?" he said, taking off his blazer and tossing it over the back of the bar stool next to me.

"Yeah, I mind." I turned back toward Rainey and lifted my empty glass. "Another."

I caught Brody's subtle shake of the head and Rainey moved down the bar to help other patrons.

"Hey," I called after him.

"Let him go," Brody murmured.

I turned to look at him but too fast. The low lights were bleary in my vision and everything trailed for a few seconds before it settled on Brody's concerned face. "I know why you're here. I don't want to hear it."

He rose his eyebrows and put his hands up in surrender. "I don't know what you're talking about. I'm here having a drink with a friend."

Rainey returned, plunking down a red ale in front of Brody. He lifted it and took a long sip. The scent of the hops reached me and strangely made my stomach turn. I stood up and my feet refused to cooperate.

Brody caught my arm as I headed down, and straightened me, suddenly at my side. Bills rustled and change clinked as he set some cash on the countertop. "I think you're done."

Moments later, we pushed through the heavy oak door and into the quiet fury of a snowstorm. I shivered, pulling my sweater close as I tried to get my bearings. I didn't remember whether or not I'd had a jacket with me. "My car is down here," I said, starting toward it.

"Nope," he answered, giving me a tug back toward him. The jolt was enough to knock loose the nausea I'd tried to reign in. I jerked away from him, collapsed on all fours on the sidewalk and puked into the storm drain over the curb in front of me. Acid stung my throat and the roof of my mouth. I looked up as Brody leaned over me, his hand on my shoulder. People sidestepped us; their faces scrunched up in disgust.

"You finished?" Brody asked after a moment, his tone still as patient as ever.

"I think so." It took me a moment to get to my feet.

"Okay, let's go." He took my arm and led me toward his Charger. I didn't remember the whole car ride, only the never-ending sickness. A few times as I watched the holiday lights flash by on the street, I had to cough to keep from losing my composure completely.

"Hey, please, not in the car," he said at one point. "We're almost there."

"Fuck you," I said, reclining the seat and lying back.

The next thing I knew Brody was guiding me up a set of stairs. They creaked loudly beneath us. The stench of cigarette smoke was like a finger down my throat. By the time we got to his apartment, I had to puke again and barely made it to his toilet.

"You want me to hold your hair back?" he asked.

"Fuck you," I repeated, spitting.

"All right." He backed out of the bathroom. "When you've cleaned yourself up, I'll have a pot of coffee waiting for you." He closed the door behind him.

I sighed.

He opened it suddenly and added, "And a donut," before shutting it again.

The thought of food made me retch again.

For the longest time, I sat curled up like some kind of snake, the only defense mechanism that I had. If I'd had the energy, I'd have gone out to his kitchen and torn into him, called him out on the hypocrisy of him coming to deal with my life when he was ignoring his own.... But the longer I spent there, the more those thoughts receded and shame filled their place.

I fiddled with the shower until I got a warm enough blast, stripped, and slithered in beneath the torrent. The water woke me some, and dulled the headache beginning in the background. After another ten minutes, I dried, redressed, and hesitantly joined Brody in his tiny apartment kitchen. He was sitting at the table, filing through a newspaper's listing section when I shuffled in.

He looked up and hummed. "She lives."

"Hi."

"You want some coffee?"

I nodded and immediately felt like a child.

"Have a seat." He stood up and scraping a mug out of the cupboard.

The smell of the coffee nearly set me on fire. Or maybe it was that disgrace, still clouding my every thought. When he set the mug down in front of me, I grabbed his hand. "Brody, I'm so sorry. I was...."

He rose his brows.

"…awful."

He put his other hand over mine and said, "Forget about it." He pulled away and sat across the table from me. "You're going through a rough patch. We all do."

I thought back to not a week ago, when I'd learned about his and Carmen's separation. I glanced around the kitchen. There were still cardboard boxes of his stuff stacked by the door to the living room. "So, these are the new digs?" I asked.

Brody looked around. "Yeah. What do ya think?"

Velcro held his cabinet doors closed. The horrible white lights in the old ceiling fan made Brody look the whitest shade of pale, which was an accomplishment. His shower head had leaked and was held up with duct tape… The fact that he'd rather dwell in the shittiest apartment this side of Olympia Junction than try to patch things up with Carmen confused the hell out of me, but I understood that I probably didn't understand at all what they were going through. I studied the mattress on the living room floor in the next room. "I take it didn't come fully furnished?"

"No. I figure if I order pizza every other night, I'll soon have enough boxes to make a couch."

I scoffed. "Good luck with that."

Silence ate at us and I took a sip of my coffee, and spit it back in the cup. I wiped my mouth. "How many scoops did you put in?"

"I thought you could use an extra kick."

I took another chug and made myself swallow.

"You want to tell me what happened?"

Looking back on it, I couldn't help but snigger. "It was a fight." The smile sank away from my lips. "He was offered a job in California. He wanted to move. I didn't."

"So, you decided that quickly?" he asked.

"He was offered the job weeks ago. I've been wrestling with the choice a long time. I made my decision tonight."

Brody took a swallow of his own coffee. "That explains some things."

"Everything Josh does is about movement. It's about going

somewhere he's never been before."

"You make him sound like Captain Kirk."

I smiled. "In some demented way, he is. It's always about shifting; never staying long enough in one place to make a home though."

"Did you tell him that?"

"I tried to but I don't think it did any good. He thinks I'm too afraid to move on from here, that that's the reason I won't go."

"Is he right?"

I looked up at Brody. His head was cocked and his questioning eyes stared me down. "No," I answered hesitantly. When he didn't look away, I relented. "Maybe."

"So, is this the end of you two?"

I nodded. "I think so. It happened in fewer words than I'd have liked. I told him to leave. So, he did."

He inhaled and sat down at the table again, his stare on the floor. "I'm sorry, kiddo."

"Me, too."

I glanced at the clock in the kitchen and shuddered. Eleven-thirty. Right now, Josh was on his flight to Los Angeles to confirm his deal with Earth Exploits magazine. I tried to imagine what he was experiencing right now: the lurches of the plane as it soared through smoke grey clouds and icy air.

"How's the job?" Brody asked suddenly, soaring me back to earth. "What can I look forward to coming back to next week?"

"Two homicides; a jogger out for his early run and a drug dealer kid barely out of high school."

"That the one with the missing middle finger?"

I gave him the side-eye. "You've been listening to the scanner?"

"It helps relax me."

I pushed the coffee away, thinking about the phone call I'd gotten earlier this afternoon. "Carmen called me."

He perked up slightly. "Yeah?"

"She wanted to know how you were."

"She couldn't call *me*?"

"I don't know if she's ready yet."

Brody nodded, taking a large gulp from his coffee. "What did you tell her?"

"That you were miserable."

He straightened. "What the hell did you say that for? Are you out of your mind?"

"Let's be honest, Brody: you *are* miserable. Anyone who eats this much pizza in a week has to be."

He snorted. "I think we've said everything that needs to be said to one another."

I stared at him a long time. "I don't get what happened with you two. I always thought you and Carmen were the indestructible ones, that nothing would break you."

Brody took a deep breath. "Me, too. Things change. I think the house might have been a mistake."

"You're blaming this on the house?"

"Not only the house. It was part of it. The construction, the roof falling apart, the water heater, the bathroom prefab.... We couldn't agree on anything. We couldn't pull it together like we always used to. Everything little thing became an argument and both of us said things we regretted. The job keeps me away from home and away from her. She doesn't like that anymore."

I frowned. "I always thought Carmen had your back as far as the job went?" I remembered times Brody told me he'd come off shift and spill to Carmen about how horrible a particular case was that day, how he had considered packing it in. She'd always encouraged him to go back. Hell, she'd done it for me a couple times.

"We're getting older."

"What are you? Forty?"

"Forty-eight."

"This isn't about you two getting older."

He huffed. "Carmen wanted kids."

My face slackened. "What? I thought she hated kids."

"No. We had a talk a long time ago and I wasn't ready to be a dad then. We talked a couple of years ago and we tried. After a year and no results, we did some tests and as it turns out, Carmen, she...." He swallowed hard.

His face made my heart ten times heavier.

"It's not going to happen," he said.

"What about adoption? Or a surrogate?"

"I brought it up. I think something in Carmen broke the day we found out though. She was never really the same after that. I guess I wasn't either. It's been a downhill race ever since."

The wind picked up outside, rattling the glass in the window frames. Brody dumped our coffee in the sink, neither of us having drank any after that conversation. I held my forehead. The headache was only getting worse. My mouth was sour from the aftertaste of coffee and the mint toothpaste I'd hurriedly scrubbed my mouth out with after my puking adventures.

"Look, you can stay here the night, sleep off the rest of that nasty hangover. I'll take you back to your car in the morning."

I stood. "Thanks."

He led me into the living room and pulled some folded blankets off the couch. "You get the wonderful mattress of old."

I accepted the blankets from him. "Where are you going to sleep?"

"I've got some stuff to work on," he said, pushing the blankets into my arms.

I took them, my hand rubbing his. That connection, that tiny flicker where we looked at one another and read not the faces we knew but ones we didn't. It was the first of realizations, both painful and brilliant.

Brody let go of the sheets and took a step back. "I'll be in there if you need anything," he said, and walked into his office. I sat down on the bed, laid out the blankets and snapped off the closest light, plunging me into blackness. But instead of lying under the covers, I sat on them, my mind unable to turn off completely.

I'd made a mess of everything with Josh. He was gone. I'd collapsed. I'd told myself I'd never run to alcohol for any kind of comfort and I'd ignored that promise so I could hide from my mistakes.

And here was Brody going through a separation that could be permanent. They had dealt with that painful lonely idea of barrenness and I hadn't recognized either of their struggles. Yet, Brody still had the patience to deal with me, to let me in to what little space he had because of my own problems.

I lay on the bed without those thoughts ever stopping for a moment. Nearly an hour later, I finally stood up, collected my sweater from the heap it sat in on the floor, and squeaked the door open to Brody's office.

He was hunched over some paperwork, his head propped on one of his hands. He swiveled in his chair at the sound of the door opening. "What is it? Can't sleep?" he asked, his own voice stained by tire.

"I'm actually going to go," I said.

"It's after one in the morning."

I nodded, my mouth a straight line. "You've been great. It's not fair of me to invade your time and space. It's better if I go." I spun around.

I was to the door when Brody's footfalls stopped behind me. I turned. "Brody, you don't need to—"

Brody stepped into me, his hands taking hold of my face, his lips pushing gently against mine. I wrapped my arm around his back, his suit shirt warm and soft against my skin. His chest pressed against mine and I leaned further into him, tasting the same black coffee on his tongue that I'd tasted on mine. For a few moments, I almost forgot where I was.

Then the horror: the thought slashed angrily across my thoughts. This was wrong. So, so *wrong*.

I pushed him away and he thudded against the opposite wall in the tiny hallway. The shock in his eyes brought all the nausea back to me.

My lip shuddered as I tried to say something, anything for what had happened between us. But all I could get out was: "What the fuck?" A big question in a tiny and hoarse voice that didn't even sound like my own.

He didn't say anything. I didn't want to hear it anyway. I turned and yanked open the door to the smoky hallway and didn't look back. I wanted to think he said my name but I couldn't tell. My heartbeat thundering in my head was too loud.

NOW

It didn't take much longer before the snow thickened, falling like torn shreds of confetti. We'd gone about an hour, passing through an empty North Conway and crossing over into Maine before the winds resumed their terrorizing of the car and the forests. Soon everything was masked by a film of white as the blizzard fully engulfed us.

We stayed along Route 32, snaking our way over hills, through tiny villages that exuded a type of silence that left me paranoid, and through miles and miles of woods. These woods were oppressive and looming, much more sinister than ever before. I didn't know what was going to appear from them at any turn in the road, or if the road would end like it had near Cardend.

I kept the car going at forty, still able to make out the road ahead but only barely. We'd gone fifty miles before the snow thickened underneath us. The car slid on a corner and I took my foot off the accelerator, slowing it down enough to keep us from going off into a ditch. *It's only going to keep getting worse and worse*, I realized.

Soon, we were driving only twenty-five miles an hour. The world ahead was a blank slate. I couldn't even tell where the road was. The trees on either side of us were the only guides.

Nearly two hours after leaving Cardend behind, we reached the point where we passed under the interstate on our way toward Portland. I hit the brakes as we came around a corner and I stared; my jaw clenched at the sight before me. Through the whiteout of the squall were hundreds of cars, jam-packed along the I-95 south bridge as if connected like train cars in a variety of colors and sizes. I couldn't tell if there was anyone inside of any of them.

They were all in the opposite lane heading toward the southern tip of Maine, away from where I needed to go. Two cars had gone off the bridge and landed upside down on the pavement in front of us, effectively blocking us off. The top of the car and windows were already buried by snow.

"Holy Moses," Brody whispered.

"If only we were so lucky," I muttered. "At least he'd be able to part it like the Red Sea."

I pulled the car up to them and nudged, the grind of metal-on-metal screeching in my ears. The tires spun underneath us, unable to get any traction. I tried to back up in order to pull around and the car sat in place, the back end fish-tailing slightly. No dice. We were stuck.

"Don't suppose you could have hijacked a snowplow," Brody finally murmured.

I slumped back in the driver's seat. "There's no way we're getting through here."

"Those cars up there were all headed south, Liz."

I swallowed. "Yup."

"It means that whatever they're driving away from must be a lot worse than what we left."

I knew the sensible thing to do would be to turn around and find an alternative route out of New England. But all I could think of was Flintland.

"What's our plan?" Brody asked.

"I'm thinking."

"Better think fast. The storm is worse than it was an hour ago and we don't want to stay here."

I killed the engine and nodded. "We need to find shelter."

"All right." He waved his hand. "Looks like we're walking,"

"We could wait it out," I ventured, despite knowing what he'd say.

"Unless you want to dig yourself out tomorrow, you should get out while you still can."

Realizing this made my heart thrum three times faster than it was already: stranded out in the middle of nowhere in a freak snowstorm. *If God has a sense of humor and he exists after all, he'll strike me down with a lightning bolt now; or if he's merciful.*

I climbed out of the car. Brody passed through the wrecked cars, while I struggled to climb over the slick hood of one. The snowfall kept the car from rocking and I was thankful for it until I reached the other side and sank into the snow up to my knees. Icy cold pricked its fingers inside my boots and I climbed out. Despite knowing we wouldn't be covering much ground, I gritted my teeth against the snow and followed Brody's hazy form, his image fuzzy like staring at an old television set.

I stayed on the road for a time. We should have been getting closer to the city, but I realized within twenty minutes that we were once again surrounded by woods on both sides. My hands had turned red and shook furiously. I shoved them into my pockets, trying to make out anything in the squall around us. Only the towering pines stood out against the grey sky and the furious storm. "Maybe we should go back!" I shouted, looking up to where I'd last seen Brody. He wasn't there.

"Brody!" The snow was solid on my legs as I spun around, searching for any sign of him. But he didn't leave tracks in the snow.

He must have been pulled back into purgatory. Don't panic. Retrace your steps. Get back to the car.

I prodded with my hands for the holes in the snow that my feet had left and worked my way back through them. But as I moved, they filled until finally I found myself at a dead end with nothing but immaculate snow all around me. "Brody!" I screamed again.

I was blind. I had no idea which way to go and the cold was eating at me. I'd already lost days staying in that house with an illness. I couldn't afford to lose any more precious time. I had to find some kind of shelter. I kept going back toward where I hoped the bridge was, the route painstaking as the snow now reached my waist.

Another step and suddenly the earth dropped out from underneath me. I fell hard, tumbling through white powder, my legs and arms upended as I screamed. I rolled against the snow, finally sinking into it as I stopped. The grey sky glared down at me, flakes tossing in my vision.

Get up. Get up.

The snow held me, sticky around my arms and legs as I tried to find something to leverage myself with. My fingers clawed at the snow around me until I had enough of an opening to get to my feet once again.

My neck screamed and my fingers itched as I looked at the wall of snow behind me. Where the hell was I now?

I took a step and I sank even further down to my waist. The snow was deeper down here and I had no way of getting out of here without freezing to death first. *This is where it's going to end,* I mused. *Here. Where no one will know where I—*

"Hey!"

I turned suddenly, noticing a small smudge of a shape appearing out of the snow ahead of me. The closer it got, the more I marveled at how tall it was. Whoever it was trudging through this snow would have had to be the size of a professional basketball player to be able to get through this. Then I noted that the person wasn't walking *through* the snow, but *on* it instead. By the time he got close, he was actually a lot shorter.

"Hey! Are you okay?"

From beneath the fur-lined hood of a down jacket, a boy's eyes stared at me, the rest of his face covered by a balaclava. Two old-fashioned snow shoes spread underneath him on the snow, distributing his weight.

"I need help!" I yelled over the wind. "I'm lost!"

He reached out a gloved hand to me and I grabbed it.

"Spread your legs further and take light steps!" he said. "Otherwise, you'll sink again."

I did as I was told, planting them at either side of me. Despite living in Maine for so long, I had never once used snowshoes.

"Now, follow me!"

He took off and I carefully followed, fear rushing through me at the idea of falling behind or losing his form in the blizzard. Every few moments, the kid would look behind him to make sure I was still there.

"What's your name?" I yelled finally.

"Jake," he answered. "Come on! It's not too much further!"

We trudged through the snow. As the cold overwhelmed me, I noticed the slight orange glow of lights coming from the gloom ahead. Soon enough, the outline of a cabin appeared. I smiled and promptly lost my footing. I cried as one of my legs dropped through the snow

Jake turned at the sound of my scream and made his way back to me, grabbing my hand to help me out.

"Are you out here all by yourself?" I asked him once I'd gotten out.

Suddenly behind him, the cabin door opened and a figure appeared with a lantern in hand, trudging toward us. They shouted something that I couldn't make out in the howling wind.

Jake stood up and said, "My grandpa. I'll get him to help." He took off toward his grandfather. I watched him go and tried to climb up into a standing position again. Half way to his grandpa, Jake suddenly dropped through the snow, his entire body vanishing beneath it.

I scrambled through the snow, my feet tripping me up as they punched through the crusted layer above me. I tried making a path through with my hands first, but it didn't make a difference. The closer I grew, the more frantic the other person's cries became.

"Jake! Jake!" A man as heavily dressed as Jake was, dropped the lantern nearby and fell to his knees above where the boy had fallen. I came up alongside him, making to go around to the other side. He grabbed my leg and forced me back. "Don't! You'll go through!"

Only then, I noticed the water: a thin, silver layer in the hole where Jake had disappeared.

"Shit! Oh shit!" We were on the edge of a lake. That was why there hadn't been any trees nearby, or anything for that matter.

"Jake!" the man yelled again, submersing both arms in the icy water and flailing them around.

I held my breath, hoping his head would surface, hoping I hadn't been the reason for this boy's death. But my hope deflated when the man screamed, an unhinged and terrifying slit of rage that completely numbed me.

He lunged at me, his icy fingers stabbing into my shoulders like knives. "It's your fault!"

We floundered in the deep snow. The white swam in my vision and I spit it out as I struggled to get my attacker off me. I finally found leverage and kicked him in the chest.

He collapsed back, his form nearly vanishing in the snow.

I righted myself, trying to get onto my feet in order to prepare for the next attack.

Behind my attacker, Jake's skinny little arm burst through the thin layer of ice that had crisped over the hole. I shot forward, grasping the hand and pulling with all my might against the weight of the water. Moments later, two more gloved hands grabbed hold from behind me and helped me wrench Jake from the lake's icy embrace. Jake's head surfaced, coughing and sputtering.

"It's all right, Jakey!" the man cried. "I've got you! I've got you!"

Together, we hauled Jake up onto the snowy bank. The grandfather cradled him in his arms and the boy shivered against him.

The man shoved the lantern into my arms. "Take this!"

I grabbed the handle and held the lantern up against the white force. The miniscule light rushed energy into me. I spun around, searching the featureless landscape for a sign. The squall was at full force, completely masking the world around us. The cabin had vanished. "Which way?"

"West!"

"Where?"

"On your right!"

I struggled through the blankets of snow. The man grunted behind me. Every few moments, he said something to Jake, though it sounded barely over a murmur. The wind would eat the rest of the sound. Several times, I thought there was a dark shape in the middle of the snow field and panic would surge through me. I hadn't encountered one of those wolf creatures since Maynard's house but I knew they were still out here, probably unburdened by the heavy snowfall.

Brody was still out here, too.

I thought about what he'd told me only a few hours ago. He was slipping away, finding it hard to hold on to something in this realm that could keep him here.

Part of me had wanted to tell him to hold on to me. The other questioned whether or not that was a good idea.

"There!" the man shouted. "There it is!"

I looked up.

Only a few feet away, the dark shape of the cabin materialized from the thick air as if it existed on a different plane. We crossed the distance to it and I held open the door while he pulled Jake in from the cold.

The scream of the wind muted as I slammed the door behind me. I collapsed on the ground by the door, exhaustion and cold itching on my fingers and toes. Winter had sunk its claws into me deeply. It was as if warmth couldn't touch me.

The man dropped Jake into the nearby couch, and immediately yanked off the boy's drenched clothes. "We're going to warm you up. That's it."

He turned toward me, his expression less than thrilled. "And you," he growled, stomping to a closet nearby. "You nearly got my grandson killed."

"He helped me," I said, my mouth barely able to get the words out. "He saved my life."

He scoffed, pulling a thick comforter from the top shelf and tossing it at me. I unfolded it, cocooning myself in it as quickly as I could.

Wrapped in that shell, the vestiges of clammy heat ebbed into my skin.

"You'd better take off your clothes."

I looked up at him.

He was stripping Jake's sopping clothes from him before wrapping him in a swath of blankets. "Your clothes are drenched. All you'll do is soak that blanket through if you keep them on."

He tromped into the kitchen, banging a steel tea kettle with some water on to the stove.

I shivered hard and knew he was right. I unzipped my jacket, my fingers trembling as they picked ice from the metal teeth.

"Aw, hell!" He slammed a spoon down on the stove top. "We're low on wood."

He stomped to the door. "When that water boils, fill those rubber water bottles, and make sure he gets them under the arm pits." He pushed out, the wind nipping at me for only a moment before he pulled it shut behind him.

I pushed the jacket off my shoulders and unbuttoned my shirt. I peeled it off, catching a glimpse of the white jagged scar on my shoulder. I laid the shirt out on the floor and pulled the zipper down on my pants.

A sound from the couch made me look up.

Jake was peering back at me over the back of the couch, still shivering.

I pulled the blanket close to cover me up. "Jake, you should lie back down. Your grandpa's going to—"

"Liz."

My name sounded so innocent coming from Jake's trembling mouth.

I'd never told him my name.

I recognized it slowly. The same dark gaze in the boy's eyes that fixated on me. His mouth twitched and his head slightly cocked. I knew who was looking at me, but I still asked. "Brody?"

"I'm here."

The second realization hit me. Jake never made it out of the lake alive.

I struggled to remember how to breathe. This kid, maybe ten, had risked his and his grandfather's life to rescue me. And now Jake was dead. Brody stared at me the entire time with a knowing sadness but nothing more.

"Why?" I finally asked. "Why did you take his body?"

"If this kid had died in that lake, his grandfather would have killed you without hesitation."

He was right. He would have.

"So, you're lying to him? Convincing him that his grandson is still alive?" I said instead.

"What would you have me do?" Coming from Jake's fragile voice, the gravity of the question was as heavy as bricks. "I had to make sure you would be all right."

I wanted to say more, but the door opened once more and the man entered again, carrying a load of firewood. He dropped it all into the metal wood box with a rumble and went over to his grandson, patting him on the head. "Rest now, Jake. Hot water bottles are a-comin'."

Brody's eyes disappeared behind the cover of the couch.

I shuddered, my heart breaking open as I thought about what he had done and my responsibility for it.

FIFTEEN

Darkness collapsed around the cabin in a matter of hours. Jake hadn't made any noise in a while and it only made sense that he'd fallen asleep. His grandfather had given him a couple of hot water bottles, the red rubber ones like the ones my parents had kept at our cabin in Middlehitch. That, along with some hot chamomile tea, had brought his temperature back up. Every time I looked at him, I got sick to my stomach. He wasn't a child anymore. Brody had taken hold, had crawled inside in order to save my life. I stared down at my quilted blanket, at the infinite swirls and patterns on it as my hands shook. That poor boy. His poor grandfather. It was my fault.

The grandfather, Elden, was outside shoveling around the house's perimeter and clearing out a path to the storage shed. He hadn't been eager to chat and I was in much of the same mood. I worried that something in my tone would give away what had happened. I knew that it was only a matter of time before Brody gave himself away.

As I mused, the door suddenly opened and Elden tromped in, snow whistling in behind him. I pulled the blanket closer to me to block the frigid air until he closed the door. He peeled off his hat and gloves, glancing at me out of the corner of his eye. "You're still awake? I thought you'd have passed out by now."

I swallowed. "It's been a long day."

He hung his jacket up on the nail next to the door, then sat on the bench underneath and picked at the ice-crusted boot laces with his fingers. "So, let's hear it then."

"What?"

"I'm assuming you weren't flailing around in the worst snow storm of the season for kicks," he grumbled.

"No. You'd be right."

He stared at me. "So?"

I decided that the abbreviated version would be better than nothing. I didn't want to end up on my tail outside again. "I was traveling north. The road was blocked so I had to continue on foot and I got turned around in the blizzard." I glanced over at the back of Jake's head.

"He found me after I'd fallen down a hill and was leading me here."

He sighed and kicked off the first boot. "That's Jake. He means well but he doesn't know any better half the time. Just like his dad."

I squinted. "Well, I'd be dead if it wasn't for him."

Elden tugged the second boot off and stood. "I think that would have been better."

Me, too, I thought, though I didn't say it out loud.

He collected a couple of mugs from the kitchen and returned to the living room, pouring hot water into them from the kettle on top of the woodstove. He dunked a couple of tea bags in and handed me a mug which I took hesitantly. The strong scent of chai lifted my brain from the snarls of exhaustion and the warmth from the mug brought my fingers back from the brink of cold.

Elden settled in the rocking chair next to the woodstove and cradled the cup in his hands. "Where were you traveling from?"

"New Hampshire."

"Why'd you leave?"

I thought back to the hydroelectric plant, to Hank and Evie. "I was with someone else. We got separated and when we tried to get back, the road was blocked."

He straightened a little in his seat. "'We tried'?"

"Huh?"

"You said '*we* tried to get back'."

My eyes rested on Jake for a moment before I shook my head and scoffed. "I'm tired. I meant 'I tried'."

Elden didn't take his eyes off of me as he took a large sip from his tea. After he swallowed, he put the mug down and clasped his hands together. "Why are you heading north?"

I sipped my tea. "I'm from Flintland. I'm trying to get back to make sure friends are all right."

"We haven't run into anybody in nearly a week," he said. "Like everyone up and left."

"It's a little further north from here. They might still be there."

He closed his eyes. "Anyone who could get out of Maine probably got out when they could. The government issued orders for people in the Northeast to leave their homes, only bring their most important possessions. They've set up a community in Boston and surrounding areas where the National Guard and law enforcement can adequately protect citizens and where the CDC can establish a treatment facility. That was a week ago. I doubt there's anyone even left north of Brunswick, much less north of us."

I gritted my teeth. "I still have to be sure."

He shook his head. "Do you even know what's happening out there? The total breakdown of society as we know it! Chaos, murder, looting…."

"I saw enough of that in New Hampshire."

He leaned forward in his seat and spoke softly, as if he was afraid to say his next words. "You know about Them, right?"

I kept myself from looking at Jake. "'Them'?" I parroted.

"Spirits. Phantoms. Ghosts. Call them whatever you'd like." His eyes drained of their strength and he whispered, "They're evil."

My grip around the cup tightened. "What do you mean 'evil'?"

"They latch onto you, something that *looks* like a loved one you've lost. Could be an aunt, a best friend, or even your own mother. They pull the wool over your eyes and make you believe that it's them. Then, when you least suspect it, they climb inside you." He reached his hand into the air and suddenly snatched at something invisible. "They take you over. When they've used you for whatever they need to, they leave you like a dried-out husk."

I pulled the blanket closer to me, frigid despite the warmth in the room. I didn't dare look at Jake for fear of giving Brody away. I glued my eyes to the cup in Elden's hand and followed it up to his face as he took another sip. "So, you don't believe this is a virus? Or a mass hallucination?"

Elden sniffed and pointed to the blanket wrapped around me. "My wife, Margie, made that quilt a few years ago for me and Jake to take with us and put up here in our winter ice fishing cabin. About ten days ago in the middle of the night, she got up from bed and went to the window that looks out on the front of the house. She said her mother called to her from the garden. She went out to look and I was still half asleep. When she came back in, she wasn't Margie."

I stared at the shadows playing with the firelight on the wooden floor, unable to make myself meet his eyes.

"She kept talking to me about how she was sorry she'd done it, that she hadn't meant to. Kept asking after our son like she didn't know he'd died. Margie's mother died from lung cancer in '85. Our son died last year in a motorcycle accident. She didn't remember," he repeated.

For a time, he sat there, staring down at his lap and not saying anything.

This didn't match up with what Brody had told me. He'd said that he been pulled into the body he'd inhabited the first time, a body that was dying. Jake had also been dying. But if what Elden was saying was true, it meant ghosts could possess someone whenever they wanted. I needed to know more.

"What happened then?" I asked carefully.

He cleared his throat. "I took Jake and we left. He didn't understand and I couldn't be there in that house. I went back eventually. I had to. Found her lying in the middle of our bedroom with not a mark on her. The ghost had left her and took Margie's soul with her." His voice shook as he forced himself to swallow more coffee.

"No injuries or anything?" I prompted.

"None that I could see."

Well, this is a twist, I thought. "I'm sorry," was all I could manage aloud.

"You've managed to avoid it for as long as you have. You're lucky you aren't attached."

Attached. I suddenly realized what he meant. Brody and I. It was why I was the only one that could see him.

Taking my silence for confusion, Elden plunked the empty mug onto the table and said, "I have this old army buddy of mine, Ismet. He was always a talkative son of a bitch, frequently gave me advice while we were stationed overseas in our hay-days. Hard to believe I actually miss it.

"This thing about being attached to someone's ghost was something Ismet believed in. Call it unfinished business, or soul mates, or whatever the hell you want. There is always some reason for the dead hanging around the living."

"But ghosts can't touch anything? So how can they possess us?"

"'The wound is the place where Light enters you.' It was an old phrase from Rumi, someone whom Ismet gleaned a lot of wisdom from."

"'The Light?'" I questioned.

"I always assumed they meant God or Allah or whoever. Or maybe he meant the loved ones we've lost who help us to heal, the people who were the light in our lives before they left."

Brody. My friend. The one person who knew everything that was happening to me when he'd been taken away. I couldn't imagine a person with more radiance than him in my life, though it pained me to think of those last few weeks with him now.

I focused back on the quote Elden had shared. "You said a wound?"

Elden straightened in his seat, his face dropping. "If you find yourself on the brink of death, like you were out there, that's when they come. I've followed stories being shared on the internet. That's the connection. That's when they get inside and worm their way all through you until they've felt, seen, tasted, and touched everything they need to. Then, they leave." He shrugged and grabbed a blanket from the top of a chest nearby, spreading it over him. "Who knows where they go from there."

"But you said that your wife didn't have a mark on her when she was possessed. I don't understand."

"My wife had metastatic breast cancer. Doctors told us she still had several months left during her last checkup. It still meant she was dying. Maybe that was enough for that monster to slip inside."

So, dying *was* the way they could possess someone. I thought about Brody. I'd been close to death after my drop into the river and not once had he ever made a move to take over my body. I had to wonder if Elden suspected all the ghosts were malicious because of what had happened to his wife. What if it was a mistake? What if Margie's mother had experienced the "pull" to her daughter's body like Brody had to the man at the hydroelectric dam?

A sliver of me wondered if Brody was keeping any more secrets from me. I didn't know which theory I believed more at the moment.

Elden urged the blanket a little higher up on his chest until his shoulders were covered and murmured, "It's late. We're going to need to be up in a couple hours to dig ourselves out of here. We should both try and get some sleep while we still can." He didn't say anything more after that.

I laid out flat on the floor. Despite the sleeping pad, the cold radiated up toward me. I couldn't force my eyes away from Brody. Even in the darkness, I was afraid that he'd slip away from me again. Or if I woke up, I'd find that I'd lived through a terrible nightmare, watching Jake die at the hands of a friend. Elden's words didn't stray far from me even in my exhaustion.

THEN

After the kiss, I avoided Brody for a few days. Between ignoring his phone calls and being wrapped up in the job, it was good to lose track of time. When I returned home in the evenings though, that was when things slowed down and I had too much time to think. More than anything, I couldn't stand that time. I thought about Josh, about how he'd called once to let me know he'd gotten to L.A. safely, but not again since. Whenever I thought about what had happened with Brody, I'd go straight for the gin. I put on my classical music, tried to think of my family's cabin and that time when everything was perfect as I sipped. It became harder and harder to attain the peace I used to get from that ritual.

When I opened my eyes that Sunday morning, head pounding and eyes bleary, my phone was ringing. I still had yesterday's clothes on and my mouth tasted like mothballs. I'd tipped the bottle of gin by accident in my sleep, but thankfully, it was already empty when that had happened. I didn't even look at the phone screen as I answered, assuming I was going to get called into work another shift. "Raleigh?"

"Look out your window."

I loafed out of bed and over to my bedroom window. I peeled back the curtain.

Brody stood on my front step, holding a coffee tray with two Styrofoam cups, cell phone to his ear. He glanced up at me. "Morning."

"What are you doing here?" I answered.

"How long are you planning on dodging me?"

"I hadn't made up my mind yet."

Brody sighed. "Look, can I come inside so we can talk?"

I stiffened. "You been standing out there long?"

He gave me a tight-lipped smile. "Long enough."

"So then, the coffee's cold?"

"It's probably frozen, and I'm about half-way there myself. Will you open the door?"

I hung up and went downstairs to unlock the door. He stepped in and shivered, as if to brush the last of the cold off him. The aroma of coffee soon folded over me like a welcome cloud along with the scent of sandalwood and cinnamon.

"Never thought you'd be the type to stand on anyone's doorstep to deliver an apology," I said, closing the door behind him. "At least you didn't throw rocks at my window."

He handed me a cup of coffee.

I flinched. "God, that's hot!"

"Don't burn your fingers."

"You said you'd been standing out there for—"

"Didn't want to get you up too early, so I sat in the car with the heat on for a while."

"You still woke me up."

He shrugged. "I got impatient. Sue me. Besides, I know how

cranky you are when you don't get your coffee the way you like it."

I took a sip of it. Black. One sugar. "Okay."

We sat in the kitchen with the light pouring in, lemon-colored and too bright for my alcohol-soaked brain. I'd forgotten to pick up after my night of binge-drinking. I knew Brody had noticed but he didn't say anything. We sat at the table for a few moments silently. The circumstances were eerily similar to the other night at his apartment. Even with the coffee, my insides were tangling themselves up.

Brody set his coffee down and looked at me squarely. "Look, I don't want to draw this out, so I'll get straight to the point. What I did was impulsive. I regret it and I'm sorry that I put you in that position."

I stared down at my lap, trying to swallow the words. It was exactly how I'd expected him to apologize, but something about it tasted sour and unsatisfying.

"Not only was it unprofessional, it was unfair to you. You're my partner and most importantly, you're my friend," he continued. "If what I did has ruined that, I'd never forgive myself."

"Why did you?" I asked, leaning back in my chair.

"I don't know."

When he didn't say anything else, I scoffed. "That's it?"

Brody cleared his throat. "Look, Liz, I'm…confused. I'm trying to figure out what's going on with Carmen and I don't know how to cope."

"So, you thought if you kissed me, you'd…what? Gain perspective?"

"Maybe?" He put his hands up. "I'm surrendering here. I haven't talked to anyone about this. It's been eating me alive. Slowly falling out of love with someone you promised to honor and cherish forever over the course of a year… I think I wanted closeness, someone to listen."

A year? I hadn't realized it was that long. I crossed my arms. "And I would have listened if you'd told me any of this. But you never did. You kept it to yourself."

"Call it one of my fatal flaws. I never say anything until things are at their absolute worst."

"Well, your timing was pretty terrible," I said, biting my lip.

"I know."

I reached over and put my hand over one of his. "I mean, if you had the hots for me, I'd have expected that to manifest *so* much earlier."

He chuckled.

"You know, back when I was in my twenties and could actually get off the sofa without groaning."

A smile brightened his features. "I'm so sorry," he said in spite of them.

"I know. I also cussed you out in a bar and puked all over your bathroom. I say we call it even."

We didn't say anything to one another for a few moments. The ominous cloud I'd had around me for the last few days was finally slipping away. But I looked at the chair Brody sat in and immediately thought about Josh sitting in that chair only a few days ago. I thought about how on Sunday mornings, we would always cook French toast, Feist in the background. The stark emptiness of the kitchen then hit me like a baseball being lobbed at my chest.

Brody noticed my sudden change in demeanor. His brows knitted together. "Liz?"

I took his hand again and leaned in, my mind losing the war against my emotions. "I don't know what to do without him," I said, my breaths short and hard to control. "I'm so alone."

Brody put one of his hands on the back of my head and held me close to him, my face buried in his shoulder as the tears took hold. "I'm sorry," he whispered. "I'm so sorry."

NOW

I didn't remember falling asleep. Elden shook me awake. The foreign space and the dim light put me on defense at once and I bolted back from him. Elden did the same, his hand at his hip, no doubt reaching for some kind of weapon hiding there.

"Easy," he said, dropping his hand and taking a deep breath.

"Sorry." I tried to swallow, but the lump in my throat from the day before was still there. It took everything I had not to look toward the couch where Brody was in Jake's body. "How long did I sleep?" I asked, hoping to deflect any question Elden might have toward me.

"It's been ten hours or so," he said, stepping back toward the stove. "The sun's been out for a few hours now."

"Good. Maybe some of that snow will melt."

He nodded toward the temperature gauge on the window. "'Fraid not."

I glanced at it and my stomach sank. Negative ten.

Elden spooned some dried oats into some bowls. "Take it as you like; it's actually better that it's staying cold. The snow will be easier to move. It won't be wet and heavy. The light today will make for a good scouting day."

"Scouting?"

He lifted the cast iron tea kettle from the stove top and poured boiling water into each bowl. "Most everyone that had cabins down here on the lake has up and deserted. Whatever supplies they've left behind are free for the taking. If we have any hope of getting through the winter out here, we'll need to take them."

"What if you did find someone trying to eke out a living? What would you do?"

Elden brought over a bowl and set it in my hands. I barely noticed the warmth. I was distracted by his gaze, which had hardened and wouldn't connect with mine. "We won't worry about that until it happens." He returned to the stove and picked up another bowl. "But it won't."

Stepping over to the couch, he said, "There you go, Jakey. Eat up."

The idea that Brody was awake sent a chill through my body. I clutched the blanket closer to me and nodded toward the couch. "How is he this morning?"

"Cold. He's going to need some time to rest and regain his strength. He'll stay here while we scout."

The idea of being alone with Elden made me uncomfortable. Apparently, it made Brody feel the same. Not even a moment had passed before he sat up higher on the couch and said, "I'm coming with you."

Elden put a hand on his head. "I know you want to be in on the action, but you're not strong enough. You were lucky you survived falling through that ice yesterday."

I winced.

"You've got to stay bundled up. Besides, who's going to defend the cabin while we're gone?" He smiled.

Jake's head turned in my direction and I stared down at my oatmeal, unable to look him in the eyes for fear of what I might betray. "Okay," he relented. "Take care of her."

Elden's face slackened a little bit in confusion. It softened as he rubbed the boy's hair and said, "Okay."

Brody's last-ditch effort of watching out for me? There was only so much he could do in a child's body. If he wanted me to be safe, he wasn't going to blow his cover. That meant a heartfelt, childlike sentiment was as good as he could do.

After we'd eaten, we dressed in winter layers, me borrowing

some of Elden's clothes since mine were still wet. Elden pushed out first with me at his heels. Before I could get out the door, Brody grabbed my hand from inside and whispered, "Watch him, Liz," before slinking back to the couch. I closed the door behind me, my stomach tied in knots all over again.

Outside, we strapped on snowshoes to traverse the arctic landscape. The pair I had on had belonged to Elden's late wife. As I tightened the buckles, I tried not to think about the story he'd told me the night before. How long could Brody's ghost stay in Jake's body? If the body died, would he be forced out like some kind of snake shedding its skin?

"Come on!" Elden called over his shoulder. "Not too far to the first cabin!"

In the crisp daylight, the lake was a flat disc that stretched back and vanished into an eventual coastline with houses. The wind was still strong and whipped the light snow around us, cutting my face at times. Elden didn't react, only pushed into the wind and maneuvered over the snow-covered roots and uneven terrain. Sprinkles of snow fell from the cedar trees along the shoreline.

Elden glanced back over his shoulder at me and waited for me to catch up. He pointed ahead through the trees. "That used to be Norris's place there. He was an insurance broker dandy from Boston, sometimes stayed up here for weeks on end like it was his own personal paradise. Threw his trash around, never looked after anything, made a racket with all of his buddies late at night…"

I eyed the black-wooded cabin as we passed it, noting the snow drifted up against the door, the broken windows, curtains still drawn inside. "What happened to him?"

"Beats me," Elden said. "He wasn't here when things happened. Didn't really leave anything useful either. A bear got in there and tore his icebox to shreds along with most of the cabin. Only thing Jake and I found were a few tins of sardines and a rifle with some ammo."

"How far have you patrolled?"

"Quarter way around the lake, I imagine. There's a lot of fishing camps here, though most are empty and lots of shacks out on the ice, too. There's an island out there with a cabin up on it, too, but I haven't tried to get out to it yet. I'll make that trip when the lake has frozen over completely."

We continued on in silence for another twenty minutes or so. We passed homely shanties with ratty American flags flapping against the gusts and creaking front steps; trailers that looked as though they'd been fashioned from millions of tin cans that wobbled against the wind; two story cabins with icicles jutting down from the eves like teeth. The docks stretched out from their porches into the white lake as if they were bridges leading to the afterlife.

At times there would be nothing but snow, and trees and the sound of cold air rushing down on us. It made me so much more alone and so much more desperate for a warm place to huddle in. Elden was determined though; he wouldn't go into a cabin that he'd already searched, even if it was for relief against the chilling temperatures.

The tree coverage lightened and several tree stumps came into view around the next bend, followed by stacks of logs. In their midst was a cabin, with an unlit lamp hanging over the door and a sign tacked into the wood above that read, "Hershey."

I sighed. "Please tell me this is a chocolate store."

"Levi Hershey's Sawmill," Elden said, pushing through the snow toward the front door. "Bastard always knew how to wake a man too early on a Saturday morning with all that chain-sawing."

I glanced around the cluttered, desolate yard. All of the machinery was covered in snow, along with already cut lumber. A useless looking 4x4 truck was leaning pretty heavily into the side of a drift, snow spilling into the passenger side window. "He left?"

We reached the door and took off our snowshoes. Elden pulled his pistol from the back of his jeans. "Only one way to find out, I suppose." He pounded on the door with his fist and called out, "Levi? You in there?"

Seconds stretched. With each one, winter crept inside me bit by bit. The howling wind around me put me on edge. I struggled to remember to breathe despite knowing whoever was inside couldn't hear me. We waited ten seconds.

"Good enough for me," Elden decided. He twisted the knob and forced the door open.

Darkness greeted us from inside, the kind of deep blue daylight that reminded me too much of night. We filed in and I closed the door behind us, sealing out the cold. Being out of the wind was enough to make me relax. The ends of my fingers burned and my nose ran unstoppably.

Elden put a finger to his lips and pointed to the hallway on our left. "Stay behind me," he ordered and with gun drawn, he stepped into the next room. It opened up into a kitchen with windows that overlooked the lake. Things were tidy, cabinets were closed, drawers were shut…nothing out of place. I reached for a drawer handle but Elden smacked my hand and pointed to the ground. Blood and lots of it. A trail led from the front door, splotches of it here and there and continued into the succeeding room.

We swept through the living room following the trail, around to the stairs and up into the loft there. Dust floated in the air between the bedroom and us as we cautiously entered. My eyes fell on a shape hunkered by the bureau and my lip hung.

The body was clothed heavily in winter attire, the knees up to the chest, and the head sunk low. I knew he was dead.

My cheeks were burning. I couldn't move.

Elden took a few steps toward the body and crouched. He gingerly raised a hand to the head and tipped it back a little. "Yup. That's Levi, all right."

"How did he die?" I asked, not wanting to get any closer.

"He's got a nasty wound on his leg here," Elden said. "Probably died of blood loss. Hell of a lot of it between the front door and here."

I stared down at the bloodied leg. The wound was ragged and deep. Even though I had an idea of what might have done it, I played dumb and asked him.

He stood and sighed. "Might be a bite. We have coyotes out here; black bears, bobcats.... Might have even been a wolf. They've been slowly making their way down from Canada over the years. He could have cut himself with one of his own saws, for all we know."

So, he didn't know about the wolves. I wasn't sure if I could even properly explain what they were, let alone if he'd believe me. But if he knew the ghosts were real, hopefully it wouldn't be a stretch to imagine there being something more dangerous than a bear out there.

As I opened my mouth, he pointed past me and said, "I'm going to go look for clothing and tools. You sort out the kitchen; see if you can find any perishables or potable water."

I turned and left, glad to be as far away from the body as possible.

The kitchen was quiet save for the shrieks of the wind cutting around the cabin outside. I peeled open cabinets and yanked drawers, checking high and low in the near dark for anything and everything I could find. I collected tins of sardines, cans of beets and pears and boxes of potato flakes.

The butcher's block on the counter had a couple of steak knives in it. I glanced toward the bedroom, where Elden shuffled through clothes in the closet. Ever since this whole thing began, I'd been without a weapon. Elden hadn't made any sort of move against me, despite Brody's assertion that I should watch him. But if he suspected anything had happened to Jake, that Brody was in there…. I had to have protection. I slid a knife out and pocketed it.

We finished up our collection and Elden inventoried the lot. "So, no water?" he asked, as we lugged everything toward the door in our packs.

"None." A sudden thought hit me. "Did you check the toilet tank?"

"Frozen. It would be less time to melt snow and boil it." He pulled down his hat and braced his hand on the door. "Ready?"

I nodded and we entered into the cold again.

The journey back was slow-going. All of the new weight made me ten times as exhausted. I was still wiped out from my trip down the river. It was hard to imagine that I'd narrowly avoided death so many times since this all began. I eyed the path ahead of us wearily and realized there was still a chance of that happening.

Our boot prints had vanished from the trip to the sawmill, the wind whipping strong enough to cover them all up. We hiked along the road for the longest time, until the drifts grew so tall, we had to break off into the woods. The tree cover was dense enough that it had kept snow from building up too high. We sank in places up to mid-calf in spite of the snowshoes and my knees knocked with the chill.

After a long time, I spied the cabin, the smoke from its chimney curling into the sky. A silvery pall had fallen over the sky once more. *Not more snow*, I pleaded. *Anything but more snow…*

We were within a quarter mile when Elden suddenly stopped and turned around. I did as well, wondering if he'd seen something I hadn't. I looked behind me, scanning the trees. There were no shapes, nothing hulking nor sinuously creeping.

I turned back. "What? What do you—?"

His gun was out of his pocket, aiming at me discreetly. There was a cold calm on his face that I recognized from the sawmill.

"Elden, what are you doing?"

"Open your jacket pocket," he ordered.

"What?"

"When we walked into Levi's place, there were two knives in the butcher's block on the counter. One was gone when we left. Your pocket was open; now it's zipped."

"Elden, listen, it was only for protection."

He fixed me with his steely eyes and said, "Take it out and throw it."

I reached a shaking hand to my pocket and pulled the zipper down. "I was never going to use it on you or Jake, you have to believe me." I brought the knife out into view. "Please."

Elden pursed his lips, as if he pitied me. He waved his gun a little. "Come on. Toss it."

It took all of my will to fling the knife away from me. It disappeared into the snow near a thorn bush. I put my hands up slowly. "I would never have hurt you both. Not after you saved my life."

He got closer, keeping the gun fixed squarely on my head. With every step, I tried to keep myself composed.

"How do I know you're actually who you say you are?" he asked. "How do I know you aren't one of them?"

"There's no way I can prove to you who I am. But we all slept together in that cabin last night. I didn't attack you then; I was never going to attack you. You have to trust me."

Elden looked down on me. "I don't *have* to do anything."

I closed my eyes, counting the seconds and recounting the cold dead eyes on Levi Hershey in the sawmill.

Seconds ticked by and nothing happened. I opened my eyes.

Elden had brought the gun down. "Come on. Get up."

I eyed the gun and then his face again.

"Call it a strike one," he said.

Footsteps in the snow alerted us both.

Elden turned and I noticed Jake coming toward us.

"Nothing to worry about, Jakey, go—"

Gunfire cracked through the air. A cry ripped from my throat. Elden collapsed in front of me, revealing the rifle in Jake's hands, hands that wouldn't have known, shouldn't have known how to fire it. In the child's eyes was Brody's solemn stare. No reaction. Not even shock.

I crawled toward Elden and slapped my gloved hands over his chest. Blood, thick and hot soaked through his coat, dying it fiery against the snow. His face was screwed up in pain and panic. "No, no!" he cried. "Jake!"

"Brody! Get me something to apply pressure!" I yelled at him.

He stayed where he was.

"BRODY!"

"You...you did this!" Elden wrenched at my arm weakly, blood bubbling up between his lips. "You knew!"

"I'm sorry," I moaned, scrambling to get my own pack off. I

yanked out a pair of flannel pajama pants and tore part of the leg with my teeth. Pressing it into the wound kept Elden from spouting his next obscenities. He hissed and sank into sobs.

"Brody! Help me!"

He shook his head. "It's too late, Liz."

I looked down.

Elden's voice had dried, and his eyes, wide and grey like the sky, stared up at me with lingering expectation. Seconds later, he went limp.

I couldn't move. I couldn't control my own body. I sat sprawled in the snow, Elden's dead weight on top of my legs and stared. When I tried to make some kind of noise, all that came out was a garble of inhuman sounds. Wails, as if they came from spirits haunting graves. It didn't sound like a sound I'd make. I didn't even make those sounds when Brody had died. I didn't have the time.

As I looked at Brody, the tears flooding my vision, it looked like he knew that. He dropped the rifle in the snow and walked to me, grabbing my arm. "Come on, Liz."

Force returned to me, energy and rage. I shoved him as hard as I could and he tripped backwards. "Why?" I finally forced the word from my lips. "Why?"

"I told you to watch him!" he yelled. "You got soft and he saw right through you."

"He wasn't going to kill me!"

"It didn't look that way from where I was sitting," he said through gritted teeth.

"He was giving me another chance." I sniffled and exhaled. "You didn't have to do that."

Brody got up and stared down at Elden. "How long do you think we could have gone on with this guy, huh? One big happy family, right? He would have found out sooner or later. You know as well as I do he'd have offed us both."

"You don't know that!"

"You know I'm right." Picking up the rifle, Brody turned and walked back to the cabin.

I remained seated in the snow, listening to the rush of winter air, watching the snow swirl in the air.

"Do you remember that time in at the East Arena? When the Rams and the Lightning were playing and that guy spilled his blue raspberry Slushie all over you?"

I remembered. A familiar anger rose in my mind at the thought of it. "Good thing it was a shirt I didn't care about."

Brody chuckled. "Good thing he was getting arrested anyway. I thought you'd take his head clean off. Hey, didn't you tell me that shirt was a gift from your mom?"

"You do realize we're in Maine, right? You do realize it's winter?"

Brody shrugged. "Maybe I run warmer than you do."

"Says the guy who owns, like, eighteen scarves."

"Those are Carmen's. I borrow one now and again."

"And you didn't think to borrow one today? Or maybe even wear a coat? It's negative five with windchill."

"What are you? My mom?"

"Apparently, yes."

"What's going on?"

"Nothing." It was a flat-out lie. I could barely keep my hands from shaking.

"It's not *nothing*."

We were in an unoccupied conference room at the police station. The lights were off. A white pall glowed from the windows, muted sunlight and snow.

"Family shit. The usual." I shrugged. "It riles me up for a little bit and then I get over it."

Brody put his hands on my shoulders. Our gazes leveled. "Tough guy, tell me what happened, hmm?"

SIXTEEN

Winter was unforgiving. My existence was consumed by snow: the act of shoveling it; of hiking through it; of trying to forget it was there. As much as I wanted to stay cloistered inside by the fire and pretend the world wasn't deteriorating around me, I knew I had to keep going out, foraging for materials, and digging out the cabin. Brody helped when he could, but being inside a ten-year-old boy had its limits. He tired easily, got colder more quickly, and couldn't lift as much back from the camps we searched during the lulls between storms.

Over the course of ten weeks, I went out in the early morning, before the sun peeked over the mountain's jagged horizon in the distance. The solitude was growing on me, nothing but the sound of the wind in my ears. But every time I returned, Brody would be watching from the windows, anxiety knit in his brows.

This time alone was a gift as much as it was a curse. My mind worked harder than ever before, unearthing memories that I'd left to molder in the furthest trenches of my brain. I remembered times that I'd once deemed insignificant with Brody. Sitting at our desks with our crap station coffee laughing over a dumb joke. Riding in the car to a scene, neither one of us saying a word but tension carved in the lines on his face. That time after my mom and I had fought and he had made me tell him what was wrong. Rarely did I linger on the time I spent alone before all of this. It was like I didn't remember it as well, as if I'd tried to blot it out like stains on white fabric. The more I thought back, the more I was reminded of the here; the now.

When I'd return from those breaches in time, I'd take what was necessary inside the cabin and store the rest of the supplies in a shed out back. Every time I'd peel open the door and let daylight into the dark space, I had to ignore the stiff lump beneath the tarp inside the canoe. Elden had deserved a proper burial. The earth was too frozen to do that for him now.

Brody hadn't understood. Would he ever be guilty about what he'd done?

We hardly spoke anymore. Besides taking stock of our supplies, I didn't have anything to say. I didn't want him to talk in Jake's voice. It only made me hate him more; hate myself more, too.

One evening in late February, I lost control.

The woodstove was constantly going. Every day, I had to forage for firewood and our supply was dwindling. A hail storm had rolled in the week before and coated everything in a slick layer of ice, including the pile I'd been pulling from at Hershey's sawmill. Taking an ax to it to try and chop it free only wore me down. I'd settled for what was knocked loose from some of the widowmaker trees around the cabin that day. After a couple of hours processing the wood into smaller pieces, I dropped the kindling into a metal bin next to the fireplace and took off my coat.

Brody stood at the stove, stirring some baked beans in a pot. He looked over his shoulder, Jake's young eyes watching me as I shrugged off my wet coat and hung it by the door. "Spotted some deer tracks behind the house today."

I tugged at my boot laces. "Yeah?"

"I think tomorrow we should head out with the rifle to track it."

"I don't know the first thing about tracking wildlife," I muttered, kicking off the first boot.

"I do. My uncle was all about it. I spent a couple hours today following the tracks—"

"Wait," I straightened. "You left the cabin?"

He put his hands up. "Yeah, what do you think? I'm going to sit around here all day, watching you do all the work?"

"The fire could have gone out, Brody!" I wrenched the second boot off and tossed it aside, trying to control my anger.

"Then we'd start another one, Liz. It's not that big a deal."

"Are you not living in the same reality as I am?" I shouted. "You have been nothing but blasé about this whole thing! You've shown no remorse, no emotion for what we did to these people… And unlike you, I won't come back as a ghost if I freeze to death out here."

Brody stiffened. I recognized anger on that little boy's face that didn't belong, an anger too hot and too serious for someone so young. He turned away from the stove and took a step toward me. "This isn't Leviticus. Keeping that fire going isn't going to bring them back; it's not going to change what happened here. It's done. You've been so busy beating yourself up for what happened that I don't think I *am* living in the same reality as you." He raised a finger at me. "What matters now is you. Your head can't be back there."

"At least I take responsibility!" I yelled. "That's more than I can say for you."

"I made a choice!" Brody snapped. "This kid was going to die anyway and that old man would have killed you if I hadn't done what I did!"

"When you shot Elden in cold blood…that was something you *had* to do?"

Brody turned away from me, returning to stirring the food on the stove.

"You remember what you told me about that guy you took over at the dam? That his ghost was suddenly gone when you entered his body?"

Brody didn't look at me.

"Did you do that to Jake? Is he now lost in purgatory because of us? Is Elden?"

"I told you I panicked," he said under his breath. "I saw that gun trained on you and I followed my instinct. Is that so hard for you to understand?"

"The Brody I knew would have shown some kind of shame."

"Maybe being dead has given me a new perspective on life. I'm sorry I'm not crying enough for you." He faced me; his eyes dark. "This isn't the same world we lived in. It's a new one. Sooner or later, you're going to have to start living in it."

Warm tears trickled down my cheeks. My teeth gnashed together as the anger built inside me. All I wanted to do was scream.

He turned away once more. "We're gonna run out of rice and beans eventually. If we get that deer, that could feed us for a couple weeks. That'll be good for us. Soon, we'll have to get the hell out of Dodge."

More than anything I wanted to argue, but I knew he was right. We had reached the limit of our supplies on the lake. There hadn't been a major weather event in the last several days. The temperatures had actually been quite temperate for Maine in February. The sun had warmed and thawed out most of the snow. With Elden's truck, we could plow our way back up to the road and hopefully continue north to Flintland.

No matter how rational his statement was, I didn't want Brody to have the last word. "If we leave, you leave Jake's body behind."

"You know I can't do that. How am I going to protect you?"

"As a child? You can't. I am the only one who can protect me."

"Then why the hell am I here?" he yelled, letting the wooden spoon drop on the floor. "What good is it to be here, existing when I can't fucking touch anything, when I can't smell, or taste anything? Why the unnecessary torment of watching someone I care about fight for survival if there's nothing I can do about it?"

I sighed and locked my eyes with his. "I can't go on with the constant reminder of what we've done always being with me." Not after everything else I'd been reliving. Not after the reminders of Brody's own death. "If you want me to live, you'll leave Jake behind."

I turned away from him and grabbed the kindling from the box to feed the fire in the woodstove. I'd figured he'd keep going, as Brody had always been apt to do. But he didn't say anything. Instead, he grabbed his jacket from the hook by the door and pushed out into the twilight, slamming the door behind him.

I ate on my own, the beans burned but filling me. I couldn't keep my eyes away from the windows, searching for Jake's silhouette against the snow and the blue evening. I debated about going out to look for him but didn't. He needed to know that I was right. He had to feel *some* kind of responsibility for this.

In the morning, I woke up to sunlight, fresh orange reaching its fingers through the windows. I sat up and checked the fire, adding another log to it. Elden's bottle of brandy sat on the counter top, the amber liquid glowing in the sun. I was tempted several nights by its promise of blurring the past and the pain. I never touched it though. I swore I'd never touch alcohol again, not after how low it brought me before.

I moved over to the kitchen, put the bottle back in the cabinet and tore open a package of coffee crystals. As I took up the cast iron teapot from atop the woodstove and poured in my water and the crystals into a mug, I noticed Jake's coat was still missing from the hook by the door. I glanced at the couch. Brody wasn't there; his fleece blanket lay tangled on the cushions from where he'd left it yesterday.

Did I actually fall asleep and not realize that he never came back?

I set the mug down and moved to the window, gazing out at the front of the cabin. Boot tracks had pushed through the snow and rounded the building.

I threw on my boots. Not bothering to lace them, I shot my arms into my jacket, opened the door to a blast of cold air, and caught a scream in my throat.

Brody was standing there, looking like he used to before he'd died.

I coughed, the realization hitting me like a club in my stomach. I followed his gaze to the boot prints. Brushing by him, I rounded the cabin, my boots crunching in the snow. I didn't need to look behind me to know Brody was following me.

The tracks led to the storage shed. The wooden bar was pulled back and the door was ajar. I didn't want to look, but I pulled the door the rest of the way open and stared.

In the canoe, lying next to the Elden's tarp-covered body was Jake. His eyes were closed and his hands lying flat at his sides, his skin grey and pale.

I couldn't look away.

"You made an ultimatum," Brody said behind me.

It was sobering; the realization that I had gotten so used to Jake's voice and now there was an emptiness there that Brody's couldn't fill. The physicality of having another person in the room was something I'd gotten used to…something that I didn't think I would miss so much. Isolating myself in the White Mountain woods was what I thought I'd needed months ago. Now I longed for someone real; *anyone* real. Even though Brody and I had had that argument the night before, even though I knew I had wanted him out of Jake's body before we left, I missed the thought of someone I could hug, or pour coffee for…

"Liz," Brody said, this time closer.

I glanced at him over my shoulder, meeting his dark eyes.

"Let's track the deer, shall we?"

THEN

"Liz!"

Brody's voice called to me through the cobwebs of sleep. I sat up too quickly and the room around me spun. Sun barely peeked in through the curtains over the living room window.

Bang, bang, bang!

My door rattled with the incessant knocking. It sounded like a herd of elephants trying to break through.

I pushed myself up from the chair and staggered through the living room to answer the door. I opened it as Brody was in mid knock.

His eyes were wide with surprise.

"Where the hell have you been? I've been trying to call you all morning!"

I closed my eyes against the bright light behind him. "Don't…yell."

He furrowed his brows. "What's the matter with you?"

"I slept in."

"Slept in? It's nine o'clock. When you didn't show up at the station this morning, I thought something had happened to you."

Panic seized me. I'd forgotten it was Brody's first day back on the job. "Damn it. I'm sorry. Give me a minute. I need to take a shower."

"Liz, you don't have time for that. We've got to go. We have a B and E on Clairmont to get to."

"Five minutes," I said over my shoulder as I disappeared back inside.

The front door closed and Brody sigh. "I'm going to count," he called after me.

I looked over my shoulder at him leaning against the door with arms crossed.

The shower didn't clear away all of the sludge in my head nor the sense that my whole body was still asleep. But it had felt good and was enough to shove me ahead into my work clothes.

I came downstairs, wrangling my hair into a wet ponytail. The sound of clinking from my kitchen sent a bolt of panic through me. I followed the sound and stopped in the kitchen door.

Brody had pulled bottles out of my cabinet: gin, vodka, white rum, even the margarita mixer and was stuffing them into a black garbage bag.

"What the fuck do you think you're doing?" I snapped.

"I should be asking you!" he barked, letting go of the bag and taking a step toward me. "I thought we'd talked about this. Now I find you hungover like some school girl crying over a boy?"

I glowered. "That's not fair."

He waved at the mostly empty bottles on the counter. "Look what you're doing to yourself! I thought you were smarter than that, that you of all people wouldn't let some guy put a chink in your armor. You've picked yourself back up after tougher shit than this!"

I threw my hands in the air. "Fuck, I don't know! Maybe it's because Josh wasn't 'some guy'!"

He shook his head and put the last few bottles into the black bag. "You're not working today."

"Let's go." I shook my head. "I don't want to talk about this anymore."

"You haven't been walking straight since I came through the door."

I self-consciously straightened my posture.

"And, no offense, you look like you crawled out of a grave."

I glared at him. "I showered."

"And into the rain."

It was getting steadily harder to focus on him and not on the fact that I wanted to sneak into bed. Keeping my eyes open was enough of a chore. My anger was the only thing keeping me vertical and even that was waning. He was right. I was in no shape to be on the job.

I sighed. "What am I supposed to tell Vance?"

"Whatever the hell you want. Tell 'em you've got bronchitis, you fell down the stairs, you got food poisoning…but you can't get in the car and be my back up when you can't even walk in a straight line."

Pulling a chair out from the kitchen table, I sunk into it and tried to focus on the bowl of bruised apples. "What the hell are you going to do then?"

"Never mind what I'm gonna do." Tying the bag at the top, Brody stalked to the back door and yanked it open. Sunlight gushed in and I squinted against it.

Brody lifted the lid on the metal garbage can and stuff the bag inside, bottles clinking loudly. When he returned, he grabbed a glass from the cupboard, filled it with water, and set it in front of me. "I'll be back tonight. If you go out and buy more booze, I'll pour it down the drain."

I felt like a child being admonished by a teacher. Worst was the disappointment in his eyes. "I won't."

Without another word, he left. His car pulled out from the driveway. I stared at my own distorted reflection in the water glass. The circles under my eyes were massive. I looked like I hadn't slept in a thousand years.

NOW

"Hey."

I opened my eyes.

Brody was crouched beside me in the brush. "Focus, eh?"

I looked down at my hands, clutched around the rifle, the butt cradled under my arm close to my chest.

We'd tracked the deer prints for about a mile through the woods away from the camp. They ended in a small glade where we stayed huddled in the shrubs for over to an hour. The temperature was bitter despite the sun. My fingers and toes were beginning to go numb.

"Right there," Brody whispered and I turned my attention back to the opening.

The thorn bushes across from us moved. The deer's head lifted, chewing grass. It looked at ease; as though everything was still right in the world.

"Not yet," Brody said as I raised the rifle. "Wait until you've got a clear shot."

I stared down the sight at the deer. The body was obscured by bushes and the head kept dipping up and down, in and out of view. It had been a long time since I'd fired a rifle. Elden's gun, a Browning thirty ought six was an older model and was hard for me to shoulder and keep the sight in line with the target.

"Probably should have had you practice before we came out," Brody whispered, despite knowing I was the only one who could hear him. "That rifle is going to have a hell of a kick."

I steadied myself in the dirt as best as I could and took a deep breath. The deer took a few steps out into the clearing, head erect and ears perked. It was listening.

My finger tensed on the trigger.

In a blur of blackness, the deer was replaced with a hulking woolly mass.

I froze and forgot to breathe.

Brody went rigid out of the corner of my eye

The creature tore at the deer on the ground, jowls bloodied and loose flesh hanging from between its teeth.

My arms shook as I tried to keep the gun trained on the new target. The muzzle of the rifle snagged on a twig in the bushes in front of me. Without thinking, I pulled back and they snapped.

The creature whipped around.

"Don't move," Brody murmured, reaching over to me. The tips of his fingers were like ice cubes in my arm.

The wolf howled. The guttural sound was like the rumbling of thunder from the shadows of the trees.

"It's not going to cross the field, not if it doesn't have to. It's too bright out," Brody said. "Don't give it a reason to try. It'll find a way around if it has to."

I stared through the sight, lining it up with the monster's face. The creature was still in shadow, but I thought I could make out the gleam of its eyes in the darkness. "I can kill it," I said under my breath.

"No!" Brody whispered urgently. "Don't. You're going to miss."

"You said it yourself: I've only ever missed a shot once in five years."

He shook his head. "I'm not even sure a gunshot would bring one of those things down. Don't risk it."

Its breast and front legs were clearer now. If these things could be killed with a gun, I would have a way to defend myself against them in the future. If I sat here like Brody wanted me to, there was still a likelihood that it would notice us anyway, and if it charged, there was no telling whether I'd actually be able to shoot it. I had to take this chance.

"Liz, listen to me: don't do it."

Its golden orbs stared straight down my sights.

Oh god. It can see us!

I fired. The gun bucked and an explosion ripped through the air. I found myself on my back, one arm still awkwardly gripping the rifle. My chest screamed and I gasped for air. The panic whirled around my head as I desperately tried to sit up. Had I gotten it? Was it dead?

An ear-splitting roar resonated through the sky before I could right myself.

No.

I'd missed.

Brody swiveled his head between me and the monster across the clearing, his mouth agape and figure frozen.

I tried to speak and all that came out of me was a groan. Wind knocked out. Couldn't breathe…

"Stay right there," he ordered, standing up. "And don't you dare make a sound."

Brody ran from my sight.

I scrambled to try and flip myself over. *What the hell was he doing?*

Brody's voice rose up over the grunting and shrieking of the animal. "Hey! Over here!"

Fuck. He was distracting it.

I tried to call his name but no sound emerged from my throat. My lungs panged with the effort. The world tilted, the grass climbing sideways up my vision as I rolled and found my footing.

The monster was running, claws scraping snow and brittle grass. But it wasn't coming for me. It was bolting into the trees to my right toward another target.

Brody.

"Stay away, Liz!" Brody's voice echoed back to me from somewhere in the trees. "Stay away!"

The creature howled as it vanished into the thicket.

Alarm bells shrieked in my head as I struggled to get back to my feet. Air punched through me and filled my lungs. I gasped.

Able to stand after a few moments, I realized that the sky had gone darker. The sun hadn't gone behind any clouds but the light was fading. The forest in front of me had also changed, its brown snow-blown ground was crawling with verdant vines and gnarled roots. A thick haze hung between the trees and tumbled closer.

And closer…

I ran in the direction of the cabin. The wind roared in my ears and the ground teetered, as if the earth would fall out from under me at any second.

I didn't dare look over my shoulder. Any second of hesitation would make the difference between reaching safety and being overtaken.

My foot sunk in a deep patch of snow and I stumbled forward. The darkness was at my back. My insides were being pulled toward my feet. I leapt up and tore myself away from it, sliding down a steep hill.

The cabin loomed ahead of me through the trees, safety mere feet from me. I bounded around the front to the door, ripped it open and fell inside, slamming it closed behind me with my boot.

Darkness rushed over the windows, erasing the light. A sound like glass scratching metal bombarded me as I closed my eyes and waited for it to end.

SEVENTEEN

THEN

I'd tried to fill my day doing mindless chores: laundry, dishes, vacuuming.... I even cleaned the fridge which I'd done recently enough that it didn't need to be done again. I wanted to stay focused and keep my hands moving. It was sitting idle that I thought too much about Josh. The dusting hadn't helped with that. I'd ended up in the hallway, looking at all of the photos in the frames. A kind of fierce anger hit me and I pulled every photo out of every frame and left them piled on the table. Not wanting to put other photos in, I hung them back up and moved onto other chores. I went outside and shoveled the walk, even as the snow filled it in after an hour. Finally, arms tired and without any other things to do, I dropped into a chair in the living room and shut my eyes.

It had been a full two weeks. Still nothing. No calls or texts. No evidence that Josh had made it past that first day in Los Angeles. Maybe he hadn't. Maybe a place as hungry as that had swallowed him in one bite.

Incessant knocking at my door pulled me out of my daze. It was nine. I hadn't made dinner, nor had I turned on any lights. The heater was running and I was sitting beside it in the dark, contemplating everything.

I got up and answered the door, knowing it would be Brody.

"I thought maybe you'd have headed home," I said, waving him in.

He handed me a warm paper bag which I took cautiously before he stepped in, shaking the snow from his coat. "I did. Finished unpacking some more things. Got hungry. Figured you hadn't eaten, so I stopped and picked up somethi...." He trailed off, noticing the lack of lights. "Did I wake you up?"

"No, I was getting ready to head up to bed," I lied.

He flicked the switch next to us. The entrance hall lit up and illuminated the empty picture frames lining the hall. I noticed his gaze drop on the pile of photographs sitting on the table.

"Mmhmm," he hummed, shrugging off his jacket.

"Listen, I appreciate you coming and checking up on me," I said, trying to refocus his attention. "But you don't have to stay. I'm sure you've had a long day."

He kicked off his boots and nodded to the bag. "You haven't eaten, right?"

I sighed. "I wasn't too hungry."

"Well, I've got the cure for that. Come on." He walked with me to the kitchen and took the bag from me, producing Styrofoam boxes from inside.

I took one, inhaling the salty spice and smiled. "Cantina Verde."

He grinned. "Look at you now? You're practically drooling."

Scoffing, I tore some paper towels from the roll and we settled down in the living room. It was amazing how the smell of food could rewrite a tired and sorrow-filled mind. Minutes ago, I'd resolved to go to bed without so much as a cup of tea. Now, I was staring at what could only be described as a boulder-sized burrito, smeared with sour cream and guacamole.

By the time we'd both finished, I imagined I was ten pounds heavier and could barely lift myself out of the chair to clear the plates. Brody rested on the couch on his back in a food coma, groaning.

"All right," he mumbled, "It was a good idea then. I'm starting rethink that now."

I chuckled. "Now that you can't move, right?"

"Exactly." He sat up and cringed. "So, question now is: do I want to put all my shit back on and go for a run to work it off? Or do I want to wake up like a slug tomorrow morning and do it then?"

"I vote neither."

He glanced at me. "Oh, yeah?"

"Yeah." I heaved myself out of the chair. "Hang on a second."

Crossing the room, I grabbed my phone and cued up a playlist on my music player. Then, I set it down in a bowl on the coffee table to amplify the noise.

In the midst of guitar, piano, and drums, Shirley Manson and Marissa Paternoster belted out "Because the Night".

"Oh no!" Brody lamented as I returned to him and grabbed his hands, yanking him up from the couch. He stood there as I swayed to the beat. "I thought you were exhausted. You were practically asleep a second ago."

I couldn't explain it. I was *tired* of being tired. I was *angry* about being angry. I wanted to get up and do *something.* "Must have been something in the food," I said.

"You know, just because I'm Puerto-Rican doesn't mean I automatically like to dance, right?"

"Why not?" I said, swinging my hips and arms to the beat. "You must have danced at your wedding?"

He chuckled. "Not like this."

I took his hands and guided him along with the music.

"I didn't think you were much of a dancer either," he said, as he put his hand at my hip and wrapped his other hand around mine.

"I took a few dancercise classes," I said, pulling him along with me.

He blew a raspberry.

I smirked. "Okay. I danced in college."

Brody squinted.

"Not *that* kind of dancing. The theater department put on community dance lessons. I learned them all in between classes. That was before I decided to join the academy."

Brody whistled. "And to think all *I* did in college was play cards." He spun me away.

"Ah, so that's the explanation for your masterful poker face," I said.

"Helped pay for my tuition."

I smiled. "You're getting the hang of the beat."

"You do this every night?"

"I haven't done this in months."

The music faded.

"Did Josh ever do this with you?"

Yes. But that stopped. I didn't have a chance to say it.

Finger snapping made me whip my head toward the stereo. Sam Smith's harmonious voice brimmed from the speaker. "Damn it. I guess he added some slow songs to my playlist." I pulled away to go change it.

"You know, I can actually dance to this," Brody said. "My stomach can only handle so much bouncing around."

I put one of my hands around his back and held the other as we swayed with the beat to "Dancing with a Stranger". I thought about the stack of photos sitting on the table in the hall, the empty picture frames hanging.

"There something interesting about the floor?"

I glanced up and noticed he was watching me closely.

"Sorry."

"Listen, when I got here this morning and saw you like that…."

I scoffed. "I didn't want anyone to have to see that."

His brows furrowed. "You can talk to me about this. Why are you always trying to work through this shit alone?"

My grip on his hand tightened. "I used to be able to channel this anger into the job but even now, it's not enough."

"You think I don't get that?"

I nodded, probably too quickly. "I think you get it more than anyone. But you don't need a constant reminder of it every time you look at me."

"That's not what I think about when I look at you."

My hand on his back stiffened. "What do you think about?"

We were standing now, not moving to the music. It was like it had disappeared and it was only us and those words lingering in the air between us.

Brody's face twitched. "I…." His hot palm on my back, his fingers pressing.

I kept my eyes on his mouth, waiting for something to emerge, anything that would validate or criticize or explain what that kiss was about a week ago.

The telephone rang and ripped us out of the moment.

I stepped back out of his embrace and went to answer it, trying to bring my voice back from the choking point. "Hello?"

"Hey." My stomach bottomed out. It was Josh.

"Hi," I said, my legs having suddenly turned to Jell-O.

"Did I wake you up? I forgot about the time change."

I looked over my shoulder. Brody was looking at the ground, with a look on his face that I could tell was full of irony. He knew it was Josh.

"Liz?" Josh asked.

I cleared my throat. "No. Brody and I were finishing up some dinner."

Josh was silent for a moment. "Oh, well, I'll call back tomorrow then."

"It's been two weeks," I said.

"I know. I've been in back-to-back meetings with photographers and travel agents. The airport lost one of my bags and I've been trying to track it down…."

"Bet you haven't even had time to brush your teeth or drink your coffee." My tone had gone sour.

"I've been on the go constantly, Liz. I'm sorry I haven't had a chance to get in touch with you."

"Well, you're not obligated to, right?"

Josh paused. He paused for a long time.

I glanced over at Brody. He had grabbed his boots from the front door and was beginning to put them on.

"Go finish your dinner with Brody," Josh said. He sounded exhausted. I didn't want to give him the benefit of the doubt. I wanted to know if he'd thought about me like I had about him. I wanted to know if his nights were as sleepless, as drunken and impossible.

But it wasn't fair to do this in front of Brody. And I was sick to death of arguing.

"Okay," I said. "Bye."

I hung up the phone and stared at it.

"I think I should go," Brody said. He'd tied up his boots and grabbed his jacket from the door. He walked to me as he slung it on. "Are you okay?"

I nodded, my throat on fire. "I'm sorry you had to be here for that."

"Don't be."

I walked him to the front door, my eyes dropping on the stack of photographs again. The one on top was of Josh and I together at the base of Waimoku Falls in Hawaii. A wall of slate rose like a bowl behind us, the vegetation like patches of new wallpaper. The water looked like a narrow mist caressing the rocks as it rushed down. Josh's arm was comfortably around my waist and the engagement ring new on my finger.

Brody opened the door and looked back at me. "What I was going to say…."

I looked up at him.

"I think you're amazing."

The tears that had threatened to escape my eyes from the phone call were worked loose again. I looked down at the ground, trying to hide it.

"You're as tough as nails and the best partner anyone could ask for."

I closed my eyes. "Ditto."

He continued out and closed the door behind him, leaving me in the too quiet house with too much on my mind.

NOW

Darkness encompassed the cabin. The only light was from the lingering embers in the woodstove. But unlike the darkness from previous snowstorms, I wasn't cold. It was surprisingly muggy in the little cabin and I had to take my heavy jacket off for relief. I glanced up at the one window but there was nothing but a grey haze beyond it. A sickness rushed down over me as I stood and searched the cabin for a weapon.

I'd dropped the rifle in the hurry to get back to the cabin. There was a chance it was still right where I'd left it, but I wasn't sure the world outside was the one I remembered. Pawing at the sleeping bag in the corner, I found Elden's gun which I'd tucked there after he'd died. Hopefully, I wouldn't need to fire it at all, but it was better to be safe than sorry.

Stepping up to the cabin door, I nudged it open with my foot, expecting the familiar sight of snow and the lake, and the silhouettes of bare trees. Instead, there was green. I took a few steps further away from the safety of the cabin, my mind trying to rationalize what was in front of me.

Not the faintest bit of snow remained on the rich earth. Instead, there was chocolate-colored soil. Countless trees had sprouted and grown, their tops vanishing in leafy canopies high above. All of them had grown in parallel lines, as if they were simulating grand architecture. The branches curved into great buttresses and apses and the openings beneath the leafy roof were wide enough for combs of strange blue light to filter through. It was beautiful and terrifying, this forest cathedral.

I stared down the line toward a pale light in the distance: snow. Was that where it had stopped? Was that the way out of this place?

Instinctively, I turned in the direction from where I'd run, the direction where Brody had led the monster. I couldn't leave without him. Brody had sacrificed his life for mine…again. After I'd blamed him for everything that had happened with Jake and Elden. I needed to find him.

I walked away from the light into the darkness. After a minute, I collided with a tree trunk once, then twice. It was nearly impossible to tell the trees apart from the blackness around me. The chances of me stumbling across the rifle I'd dropped were slim. I wasn't even sure I had gone the same way I'd taken before. I relied solely on my memory of the land before to guide me. Nothing else was familiar enough to relate to.

When light did return, it did so gradually. A kind of soft green emanation pervaded the mist enough for me to glimpse my surroundings in detail. The soil and vine covered ground had morphed into a strange stone, brittle enough that it crushed under my boots and let me sink slightly as if I was walking in sand. The trees had grown a strange lichen, like a sinew that coated them and breathed as though it were alive. The sky, which I hadn't been able to glimpse until now, was a swirl of grey clouds, rain and lightning choked inside of them. A sound I assumed was thunder rumbled in the distance.

There were no signs of life, not those monsters, not other ghosts…nothing. A horrifying thought stretched across my mind. *What if I'm the only one in here?*

A hollow scream scraped against my ears and all the hairs on my arms stood.

I wasn't.

Other cries rose up to join the first, echoing into the sky from somewhere far off. Despite every instinct to run back in the opposite direction, I forced myself to continue.

I hiked for another mile, climbing over gargantuan knotted roots. The fragile stone beneath me was a guide. This hadn't been a remnant from the woods by the lake before; this had come with The Woods. What if it was a trail? That would mean that something lived here once. It didn't seem like the place for industry or cultivating quaint garden paths. It was ancient, beyond time.

The green eventually faded into a deep orange. The plant life turned black and shiny, each leaf giving off a lethal-looking purple sheen as I passed. The sky took on the same toxic ochre color as the mist and walls of crumbling stone rose out of the ground on either side of me. I was being funneled toward the sound of the screams, into a potential trap. I didn't like having nowhere to hide, but I also knew that I couldn't stop. Brody needed me. I couldn't let him suffer in here alone.

At the top of a hill, I looked down into a forested valley. In the middle of the trees was a building of grotesque architecture. The roof looked like it was made from the ribcage of several giants piled together. The whole thing was covered in a kind of mud that had dripped and dried over the bones, creating a hellish sandcastle. Two tall spires jutted from the top, each pinpricked with a fiery light in every hollowed window.

The screaming came from there.

Sandcastle. This was the place Brody had spoken about when he'd mentioned being in purgatory. Which meant he was right: purgatory was slowly taking over the earth.

A burning sensation filled my head. I couldn't focus and found myself crouching toward the ground, trying to take in a normal breath. After everything that had happened, I'd figured that this revelation would have been proven false. I'd wake up from some kind of coma and suddenly be back in real life, where I was alone again and though Brody would be gone, everything else would have this blatant normalcy to it.

That wasn't going to happen. This place was impossibly real. Down to the strange smell of the acrid plants, the charred earth, the rotten architecture.... I had to accept that all of these things I'd been running from my whole life, the idea of Heaven, of Hell, of the in between...that it was somehow all real.

I swallowed hard, tears searing for an escape as the other realization I'd fought since I was a kid came crashing down. What if Dad was here?

I shut it down as hard as it had come bubbling up. No. He wouldn't have been here.

But Brody was. He'd mentioned that the wolves were trying to bring the souls back here. Had it brought them to this insane building? Was this some kind of demented prison for those lost souls?

Beyond it, I recognized more outlines of buildings, all twisted and terrifying, none looking the exact same.

Brody was in there, somewhere.

I made myself stand, made myself take the deepest breath I had in minutes, made myself concentrate on what I needed to do. Brody had come back to me. I didn't want to lose him again.

How the hell am I going to find him?

Then, I remembered waking up in Maynard's house. I remembered my conversation with Brody. Somehow, after losing me at the water mill, he'd been able to find me. Somehow, we were unable to be severed from one another by whatever cosmic fate had bound us together. That meant that for all my wandering, I must have been getting closer. I reasoned this despite having no evidence that I was anywhere near him.

I forced myself to close my eyes in this strange and terrible place, forced myself to try and picture my friend as he was before, when all was right. I thought about that Thanksgiving dinner we'd shared, the cup of coffee on the patio, then the conversation in his kitchen under the bright lights, our strange kiss in the darkened hallway...

I opened my eyes and let out a frustrated growl. Damn it. This was ridiculous, the thought that maybe I could *sense* him nearby. I leaned against one of the stone walls next to me and slammed the bottom of my fist against it in frustration. I didn't have time to be fantasizing about mystical forces. I needed to—

Liz.

I gasped. His voice was as clear as day, like he'd whispered in my ear.

"Where are you?"

I waited a second.

Two.

Three.

Four.

"Brody!?"

The forest around me didn't respond, my echo chasing into the sky.

I took a couple of deep breaths through my nose, my eyes searching the landscape for some sign that something had changed.

I'm here.

The voice nearly made me jump. "Where? Where are you?"

Monolith.

I blinked. His voice had sounded weak. "Monolith? How do I find that? What does that look like?"

No response. I said his name a few more times while scanning the scenery before me. Monolith. Usually like a stone pillar or large singular monument. I scraped for the definition in my head as my eyes caught on something in the woods about a mile out. Unlike the alien-like buildings in the distance, this was squarer. A large moss-covered hump with angular corners cut up from the ground off to my right, like someone had thrown a green blanket over a dining chair. It was as titanic as the Gavea Rock next to the city of Rio de Janeiro in Brazil, a huge mass of stone towering over already gargantuan skyscrapers and surrounded by the ocean.

It was the only thing resembling a monolith on the horizon and the only thing I had to go on. I broke trail, leaving the path behind as I headed back into a mess of scrabbled black trees.

The moisture in the woods reminded me of the jungle in Hawaii where Josh and I had taken a vacation a few years back. Within a few moments of breaking trail, I had rolled up the sleeves on my shirt and gathered all of my hair up into a bun under my winter hat. Sweat beaded on the back of my neck and soaked my under arms. This climate was so unnatural for Maine, though I wasn't even sure this qualified as being in Maine anymore.

Within a half of a mile from the monolith, a cry rang out: Brody's. This hadn't been in my head, though the sound triggered a memory into action and halted me in the middle of the woods.

Blood on my hands, screaming for help, Brody's weight in my arms.

I pinched myself to come back to the present. *Not now.*

I zigzagged through the trees, carefully threading through their trunks and over roots that spanned the rich earth like nerves. The closer I drew to the monolith, the more I noticed a stone structure emerge at its base. Smooth pillars of rock emerged from the earth lined up in a circle. The highest points ended in serrated edges, pointing in haphazard directions. A stone table was set in the center of the pillars. Maybe it was once a monument of some kind. I couldn't tell. I was barely holding onto the tenuous understanding that this was all really happening.

Brody yelped again. The sound made a part of me shrivel up.

Focus.

I stayed well within the darkness that the forest offered, hoping to stay out of sight until I knew what the best way to get to Brody would be. A low growl froze me against the base of a tree. When I gathered the strength to look out from it, I noticed one of the wolf-like beasts. It was walking away from me, the lithe form bobbing up and down. It turned to one side briefly and I caught a glimpse of its golden eyes, glowing like lamps against the ominous landscape.

I waited until it left before I moved forward.

The pillars were set on a circular dais inscribed with small lines. It reminded me vaguely of a Mayan calendar though not as intricate, not as meaningful. The lines here were more haphazard, made without intention or design. The thought of a sacrificial altar suddenly came to mind and chilled me. Was that what this was? Were souls tortured here?

I finally noticed Brody. He was tied to a pillar behind the stone table at the edge of the dais, the monolith overshadowing him. Making sure that I was in the clear, I pulled Elden's gun from the small of my back. The comfort it provided me was quickly snuffed out by the thought that I had missed shooting one of these monsters with a rifle already. Or had I? What if bullets did nothing to them?

Crossing the dais, I approached the pillar. Brody was slumped there and lifted his head as I stopped in front of him.

"I'm dreaming," he muttered to himself. "You're not really here."

"Oh, I'm here," I said, coming up beside him. My stomach turned.

His arms were locked behind the pillar by more of those black vines from the forest. It was as though they had erupted out of the ground at the edge of the stone dais, wrapped around each wrist several times.

"I'm going to get you out of here," I said, making to grab at the vines. I gasped when my hand phased through them. I made another attempt.

Brody shook his head. "It's no use. You're corporeal; this place isn't."

"What the hell does that mean?" I tried to touch the pillar. Nothing. There was nothing I could interact with.

"I'm a spirit," he said weakly. "This place houses spirits. It's not meant to house the living. You and it don't mesh. So, you can't touch anything, like I can't touch anything outside of here."

"Those wolf things can do both, can't they?" I pressed. "There has to be some kind of exception."

"I told you not to come here," he growled. "You need to go."

"The hell with that. I'm not going to let you suffer," I answered.

Brody stood cautiously. The vines strained as he pulled against them. "These creatures will kill you if you don't leave."

"Help me find a way to get you out of this."

"Damn it, Liz!"

"You would do the same for me!" I snarled at him. "Forget about me leaving because it isn't going to happen. Now tell me what I'm supposed to do."

He sighed and I detected the resignation in it. "I don't exactly know."

"Even if I could touch them, these vines look like they're made of stone. I don't think I could cut them. What else could I use?"

"Short of getting the attention of one of those wolves, I don't think there's anything you can use."

I glanced in the direction I'd watched the creature go. The brittle path resumed there, winding around toward the other side of the green monolith behind us. "I'm going to investigate."

Brody shook his head. "That's a bad idea."

"Well, you know me. I thrive at getting into trouble." I started toward the path. "Wish me luck."

"If you get yourself fucking killed because of me…," he muttered under his breath.

I glanced over my shoulder. "We'd be even." I walked toward certain doom.

IGHTEEN

The longer I spent inside the Woods, the more I fell in on myself. Everything in this place appeared to be made of either rock or bone, punching up out of the landscape like calluses the further away from the Woods I walked. Even when I had thought I was beholding death in those trees, there was an ever-present reminder of life, of simulated greenery and lushness. Following the path further into the shadow of the monolith and deeper into the realm, everything had changed.

The ochre sky I'd noticed from overlooking the monolith before had completely coated the sky above like wool. The only light filtering through bathed everything in orange. Was there a sun behind it somewhere? I wasn't sure. The landscape reminded me more of a desert now: no growth and no places to hide other than in the menacing shade of the monolith. I wondered where the wolves had gone and whether or not they were now stalking me, awaiting the right time to plunge in for the kill.

With every step, that trepidation ramped up. How was it going to happen? If I died here, what would happen to my soul? Would I appear to my sister as a ghost like Brody had appeared to me? Would I stay here lost in these woods without an escape?

I couldn't turn back. I needed to find a way to break Brody free and get us both out of here.

The monolith was much larger than I'd expected. What I had thought was greenery coating it was more like shards of broken glass. The monolith bristled with them, the wind whistling through its jagged fur. Occasionally, they'd crack. Pebble-sized pieces would ping off shards high above before raining down around me. No matter how wide a berth I tried to keep from the wall, they fell too close for comfort.

After some time, the path circled around to the opposite side of the monolith from where I'd found Brody. I stopped at that final turn and gazed at the spectacle before me.

Bones swept like fabric down from the top of the monolith and bowed out on both sides of the back entrance like gothic buttresses. Skeletal filigree wrapped around the breadth of a cavernous opening like a collar and twisted down each side into thick columns. Where I'd expected a dark interior, I was transfixed by warm blue light coming from where the ceiling should have been. I looked back and forth from the outside zenith of the monolith brimming in glass and deathly architecture, to the formless span of blue within. From where I stood, it looked like there were stars faintly glowing within its impossible depths. It was the most beautiful thing I'd witnessed since arriving here and I didn't trust it one bit.

I scanned the area around me before looking back into the opening. The cavern dipped down inside toward an unknown nadir. Even as the prospect of heading into a dark cramped space hit my thoughts, a deeper sense of wonder tugged at me, a need to know what lay inside. The blue wonder above me had only spurred on what remained of my curiosity about the afterlife, of why this place was consuming everything I knew and loved. Even if there wasn't anything in here that would free Brody, I needed to go in. For my own sanity, I needed to try and understand something about why all of this was happening.

The gun firmly in my grasp, I stepped inside.

The ground sloped down into the earth and pumice-like walls closed in on me within moments of reaching a sublevel. I was again surrounded by a strange unbearable heat, this time drier and one that closed on me like a blanket. I yanked off my winter cap and tucked it into the pocket of my jacket. My hair fell down across my shoulders. I wished I had something to tie it back with, but the hat was too hot to stand anymore.

A flickering light came into view around the next bend. Torches snapped and hissed against the walls, illuminating a narrow hall filled with barred doors. I was aware of noises: whimpers, grunts, the tearing of something that sounded like someone cutting into a steak. Against all my better judgement, I entered.

My footsteps sounded like cannons in the cramped space. The first gated door looked into a small room, about the same size as our holding cells back at Flintland PD. There was a body sitting in a chair in the middle of the room, slumped forward. What didn't make any sense was another figure sitting in the same chair leaning back. I blinked, hoping I had mistaken something but it only got clearer the next time I opened my eyes. The figure slumping was ashen, long dead; traits that distinguished any humanity on its face gone. There were no eyes, no nose, no lips; only decayed skin. The thing leaning in the opposite direction shared the same legs as the body, but melted into a new torso, a new neck and head as dark as a hole. It flexed against the corpse in the opposite direction, as if trying to pull itself free.

I backed away from the bars and straightened, taking deep breaths through my nose.

Fuck, fuck, fuck!

I ran. I wanted to get to the other side of this sadistic hallway as quickly as possible. But as soon as the next row of cells came into view and the eerie noises intensified, I knew I'd only dropped further into insanity.

The cell on my right contained a plaster square pillar in the middle, overgrown with black vines and creeping roots. They combined in a cluster of lichen and black moss in the middle and as my eyes traveled further up, I realized a body was forming—

No.... A body had *transformed* into dense black clumps. The arms, once wrapped around the pillar, as though to hug it, had forested into florae.

In the next was similar, though two bodies were chained to either side of the pillar, their arms grasping each other's while their faces and torsos melted into the plaster.

The room was spinning. I took a step and the ground rushed up at me. My palms slapped the floor, barely catching myself. My gun skittered off somewhere to my right. My face tingled uncontrollably and the heat in the room had become stifling. I threw up, though it was mostly dry heaves. I hadn't eaten that morning and I was pretty sure this place had sweated out whatever water I'd had.

As I wiped my mouth, a moaning sound brought my head up. It was coming from the last cell in the row and the darkest one. Picking myself up, I cautiously walked toward it. My gun had slid right up to the cell door. As I scanned the blackened space, a figure crept forward, crouched on the floor on hands and knees. I knelt down, never letting my eyes leave the figure and grabbed my gun.

The figure shot forward; taloned hands outstretched at me.

I fell backward as the metal bars juddered with the impact of the creature smashing into them. The monster looking at me, if one could say "looking", was as faceless as the poor creatures in the other cages.

Its body was a gangling mass of inky flesh pulled tightly over spindly bone. The head was bone white; a red smear the only distinguishing feature for a face. The sounds it uttered reminded me of someone bound and gagged. I knew those sounds from the job. They were too real and too horrible to think back on.

I aimed my gun at it and immediately fired off a round. The bullet struck, though I wasn't sure where. The thing immediately scurried back into the shadows of its cell and I ran past into the dark room that awaited at the end of the hall.

The room wasn't much of a room at all, more a threshold leading to a set of floating stairs. They descended though an open chasm, the walls that same porous stone at the entrance to the monolith. A black abyss glared up at me from below.

How far down did this go? Did it ever end?

Even as I debated turning around and heading back, I knew that I hadn't come this far only to turn back without learning anything. There had to be something to this, *some* meaning. Didn't there?

The stairs retreated into an opening on the rock face opposite me. I slipped through a small crevice at the end of the stairs and entered total darkness for a brief moment. A torch crackled ahead of me and I didn't breathe until its familiar light swam into my vision. A perfect rectangular doorway sat between two torches, the sound of tap-tap-tapping echoing from within. There was no light inside.

I reached up to unholster one of the torches from its sconce and I was surprised when it come loose in my hand. I could touch this. Holding it before me, I went inside.

Another small room with no ceiling. There was a sky, which didn't make any sense, like the blue aura at the top of the cavern I'd entered hadn't made any sense. The only thing in the room was a strange looking table, slanting to one side. It looked more like an ornate cradle, with rockers on the bottom that let it sway to the left, then to the right. A blue hooded figure towered over it, its bony fingers caressing the wood as it tipped the cradle table back and forth and stared at something on its surface.

I stopped immediately, questioning whether it had even seen me come in. It didn't act like anything had changed, didn't hesitate or look up. There were no other doors. It was this room and this thing and that table.

A strange static buzzed in my ears. I cautiously took a step forward, trying to get a better idea of what this creature was looking at.

"Who are you?" I asked, finally finding my voice. "What the hell is this place?"

The buzzing intensified, a radio-like fuzzing that reminded me of our family's old television in the Middlehitch cabin. I soon recognized that there was a voice beneath it all, a deep and withered sound that I struggled to make sense of. Only after a moment could I finally discern some of the words being said.

The Great Corruption.

I blinked. "What's that mean?"

Souls are no longer recycled. They've escaped. Existence is at a standstill. Death is meaningless. Life is meaningless. Souls are corrupted by the living earth. The blue robed figure finally lifted its head. Inside its hood was complete blackness. *The souls can no longer spin. They can no longer be recycled.*

I shook my head. "What does that even mean? 'Recycled'? What about Heaven? What about Hell?"

Constructs of the living. Made to appease the living. The dead have no need for placation. They are recycled. Life is reborn. The Great Corruption has stopped this.

I took a deep breath and the air fluttered in my chest. "Why did you cause the Great Corruption?"

The buzzing ceased. The figure stopped rocking the table back and forth. In the silence, I recognized that my heart beat harder, faster.

The cause of the Great Corruption is unknown.

"You don't know?"

The figure said nothing.

I stared at the table cradle. On it was a sheaf of paper with millions of tiny scribbles on it. They were in geometric shapes, letters, numbers… It was like looking at an advanced formula on a page but there didn't seem to be any calculations. Lines and lines of meaningless jargon.

"How do we fix this?" I asked. "How do we make it stop?"

Silence.

I took a step toward it. "Answer me, God Damn—"

GOD IS A CONSTRUCT. The words were like cannon fire in my head. I backed away, holding a hand to my head as the sound reverberated through it.

The floor beneath my feet shook with the tremor in my head.

The souls will pervert. It is too late. They cannot reenter the cycle.

"I don't understand what that means!"

Your comprehension is insignificant.

The crumbling of rock made me look up. It sounded like a cave-in on the other side of the noxious colored sky.

"Tell me what I need to do to stop this!" I roared. I didn't want to give up. I didn't want to surrender to the idea that there was no answer for this.

The humming of static faded. The rumble of rocks grew.

The figure bent its head back toward the sky and for a brief moment, I saw the faintest outline of its fleshless, contoured chin.

Too late. It's too late.

I turned and fled the room. Holding the torch above me, I wove through the crevice, scraping my arms on the jagged rocks until I emerged in the vast cavern. Long fissures crept up through the cavern walls on both sides of me and pieces were beginning to collapse up above. I raced up the narrow stairs, taking two at a time, my sights locked on the opening to the torture cells ahead of me. One slip of a foot could send me careening into the void below.

A chunk of rock as big as a car slammed down into the stairs behind me, severing the route and sending me falling forward onto my hands and knees. The torch cascaded across the steps in front of me and down into the hole below, soon a matchlight against the darkness. Jumping to my feet, I ran harder, listening to the grind and crush of the rock staircase collapsing behind me.

I bolted into the torture cell doors as the last step dropped out beneath me. I didn't stop to consider what would have happened if I'd been any slower. I scrambled through the hall of cells, not stopping to look at the bodies, my heart thrashing in my chest harder and faster than I ever thought possible.

Movement out of the corner of my eye made me jump back as the taloned monster slashed out at me, its claws scraping through my forearms. I threw myself to the floor away from it, my gun vanishing into the shadows.

The creature snarled and swiped at me from the partially collapsed cage door.

I pushed myself to my feet, my arms burning, teeth grinding past the pain. No time to look for the gun. I had to move.

At the end of the hall, I yanked a torch from the wall and swung back around, the flame colliding with the creature's head and resounding with a THWACK! It immediately was drowned in flame. Its muffled screams driving me toward the next set of cells and toward the entrance of the monolith. As I followed the rising earth toward the blue rapture, all I could think of was getting as far away from that hell as I could. I burst from the darkness into the orange world above, collapsing on my knees at the top and sucking in gulps of air. I listened for the sounds that that creature could be chasing me, the sounds of its claws skittering against rock as it raced toward me. But there was only the distant sound like thunder in the earth below me, of the tunnels and pathways and rooms collapsing on themselves.

I got to my feet and followed the path back around the monolith to Brody, aware of the idea that the entire monolith might also come down in light of everything happening inside. If it did, I needed to be as far away from it as possible.

When I'd traversed this path before, it had taken longer because of creeping along, making sure I wasn't spotted by anything. I flat out ran now, the monolith beside me rumbling, the glass on its edges chiming with the intensifying tremors. Shards fell like swords behind me, beside me, in front of me. One sliced down into the heel of my boot, and I screamed before I realized that it had hit the rubber of my sole and not the leather.

Clearing the eastern wall of the monolith, I found myself surrounded by inky trees once more. The sound of Brody's panicked breathing fluttered in the air before I reached him. He was still tied to the pillar, though he was turning his head this way and that, trying to see what was going on behind him. As soon as I reached him, the torch still billowing in my hand, he let out a relieved gasp.

"Lizzy! What did you do?"

"Don't ask, don't tell. Remember we had that policy for a while?" I held the torch up to the vines tied around his wrists.

"Fuck! You're burning me!"

"Hold still!"

I hadn't known if it was going to work, but the longer I held the torch to the vines, the more they began to wither and break apart.

Finally, Brody was able to pull his hands away and collapsed on his stomach on the stone dais.

"Come on," I urged, moving up in front of him. "We need to leave before this whole monolith collapses."

Brody slowly picked himself up and nodded. "Okay, you lead."

We crossed the dais and descended the steps at its edge. I checked left and right for the wolves. They weren't in sight and little could be heard over the now cacophony of the crumpling monolith. Billowing dust had encircled its base as the rock dissolved into the earth and was wafting toward us.

I waved Brody forward and let him cross into the woods before I did. Under the cover of the bizarre wilderness, breathing came easier. At least now, we weren't in the open. All we had to do was get back to the cabin.

The return trip was slower going than I would have liked. Every minute that passed, it seemed like we'd only moved a few feet.

Brody lagged behind. "I'm with you," was all he'd say whenever I looked back.

After about twenty minutes, we were finally back on the stone path over-looking the scores of horrendous buildings and the carnage of the monolith sinking into the earth.

We followed the road until we were once again thrust into the green. I held the torch carefully, making sure not to set anything alight. I wasn't sure I really could. It was so damp here; I was more afraid the torch would go out from the moisture in the air.

"I know you're hurting, but we have got to move," I finally said, when Brody leaned against a tree for support.

His eyes were glazed over. "I'm going as quick as I can—"

An ear-splitting howl cut him off.

All the hair on my arms stood. "They're coming."

Brody righted himself and waved me on. "Go, Liz, I'm right behind you."

The trail felt wilder than when I'd first explored it. Thousands of roots had risen up from under the mist to trip us up. I watched as Brody stumbled on one and caught myself before I could try and help him, forgetting there was nothing I could do.

Finally, I recognized the shape that didn't belong amidst the tall tree cathedral. "There's the cabin."

Once we were up alongside it, I left the torch sputtering on the ground nearby and opened the door. Inside, I slammed it shut behind us and took my first real breath since I'd walked into this purgatory.

"We can't stay here," Brody said, having fallen to one knee. "Those things will smell us in here."

"We need supplies. It's still the middle of winter out there and everything we have is in this cabin." I grabbed a blanket from the bed and tossed it toward Brody as I moved to the kitchen to collect food.

"Liz," he said.

"I've got to get everything packed. We can't go out there unprepared. We can't—"

"Liz." This time his voice was insistent.

"What?" I looked over my shoulder and I froze.

Brody was holding the blanket, staring at it like it was something alien. He wasn't supposed to be able to touch it and I'd forgotten that. But he was. I dropped the can I was holding on the ground and moved toward him.

"Can you…?" I couldn't even finish my sentence.

I reached out a tentative hand toward him as he did the same.

Our fingers touched.

I grabbed and held him, burying my head in his shoulder.

His fingers clutched at my back and his warm breath at the base of my neck sent chills down my spine.

I could barely breathe, and I couldn't think of anything to say. Here in the material within the immaterial, Brody was more than an image, a hallucination of my past and what I'd lost.

Brody was the first to pull away. He took my chin in his hands and said, "We have to go. They'll be here soon."

In the blink of an eye, the dream was over. This small window was all we had. Once we stepped outside, it would be the same as it had. We'd be unable to touch one another.

I forced myself to nod and we broke apart. I grabbed the water bottle from under the sink and stuffed it into the rucksack filled with canned goods. My thoughts were spinning, trying to figure out all the things I needed. Those monsters would be here any minute. What else? What else?

"Axe!" Brody yelled, and I snatched it up from near the woodstove. "Can-opener, med kit, sewing tools…."

I grabbed things as he listed them off. Once I had what I thought was everything, I slung the bag on my back and we approached the door.

"Don't forget this," he said, handing me a knife. I took it, holding his hand briefly. I didn't want to let go. I didn't want him to.

"Now!" he barked and I pushed open the door.

The green outside had only grown eerier and it was ten times harder to take a breath in without imagining like it was all water. I picked up the torch from where I'd dropped it, fluttering and nearly extinguished. We ran toward the white light at the end of the forest cathedral. We were so close that winter's cold hand reached my skin.

Behind us, claws tore at dirt and foliage.

"Don't look back!" Brody shouted.

The chill overtook me. Snow glimmered on trees. The ice shone on the lake beneath the afternoon sun.

Branches snapped and I looked over my shoulder.

The golden eyes were right there.

My feet slid out from under me and I fell forward toward the white. Brody appeared in the corner of my vision, throwing himself between me and the creature.

Snow caught me in the face. I spun around. Brody lay on his stomach nearby, his eyes dizzy with pain. Gut instinct made me swing the torch up as a defense.

The monster was shrieking, the sunlight scorching its face. It had stepped halfway through the portal. The only thing keeping it from attacking us was the light. It backed away into shadow again, shaking its head and howling.

I kept the torch braced between us.

The monster stared at me. It didn't have an animal's eyes. These were filled with emotion, with hatred and torture. It wanted us. It was being denied its sole purpose. That cold-blooded, primeval countenance seared in my mind. I couldn't look away.

I slowly moved toward Brody and made the mistake of trying to help him up. Again, my hand slid through his arm.

He winced and our gazes connected.

"The fairytale's over," he said, getting to his feet.

I shook my head.

He looked back at the beast in the shadows, watching our every move. "Let's get out of here. Come sundown, that thing's going to come for us. Let's make sure we're far away before that happens."

NINETEEN

"Liz?" Brody's voice whispered in the dark.

I didn't know what time it was. I didn't care. It was still dark. I'd been laying there, clutching at my sleeping bag shivering for hours.

We'd found the main road after a half an hour of trudging through snowy heaps. Thank God, it was a clear day. Thank God, the temperatures were pushing forty. The arrival of the forest had a way of changing the climate of the space around it. It was the only way we'd have hiked as far as we did that day.

Elden's truck was swallowed by the green world and that had been our only shot of getting anywhere far in a short amount of time. Thankfully, there were signs for a gas station not too much further down the road. If we couldn't find a car, at least we'd have a place to hole up for the night that could be fortified. After hours of walking and finally leaving the lake far behind, we found the gas station, unoccupied with few supplies left. Apparently, everyone else had a similar idea to ours and ransacked it when things had first gone to the pits.

The temperature dropped in the night and the steam of my breath unfurled into the air. I snuggled as far into the sleeping bag as I could, though it didn't stop me from shaking. The down in Elden's sleeping bag must have been old and the loft was probably gone. I wished for my fifteen-degree Mountain Hardwear bag and silk liner locked in my closet at home at least seventy miles north west of us.

"You awake?" Brody whispered. His voice made my throat thick. I didn't answer. Embracing him in the cabin felt as if it had happened long ago. I'd begun to forget people, about how warm they were, and how they smelled so distinct. I didn't want to think about this tonight. All I wanted was to sleep and not dream, to fall into oblivion and awaken with purpose once more.

Morning light woke me too soon. The night didn't last long enough to placate my wild thoughts. Brody was oddly quiet as I collected my gear and we headed out. It was as if he knew I had been ignoring him last night. I hadn't wanted to linger on what we'd experienced. Neither did he. It was all too painful, being allowed such temporary contact only to have it stripped away again.

We walked for a few more miles until we came across a house with a closed garage. A car was nestled safe from the snow inside. Chances were if there was gas in the tank and we could find the keys inside, it would still run fine. Judging by the open curtains, lack of noise, and unlocked doors, there hadn't been anyone home in a long while. I collected what canned goods I could find from the kitchen pantry and followed Brody into the garage. There were no keys hanging inside, nor tucked in any drawers.

"I think our luck ran out on this one," I told him, as I shut a drawer in a tool bench nearby.

"Where's my brother when you need him?" Brody muttered.

"Why? Is he a car specialist?"

"If, by specialist, you mean a thief and an asshole, then you'd be correct."

I tried another drawer but found it locked. "In all the time I've known you, you've never talked about your brother."

"Javi died when I was at the academy. He'd swiped some guy's F-150 and plowed it into a tree. Had a blood alcohol level of point two-one."

I looked back over my shoulder at him. "I'm sorry."

He shook his head. "Don't be. I stopped getting angry about it a long time ago."

Returning my thoughts to the drawer, I grabbed a flathead screwdriver from the tool bench and jammed it into the crack of the drawer, trying to wedge it open. "What was he like?"

"Javi was a kind of dumb. One of those people that never learned from their mistakes, no matter how many times he made the same ones. Good at hoops though and liked science 'because he was weird like that."

"I liked science."

"You're hardly normal yourself," he joked.

"What else?"

"We were never really close as teens but when we were younger, he was…good. We used to stop by this ice cream shack on the way home from school. Javi would knock the trash over in the back, make the guy come out and clean it up while he lifted us some bars from inside.

Worked for a couple weeks before the guy got wise."

I chuckled. "So, your brother was born with quick hands."

"Nah, he got in with a shitty crowd. Could have just as easily happened to me. Pops and Ma tried their best, but working two jobs each and taking care of two kids is as hard as it sounds. I always got caught though, got the brunt of their anger. It's what kept me straight."

"Was Javi older?"

"By a few years."

I noticed a wider gap in the drawer and jammed the screwdriver there. "My sister once broke the glass door on my mom's antique cabinet. She blamed me. No bread and butter for a week."

He scoffed. "Harsh punishment."

"I was only seven. It was my favorite thing to eat so…it was torture."

The drawer juddered open under my force and I groped inside. My fingers slid over the cold blade of a key.

"You know the strangest thing about it is that Javi *is* probably out there somewhere walking around like me when he shouldn't be." Brody hung his head and gave a humorless chuckle.

I approached him, holding up the key for the car. "Come on. Let's fire this thing up."

Brody simply nodded and I unlocked the car. "Don't forget the garage door," he said. I flipped the switch on the wall nearby and the door roared to life, lifting to reveal the white land outside.

Tossing the rucksack, sleeping bag and essentials inside, we coasted the car out of the driveway and onto the open road. There was a half tank of gas inside, plenty to get us to Flintland if the roads were clear.

It was a quiet car ride. Thinking about the cabinet incident reminded me of my sister, reminded me that all of this time I'd barely thought about her, about what may have happened to her and her family. I hadn't seen them in over a year. But Dana…. In the last year, she'd had this indeterminable goal to somehow bring our family back together again, to try and mend old wounds that were better left shredded in my opinion. The two of us had lived within a half an hour of each other since she graduated college and we still didn't visit each other more than a few times a year.

My mom and I spoke here and there and never for longer than twenty minutes at a time. She decided I wasn't worth the time to try and figure out and moved to California to live on a vineyard with her new husband when I went to the academy. While I tried to search for some meaning behind losing my dad and tried to cope with the hole in our lives, she forged ahead resolved to not let his death wrench open any kind of chasm in hers. She spent long nights away from home, out to dinner with friends. She joined every community class she could find, from learning to basket weave to belly dancing. She never sat still for long enough to really let anything touch her, I thought. Somehow, she was simultaneously there for my sister and not for me.

Still, Dana tried in spite of it all. I hated that I had barely thought about her since all of this had begun.

THEN

Laura Cole Park was undoubtedly one of Flintland's prettiest parks in the summertime. The one and a half acre greens south of Main Street ran along the Ohtuk river. In memoriam to one of Flintland's largest natural philanthropists, the city had paid for the park to be renamed, and landscaped. Two years ago in the spring, gardeners had gone in and planted a variety of foliage to beautify the otherwise ragged piece of land. Hostas were planted around the bases of most trees, tiger lilies rimmed the edges of the park next to the hand-built knee-high stone walls, and new seed was thrown down to try and flush the deteriorating grass-cover.

The campaign to spruce up the park had made it completely normal for people to spend their entire days there, playing with dogs, letting their children run free, and playing frisbee or picnicking. In light of this, we received fewer calls about homeless people camping there, and drug-related offenses had all but come to a halt in the near vicinity.

On that late December day though, Laura Cole Park was as desolate as a winter tundra. The only allure was the wooden jungle gym where Dana's husband, Mark, stood watching Michael as he clambered up the wooden ladder to the top of the slide. Dana and I watched from the bench nearby, all of us ready to jump up at the slightest slip of a boot or hand on an icy rung.

"What did you end up doing on Christmas?" Dana asked me, taking a sip of her turmeric tea. The potent smell hit me whenever she tilted her cup back. I'd thought about stopping for coffee on my way to meet her but had decided not to. I was regretting my decision.

"I watched some movies. Cooked myself a rack of ribs. Bought myself that new Peloton I'd been dreaming of."

Dana took a deep breath and tucked a blonde whisp of hair behind her ear. "Mom wondered why she couldn't get through to you."

"I left my phone at work."

"Is that really true?"

We stared at each other. Her blue eyes searched me. I rolled mine. "What if it's not? Would you really be surprised?"

She smiled ironically and shook her head. "She's trying, you know."

I threaded my hands together and put them behind my head. "Maybe I don't want her to right now. I've got too much shit going on."

On the playground, Michael had gone down the slide and Mark had caught him at the bottom and spun him around. They were moving over toward the seesaws.

"I told Mom about Josh and you. She was sorry."

I let a blast of hot air seep through my teeth. "Am I allowed to have any autonomy over what parts of my life Mom knows about? Jesus. I haven't even finished processing it myself yet."

Dana squinted. "What am I supposed to say when she asks? It's not like you're giving her any kind of a chance."

"You could say 'Maybe if you had given a shit about your oldest daughter before adopting a new religion, you could have mended things long ago'."

My sister sat there, her eyes wide with some form of disbelief or uncertainty. I wasn't sure which. Her teeth ground together behind her closed mouth. "Stop doing that," I said. "You'll ruin those perfect teeth that Mom paid for."

"I'm surprised you didn't refer to them as 'chipmunk chompers'."

"I never called them that," I said, trying really hard not to let my laughter slip out.

We locked eyes and my smile escaped. She reached a hand over and put it on mine.

We sat that way for a long time, watching Mark and Michael play, not saying anything. The light from the setting sun was twisting in and out of the blue clouds on the horizon, the orange bleeding into the fading sky.

"I am sorry," Dana finally said. "I really liked Josh. I thought he was going to be your other half for a long time."

"So did I," I said. "Suppose the domestic life was never going to be for me."

More silence. I wasn't sure what Dana was thinking now. Despite growing up together, she was never someone I could anticipate, someone I could figure out. I suppose she thought the same about me. I knew this whole get together was because she'd wanted to exchange Christmas gifts. We hadn't even done that. It was this quasi-interested conversation we had where we pretended to care about what happened in the other's life. Maybe we did care. But we rarely interacted, we rarely made it a point to jump into action. Until recently anyway. Considering everything I had going on, her timing was horrible.

"We're having a small get together on New Year's. You could come by, stay the night, spend some time with your nephew."

Michael pumped his legs on the swings, Mark pushing him from behind.

"That sounds nice," I said, thinking of the first excuse I could. "But I'll be on call."

The hope in Dana's eyes deflated. "Well, can't say I didn't try to socialize you."

"What am I? A dog?"

Her mouth straightened. "Sometimes, I think so."

I shot her a sarcastic smirk.

Dana waved to Mark and Michael. "Time to go!" she called.

Mark dutifully swept Michael up from the playground and carried him back to their car, even as the boy whined loudly.

"Do me a favor," Dana said, as we stood up from the bench. "Don't isolate yourself. Don't stop going out and doing things because it's easier than dealing with him being gone."

I nodded, an automatic response, one I made before I even fully processed the sentence. "Don't worry about me. I'm fine."

We hugged. I watched them all pile into Dana's car and leave from the bench and then watched the sunset fully descend.

NOW

Hours slipped by as Brody and I were lost in our respective thoughts. So many times, I'd notice him turn toward me, lips pursed as if he was about to ask me a question. He'd hesitate and the desire for any speech on my part would dissolve.

What was there to say? Every single atom in my body wanted to touch him, to be in his arms again. But he didn't remember the night we danced. He didn't remember what had happened the day he'd died. To give him those memories would be like sharing my torture. I didn't want him missing anything more than what he'd already lost. I *had* to endure this alone.

We exited the highway onto Route 1 and traveled further up the coast, through pale grey towns buried in snow, only hints of a life that once thrived there peeking out of the white drifts. Towns sat still, empty of people and activity. Usually, lit signs in store windows were off, sidewalks were empty, and traffic lights still blinked from green to yellow to red even though we were the only car moving anywhere nearby.

The road was still covered in several inches of snow and ice in places. It was only by sheer luck that the tires found traction and we continued, albeit slowly. Driving over the bridge that towered above the Kennebec River, I held my breath and hoped we didn't careen into the water below. It was a weird thought, knowing that the bridge was four car lanes wide and had plenty of stone barricades to prevent any such thing from happening. I couldn't help but think that this reality might break apart and toss me into another place and time. Nothing was real anymore.

The twists and turns in the road ahead of us I'd known so well. Having not driven them in several months made the realization of what we were driving back into all the more real. Prickles covered my neck and shoulders. A chill spread over me despite the heat blasting from the vents. I didn't want to know what had become of my hometown, but I had to.

We were half an hour from Flintland when the sky turned grey again. Snow flurried, blurring my view of the nearby town of Brummel. No other cars on the road, no sounds of traffic, not even the gulls. It was dead silence. Every black window of every building stared back at us ominously, and every time I tried not to imagine what could be inside. I followed the main drag around the center of town, passing the immaculate snow-covered lawns and pristine Victorian and colonial gems.

I turned the car onto a side street.

Brody frowned. "What are we turning off for?"

I didn't look at him. "I need to check something."

All the oak trees on the block where my sister lived overshadowed the road, as if they were waiting to tell on me to the force that had prompted this chaos.

I narrowed my gaze as I approached my sister's two-story plum-colored house. She'd painted it a couple years ago, much to the chagrin of her husband, who would have rather had them blend in with the rest of the quaint, white capes on their street. Even with the daylight fading into night and the snow, I recognized the pumpkin orange pop of her shutters and slowed down as we approached.

"Oh no," I moaned under my breath, noticing that her Honda Civic was there in its usual spot. I screeched the car to a stop in front of the neighbor's house and jumped out.

"The keys!" Brody yelled after me. "Liz!"

I ran, my chest tight, every muscle seizing. "Dana!" I called, crossing the frost heaved lawn to the front porch. Pounding up the steps to the door, I shouldered through the front door. "Dana!"

Silence answered me.

Please say you made it out. Please say you're not still here…

The carpet in the front hall was wrinkled and tilted off center, one corner flipped over. I ran into the living room; nobody. "Dana!" I checked the dining room. A mug was sitting on the table with cold turmeric tea in it. My sister's: she had several cups a day.

I poked my head into the kitchen. Nothing. I thumped up the stairs to my sister's room. A few shirts trailed from a suitcase on the bed. Her ridiculous high heels were kicked off in the middle of the room. Clothes spilled over the sides of drawers, yanked half-way from the dresser and looked as if they'd tried to make a desperate escape.

My nephew's room was in the same state. His bureau was completely empty. Toys littered the carpet. I had to tip-toe around them so I wouldn't trip. The covers on his bed were twisted. I pulled them back, searching for his favorite stuffed animal, a panda named Dizzy.

"Come on!" I urged, stripping blanket after blanket from the bed in an effort to find it. Did he even have a favorite stuffed animal anymore? Had he grown out of it? I hadn't seen my nephew in a year. Maybe he wasn't the kid I remembered anymore.

There was no panda.

Stiffly, I made my way down the stairs and sat in the middle of the living room. They were gone. They'd made it out of here alive. My relief was soon replaced by worry. Where had they gone? And with who? Their car was still in the driveway. I dug my fingers into my scalp, trying to keep myself from screaming.

If they had left with someone else, there was no telling where they could be now. I was on my own.

"This is your sister's place?"

I lifted my head. Brody was standing in the doorway to the living room, brows knit. His expression was laced with caution, as if getting closer was somehow dangerous.

I didn't say anything, couldn't say anything. My face was frozen and my lips numb.

"Liz? Talk to me."

"She's gone..." I said under my breath, hardly believing my own words. All the strife and the death and the conflict...all for an empty house. "They're all gone."

"They're still out there somewhere. I'll bet they're safe."

"We don't know that! Anyone could have taken them. They could be in trouble!"

Brody took a step back. "Easy. Consider the surroundings, *Detective.* There's no evidence of a struggle. No signs of blood..."

I forced myself to listen to him. It was true. Aside from the tea on the table and the rooms in disarray upstairs, it didn't look like anyone had broken in. It looked like they'd left on their own. Despite the rationality, it grew harder to breathe.

"I should have been here," I whispered. "I should have been here."

"But you weren't," Brody interrupted. "There's nothing that can be done about that now, Liz. There's no way to change the past. All you can do is the same thing that she did, and that is to get the hell out of here."

"And go where?" I shouted.

"Don't you still want to know what happened in Flintland? Isn't that where you've been trying to go?"

"I don't know if it matters anymore." I moved backward to the couch. I picked up my feet and lie across the soft brown cushions. Their comfort under my aching body was like a cloud. It was the only thing supporting me.

"No." Brody knelt by the couch, eyes pleading. "Don't do this. Don't curl up and decide it's over. Not here; not now."

"I'm too tired to decide anything."

"We don't even know if this is a safe place to stop. We should keep going until we reach your place in Flintland. We're so close."

"Fine. You go. I'll stay here," I murmured, closing my eyes.

"Get up, Liz," Brody ordered.

I peeked through my eyelashes at him. His mouth had formed a grim line, and his dark eyes had lost any sympathy, any understanding. He was as cold and aloof as he'd been when he'd killed Elden.

"No," I answered.

"Damn it!" he shouted. "So, you are going to give up? You're going to sit there and wait for those things to come and take you; take us both? You saw how horrible that forest was."

I opened my eyes fully. "And I finally felt you. I finally got a chance to exist with you in the same time and space. We had, what? Four seconds? Four seconds of a reminder that I've lost you. That it wasn't an illusion. That I'm not losing my mind. And then, poof! It was over."

Brody looked away, his jaw set. He focused on a spot somewhere to my right and fixed his gaze on it. "I know," he said, his voice tight.

"Dana is gone. Everyone I care about is gone. If the only chance I have to be with you again is to sit here and wait for the forest to come so you'll be real…so that I can touch you, I'll do it." I tried to swallow back the fear of what I was about to say and failed, my voice trembling. "I'd do anything to go back and change what happened that day."

He looked at me, his eyes wet and his mouth slack. "When we hugged in that cabin, all I could think about was how I wanted to protect you, how I wanted to keep you safe, and not let anything bad happen to you. It was so unexpected and short. I let go of you and suddenly, I didn't understand." Brody stood and paced. "Why did I appear to you? Why not to Carmen, to my wife? To the woman who was the love of my life? Why is it that whenever I try and think about her, why I'm not with her…I think about you instead."

Everything inside was spinning as if I'd come off a dizzying ride and couldn't find my balance. Any and all tiredness was gone and replaced with anxiety.

Brody regarded me, nodding slightly as he always had when he was putting the pieces of a mystery together. "You won't tell me what happened before I died. But I know…something happened, didn't it?"

I couldn't answer without the familiar hollowness in my gut. I couldn't tell him. I didn't want to remember.

"You died," I said, hoping I could deter any further questions. "Isn't that enough?"

His eyes narrowed and I could tell he was questioning. Instead of saying what I knew he was thinking, he sighed and said, "Take some time and rest. Maybe there's something that your sister left behind that we can take with us. Food. Clothes. Something."

"Yeah," I said.

"You left the keys in the car. You should go get 'em. Make sure no one takes our ride."

I forced myself onto my feet and moved to the door. "There's no one around to take our—"

Something metallic slid, like someone scraping a pan with a spatula. I only had a moment to duck and it wasn't fast enough. The gunshot exploded across the sky as my leg erupted in pain. I fell against the porch, my hands slapping the wood and barely keeping my face from doing the same.

"Liz!" Brody yelled from inside the house.

Dazed, I tried to get my bearings. Blood raced from the wound in my thigh. The shot ricocheted beneath the overcast sky, bouncing off the buildings. Where had it come from?

"What happened?" Brody appeared in the doorway, swiveling his head this way and that.

"Got shot. Someone's out there," I panted, as I army crawled back into the safety of the house again. "Can you find them?"

Brody nodded and ran out, bobbing up and down to look over the hoods of cars and around fences. I watched him as I peeked from behind the door. I scrambled to pull my belt off. The pain was incredible, the force threatened to retreat me into unconsciousness to escape from it. I somehow got the belt off my waist and around my thigh, tightening it as a howl escaped my lips.

"Oh shit!" Brody yelled.

I peered out, noticing him backing toward the house. "Liz, get out of there. It's a trap!"

His words sent ice through my veins. I tried to stand but the entire world teetered and I collapsed on my stomach. Unconsciousness won as I sank into an inky black sleep.

TWENTY

THEN

I turned on the siren while Brody answered dispatch. The scene was only a block from our current position. We were coming back from court, testifying our evidence and procedure during a case against an abusive husband. The wife, Adair, recanted on her earlier statement, and her husband, Rafe, went free. Both Brody and I watched them reuniting in the hall as we left, both too frustrated and exhausted to say a word. We had answered a number of domestic disturbance calls from the Dolan address over the last ten months. I'd finally talked Adair into pressing charges, talked her into going to a shelter while we convicted Rafe. All of that strife, all that good that we thought we were accomplishing had slipped through our fingers like the sunlight that evening.

It was a convenience store robbery on Giroux Street. The place had a pharmacy in the back which had made it a target for theft before. Brody pulled his Charger up onto the sidewalk behind another patrol car, its lights spinning in the new darkness, bouncing off the nearby buildings. A few people stood nearby and were watching expectantly.

The officers, Jackman and Stoddart, were already inside. Stoddart pushed open the convenience store doors as we approached. "Guy got away before we could even get here," he said, his breath rolling into the wintry air. "Looks like he robbed the till. Good thing the owners keep a camera."

"They bought it after the last robbery," I said. "We'll take a look at it back at the station."

"Everyone inside okay?" Brody asked.

"Freaked out. Jackman is gathering eyewitness reports now."

We followed Stoddart inside and the bleary ultra-white lights were like a whole new wake up call. A bag of torn Skittles lay on the floor in front of the register, the colored dots sprayed across the scuffed linoleum. Jackman was interviewing the cashier, a teen with smooth long amber-colored hair in a university sweater. She had cried but her eyes were drowned in disappointment now.

"Owner's daughter?" I guessed.

Stoddart nodded. "Turned eighteen a couple weeks ago. She was watching the place for the first time by herself."

The other witnesses were standing off to the left side of the store near the liquor: an older guy with a beet red face, a couple of college age boys and…

I blinked. "Carmen?"

Brody's head whipped around as I said the name.

I hadn't talked with Carmen in weeks. The last time we'd conversed was after learning that Brody and she had split. Even then, she had looked put together. Carmen had a way with adversity, which was probably why she was so good at her job on the city's planning board. But the Carmen before me barely resembled the one I'd known for almost ten years. Her normally full-bodied dark hair was limp, tucked behind her ears. Her eyeshadow and mascara had smudged as her teary eyes stared up at us.

Brody rushed forward and took Carmen in his arms. She cried and a part of me cracked as I watched them together, as if they'd never been apart.

Then, Carmen pulled back from him, a fury crossing her face immediately. "Where were you? I've been calling you and calling you!"

I watched him dig into his pocket for his phone. "I've been in court all afternoon. I silenced my phone."

"I needed you," she sobbed. "I *needed* you!"

"Shh, shh, you're okay," he said. "You're okay."

She shook her head. "I'm not. You don't get to tell me that I'm okay. You weren't here."

Brody took a deep breath. "Babe, I'm sorry I wasn't here. But it couldn't have been helped."

Carmen shoved her purse toward him. "He stole my money, Brody. He stole my credit cards. He stole my earrings."

"What?" he muttered.

I turned to Stoddard. "The perp stole everyone's stuff. Why didn't you mention that?"

"I'm st-still gathering details. It hadn't come up yet!" he sputtered.

Brody walked to one of the coolers and grabbed a water bottle. He opened it and handed it to Carmen. "We'll call the card company and get them cancelled. My bet is that this guy is too stupid to know what kind of mess he's gotten himself into. He'll try to pawn the earrings and the first time he tries to use one of the cards, we'll nail his ass."

Carmen took a long swig from the bottle and held it, crinkling the plastic. "Okay. Okay."

"I can check in with the pawn shop around the corner," I offered. "Make sure that they know what we're looking for. They could tip us off if he shows up."

Brody nodded and I stepped back outside into the frigid air. The small crowd outside had left with only a few passing bystanders pointing as they went on their ways. Ace's Pawn shop was a glaring red beacon in the darkness of Giroux Street, the gritty old neon lights barely illuminating the caged windows and the scratched front doors. After filling in the owner on what to look out for, I spent the next few minutes returning to the convenience store and trying to forget the stench of cigarette smoke and grime that permeated the pawn shop.

I was nearing the front of the store when Brody said, "What are you even doing out here anyway?"

"What does it matter?" Carmen responded; tone guarded.

"This isn't exactly near the house or your job." Brody had his arms crossed. They were standing off to the side of the doors. Stoddard and Jackman had finished interviewing all of the occupants and were now talking with the owners, who had finally shown up. The father was holding his daughter, while the mother yelled about how we still hadn't caught the first offender to steal from their pharmacy.

Carmen stiffened. "I was on my way back from an appointment with a committee member. I needed to stop and get a bottle of Advil. My head's been killing me all day."

"Which committee member would that be?" Brody asked.

"What the fuck does it matter?" she snapped. She looked at me. "Are you listening to this?"

I took a few more steps toward them. "Brody, we should head back to the station."

Brody didn't look at me. "Why aren't you telling me the truth, Car?"

"Why do you assume I'm not?" She stared him up and down. "And how dare you interrogate me on the street like a common criminal."

Carmen turned toward the crosswalk. On the other side of the road, I recognized her black Subaru wagon. "I'm going home."

I grabbed Brody as he took a step after her. "Cool down. Let her go."

He closed his eyes and stalked toward his car. I quickly checked in with Stoddard to make sure they had everything they needed before following my partner. The engine was already going when I climbed into the passenger seat. He pulled out into traffic, cutting off a car. The horn blared at us.

"What the fuck?" I asked him. "She's been through a traumatic experience. What the hell were you thinking?"

"She had a wine bottle in her basket," he growled. "She wasn't stopping to get Advil."

"So what? She wanted some wine."

"She's shopping for it here? At this convenience store in the Reef? No. Carmen would have gone to that boutique on Main."

"I saw it, Brody. It was fucking Moscato. That's the kind of wine I drink in a night if I'm ugly crying and watching 'P.S. I Love You'."

The entire ride back to the police station, he didn't say anything.

He parked next to my car and we sat there with the engine idling.

"You have any plans tonight?" I finally said.

He shook his head. "Probably turn in early."

"On the horizon of a brand-new year? Doesn't sound like a whole lot of fun."

"Well, I'm not much fun to be around now adays anyway," Brody said, cutting the engine. "Besides, I should probably call Carmen and apologize."

I rested my hand on the door handle. "Or you could not exacerbate things and come with me to my sister's."

He glanced at me.

"I know; it doesn't sound like much fun either. There will probably be many rousing games of Uno ahead, at least I think that's still my nephew's favorite game. Probably some killer sparkling apple cider, too."

"Why would me calling my wife to apologize be 'exacerbating things'?"

The sentence had a cutting edge to it, once that I hadn't anticipated. I sighed. "I meant—"

"Don't." Brody unclicked his seatbelt and opened the car door.

I opened my car door to follow but realized I was still buckled in. "Hey!" I punched the button with my thumb and the belt slithered off. By the time I got my door open, he was already half way across the lot. "That wasn't what I meant!"

"Don't," he yelled back, not turning to face me. "I don't want to hear it."

I watched him walk into the station and stood there in the lot, the cold bristling against my skin. I unlocked my car and threw my stuff inside before slamming the back door.

Son of a bitch.

NOW

Consciousness returned before my vision could. There was only grey, but no definitive shapes in it. The unpleasant memories receded as I remembered what had happened and then the pain hit me. My leg throbbed. Every attempt to move it was in vain, like it was trapped under a concrete slab.

"Don't do that," someone ordered and my eyes snapped open.

I scooted backward, my back connecting with the wall and quickly took in my surroundings.

An Asian woman lifted her hands up. "Whoa! You're okay!"

I spun my head. "Brody? Where are you?"

"I'm here, I'm here," he said from my other side. He was leaning over me, concern puckering his brow.

"Where am I?" I asked. "Who is that?"

"You're all right and she's okay. You can trust her."

I glanced at the woman and she slowly put her hands down. "We won't hurt you. I assume Brody told you that."

I blinked. "Can you see him?"

She shook her head. "But that doesn't mean I don't believe he's there. Your friend has been entertaining, my husband, Ty for the last day with the story of how you got here."

Her words struck me slowly. *Brody entertaining her husband. No one else can see Brody unless they are also already dead, like Edith's ghost at the dam.*

This woman was like me. Her husband was a ghost.

I glanced around. We were in a small room, white walls, bare furnishings. I sat on a mattress in the corner furthest from the door, white gauze hung above it. "Who are you?"

"I'm Tamiko. You're in a safe place now. There's no need to be frightened."

"I was shot. I'm not exactly feeling safe." I shook my head and tried to sit up straighter. My leg burned with the effort.

Tamiko reached behind her and I tensed, half expecting her to come out with a gun. I relaxed when she produced a bottle of pills and handed me a couple. "Acetaminophen. Don't have anything stronger, I'm afraid."

I took it with a "thank you" and swallowed them. "Am I a prisoner?"

She shook her head. "You misunderstand: we didn't shoot you."

"Then, who did?"

"Trackers. We hadn't run into any since leaving Bangor. We barely got out of there before the forest overran it."

I frowned. "Trackers?"

Tamiko frowned. "You don't know about the government trackers?"

Nothing she said meant anything to me. "I've been…isolated these last few months."

"Understatement of the year," Brody said under his breath.

About a second later, Tamiko nodded. "To put it plainly, after the 'outbreak', the government organized a recruitment of everyone not suffering any symptoms. Some people affected were nervous wrecks: dangerous and self-damaging. Local law enforcement broke down in a matter of hours. Even some of the police on duty were afflicted."

I thought back to Flintland's force, to Brody's and my fellow officers. The people I'd left behind after I'd quit. Were any of them still around? Had any of them made it out alive?

"Anyone who wasn't seeing things was allowed to join a specially trained team in charge of segregating the population. Anyone experiencing hallucinations as they deemed it, would be taken to a special facility called Gideon in order to be…," here Tamiko paused and I noticed her expression dim a little, "…studied."

"Why do I get the idea that isn't a good place to go?"

"Because it isn't. Gideon isn't so much a quarantine zone as much as it's a concentration camp. I don't believe for one second that they want to 'bring people back' as their mission statement suggests."

I stared down at the bandage on my leg.

"They sure have a funny way of trying to help you," Brody said before I could.

"So, these trackers shot me. How did I end up here?"

"You had barricaded yourself in the house. We'd watched

everything happen from across the road. We were out scouting for supplies when they rolled through. Normally, we don't engage. We're not strong enough to hold off a group of trackers. But the dogs came. Do you know about the—"

"I do," I said shortly, not wanting to think about my awful encounter with one in the house or the horrifying close call in the woods.

"Well, the trackers couldn't hold them off. They had to retreat. As soon as the dogs were out of sight, we got you out of there."

I rested my head back, processing all of the information. "How has society fallen apart so fast?" I said more to myself than to her.

"There are other places faring better than we are," Tamiko said, putting the pills away. "At least, that's what I've heard. We've been trying to get out of Maine for a while now with no luck. The Woods have closed us off in most places."

"How long have you and…Ty, wasn't it?" She nodded. "How long have you been traveling together?"

"Since that night. There are times I think I need to let him go. But I can't."

I suddenly understood.

"Do you mind if I ask how he died?"

Tamiko's face pinched for only a moment, something that didn't belong on her soft delicate features. "He had an aneurysm. Ty was brilliant; a heart surgeon at the hospital where we both worked. He was in surgery when it happened. Two years and seven months ago. We'd only been married a year."

"I'm sorry," I said, my voice unable to carry a tone.

"And your Brody?"

"He's not mine—" I stopped, trying to control my voice. "We're not…. We were police officers. He was my partner and a close friend. He was shot and killed in the line of duty last year."

I felt Brody's eyes on me.

Tamiko bowed her head. "I think I remember that story on the news. I'm so sorry."

We sat together in that silence for several moments, drinking in each other's pain. I finally cleared my throat when the tears begin to form and said, "You and Ty have been traveling by yourselves this whole time?"

"Oh, no," she said, glancing toward the door. "We wouldn't have made it this far without Lennox and Prisca. Or their loved ones." She stood. "Once you're up to it, they'd like to meet you."

That name struck me like thousands of needles pressing into my chest. "Lennox? Jack Lennox?"

"You *do* know each other!" Tamiko smiled. "I thought Lennox was lying, but that look he gave when we found you was so unmistakable."

One of the only people that I hated more than myself for what happened with Brody was alive. He was *here*. I didn't want to have anything to do with him.

"I'll leave you so you can dress," Tamiko said. "We'll be eating breakfast soon if you'd like to join us."

"Thank you, Tamiko."

She left, closing the door behind her.

"Where are we?" I asked Brody who was standing nearby patiently, allowing me to wrap my head around everything.

"The Brummel elementary school. We're in the principal's old office."

I glanced around, taking in my surroundings again. A desk was shoved up against the wall nearby and a bulletin board was tacked with numerous papers in varied colors. I had been here once before: to pick up my nephew when he'd gotten sick. Dana was stuck at the airport on her way back from a business trip and Mark was out of cell reception on a jobsite. I remembered doing the walk of shame with him to the car, vomit all over his clothes and tears in his eyes.

"These people are okay," Brody said bringing me back to the here and now. However, his eyes belied him.

"You don't remember Jack Lennox, do you?"

He rolled his eyes. "Of course, I do. The guy like a cross between a stop sign and an oil slick? Yeah. Who could forget him?"

"You don't remember how much of an asshole he was though."

"Sure, I do."

I raised my head. "Wait, you…do?"

Brody stared into the shadows past me. "Yeah. Kind of came to me when I saw him again. When you were out. The missing kid: he pulled out of the search. You were livid."

My breath caught in my throat. Brody hadn't remembered this when I'd asked him about it months ago. What else did he now remember?

"Here's the thing," He held up a thumb and forefinger. "This group is about this far from breaking apart."

Brody left to give me some much-needed privacy. I finally had a moment to assess myself and think about all that had happened in the last day or so. Thankfully, these people had recovered my bag from my sister's house along with me, otherwise I'd have no choice but to go back there and get it.

I thought about Dana's empty house, about where she could possibly be now. I couldn't help but think she would have left something behind, some sort of clue to identify where she'd gone. Otherwise, how did she think I'd find her? Had she even suspected I'd try?

That thought was the hardest. I hadn't been the closest sister. I hadn't even been there for her when she'd had Michael. I was on the job, couldn't even remember the case. The last meaningful thing I'd been present for in her life was that New Year's Eve, the night that Brody and I had argued. I'd gone to Dana's and distracted myself with games and buffalo chicken bites and white grape juice and ignoring the offers for prosecco as the ball dropped and the new year started.

Before that, her wedding. I'd missed the actual ceremony, which I was supposed to be a bridesmaid in. I wasn't dating Josh back then; I only had myself to blame for getting the time wrong and not trying on the dress I'd picked out at the Evening Boutique until that day. As it turned out, it was too big, like I was being swallowed by a killer whale. I made it to the reception in time for my mother to chastise me about being late. I'd eaten too much cake and drank too much from the bar and danced like an idiot to all of the DJ's songs before Dana called Brody and Carmen to pick me up.

Of course, she hadn't expected me to come. I had retreated into the woods like a coward for a month before all this happened. I wouldn't have expected me to come either.

Opening my bag, I peeled off my sweat-soaked old shirt and slid into a clean one. Months ago, a medium sized t-shirt would have fit fine. Now, it hung off my frame as if I were made of wire. I hadn't wanted to look at myself in the mirror for months. I was afraid of picturing myself as anything less than the me I used to be, the me that had existed before Brody had died.

Finally, I got the courage to open the door. Negotiating the empty school corridors in the darkness, I couldn't keep the goosebumps from creeping from my arms to the back of my neck. It was hard to think of this place in the light, imagine the giggling of children and think of their eager and excited faces. My stomach hollowed and the thought of eating made me nauseated.

Following the hallway to the entrance corridor, I stopped and studied the signs for the various classrooms. The school's logo spread out on the tiled floor below me; a large italicized B over "elementary" in cursive. At the bottom was a stylized cartoon of a lizard, the mascot. The narrowed eyes immediately reminded me of those monsters hunting for us out there.

I followed another hall off to my right. The murmur of voices got louder. Soon, I was standing at the glass teacher's lounge doors. I studied each of them from outside.

Tamiko was sitting by the window, a smile lighting up her face. She was pretty, though she appeared exhausted. Her dark eyes coupled with her black bob haircut gave her a sophisticated air in spite of their current surroundings. She was looking at no one and every time her lips moved, I realized that she was talking to her dead husband.

I moved my sights over to the man leaning against the wall at the back of the room. His white shirt sleeves were rolled up over his lanky elbows and his brown hair was swept to one side back behind his ear.

Lennox.

I studied him. Somehow, even in a place surrounded by turmoil and disorder, he was tidy. He wore a pair of jeans and a black leather jacket and had grown the beginnings of a mustache and beard. How strange, viewing him without his usual suit and tie, even here, even with the world in the state it was now. Somehow, I had expected him to carry on the way I'd always seen him: nonchalantly and without much deference for anyone else. His eyes appeared calculating but callous.

Worse than seeing him again was the realization the he knew what had happened that day when Brody died, something that I had left Flintland to escape the reality of, something I'd hoped I'd never have to tell another soul again, including Brody's. I didn't want him to know.

I'd been out for a long time, and Brody had clearly connected with some of the other ghosts in this group. I needed to know if he had spoken with Lennox's and if he had, what they'd talked about.

"Who is it, then?" I'd poked Brody when we were talking in the principal's office. "Who is Lennox attached to?"

"Some girl. Probably mid-twenties. I'm guessing a sister, but who knows these days." He squinted. "Not all there, that one. When I tried asking her name, she started going on about the flamingos in the kiddie pool."

Lennox suddenly pushed off from the wall and walked away toward the other side of the room to look out the window.

I passed my gaze over to the shorter woman toward the front of the room. She was seated at the table there, a serene look on her face, a smile stretching over her full lips pleasantly. Her course brown hair was cut close to her skull. Looking at her made me relax a little inside. That is, until I remembered what Brody had said.

"Prisca is the defacto leader," he'd explained. "She might look like the kind of mom who'd sooner give you cookies and kiss your cuts and scrapes but that's not her. She's a tough one. Really has to be, considering she lost her kid."

I'd looked at him, forcing myself to focus. "How old?"

"Five."

I could only imagine how hard it was to lose a child, someone only beginning to become a person, an individual with likes and dislikes and questions and thoughts about how things worked and lived. To be reminded of that at every hour of every day in this new existence... Brody was right. She must have had nerves of steel.

Prisca turned her head and our eyes locked. I steeled myself for the inevitable interrogation and pushed into the teacher's lounge.

The reactions were mixed: Tamiko's kind smile remained, Lennox's expression shifted briefly to fear before resuming his cold demeanor, and Prisca kept a guarded eye on me, as if I might suddenly pull out a gun and blow everyone away.

"How are you feeling, Elizabeth?" Tamiko asked, clearly the only one who wanted me here.

"I'm upright, which is a start," I said, returning her smile.

"What were you doing in that house?" Lennox asked point-blank.

I frowned. "That's none of your business."

He stood straighter. "It's *my* business when it endangers *my* life."

"Leave her alone, Nox," Prisca commanded, her voice powerful. "Let her get some food. Then, we'll talk."

I nodded respectfully to her and went to the open cans on the counter. It was practically a smorgasbord compared to how terribly I'd eaten these last few weeks. A pot of rice and beans bubbled on a hot plate next to two large cans of sliced pears and fruit cocktail. I spooned a helping of canned beets onto my plate along with the pears, beans, and rice and retreated to my own corner of the room to eat.

Brody, who up until then was standing back, joined me. I ate in silence. Someone had added red pepper and paprika to the rice. It was divine, so much more flavorful than the bland rations I'd consumed at the cabin.

"Go easy," Brody said. "You don't want to choke on that."

"I haven't eaten in days," I reminded him.

"And it might be a few more days until you eat again. These guys have been living like nomads, frequently on the move, usually not trustful of outsiders."

"You learned all of this while I was out?" I whispered before taking a drink of water.

"Ty's been pretty forthcoming, even if the others aren't so much. Doesn't mean they won't do what they have to for the safety of the group."

I read his expression. "They killed someone?"

Brody tilted his head. "Not exactly."

"So," Prisca's voice called from across the room. "Are you ready to tell us what you were doing in that house?"

"Yeah, why don't you sing us a song about that, Detective?" Lennox added.

"You wouldn't like it if I sang. I've been told I'm tone-deaf."

He chuckled. "So, it's all one big joke to you?"

I somehow kept my tone even. "Hardly."

Prisca rolled her eyes. "If the both of you don't knock it off, I'm going to toss you outside and let you deal with the hunters and the dogs by yourselves."

I glared at Lennox.

"Hey, Raging Bull," Brody said, making me turn to him. "Answer their questions."

I locked eyes with Prisca. "That was my sister's house. She's gone: her, her husband, and my nephew. I don't know where they went. I didn't even know there were people hunting other people until today. I still don't understand what's happening out there. I don't have any answers."

"Neither do we," Prisca said.

I frowned. "What about FEMA? The Red Cross? United Nations?"

She shook her head. "Everyone was affected."

"No one was immune to this," Tamiko spoke up. "At the hospital, one hundred and nine of our one hundred and twenty-seven patients saw someone there that we couldn't. Roughly ninety members of our staff said they were influenced, including myself. The ratio isn't good."

Lennox stared out the window. "While no one was able to get an official count, the likelihood is that over eighty-five percent of the population were afflicted."

I swallowed hard. If that was true, what if my sister had become disturbed? What if Dad had come back to her? A small flame lit up inside of me at the thought, a strange jealous pinprick that I was immediately ashamed of. This was nothing to be resentful over. None of this should have been happening at all.

"You'd think that some semblance of society would have remained intact, but…." Prisca shook her head. "People lost it. They couldn't handle it."

"It's like someone took a baseball bat to a mirror and BAM!" Lennox clapped his hands, making everyone jump a little. "We're all in pieces. People acted out. Violence escalated. There was confusion, panic, and those who couldn't cope ended it."

"Society fractured," Prisca said, pulling her threaded fingers apart. "There were the likely groups; the conspiracy-theorists convinced this was something the government did; the religious nuts who say it's some trick of the devil, or the end of times; the militant assholes rushing in to gain control and the scientists who are convinced we've all fallen victim to chemical warfare."

The things I'd witnessed in Cardend mirrored what had happened in Brummel and likely, the rest of the world. Both were only small towns, probably fifteen thousand people between them. I couldn't imagine what the scene would have been like in cities ten times our size, places like New York, or Chicago, or even D.C. I was scared to even try.

"It wasn't only people who saw the ghosts; it was people who couldn't, too," Prisca said. "Some of them were envious and angry and lost. One was a woman in the eastern side of Flintland who lost her husband last year and didn't see him when the change happened."

My eyes widened in realization. Brody's wife lived on the eastern side of Flintland.

"Carmen," he muttered before I could.

"What happened to her?"

"Blew out her brains with her husband's old pistol," Prisca stated, somehow keeping her voice even.

All of the knots in my stomach suddenly bunched up. I put a hand over my eyes and tried to keep breathing. When I looked at Brody,

I noticed he was staring at the floor, his fists clenched. Were it possible for him to look any paler, I imagined he would have turned as grey as winter.

"Prisca," Tamiko reproved.

She studied me a moment and said, "You know her."

Brody stalked out the door suddenly.

"Brody!"

"Better for him to know now than find her like that," Prisca said.

"Fuck you," I growled at her. I followed Brody out the door of the teacher's lounge. My eyes were drowning and all I could think about was how much I hated myself. Maybe if Brody had appeared to her instead of me, she would be here with these people instead. And maybe I'd be the one lying in a pool of blood unable to cope.

I stood in the central corridor and glanced around, not sure where he had gone. I caught a glimpse of his arm as he vanished through a door to the school's courtyard. I followed; the door was heavy as I pushed it open. I had to lean on my injured leg for support and it was like sticking my finger in the bullet hole and jerking it around.

Outside, in the plume of fog, Brody stood with his back to me, staring at the overcast sky.

"I'm so sorry."

"She can't be dead."

"What?"

"I said, "She can't be dead." Carmen would never do that to herself," he said, turning to face me. "Besides, Prisca didn't say her name. It could be someone else."

I thought of Carmen in the weeks after Brody had died. We didn't speak to one another. There was enough guilt on my part and anger on hers that it separated us. The one time I did come across her, I'd run into her at a café by accident, months after the funeral. There was worthlessness in her eyes. It was something I immediately loathed, something I wished I could tear from her like a parasite. The bold and confident woman I'd known for so long had changed, probably even before Brody had died. Their relationship had grown emaciated in the time the couple had spent apart. Brody didn't remember that or wouldn't remember; I wasn't sure which.

"She changed when she lost you," I said, hoping the words struck him. "She was listless for a long time. You have to prepare for the inevitability that she did this."

"I know my wife. I can't accept it until I've seen it for myself."

"What do you mean?"

"I have to go there."

My leg throbbed with the effort to keep standing, but I ignored it. The words made every inch of warmth retreat from me. The thought of Carmen lying on the floor with a hole blown in her head made me want to throw up or run for cover or both. I shook my head. "You don't know what you'll find."

"I need to know." His eyes had somehow grown darker but not wetter. Not the sad kind of darkness that came with grief or sorrow. It was a mixture of confusion and morbid curiosity, one that I'd never before recognized in him.

"That's going to be hard, considering the fact that there are now people out there hunting us," I hissed. The mist around us made me uneasy. Who knew what was lurking inside of it waiting to pounce...? I wanted to be safe, even if it was only for one more day.

"She's my wife, Liz."

"I know."

"What if it was your sister? Huh?"

My stomach flipped. The gunshot was on fire and so was the rest of my leg.

He took a step closer. "What if it was Josh?"

Before I could keep myself, I stumbled toward a nearby bush and puked. Landing on the ground only reinforced how exhausted I was.

Brody approached from the corner of my vision and I held up a hand, spitting the last of the bile.

Brody's eyebrows knitted. "You should stay here; you're in no condition to be out there by yourself."

"What does that mean?" I looked up at him.

He'd turned away and was walking down the cement walkway. "Means I'm going on my own."

Gooseflesh rose on my arms as I staggered to my feet. "Brody, you can't." I took a step after him.

"No!" he commanded, spinning and walking backwards away. "Stay there."

I dropped back down to my hands and knees. The world teetered around me. "Remember what happened last time we got separated?"

"I'll need to find some camouflage this time," he called over his shoulder.

In spite of my body crying for rest, my mind was vibrating with his words and their implications. "What do you mean?"

Brody's figure vanished into the fog.

"Brody!" I shouted after him but he didn't reappear.

The push doors squeaked open on my left. "Elizabeth!" Tamiko exclaimed before her hands reached under my arms. "I've got you. Let's get you back to your bed."

In a haze somewhere deep underneath pain's thumb, I pushed my body back toward the school and away from the ghost of my friend.

TWENTY-ONE

THEN

Time and a hunch kept my brain rattling for nearly a week after the convenience store robbery. The job had kept Brody and me busy, leaving hardly any idle time. There hadn't been much opportunity for an in-depth conversation which only frustrated me more. The tension that rested between us had become an elephant in the office, in the car, and everywhere else we were together. We hadn't made an effort to meet up for drinks or food and coffee together was essentially had at our own desks, deep in writing our reports.

He didn't talk about Carmen. I didn't talk about Josh. Our talk was about work and work alone, a formal and dry dictation that hollowed me out more and more as the days passed. Every time I looked at him, I wondered how our friendship had sunken into this pathetic mirage of one. We were both watching it drown and doing nothing to save it.

One thing was clear to me though: Brody acted different around me than he used to. I could sense it in little things. The lingering touch of his hand to my back as I went through a door ahead of him, or whenever we were talking; he'd watch my mouth as if he was waiting for me to change the topic.

It wasn't only how he behaved with me; it was how I reacted to him in return. I became upset when I didn't hear from him on my day off, but was too stubborn to call him first. Sunday morning when I drove into the station, I found myself nervous to see him, and when we did lay eyes on each other, a kind of relief washed over me that I couldn't place.

Whatever our friendship had morphed into, I needed to understand it. To do that, we needed to talk about it eventually.

We were ending our shift on Friday after a going through mountains of paperwork. The sky had turned purple black. Thick snow had fallen for a while and the roads were a mess. I walked to my car and unlocked it when I noticed Brody sitting in his Charger only a few spaces from mine. He was looking at his phone, clearly reading a text or post. He caught me watching and put down his window a little to call out.

"I'll see you tomorrow," he said. His voice was racked with tire.

I didn't move. "Can we talk?"

He closed his eyes. "How about tomorrow, okay?"

A humorless smile broke on my face. "I *can't* handle another day of this weirdness..."

He stared at me. "What are you talking about?"

I crossed the lot to his car and got in the passenger door. He turned on the engine to his car and the heater blew cold air at us.

"What weirdness?" Brody asked again, turning down the blower on the fan.

I shook my head. "Don't act like you haven't noticed."

A couple people emerged from the elevator in the parking garage and crossed to their cars nearby. "This is work," he said, keeping his voice low. "This isn't the place."

I waited for the other people to climb into their cars before saying, "I only want to know what changed between us. I'm not going to hold you down and beat it out of you. I don't want every single day to be so...empty."

Brody set his jaw. "Oh, so, our partnership is *empty* now?"

"That's not what I said."

"This isn't about you and me as friends, or as partners, or...." he drifted off. "We're both dealing with our own shit. I don't know about you, but last week was a reminder that I need to deal with it another way."

"I thought we *were* supporting each other as friends. Hell, I'd still be down at the bottom of a bottle if you hadn't stepped in."

He reached over and took my hand. The warmth rekindled dread inside.

"I hate seeing you in pain. You know that. But my marriage is crumbling. I need to take a step back. I need to figure out some things. You understand?"

"No, I'm not sure I do."

He sighed. "You want me to say it out loud?"

My insides were fluttering. "I'll never know what "it" is unless you give it a name."

He stared at me and the look held between us made me want to stop breathing. "I'm not sure I should. I'm not sure that's a good idea for either of us."

What I'd been assuming for weeks was confirmed: my partner and friend of ten years had feelings for me. The car became stifling in only a few seconds and I secretly wanted to open all the windows and let the winter storm envelop me. But I couldn't move, couldn't make myself look away.

"Why didn't you tell me?"

"I tried to, lots of times. I thought better of it each and every time. It wasn't fair to you. It wasn't fair to Carmen or Josh. I wasn't even sure I knew what I was thinking half the time."

I let go of his hand and the warmth receded. "That night in your apartment, you…kissed me. I didn't know how was I supposed to take it."

"I wasn't thinking. I never should have done that, especially after the night you had." He caught my look and backpedaled, hanging his head. "We're partners. We're responsible for each other's well-being on the job, and being friends means I'm responsible for your well-being off the clock as well."

I studied his gaze and frowned. "How long have you felt like this?"

Silence pervaded the small space. Every second I waited for an answer was another that I couldn't sit still in my seat.

Brody stared at the dark space down by his feet. "A while," he finally uttered.

I didn't know how to react. It was more than an admission of affection. It was the realization that Brody had cared for me as more than a friend and that he'd been struggling with it silently while I never even knew.

"I'm not the reason you and Carmen broke up, am I?"

He shook his head. "No. I told you the truth about that; we've been having problems for a long time."

We sat in the growing darkness, the heat stifling in the car. I'd forgotten about the building snow, the call I was going to give my sister when I got home, the grocery shopping I needed to do on the way there. I was afraid that once I left this car, nothing would ever be the same again. How could it be?

"So," he said, breaking the silence again. "Now, what happens?"

My throat was tight. I tried to take a deep breath but it ended up being shallow and shuddery. "I don't know."

He frowned. "This is what I was afraid of."

"Maybe you need to transfer partners then?"

The moment I said the words, a wounded look crossed Brody's face. I could sense everything in that look, every iota of shame and guilt about ever starting the conversation bubbled up into my head. I could have handled awkward conversations, a gradual return to our status quo. I wasn't sure I could handle this.

"I don't like the idea of one of these other guys having your back out there," he finally said. "I don't like not knowing whether you're safe or not."

My eyes were brimming, my chest tight as I forced myself to keep talking. "I can handle myself. What you need to decide is if your marriage is worth saving. I'm a diversion. I'm a block on your path back to her. If you still love Carmen like I know you do, then make the transfer."

I opened the car door and pushed out into the snow storm. The blast of cold air against my wet eyes grounded me. I moved with all the fluidity of a robot, my arms and legs heavy and my shoulders carrying the brunt of the weight. I got into my own car and left.

The journey home was slow-going. The plow trucks hadn't come out yet and with a couple inches already on the road, people were driving as if they'd never encountered snow before. I finally inched my way through town and down the cul-de-sac to my home. I didn't bother shoveling the driveway, or the walk.

Taking off my boots and dropping my coat in the entryway, I walked into my living room and laid down on the rug. All of the emotions escaped. Josh was gone. Brody would be gone. I'd never be able to look Carmen in the eye again. It was like being trapped in a tank with the water slowly rising. How had I put myself inside of this? How would I get out?

Eventually, I got up and went upstairs to the bedroom. I stared at the bed before putting on sweatpants and a t-shirt and going back downstairs. Sleep was elusive. I had to calm the whirl of thoughts.

Going downstairs, I jumped on my new Peloton and peddled. I didn't need music or the guidance of a video. Each and every time I closed my eyes, I thought of what had happened in the car, what I'd said, what I should have said.... Soon, my blood was pumping hard in my ears as I moved and it drowned out Brody's voice and mine. After I exhausted myself, I jumped off the machine and downed a glass of cold water.

It was after ten. I grabbed a kitchen towel and quickly wiped my brow and face. I was gross again, covered in sweat, my limbs exhausted and begging for rest. As I ascended the stairs for the bathroom to wash my face, someone knocked on the door.

Damn it, I realized. I'd forgotten to call Dana. I'd talked to her that morning, mentioned I might be receptive to a conversation with Mom on her birthday in a few weeks. She was planning a surprise Zoom call between family members. She wanted to work out the details with me. I'd left my phone in the bedroom upstairs in my blazer pocket. She'd probably been trying to get ahold of me for hours. Still, it was strange for her to drive all the way over here from Brummel though, especially at this time of night.

I ran to the door and peered through the peephole, my apologies screeching to a halt. It wasn't Dana.

I opened the door to Brody, his shoulders and black hair topped with snow.

I stared dumbly. Had he forgotten we'd had that horrible conversation, one where I'd made the decision for both of us that he needed to stay away from me?

Everything inside of me screamed. My heartrate increased tenfold. For a moment, I was swarmed by all of my thoughts that had bombarded me in the shower. I lost control. "I don't want to be this person," I said. "But no matter what I do, I keep ending up alone."

Brody stepped forward, his hand cupping the back of my neck and his lips touched mine. I put a hand to his cheek, his stubble rough under my fingers. I breathed in his smell as our lips crushed together. With the snow falling behind him, it was as though we were hovering in space, lost in a vast blackness of falling stars, surrounded by cold and eclipsed by each other's warmth. He put his other arm around my back and pulled me closer.

This was what he had wanted. Maybe this was what I'd wanted all along. Or maybe I wanted closeness, some connection with someone. It didn't matter in those moments what the difference was. His chest pressed against mine and his hand caressing my back made me want to forget about it all. I wanted to lose myself in the moment. I wanted there to be some kind of hope.

He pulled away first, his near black eyes searched mine. "I'm here. You're not alone."

"Stay."

Brody leaned in and captured my lips against his again. He

kicked the door closed behind him. We sunk toward the living room floor, entangled in each other, his arms around me to cradle my landing, and mine to guide him after me. His hands on my sides, sliding over my hips spurred a kind of sensation in me that I'd never had for him before. Those abrasive and rough hands that I'd watched for years on the job were hands that had belonged on someone else's body.... I'd never thought about how they might feel on mine. I'd never wondered how they'd touch my skin, how tender a trace they might actually give.

His hand moved lower, cupping between my legs and a primal urge awoke within me, a force that beckoned and I arched my back with need.

We undressed in the bedroom upstairs. A dark pit had yawned open inside me, something bottomless, something ravenous. I didn't recognize myself and shut off the part of my brain trying to. I was tired of overthinking things, tired of never taking care of myself, tired of losing everyone that meant something to me. By the time we were breathless and I was lying in his embrace, I actually experienced real release, real ease, actual serenity in my own head. I slept, Brody's arm around me within the blue dark night amongst a welter of blankets.

NOW

I awoke. It was dark now and Brody was still gone. I didn't know how long I'd slept. The memory of my dreams rushed through me at full force, pushing me to the brink of losing it. I thought of Brody's embrace, the way his fingers had trailed over my skin and how safe I'd been with him...and how wrong that was. He'd left me to go find Carmen's body. What if the wolves found him? I might lose him again.

Those remembrances were slashed further by the thought of Carmen dead, the thought that Josh might be dead somewhere, too. I wanted this pain to end. I wanted to forget how much those memories hurt, especially this one: a memory that I couldn't even share with Brody, because he didn't remember it and probably wouldn't accept it.

I pushed the blankets off of me and stretched my injured leg out in front of me. I was exhausted. Standing was the most difficult task in the world. But I had to gather my things and get after Brody. I had been thinking about what his camouflage remark meant and when it dawned on me, it nearly knocked the wind out of me. He was looking for a human body to take over.

The door squeaked open and Prisca's stout and commanding

presence stood there. "So, I take it your friend is going to check up on his wife?"

"Yeah," I said, clearing my throat. "Thanks for being *so* delicate about that, by the way."

Prisca rubbed an eye as she stepped closer and sat in a swivel chair nearby. "I'm sorry that was how you both had to find out."

"To be honest, I didn't even think of Carmen until a few days after Brody showed up. Even then, I hadn't thought about what she might do. Brody should have appeared to her; not me."

"He's with you for a reason. They all came back to us for *some* reason. At least, that's what I assume."

I sat with my back to the wall on the mattress, letting the plaster support my tired frame. "What do you mean 'a reason'?"

"There was a member of our group before who believed that each returning spirit had unfinished business with whomever they are attached to. It made sense, at least, it did to us. Is there was something between you and your partner that needs to be addressed?"

Her eyes studied mine in a way that was all too uncomfortable. I flipped the question back on her before she could ask me anymore about Carmen or Brody. "Who is this group member you're talking about?"

Prisca took a deep breath. "His name was Astor. He was a literature professor on sabbatical from Oxford. Seemed nice enough but could have a temper, definitely suffered from that superiority complex thing. He thought he was a real smart guy."

"Who was he attached to?"

"We never really found out. Tamiko mentioned that Ty had noticed young man once but he could have been anyone and…I didn't get the impression that he and Astor were on friendly terms."

I frowned. "Why would you say that?"

"Well, he killed him for starters."

"What?" I was suddenly charged again, my alertness fighting through the nausea and exhaustion. "Astor murdered this guy when he was alive?"

"No. That's not what I meant," Prisca said, waving a hand. "Astor found a way to detach himself from his specter. We still don't know how. All we know is that it happened after Astor's ghost inhabited another person."

I stared at the floor. "You guys know about the possessing thing?"

"Happened by accident once. Lennox's..." Prisca paused. "...whatever she is... She got pulled into a hunter."

"You guys injured one of the hunters?"

"Not on purpose," Prisca said quickly. "He fell into a ravine while chasing us. Broke his leg. The hunter kind of jerked around like a fish on the riverbank for a moment and then, he was singing the Care Bear's theme song. Lennox got angry; angriest I've seen him."

I chewed on that information for a moment. Instead of focusing on Lennox though, I was thinking about Prisca's earlier revelation: there was a way to separate Brody from me.

If I hadn't gone into the Woods to find Brody, I might never have seen him again. But I wasn't sure how many people knew about those altars, or the Great Corruption as that thing deep below the ground in the Woods had talked about. I was probably the only one.

Brody's words from earlier returned to me. I'd asked him if Prisca's group had killed someone to protect themselves.

"Not exactly."

"What happened to Astor?" I asked, dread creeping along every word.

Prisca closed her eyes, her fingers massaging her forehead. "He was going on about how the ghosts changed, they weren't who we thought they were, they were dangerous...." She glanced over her shoulder at the door and said under her breath, "My boy was five when he died. He's *still* five when he appears to me now. How dangerous could he be?"

"And?"

"Astor said he had destroyed his ghost in order to protect himself and wanted us to do the same. Naturally, we wanted to spend more time with our loved ones and they have never once seemed unsafe. So, we ignored him. He didn't like that."

"What did he do?"

"He wanted to convince my son to possess Tamiko. He was going to tell him that it wouldn't hurt, that he'd be able to hug and be with his mommy again. Then, he could prove to us that he was right, that our ghosts were dangerous." Prisca's lip curled. "He'd left this stupid journal of his out. He'd been acting strange. I didn't like it. And as it turned out, I was right about needing to watch him."

I watched Prisca as she stopped massaging her head and slid her palms down to her cheeks, her eyes locked on the ground.

"Did you kill Astor?"

"No." Prisca stood and paced from one end of the room to the other, as if she was trying to walk off an invisible malady. "Lennox knocked him out and we left him for the Woods and the dogs."

"You left him to die."

"Only because I couldn't kill him myself," she growled. "If I'd been stronger, I might have. But this whole society has become about killing people who are different, using violence to exercise their opinions about race and religion and sexual orientation and even fucking politics. I don't want to be one of those people."

"You have any idea what happened to Astor?"

"I've tried not to think about it."

The world outside was deadly. The more the Woods took over, the more it seemed only the strongest were destined to survive. But Astor had had the mental and emotional fortitude to kill his own attached ghost and even the duplicity to try and kill more. There was a chance he'd made it. If he had, Prisca and her group had a target on their backs. Only one more reason not to stick around them any longer.

Prisca stood up. "You stay here as long as you'd like. We're going to move out of here as soon as we have a clear path to do so. You're welcome to join us." The invitation was hesitant.

I cleared my throat. "Brody left to investigate Carmen's death on his own. I have to follow him."

"Forget it. Most of Flintland has been swallowed by the forest and is probably crawling with dogs."

The words clunked hollowly against my skull. The place I'd called home for so long was overtaken. I might not even have a house to go back to, one that was safe anyway. I needed to find Brody before he ended up in the jaws of a wolf.

"Means I'll have to get going now then." I got to my feet, albeit struggling.

Prisca scoffed. "It's your funeral."

"It would be easier if I wasn't alone," I added.

She looked over her shoulder. "Are you suggesting what I think you are?"

"You said it yourself: the place is a death trap. If there was another set of eyes to watch my back, I could—"

Prisca's eyes rounded. "I didn't think you'd hit your head or anything but maybe Tamiko was wrong, because you must be out of your damned mind."

I paused. "Have you ever been inside?"

"No," Prisca said. "But those I've watched get lost in it have never returned. I don't want to know what kind of hell is in there."

"You might," I said before I could stop myself.

She gave me a quizzical look.

"I got trapped in the Woods. When I was in there, I saw all kinds of things that I don't want to remember; things that belonged in a nightmare. But I got to touch Brody. I could hold him in my arms as though he were alive again. Even though it was only for a few seconds, it was like I'd traveled back in time, that I was far away from all of this chaos."

Prisca's eyes watered. "There was a time when I'd have given anything to hug my Anthony again. Every time I look at his face, I think if I still would…."

I looked her in the eye. "It's possible. It's risky but it's possible."

Prisca shook her head. "I won't put Lennox and Tamiko in danger because of my selfishness. If you go up there, you go up there alone."

I jumped to my feet. "What if the key to stopping all of this is inside the Woods? You don't think it would be worth at least trying to find out?"

Prisca's fists clenched and unclenched. "There's nothing that can stop this."

"How do you know that? All you've been doing is running."

Her eyes narrowed and filled with a cold and penetrating ferocity. "You're tempted by that place. You're tempted by that idea of having him back. It's all an illusion. It's a lure and you're getting ensnared in it. You said there were terrible things in there, things you'd 'never want to remember'. Yet, here you are, ready to throw yourself down in harms' way for a chance to touch something that you can't keep."

The last words were said with so much weight that my knees buckled slightly. "I'm not losing sight of the bigger picture. There has to be something that can end this. Don't tell me that you want to live the rest of your life with Anthony's ghost hovering around you every second of every day, a living memory that you can't turn off or mute."

"Cancer took him from me," Prisca spat. "Vile, poisonous cancer. It wasn't his time to go. It wasn't his time to say goodbye. You think what's happening is a curse, some kind of hell where you'll always be reminded of what you lost." She shook her head. "Not me. This is our second chance."

I stared at her, acknowledging her pain and trying to keep my own at bay. "Your illusion isn't any different than mine."

She watched me blankly. "You have my permission to leave. I'd prefer it be sooner rather than later." She turned and left without another word.

TWENTY-TWO

When the night burned off into dawn, I made my way from the school back toward the center of Brummel. I didn't bother saying goodbye, even if I had wanted to thank Tamiko once more for patching up my leg. It was like a colony of fire ants was living inside of it and every time I took a step, it shook the anthill. I took more painkillers, hoping it would dull the pain enough. I couldn't afford to let it slow me down, not when I was heading straight into Flintland and the Woods, a place where danger was always looming.

Brody was way ahead of me, at least several miles. Who knew what obstacles would be in my way that he'd been able to walk right through? Meanwhile, all I could think about was his goal: to check if his wife was dead, something that made me sick to my stomach. After witnessing Brody shoot Elden in Jake's body, I never wanted to see another dead body. I knew that was unlikely though.

By the time I made it back to my sister's house, I was huffing and I'd sweat through my new shirt. I took a few moments to pilfer some clothes from Dana's closet. I found one of my cardigans that I had worn to mom's wedding back when I went to college. Not sure why my sister kept it; maybe because she liked the style? Dana ended up inheriting most of my old clothing when we were children which made me a little sad for her. Whenever Mom took me shopping, I ended up picking a lot of what I thought Dana would like, even if it looked too girly for me. I think I actually may have liked some of the frilly, glittery things at some point. Her taste rubbed off on me.

There were no frills on any of the things I took now. Plain t-shirts, her one pair of yoga pants, jeans, and her only pair of hiking boots. The ones I'd taken from Maynard's house back in New Hampshire were beaten all to hell.

In the kitchen, I rifled through what canned goods and dried pasta I could find and packed it into every nook and cranny in my bag that I could. Then, I left.

My sister's car was gone. I hadn't even noticed it upon returning. The hunters probably took it, along with the truck Brody and I had used to get here. It meant I'd be traveling on foot to Flintland. It was a fifteen-minute drive between my sister's house and mine in Flintland which meant at least a couple hours on foot. At the rate I was moving, it might be longer. At least I was heading out early.

I followed the road out of the burbs where Dana's house was and toward Route 1. Even though it was one of the more well-traveled state routes in Maine, it was so foreign now. I'd never seen it so completely empty. Normally, it was choked with traffic moving north and south, especially in the summer months. Aside from the snow-drifted pavement and the occasional downed trees on the sides of the road, it felt as though I was in a dream.

After an hour, I diverted onto a western exit for route 127, which was surrounded by natural woods on both sides. I stayed vigilant; my steps as soft as I could make them. While the trees weren't close on either side of me, I still got the impression that I was being watched from them, the mist cloaking their innards from me almost completely. Reaching the top of a bluff, I finally glimpsed the tips of buildings emerging from the mist below me: Flintland. Woods surrounded it while the Ohtuk River sliced a jagged swath through its left side, running off of the impressive Kennebec. I recognized the fields on the northern border of the city where Brody's and Carmen's house lay. Cutting down across the snow, I left the main road that led into town, in favor of shortening my time and distance following its zigzagging. I turned my head back toward the road I'd come from.

There was nothing but the wind shaking the trees, the limbs knocking together.

Being truly alone in the midst of this silence, it was easy to be paranoid. It was easy to think that the sounds of the forest were something much worse. I dreaded the moment when I'd look behind me and actually notice something there instead of chalking it up to my terror getting the best of me.

Crunching down to the snow-drifted road at the bottom of the hill once more, I followed it as it snaked down and up a smaller knoll toward the outskirts of town, otherwise known as Mottershill. The houses there were grim reminders of a time passed. I remembered them festooned in holiday decorations, warm light gleaming from the windows. The Mottershill community was always the envy of the town during Christmas, with elaborate displays that brought people from all over the city for nighttime drive-bys. They hadn't even made it to Christmas before the ghosts came. The only thing reflected in their windows now were the overcast skies and bleak doorways of other homes.

By the time I reached the top of Mottershill Road, the painkillers had worn off and my gunshot wound was fiery and sore. Needing a rest, I stopped in the covered entrance to an auto parts store in one of the old white vinyl sided buildings. The glass doors were locked and scratched beyond belief. The black and orange CLOSED sign stuck on it inside blocked most of my view.

I sat as close to the wall as possible for cover from the cold, keeping watch back at the path I'd traveled. I still had to make it to Brody's house and there was a lot of city between me and it. I didn't know what I'd find on the way.

Not a moment later, someone dressed in black appeared at the top of the hill, face hidden by a winter hat and scarf.

I tensed and flattened against the wall as much as I could, my thoughts racing. Not my imagination; I was being followed. I slung my bag off my back and pulled out the knife I'd taken from Elden's cabin and dared to take another peek.

I had to find a place to hide and get the jump on this shadow. Noting a gap between the auto parts store and the garage next door, I quickly slipped inside the dark mouth, waiting for the figure to approach.

It was ten minutes before footsteps scuffed on ice and snow and salt, drawing closer. I made myself ready to take the stranger by surprise.

The moment the body was in view, I moved from my hiding spot and whipped the knife's point against the back of the figure's neck. "Move and you're dead."

The figure froze. "Jesus! It's me! It's Lennox!"

I lowered the knife. "What the hell are you doing here? Did you seriously fucking follow me on foot this whole way?"

He turned and lowered his scarf so I could glimpse his face. His stubble was dotted with frozen beads of ice and his light-colored eyes looked glassy. "I overheard you and Prisca talking. If you think there's a way to make this whole thing end, I want to help."

"You? The guy who ruined my career? Who interrogated me back there?" I snapped.

He narrowed his gaze. "You can't fault me for being careful. You'd have done the same."

He has a point, I reminded myself.

"Why do you want to help anyway?" I asked. "I thought you were on the same page as Prisca, preferring to stay blissfully ignorant to what's happening."

"Prisca's dealing with it in her own way. Tamiko is, too. They both lost people who were taken from them prematurely. It's only natural they'd want to hold on for them as long as possible." He squinted. "Not you though. And not me."

I swallowed a lump in my throat. "Don't assume that I wouldn't want Brody back if it were possible. But he doesn't belong here, shackled to me. Just because you don't want to have anything to do with your ghost, doesn't make us the same."

Lennox stiffened.

"Who is she anyway; who's that young woman attached to you? No one back there even mentioned her name."

Lennox scoffed. "I guess it was a mistake to think that you'd need any help. Or want it, for that matter." He turned back toward the road from where he'd come.

I watched him for a few moments. It was stupid that he'd come when he hadn't shown an ounce of concern back at the school. He must have been desperate to get himself away from his ghost. As much as I wanted to let him walk away, the idea of going into Flintland alone and injured made me worried that I'd never come out of it alive.

"Wait!"

Lennox slowed and turned back to look at me.

I gave him a wave and said, "We should get moving."

No one wants to imagine their hometown in ruins. No one wants that kind of picture in their head. It corrupts all sense of peace and purity, a picture we keep in our minds so that we can live our lives, keep thinking the world is still a good place.

But, Flintland was derelict. The places I had passed by every day on patrol were locked tight and the streets were barren. In the icy chill of that mid-day, it was like the whole town was asleep, and had simply forgotten when it was supposed to wake up. It unnerved me and kept my head swiveling in all directions.

Lennox was a transplant. He worked for the Boston police department, until he decided to make a major life change and moved to Brummel, a smaller town away from the city's hustle and bustle. While no one in Flintland PD had much more information than that, they did know that he came with stunning references, was one of the Boston PD's most promising profilers and had a near perfect record. It was probably why he was chosen by Captain Vance as Flintland PD's go-to for internal affairs issues.

Flintland didn't have a large enough force to warrant an Internal Affairs Department and the occurrences of situations that would need one were so low, it had never been disputed. Brummel often assisted Flintland and vice versa.

Lennox walked quite far in front of me, his pace rapid to my hobbling one. Had he forgotten that I'd been shot?

"You want to slow down a bit?" I called to him.

He paused and looked over his shoulder, raising his eyebrow with impatience.

I caught up to him and we continued walking. "Are you ever going to tell me her name?"

He looked down at his boots. "No."

"What did she do to you?"

"Excuse me?"

"You obviously want her to go away. You don't like talking about her or even talking to her. But you stayed with Prisca and Tamiko because they genuinely care about the people they're attached to. So, you must care about her. Right?"

"Why does it matter to you so damn much?"

"Why *doesn't* it matter to you?"

"Who said it doesn't?" he said with exasperation.

"So, it does."

He shook his head. "Please. Enough with the psychobabble. Let's find Aritza and get this over with."

I stopped. "When Brody died, and you were investigating, you made my life a living hell. So, don't be surprised if I don't trust you."

Lennox's expression remained solemn. "I'm sorry you took it so personally. I was doing my job."

"And back at the school when you were grilling me? Was that a part of your job then?"

"I was being cautious. You haven't experienced what we have. You can't trust anyone."

"Hence my reason for asking you now: Who is she?"

Lennox crossed his arms. "She isn't a threat to you."

"You are. And who knows what you're willing to do to get rid of her. What you'd be willing to do to me."

He made the connection immediately. "I'm nothing like Astor."

"Prove it."

Lennox chewed on his lip; his glare potent. His voice cracked as he said, "Her name was Lynn."

"Who was she?"

He looked from side to side. "This isn't a good place to do this. We should find cover."

"I'm not going any further until you tell me."

His hands balled into fists at his sides. "She was a friend of mine. Nice girl, lived in Dorchester with her aunt and uncle. The guy used to be a cop, retired for early onset dementia but it was kept quiet, lied about it being glaucoma. He hit his wife. He hit Lynn. By the time we found out what was going on, she'd suffered head trauma, brain damage, not to mention the traumatic distress."

"How did you become friends with her?"

"It was a…weird kind of bond. This girl sat herself down at my desk one day. A precocious ten-year-old and started asking me questions. It was annoying at first and I thought she'd get tired of it. But she didn't. Every week for the next five years, this kid would hang out and play Uno with me and talk about the job. I never thought I'd get used to something like that, never thought I'd miss it.

"She never wanted to go home. She'd always ask if she could stay five more minutes. I never took a hint, never entertained a thought about why Lynn would be so upset to leave that she'd cry. The uncle retired and she stopped coming around. When I did see her again, she wasn't the same."

The pain on Lennox's face as he narrated the story of that poor girl's life pulled at a chord in me. She wasn't even his own flesh and blood: some poor girl he'd tried to help.

"The domestic disturbance call came in, right around Valentine's Day," Lennox said, taking a deep breath. "The uncle had knocked both Lynn and his wife out with a frying pan. Wife died from blunt force trauma. Neighbors heard the arguing. The call went out on dispatch and I recognized the address. By the time I got there, I saw this bloody…body strapped to a gurney being put in an ambulance. I didn't know it was Lynn until someone told me. She was unrecognizable, face completely swollen and bashed to bits. I don't know how she survived."

"What happened to her?"

"She was in hospitals and psych wards through her teens. I

visited her as much as I could. I think it helped. I know it did. Otherwise, why else would she be here now? But one day, the one day I couldn't come, another patient got hold of a pen, and punctured her carotid, and she bled out. It was all over before they could even blink."

A fierce wind pulled at my hair, and sent melted snow dipping down the back of my neck. He was guilty. I was guilty. We were more alike than I thought.

"Lynn doesn't deserve another dose of confusion like this. She doesn't deserve to be dragged around, forever remembering and reliving that pain. She doesn't even understand what's happening right now. And I can't explain it to her because *I* don't understand it! All I know is that there has to be a way to stop it." He raised his eyebrows. "Is that enough for you? Or should I keep going?"

I shook my head. "Let's get moving."

We made our way out of town toward Orange Street which cut across the fields belonging to Innes Farm Market and would take us directly up to the River Road and bypass the Reef. We trod through the muddy countryside before reaching the uneven pastures behind Innes Farm. The ground was sloppy and mud-filled. Both of us stumbled over ourselves traversing it, me especially. The extra effort only made my leg hurt more.

The handle of a baseball ball bat protruded from Lennox's bag on his back. I wondered if he had any other weapons inside in case we were ambushed. A knife wasn't exactly the best offense unless you were fighting in close-quarters or were stealthy enough. I was hardly sly at the moment, each step on my injured leg coming down heavier than the last.

Eventually staggering out of the mud and into an orchard, we crossed the lines of apple trees toward the T intersection that would lead to River. The skeletal branches looked gnarled, as if they were arthritic hands and knobby fingers twisting toward the sky to escape from the snow.

"I was right, wasn't I?" Lennox said suddenly, his eyes scanning the trees around us.

"About what?"

"You and Aritza were more than partners, weren't you?"

I moved a few steps ahead of him, not making eye contact. "We were friends."

He scoffed. "You're going to lie to me now? After I told you everything?"

I said nothing.

"You two were lovers."

This time, I looked back at him and tried to keep my breathing under control. "No."

"I don't believe that."

I fought to keep the memories from invading my head. Brody's lips tracing over my shoulder and down my arm. "It began. But we never had the chance to let it go anywhere."

"What distracted you so much that day that he ended up dying?"

The sentence resonated in me like a hum on a guitar string, the tremor reverberating and never dissipating. All I could picture were Brody's eyes as my stomach gyrated in sickening knots.

I stared into Lennox's unsympathetic gaze, somehow keeping myself from tearing him apart. "I was going to call it off."

THEN

"Hey, Lizzy."

I opened my eyes and my bedroom came into focus. Sunlight spotted the pale blue walls, the bed was warm, and there was a hand gently caressing my arm. I looked up into Brody's dark brown eyes and I smiled.

In a plain white t-shirt, Brody's skin seemed more tanned than usual, his chest muscles sculpted beneath the thin material. His usually hidden tattoo of a skull wearing a crown on the inside of his left bicep had faded to green through years of sun exposure and ink absorption. I'd joked about it being slightly emo of him to have gotten that design and he'd chuckled but never really explained what it meant.

A part of me faded as my mind caught up with everything that had happened in the last twelve hours. Even though I had thought I was more complete with another person lying next to me in my bed, I knew I was not.

"You're already up?" I said, forcing those weeded thoughts to die down into the soil.

Brody smirked. "As much as I'd like to stay in bed all day, we've got work to do."

It only took me a second, but I recognized the spark of guilt in his face as well. What was an escape for us both, a way to put a tourniquet on the wounds, had only made our descent into sadness slower.

I took Brody's hand and held it a moment, touching each callous and each line as if I were following a map.

He brought it up to my cheek and caressed it.

I'd half expected him to say something right then and there. After all, the Brody I knew was blunt and didn't believe in dancing around something, especially if it was bugging him. That was, until this whole revelation about us came out. Now, I wasn't quite sure if I did still know him.

He stood up instead. "I'm going to make some coffee."

I finally sat up. "Good idea."

I went into the bathroom for a shower. While I rinsed my hair, the door opened and I recognized Brody's figure through the pebbly glass as he entered. I turned off the water, wrung out my hair, and stepped out. He held out a towel and wrapped me in it.

"What are we doing?" I blurted out, my thoughts getting ahead of me.

"I don't know."

"Shouldn't we?"

He turned me to face him, his arms still around me. "Look," he said, "I came here because I wanted to and you told me to stay, so I did. I don't know what's going to happen. All I know is that this is the first time I've been able to sleep in weeks. But I'm not going to pretend that this is all good. We both know we crossed a line here. I'm not deciding anything. I don't want to. I think we should hang tight until our shift is over. Then, we can talk."

I took a deep breath. Despite knowing that what had happened last night was a movement in the direction of chaos, I didn't want to start the day this way. I didn't want things to be off-kilter and I was already beginning to miss the pleasantness of waking up to the sound of his voice and the sight of his face.

I leaned forward and kissed him softly, then touched my forehead to his. "Okay."

"Okay," he echoed. "Shake a leg. Let's get caffeinated and head out."

I dressed in my black blazer, white button-down, black slacks, Chelsea boots and threw my hair into a bun. When I got downstairs, my eyes fell on a bowl of black cherries in the middle of the dining room table. "Where did those come from?" I asked, a smile lighting on my lips.

"I took a run this morning. Stopped at that farm stand on Maple and picked these up." Brody plucked one from the bunch and pulled the fruit off the stem. He offered it to me.

I shook my head. "Not a fan of cherries. But if you had listened to me that time you bought me cherry cola, you'd know that."

He chuckled and ate the cherry. "Guess that means you never learned to tie a stem in a knot with your tongue, huh?" he asked while chewing.

"After last night," I said, stepping up to him and scoffing. "What do you think?"

Brody leaned in and our lips connected for the last time.

I focused on the job, forced myself to look past the eyes of the man I'd allowed to sleep next to me, a man who I had always had the deepest friendship for and trusted. Things were jumbled now and although I knew only thinking about it would make things harder, I couldn't help it.

For his benefit, Brody went about the day as if it was like any other day. He kept his gruff sarcastic humor about him, even joked with some of the guys at the station as though everything was fine. While I didn't know what they were saying, I was sure they were asking about how he and Carmen were doing in that big old house of theirs. They didn't know he was living in his own place. They definitely couldn't know about where he'd spent last night.

By lunchtime, I'd forced myself to put it in the back of my head and act as I always did. We'd gone out to follow-up on the convenience store robbery from the week before and were stopping to grab some food at a nearby gas station. As Brody went in to collect our lunch, my cell phone rang. I didn't even bother to check the number before answering. If I had, I probably wouldn't have picked it up.

"This is Raleigh."

"Hey, Liz," Josh said.

"Hey," I answered, glancing toward Brody in the store. He was at the cash-out desk and gave me a smirk which I tried to return.

"Listen, I know you're probably in the middle of something but I would really like to talk to you tonight if you're free."

I stared down at my shoes and bit my lip. "What's on your mind?"

"I was going to tell you that I got you that David Hasselhoff autograph you always wanted."

I rolled my eyes. "Gross."

"And I've been thinking about taking up skateboarding for my daily commute."

The thought of Josh and his large frame riding a skateboard made me chuckle. "Didn't think you were coordinated enough for that."

"I'm not. But rollerblading! That could work. All the cool kids are doing it around here."

I scoffed. As much as I enjoyed his voice and exchanging banter like the good ole days, my insides squirmed with the understanding of his call. "Something's wrong, isn't it?"

He paused. "Let's say that things aren't working out here."

"Oh."

"Yeah."

I looked over at Brody again as he pushed out the glass doors.

"Listen, I have to go," I said. "I'll call you later, okay?"

"That's fine. I'll talk to you soon."

I said the same and hung up before Brody climbed in and dropped a paper bag in my lap. "Here's your daily dose of mercury, with an apple to keep those pesky doctors away," he said.

I unwrapped the tuna fish sandwich and sipped my Coke, not particularly hungry.

Brody watched me, taking a big bite of his Italian sub. He swallowed. "You okay?"

"Yeah. Why?"

"You've got this sick look on your face; like you ate cherries or something."

"I'm fine," I smiled. "It's a headache."

"'A headache', huh?" he echoed. "You're still thinking about what I said this morning, aren't you?"

"No, I'm not."

"Yeah, you're real convincing."

There was static on the radio and the dispatcher came on. A domestic disturbance call toward the strip downtown. We both knew the address: Rafe and Adair Dolan. The court case had probably pushed him over the edge.

I answered the radio and Brody started the engine. As we drove, I thought more and more about Josh's phone call and knew I shouldn't keep it to myself. Above all else, we needed to be honest with each other. He had told me where Carmen stood with their separation. It was only fair to keep him in the loop concerning Josh.

The worst thing about it all was that I missed Josh like I missed oxygen. I missed our Sunday classic movie nights, our summer trips to his family's cabin in Northern Maine. I missed his Eggs Benedict, the smell of his shampoo, and the sound of his laugh. Those things were a part of my life for nearly four years and they were all suddenly stripped away from me. Talking with him on the phone now had hurt more than it had comforted me. As soothing and observant as Brody was, he wasn't Josh and that chasm that had developed from him leaving me was still there.

"Josh called me," I said, afraid to look at Brody. "He wants to talk."

Brody's expression sobered but he didn't look at me and I couldn't read his eyes behind his sunglasses. "This isn't really the time to do this."

I clammed up, knowing he was right. We were about to go into a house where we knew assaults happened often and were brutal. We weren't sure if we were going to find Adair alive or not. This was no time to think about relationship shit.

"Did you tell him?" Brody asked suddenly.

"No."

"Huh?"

"I said, 'NO'!" It was hard to hear each other over the revving engine and the blaring siren.

"*Are* you going to tell him?" This time, he glanced at me out of the corner of his eyes. I think he might have stared if we weren't cruising at seventy miles per hour down a busy road in downtown Flintland at midday.

"Were you planning on telling Carmen?"

He spun the wheel to the left at the next light, not saying anything.

"My point exactly."

"Never mind," he yelled, "I was right before: we shouldn't talk about this now."

Brody pulled the car up beside a brick block of buildings, sheltered by tall oaks. It was an area of town where several stores used to be. The economy in Flintland, like most of the Northeast, had suffered under the Coronavirus outbreak a couple years before. Most businesses were closed out, others were still in the process of flat-lining. The people who lived around here appeared to be doing the same.

I notified dispatch that we'd arrived at the location and Brody and I stepped out. The winter silence was disturbed by the sounds of yelling from inside a white two-story cape-style house opposite the brick buildings. It looked picturesque from outside: windows framed by lacy curtains, window boxes filled with evergreens and red berries under the front windows and even a little Christmas tree set up on the front porch, left over from the holiday. We knew inside it would be a completely different story.

Brody took the lead, heading straight for the burgundy front door while I followed. He must have noticed something in my gaze enough to think I was still concentrating on our conversation in the car.

Brody beat his fist on the door. "Flintland PD! Open up!"

The yelling ceased. I listened for footfalls to signal someone's approach but nothing happened.

Brody slammed on the door again. "Mr. Dolan, open up! I'm not going to count to ten!"

Glass shattered inside and a woman screamed.

I went for my gun immediately as Brody shouldered the door in. I maneuvered inside first while Brody covered me. A suede chair littered with crumbs sat directed toward a television, its volume turned down. Chairs at the dining room table were knocked over. Spotted along the floor leading down the hall were dark, wet spots of something I knew wasn't ketchup or old coffee. There was a whimper coming from the room at the end. "Down there," I whispered to Brody.

"Stay behind me," he said, moving out in front and pinning himself to the cream-colored walls. We peered into the first doorway.

The kitchen was dotted with appliances from the sixties that looked to somehow still be functioning. A woman was curled up, bleeding on the floor. Shards glinted on the laminate tiles around her. She looked up at us with teary eyes and said, "No! I don't care that they called you." Her lips slurred, dragging against her teeth as she tried to talk. "He didn't mean it! He promised he'd change—"

I snagged a kitchen towel from the rack and crouched down next to her to assess her injuries. Rafe had broken a bottle over her head. Speckles of green glass dotted her hair and rivulets of blood raced down her face. Her right eye was already swollen shut.

Brody asked, "Where'd he go?"

"No! You can't take him!" she cried.

Brody put up his hands. "We're going to have a little talk. That's all."

"Like hell we are," I growled as I pressed the dishtowel against the cut in her head. My hand was instantly stained red. I looked around the room, my eyes catching on an open drawer near the sink.

We'd inspected this house time and time again and knew that the Dolan's kept a gun, though Rafe had never been stupid enough to use it against his wife. "It's for neighborhood prowlers," he'd explained time and time again. It was registered and had never been used in any felonies. They used to keep the gun in that drawer.

I nodded toward the open drawer. "Hey, didn't we seize that?"

Brody shook his head. "It's in her name. Couldn't legally confiscate it unless it was used in the assaults."

"Well, now that scumbag is armed," I said.

"He's not a scumbag! Don't call him that!" Adair wailed, even as she leaned into me for support.

Brody finished checking the remainder of the house. "It's clear. I think he snuck out the back door. Call the bus. I'll get a look out there."

I pulled out my radio. "Wait for me. I'll be right there." When I turned back to him, he'd already gone.

I pressed the button and reported to dispatch, telling them we needed an ambulance and back up, that the suspect was likely armed. When I was finished, I forced the towel into Adair's hands. "Hold this on your head. The ambulance is on its w—"

A gunshot exploded from the back of the house. I leapt to my feet, my ears ringing, Adair's crying like white noise. Sprinting for the hall, I shouldered through the ajar back door, my stomach in my throat.

Nothing. No suspect. No Brody.

I sputtered into the radio, "Shots fired at seventeen Old Angelina Way…"

"He's running!" Brody shouted, appearing from behind a fence near the edge of the property.

"Where?"

"He went into the neighbor's yard. This way!" He took off in that direction and I followed.

My heart hammered as we passed over a hill into a yard littered with children's toys. All I could think of was how glad I was that none of the kids were outside. I updated dispatch to our position and caught up with Brody at the corner to the neighbor's house. "You good?"

"He was way off. Probably drunk."

I turned and noticed a black coat vanish behind a shed into another yard. "There!"

"You keep on him. I'm going to try and cut him off," Brody said and veered off to my right.

I charged ahead. The sounds of sirens called across the air. My hands were cold but firm on my pistol.

Rafe didn't know what he was doing. He was panicking and probably desperate. There was no way he'd escape conviction after something like this. He was going to go away for a long time if he got caught and he knew it.

I rounded the corner toward the street front and got my full view of Rafe as he ran away from me. Rafe Dolan was a big man, at least six-foot three and over two hundred pounds. It made him a slow runner but not someone I was eager to catch up to either.

"Rafe Dolan! Freeze!" I yelled after him.

Rafe turned, his eyes wild and swung the gun around toward me. I ducked behind a parked car moments before the weapon went off. The windshield in the car shattered, followed by the one in the back, the tempered glass instantly splintering over my head. I glanced out briefly from behind the fender. Rafe was running again.

If I got out to chase him, I'd lose cover. The only other car parked on the street was a few spaces from me. I had to risk it though. Rafe headed toward the main thoroughfare.

Where the fuck was Brody?

I got to my feet and ran, spewing words into my radio. "Suspect is heading north on Apollo Road toward intersection of the River Road. I repeat: suspect is heading toward River Road!"

River Road intersected with Church Street and eventually, Main. Rafe was heading into the center of Flintland where pedestrian traffic was thicker. More people would be in danger if we didn't stop him soon.

As soon as I caught up to the next car parked on the street, I planted both feet and held my weapon firmly in front of me, aiming for Rafe's center mass. "Rafe Dolan! Put your hands where I can see them!"

He briefly glanced over his shoulder as he slowed his steps.

That's when Brody made his move from behind the house in front of Rafe. He moved from cover; his Glock aimed at Rafe's head as he stalked out. "Drop the gun, Dolan!" he barked.

Rafe immediately spun back toward Brody in surprise. Throwing his hands into the air, he let the gun clatter onto the sidewalk.

"On your knees!" I yelled, carefully walking toward Rafe, keeping my pistol on him.

The suspect fell forward onto his hands and knees. Brody went in for the handcuffs. He glanced at me as he wrestled them from his belt and put them on Rafe. "You good?"

"Oh, yeah. I'm good," I panted, staring Rafe down. Once I was close enough to the two of them, I kicked the gun away. "Fucker tried to shoot me."

Rafe stared down at the sidewalk with blank eyes. I couldn't discern any emotion from them: not disappointment, not anger, not…anything.

Brody read Dolan his rights.

An ambulance siren echoed distantly across the blue sky as I turned to collect Rafe's gun. I frowned when I found it and picked it up. "Brody?"

Brody paused in his reading of rights. "What?"

"This isn't the Dolan's gun."

"On your feet!" he grunted to Dolan as he pulled the big man up before turning his attention back to me. "What do you mean?"

"They had a registered Walther P22, a defense gun. This is a Smith and Wesson 9 mil."

I hadn't actually looked in the kitchen drawer to check if the gun was missing, I realized. I'd assumed that it was because the drawer was ajar. The stupidest thing an officer could do was make an assumption, to not look, to not make sure…. I hadn't been paying attention, not fully. My mind had wrestled with romance, guilt, and selfish thoughts.

The gunshot was loud. All I remembered was turning my head and watching Brody crumpling on the sidewalk.

I swung the gun up at Dolan, screaming for him not to move, wildly searching for a hidden weapon but finding nothing in his still handcuffed hands.

Red emerged from the corner of my vision. Adair stalked up the sidewalk, holding the Walther 22 and aiming it at me. I threw a hand out mere seconds before she pulled the trigger again.

Pain erupted in my shoulder as it split open. The force of the shot sent me reeling, barely catching myself as I buckled onto the cement. Blood bloomed over my shirt. Every breath from my lungs seared. Dazed and shrouded in pain, I gazed up in time for Adair to run by. "Run, Rafe!" her frantic voice echoed against the trees as their foot falls chased up the sidewalk away from us.

Every ounce of energy forced me to twist my body so I could look at my partner. "Brody!" I tried to scream, my voice failing me.

He didn't respond. He was on his back, feet quivering.

Getting up on my hands and knees was brutal. Everything on my right side from my neck down to my right arm was throbbing. I crawled on hands and knees, my panic like a caged animal bucking for release. The sirens were so close, yet so far away. I couldn't move fast enough.

Seconds stretched. Each inch took a year to negotiate. *Come on!* I screamed at myself.

Blood rippled from the gaping hole in Brody's throat, coating his neck and his chest in sheets. He gagged as his mouth filled with the dark liquid. I fumbled for his wrist and felt his pulse, squelching beneath me. I reached for my radio but couldn't find it. It had fallen somewhere. "Somebody call an ambulance!" I screamed, swiveling my head left and right.

A few people on the other side of the street were already on their phones. No one dared move closer.

My own strength was waning. My hands were cold, even coated in Brody's blood. I fought to stay focused on him. I pressed my hand over his wound and a sob ruptured through my throat as the blood oozed between my fingers.

"Brody! Can you hear me? Brody!"

He coughed and gasped like a fish out of water. "Can't breathe…," he rasped. Red dribbled down his cheeks.

"Look at me. I'm here. I'm not going anywhere."

But he wasn't looking at me. His eyes had rolled back into his head. I pressed on his throat harder. His body settled, his hand going lax in mine.

"No! Don't! Don't you fucking dare!"

His coughing died away. His blood continued to rush through my fingers, even as I swore and pleaded, hoping, praying that there was some time left. That he wasn't gone.

I whispered his name over and over, looking for a flicker of life, a sense of recognition.

Nothing.

Time stopped moving.

And then it sped up. Suddenly, there were hands on my arms, guiding my numb legs up and onto my feet. I turned my head and the world took longer to turn with my eyes. An ambulance had arrived. Lights from a half dozen cop cars flickered all around us. I recognized Officer Stoddard's lean face in mine as he asked me questions though I didn't answer them. Pain had enveloped all of me at that point. Someone moved me to the back of an ambulance to sit. I stared at the sky as storm clouds rushed in over the buildings.

At some point, Captain Vance came. Someone covered Brody's

body with a black sheet. His hand stuck out: the hand that belonged to the arm inked with his crowned skull.

Vance rode with me to the hospital, his large, careful hands enveloping mine on the gurney. He told me they had BOLO's out for Adair and Rafe, that they wouldn't get far.

I didn't care. Nothing mattered anymore. Brody was gone forever.

TWENTY-THREE

NOW

Afternoon light deepened into a wild orange that was unnatural for a bitter winter day or perhaps it was. Everything else in the world was upset. It was hard to tell what was normal now.

I spent much of the next few minutes reminiscing on the ache and the emptiness that had followed in the wake of Brody's death. Lennox had pushed and pushed so he could be proven right and in doing so, had reopened the worst of my wounds from that day. He'd made me remember in exact detail that horrible moment when I'd lost my best friend.

While I'd lagged behind preferring to relive the horror alone, Lennox had pushed on ahead in the apple orchard, wanting to keep his attention on the road. Was he at all remorseful for dredging up these memories? I couldn't say. He hid all of his feelings behind a perfect mask of apathy.

"Hey."

I looked up. Lennox had paused.

"What's up?" I whispered.

He pointed into the distance. "See that?"

I squinted. At the T-intersection ahead of us on the River Road, there was a three-story brick motel, the Riverside Arms. It was Flintland's equivalent of a Motel 6. Lots of transients stayed there as well as a few yeartime residents who got a special rate and worked part time for it. I remembered the place from the job: numerous calls for drug-related activities. On the top floor facing the intersection in front of us, there was an open window.

"Trackers are in there," Lennox said. "And they've got a spotter."

"How do you know?"

"They did the same thing in Bangor. The trackers set up in a building on a road leading into town and watched the area from a lone open window."

I held my breath. Someone was probably watching the River Road into town, keeping guard. But why Flintland? It was strange that trackers would still be here, when they were in Brummel a couple days before. That would mean they were heading north. Why would they bother? Elden had made it seem as though everyone in Maine was trying to get south to escape. Wouldn't trackers have followed the majority of the populace trying to find attached people among them?

No, I realized, as I spotted a familiar Toyota parked in the Riverside Arms parking lot. My sister's car. They knew about me. They knew about Prisca, Lennox, and Tamiko. If we were here, there were probably others. They were probably up here searching for anyone that might have stayed behind.

"How are we going to do this?" I asked.

He shrugged. "You know this town better than I do. What's your take?"

I studied the route ahead. River Road was our straightest shot toward Flintland Greens, where the police station was, and from there, toward Brody's home in Upper Vale. If we went further into the Reef and stuck to the little back roads, there was a chance we wouldn't be spotted until we made it past The Riverside Arms. Then, again, we had no idea how many people were in this tracking group. Just because one had set himself up in the motel didn't mean there weren't others patrolling nearby.

"Stick close to the buildings," I decided. "The afternoon sun banks pretty heavily to the left side of that motel, so the right faces of those buildings will be more in shadow. Plus, the setting sun will be in their eyes. We should be able to slip through easier."

Lennox nodded. "Sounds like a plan to me."

We moved toward the west, in an attempt to move down the smaller roads in The Reef. The grove of apple trees gave us black objects to blend in with against the white snow. I held my breath intermittently, leading Lennox toward the cluster of homes behind the Riverside Arms.

There was an open section of road between the trees and the town. We had to move carefully here. There was nothing to hide behind until we got to the houses. Crouched at the base of an apple tree, I carefully checked to make sure the coast was clear before I bolted the distance to cover. My leg flared angrily with the movement. By the time

I hunkered against the asbestos siding of a blue house, I wanted to take my leg off.

Both Lennox and I stayed in our respective places for a moment, waiting for some sign of movement in the window of the Riverside Arms. We were rewarded with silence.

I waved to Lennox. He darted from his spot.

A loud crack echoed across the sky. Lennox was on his stomach, yelling. I panicked and glanced up to the building above, staying in hiding. There was movement in the murkiness there.

"Come on!" I urged.

Lennox writhed on the ground, his hands clutching at his leg. "Go!"

Descending boots thumped on stairs next door. They were coming. Soon enough, they'd reach the ground floor.

I limped to Lennox and scooped my arm under his. "Get up!"

His breaths came in short painful rasps. "Shattered…my knee."

Blood was soaking the snow beneath him.

He shook his head as I tried to get him up one more time. "I'll only leave a blood trail. They'd find us. Get out of here, Raleigh."

"I said 'Get the hell up'!" I forced him to his feet and we hobbled together.

The door to the Riverside Arms squeaked open as I pulled Lennox into cover. It wasn't over. We still had a network of homes to navigate and lose ourselves in before they found us. Now, we were giving them a trail to follow.

Lennox's weight was excruciating on my already injured leg. His tall frame leaning on me made me rub against the alley walls and kept my feet sliding against the soft snow. We turned down an intersecting back alley and our combined weight came out from under us on some ice beneath a leaking gutter. I hit the pavement hard. Fuzzy bright spots blurred my vision.

Footsteps crunched in the alleyway we'd come from, slow and cautious.

I gripped Lennox's jacket and hauled him up. He pushed me roughly away and I fell on my side. "Go! You idiot!" he exclaimed.

A shout of alarm rose up, bouncing off the brick walls.

I staggered to my feet and ran, cold pervading every inch of my body. I didn't know where I was going, panic purely driving me. I took each twist and turn I came across, squeezing between homes, cutting along chain link backyard fences, and skirting through alleys. All the while, I tried to listen. It was hard to over the blood pumping in my ears. Had they found Lennox? They had to have. They were right behind us.

As I slowed down to try and catch my breath, a clanging from somewhere behind me jump-started my heart. Scuttling into a dark passage between two buildings, I crouched down and wedged myself as close to the back as I could. My coat scraped against the bricks and I closed my eyes, praying that no one had heard, praying that they were still too far away.

The sounds got closer. There was no talking. Talking would have made me more at ease. Someone was about to come into view and I had no idea who. I'd stuffed myself in here and even if I'd wanted to take him by surprise, my rustling around would give me away first. I stayed put.

Someone passed into view and vanished as quickly as they'd appeared. I waited, silent and still, figuring they must have noticed me at the last moment. But they hadn't. After the sounds of footsteps were gone, I wiggled my way out of the narrow crevice and into the empty backstreet.

Something heavy rammed against my head and as I collapsed, I realized that the sounds of the footfalls hadn't dwindled, but had stopped around the corner. They'd been there the whole time, taking cover.

Disoriented, I blindly kicked out but missed. Seconds later, the hard steel toe of the tracker's boot connected with my stomach. The pain spread through my ribs like a burst of fire. I flipped and landed on my back, staring up at the strip of blood orange sky between the buildings.

This is where I'm going to die.

I gasped and tried to speak but the wind was knocked out of me. Every time I thought I was ready to get it back, the tracker would kick me again. The alleyway around me spun and rocked as though I were on a boat lost in a storm. I put up a hand feebly, hoping it would keep him from striking me again.

I caught a strip of a face from beneath a hood, young eyes full of fear. He was no older than twenty and scared. "Wait," I tried to say, although my voice wasn't cooperating with me.

He had paused and that pause was long enough.

A wooden bat clobbered my attacker in the face. Bones and cartilage crunched. He fell beside me and curled into himself like an injured animal, crying and yowling.

Hands gripped my shoulders and helped me to my feet.

I gasped at Lennox. His right pant leg was soaked through with red as was the right side of his face. A nasty gash stretched over his eye, bone glistening beneath the blood.

I coughed, my oxygen finally returning to me along with the hollow ache of every kick I'd endured. It made me want to drop to the ground again, but Lennox's grip was firm on me. It kept me upright. "We've got to keep moving," I gasped, taking his hand.

He looked down at it as if I'd latched onto him with a robot arm.

"Lennox, let's go!"

"I'm not him," came his meek voice.

The sound was so little. I turned back around. I dropped his hand. "What?"

"He's not me."

"Brody?"

Lennox shook his head like a child and I instantly understood.

"Lynn?"

His eyes focused a little more. Then, he nodded.

A series of shouts rose up over the buildings.

I grabbed Lennox's hand again and pulled him along behind me.

What the hell was I doing? Lynn had taken over Lennox. He was gone and she was deeply disturbed. But she had saved my life. I couldn't abandon her, no matter what my rationality told me.

Lynn stopped behind me. My arm was almost yanked from my socket. She'd fallen on the cobblestones, holding her leg. It was as if she'd forgotten how pain felt and was now remembering. She'd dropped the bat and put one of Lennox's hands to his head to caress the cut before staring at the blood on her fingers. "It's like I remember," she said.

Shadows rocked on the brick walls behind us. I grabbed Lynn's shoulder and hauled her to her feet. "We have to keep moving."

"No," she said, remaining where she was. "He's still here."

"Lynn, listen to me: Lennox is gone but you're here."

She tipped Lennox's head slightly. "No. He's not."

Someone appeared around the bend in front of us and all of my fear reached up to choke me. "Please!" I urged through gritted teeth. "Don't give up."

"But he's alone, all alone there. I can't leave Lennox," she said. She pulled out of my grasp and turned to the sounds of the advancing group. I tripped as I turned and made down the nearest crack between two houses. The last thing I saw of her was her sitting down on the pavement. Lennox's voice hummed behind me. Even as the tune faded, I recognized it: the Care Bear's countdown.

My ears burst with the sound of gunfire at number two. My boots scratched and scrabbled on the snow and ice as I ran for my life. Within minutes, I'd thoroughly lost myself in the maze of homes. I wasn't sure how much closer I was to River Road or Flintland Greens and I couldn't catch my breath. Everything hurt and all I wanted to do was drop to the ground and rest. There was no use in continuing to run. I had to find a place to wait them out.

I tried the nearest door. The knob stuck; it was locked. I moved down the road, trying several more doors. Each one was shut tight. Finally, I reached the nearest street front with a corner shop and shouldered the door open. Bells jingled above as I pushed the door closed behind me.

Damn it.

I weaved around tables and chairs and ducked behind the old fashioned wooden counter top, crouching low to the varnished floor.

It struck me in the darkness what this place was. Rainey's; the bar, the place where Brody and I always got our drinks after shift, the place I'd gone to drink my sorrows away after Josh had left, the place where Brody had found me.... The memories made me sick. On top of all those kicks in the stomach, I could barely hold myself together. I wanted to picture myself anywhere else but here, another place, another time. I didn't have the strength for it now.

But they were coming.

I searched beneath the bar, knowing the owner, an ex-cop who still wished he was on the job, had kept a piece there. It was gone. Rainey had probably taken it with him when he'd left.

Noise outside put me on edge once again. I crept along, staying low and headed for the kitchen door. There were knives inside. I'd left my bag in the alley after Lynn had saved me, my only weapon inside. I needed something to defend myself with.

The front door bells chimed as I'd passed through the kitchen door. I rounded an island counter top and sunk low, keeping my back to it. I was out of sight, but not for much longer. I glanced up at the knife block on the countertop in front of me.

There was an exit to my right. It opened up in the alley on the other side. Problem was, I didn't know if there'd be anyone waiting for me out there. I tried to steady my breath and listened carefully.

"You okay?" someone whispered.

A delayed, "Yes." A cold and eerie "yes". It sounded dead. Did they even think I was a person? A human being? Were they dogs on the scent of a fox? They had killed Lennox/Lynn in cold blood. They weren't going to take me alive, not after what had happened to their tracker in the alley.

The rustle of their winter coats was close. I desperately wanted to peer around the bar to see where they were. Maybe I could go for the knife if they weren't looking. Fear rooted me to my spot.

"Check the kitchen," the first one said. "She could have gone out the back."

I turned my head. How did he know? I stilled my thoughts. Maybe he's a townie. Prisca had mentioned that they were recruiting as they traveled. I couldn't tell anything from his voice. It could have even been Rainey if he wasn't in his sixties and sporting a new hip-replacement.

I tried to keep my wild thoughts in-check as the footsteps got closer. I needed Brody to be my second set of eyes. He had left. He wasn't here. I had to do this myself. I crawled toward the far side of the island counter top as the person came through the doorway. I moved slowly and carefully, hoping not to make any loud noises. I rounded the corner and stilled.

The tracker's footsteps crushed into the carpet as he made his way around to where I'd been sitting.

The back door was right in front of me. All I needed to do was run. My heart pounded like someone striking a kettledrum in my chest. I wasn't sure I could make it.

I clambered to my feet and slammed into the door. The cold outside encased me as the tracker yelled. Disoriented, I swung around the left side of the building and raced for the street. As I hit the pavement, the butt of a gun swung up and cracked me in the forehead.

I dropped with so much force, my bones quivered. The pain wrapped around my head and everything swam in a murky sea of snow and darkening sky. I knew someone was standing over me with a gun.

Angry shouting. He called me a bitch and his fingers raked in my hair.

There was another face. More shouting. And then, a light touch on my chin.

Then, my name. Then, white.

THEN

I was only in surgery for an hour. The bullet came out but left my shoulder a mess. The shot had grazed my clavicle and lodged in my trapezius. Two inches lower and it would have hit an artery. I got my own recovery room where the nurses tried to talk to me, tried to get me to open up to them. The culpability muted me. I should have been the one who died. I was the one who made the mistake. I was the one who hadn't checked for the gun at the Dolan's house. My mistake had cost me the one person I was closest to in the world.

Vance knocked on the door and let himself in as the last nurse was explaining the buttons to call for assistance. I'd refused painkillers. I wanted to feel it, suffer with it. I *deserved* it.

The captain sat with me for a little bit. He'd called my sister, who was on her way from Brummel. He'd also gone to Brody's house and given Carmen the news. Imagining her reaction ripped open a new wound in me. When Vance told her that I was in surgery, she'd begged him to bring her to the hospital. She was outside, waiting.

I was hanging by my fingers on a precipice. The thought of Carmen being so close after all the terrible things I'd done only made me want to crawl further inside of myself. "I don't want to see her," I said, staring at the door.

"Her husband died, God damn it," Vance muttered. "You're going to blame yourself for this as long as you live. I know you. Give her five minutes."

The captain got up and left the room. Moments later, Carmen entered.

She was wearing one of Brody's old plaid shirts, flecked with paint and torn in places, the sleeves rolled up passed her elbows. Her dark brown eyes were shining with tears and her black hair crashed down over one shoulder, frizzy and tangled. Carmen immediately came to my side and took my hand.

Tears washed over me. "I'm so sorry," I said, the words tumbling over themselves in my mouth. I couldn't stop repeating them, even after she told me to stop, even after her own sobs joined mine.

We sat together for so long. It was the most time I'd spent with Carmen in months and I hated myself immediately once again with that thought. While Brody and I were partners, I'd grown to be great friends with Carmen. We used to hang out so much, sometimes the two of us, but mostly with Brody and then, with Josh, too. Ever since Josh's job promotion and the revelation of Brody's and Carmen's failing marriage, we'd visited less and less with each other. Maybe that's why it was easier to betray her, why it was so easy to ignore the fact that she and Brody were still married.

My sister came eventually, blissfully before any questions departed Carmen's lips. She was going to have them. She was going to want to know what happened in detail, as much detail as internal affairs would and the rest of the community. Thankfully, she had enough sense to give me my space for the rest of the evening.

Captain Vance's wife had come bearing strong arms and listening ears to drive Carmen home and make sure she wasn't alone. I suppose I never realized how close the Vance's were with Brody and Carmen but that was my fault to a tee; ignoring the importance and closeness of other people's relationships. Carmen's family would be flying in later that night. At least she wouldn't be alone. That was all that mattered.

When Dana took up the vigil, she was somehow as cool as a cucumber. It was exactly what I needed; no more crying, no more being faced with my mistakes for the evening. She pulled the blanket up over me and let me sleep for the rest of the evening, even turning away an anxious Lennox, who was called in to try and get an IA statement as soon after the event as possible.

When I awoke, she was reading a copy of Down East magazine, her reading glasses down at the end of her nose. Steaming coffee in a paper cup called to me from the tray next to her. As my vision cleared, I realized that my sister didn't wear reading glasses and she didn't drink coffee.

"Mom?"

She glanced at me, letting the magazine fall into her lap. "Elizabeth."

Audrey Raleigh, now Deering, had changed a lot since the last time I'd seen her over two years ago. My mom had always kept her hair short when we were kids. "I don't have time for this," she'd say as she cut it into a bob time and time again. "I have so many more important things to do." She'd grown it out now, the blonde locks entangled with silver whisps. Her bolt blue gaze was as direct as ever, her cheek bones sharp and tanned by the California sun. Laugh lines that I had no memory of as a teenager had permanently marked her cheeks and chin.

Despite all of this, she didn't look happy now. The depth in her gaze, the one I'd always challenged in my youth, seemed bottomless as she stared at me.

My sister's purse was hanging on the back of the chair my mom sat in. A glance at the window revealed that it was still dark out. Or maybe it was dark out *again.* I had no concept of time anymore.

My mom straightened in the hospital chair. "Can I get you anything? Water?"

I was parched. But the discomfort at having my mother in the room was more pressing at that moment. I shook my head no.

"Your sister called me yesterday. I took the Red Eye here."

That explained things. She had told me so I would see how she'd dropped everything for me, something she'd neglected to do so many times in our past.

"Dana filled me in," she kept going. "I'm sorry about Detective Aritza."

The reminder was like a fresh sting in my heart. I shook my head. "You never even knew him."

"No," she said, her voice unruffled by my comment. "But I know he meant a lot to you." She reached a hand out and took mine. It was bony and cool and strange.

Normally, I would have rebuffed her attempts to try and assuage me. She usually only tried this tactic when she wanted something. But I couldn't, for the life of me, figure out exactly what she would want now. So, I left my hand where it was and uttered, "He did."

Mom brushed a piece of hair behind her ear with her other hand. The diamond ring on her finger was grotesquely huge. "I spoke with him on the phone once. He was protective of you."

"We watched each other's backs for ten years and you only had one phone conversation with him?" I asked.

"Had it been a pleasant one, I think we would have gotten along famously." She said it in a way that made me pause. Maybe she had tried to call the station looking for me and he'd answered. I'd told Brody enough about my childhood and my relationship with my mom that he probably would have said something to set her straight. In my recent memory though, I couldn't think of what that would have been. He'd only been gone for a few hours and I was already starting to forget parts of him.

She glanced over her shoulder at a familiar backpack hanging on the door to the bathroom. "I stopped by your house before coming and packed you some new clothes. The doctors threw away your old ones. They were covered in blood and the shirt was cut to ribbons."

I froze. "How do you know where I live?"

"Your sister gave me directions."

I didn't remember how I'd left the house that morning. The only thing I knew was that Brody and I had spent the night together previously, and I hadn't bet on anyone else walking into my personal space.

As if she knew what I was thinking, my mom gave my hand a gentle squeeze. "You loved each other. I see that."

The words deflected off me. Suddenly, all my shields were back up, my back bristling with the revelation. "What do you mean?"

"It doesn't take a detective to know what happened in your house last night, Elizabeth. Two coffee cups at the kitchen table, a bowl of fruit you've hated since you were a child, a man's shirt on the bed and his deodorant in the bathroom... Unless Josh is suddenly back from California and is now wearing Tom Ford's Tuscan Leather, it looks like you and Detective Aritza slept together."

I snatched my hand away from her. "Get out."

Mom stiffened in her chair. "I cleaned up. I know what this could mean for you if someone were to find out."

"What did you do with his stuff?"

"I put it in a shoe box in the bedroom closet. I put the sheets in the wash. The coffee cups in the dishwasher."

The thought that my house had been purged of Brody's presence sent new waves of rage through me. Worse, the pain in my shoulder was flaring. Tears coursed down my face from the combination. "Please leave," I gasped.

My sister opened the door at this moment. She looked between me and my mom and then rounded the bed to my side. "What did you say?" Dana snapped at our mother.

Mom stood abruptly and gathered her coat from the hook on the wall nearby. "I'm staying at the local Hilton. Call me when they release her to go home." She stopped in the doorway and looked back at me one more time. "I was only doing it to protect you." Then, she left.

Dana pressed the call button for the nurse and held me as I continued to cry.

TWENTY-FOUR

NOW

A cool wet cloth was draped over my forehead as I came to. My body ached as though I really was shattered and put back together haphazardly. My head pounded and my stomach ached with the slightest movement. Candlelight bloomed on the pale green walls. My eyes adjusted and as they did, my hope that I was once again in my own bed at home was swiftly snatched from me. It was not my house; someone else's apartment from the looks of it. The smell of tarry pungent hospital coffee from my memory was replaced by the sourness of rotting fruit. I focused on a bowl of soft-looking oranges on the tabletop next to me and the tiny swarm of fruit flies lingering there in spite of the cold.

"Liz, can you hear me?"

It sounded like my dad, calling to me from across our house. I looked down at my skinny long legs: bug-bitten, and sneaker-footed as I blazed across the grass to greet him. I turned my head and the blur of grass became the walls and my father's voice came from a face. But it wasn't him. Josh's sobering eyes were there instead.

"Josh?" I murmured, wincing as the throbbing in my head got worse. "You're not real."

He put a hand on my head, gently caressing my hair. "Slow down. You got a pretty bad tap on the head."

My eyes widened and my vision cleared. A *tap*. Not a knock like my dad would have said. "Josh?"

"Yeah, it's me."

I reached for him, my fingers clinging to his arms. He held me to him and I let him. I couldn't breathe, couldn't force my thoughts to slow down as they raced through my head. Eventually, I pulled away.

The Josh that stood before me was not the same as the one I'd known. This one seemed hollower, as if he'd forgotten how to smile. He had lost weight, his frame gaunt. His usually stubbled chin was forested by a beard, and his clothes were dirt-soiled and torn in places. I recognized the shirt; one that I'd given him for his last birthday. I'd sent it to him in Cali. I had told him I needed to be alone, that I wanted to be. I'd driven him away again.

"What are you doing here?" I finally said.

He cleared his throat. "It's nice to see you, too."

I tensed immediately, remembering the trackers at the bar. "My head," I grimaced, reaching up to my forehead. My fingers traced over a thick pad taped to my head.

"Go easy. You've been in and out for a few hours."

I ignored him and tried to stand up. "We can't stay here. It's too dangerous."

"Relax. You're safe with us."

With us? The thought poured over me like icy cold water and I understood.

"Who is 'us'?"

He groaned. "Government trackers. We were following you. We…thought you were one of the Affected ones."

I shook my head. "Affected?"

He frowned. "People who are *seeing* things. Most of them are having hallucinations about dead family, dead friends… They aren't sure whether it's some kind of chemical warfare or something viral. There's been a quarantine effective for anyone with those or similar symptoms."

Affected: this wasn't the first time someone had used that word. It was what the world was calling the people who could see ghosts. It was their word for me. But Brody wasn't with me now and Josh being with these trackers was the only reason I wasn't dead.

"You do know what's going on, don't you, Liz?"

"I know you and your soldiers killed a man back there in cold blood without a second thought." I tried to keep my voice even. "Is that how you 'quarantine' people?"

Josh swallowed. "Some of our volunteers are young and stupid. They're scared and they react badly because of that."

"There's no excuse," I said, my jaw locking. "Not for killing an innocent person."

Josh's eyes widened. "That 'innocent person' had bashed one of those kids' heads in."

"Because that kid was trying to kick a hole in my chest!"

"He didn't know who you were." Josh sighed.

I lifted my shirt high enough to show my abdomen. Purple and black bruises marbled the skin on my left side. "It was an unprovoked attack," I coughed. "Lennox was defending me."

"Jesus," he muttered as he reached out to me. "I didn't know."

I cringed. "I don't want an apology. I want you to open your eyes. Some of these Affected are people we used to know, Josh. Why are you hunting them down like they're animals?"

"Because they're *not* the people we used to know."

The seriousness in his eyes made me sick to my stomach.

I forced myself to listen as Josh filled me in on what I'd missed. Thanks to Prisca's group, I'd learned that roughly eighty-five percent of the population were Affected. Josh's revelation was much more sobering.

Much of the West Wing had been afflicted, including the President, Vice President, and Secretary of State. The Speaker of the House had taken over after a decision was made that the others were unfit to lead and immediately assumed a defensive measure by closing off the borders of the United States. His next step was quarantine, gathering as many Unaffected members of the CDC and WHO to set up centralized points for study and experimentation in each region. Since the army and military had also been upset, a nationwide broadcast was sent out to recruit civilian volunteers for the cause of quarantining the Affected population.

No one mentioned ghosts. It was an outbreak, a possible virus according to the few media outlets still able to get the word out. Those showing symptoms were encouraged to paint an X on their doors so that they could be extracted for treatment. Several people had taken to violence which recruits were told was an uncontrollable symptom of the virus. Therefore, all measures of safety and caution were to be taken, including pulling the trigger if it was necessary.

The New England states established a base to take Affected people in Boston in what was once a football stadium. They'd remodeled and partitioned it into a giant makeshift hospital. It was known simply as Gideon. Due to their limited space, several smaller centers were set up in Connecticut, southern Vermont, inland Massachusetts, and most recently, here in Flintland, in an effort to stem the constant flow of patients into Gideon.

Everything he told me was like stone after stone being set on my shoulders. There was some semblance of society still intact, however fractured it was. Everything I'd encountered in the last couple months had led me to believe that life the way I'd known it was over. It was hard to fathom that someone was still in charge, someone was still grinding their coffee beans somewhere, and cooking breakfast like nothing had happened to them.

"You were in L.A. though," I said, everything not quite sinking in yet.

"I came back a month before it happened. I wanted to talk with you. I'd hoped you'd maybe changed your mind. Your sister said you'd left for a while to take some time. She wouldn't tell me where you'd gone."

Dana had kept her promise even though I was now wishing she hadn't. She more than anyone, had wanted Josh and I to get back together, even after the whole awful truth had spilled out. I still hadn't healed and the idea of accepting Josh back into my life after Brody's death made me hate myself.

"I needed to get away from everything that reminded me of Brody and the job…." I added, realizing how it sounded. "I felt trapped. That was my life and it was suddenly all gone."

Josh's green eyes dimmed. "I never wanted to corner you. I wanted to be there so I could…be there."

"I wasn't ready to talk about it."

"Obviously," he whispered and stood up.

I tried to ignore the hollowness in his voice and glanced around the room. "Where are we?"

"You remember that old Thai restaurant that used to be downtown?"

One of our first dates. A thread of humor pulled through me at the memory. "Yeah. The lady had a microwave in the kitchen but no stove, the Pad Thai came with the option of peanuts in a can…."

"…provided by whoever that random old guy was that stood there the whole time."

"He definitely wasn't a waiter."

"He had overalls on! He was like a plumber or a farmer or something."

I somehow found the strength to smile. "Yeah. That was a date night for the books."

"Well, after the Thai restaurant left, the new owners remodeled the space into a tea shop. We're in the upstairs apartment."

That was near the Commons and my home. I desperately had

the urge to look out the windows and take in what had once been my neighborhood, houses I'd driven by on a daily basis, neighbors I recognized but never learned the names of. But it would be empty and nothing like my memories.

I put a hand to my head and laid back down on the bed. "I feel sick."

"You've probably got a concussion. Not to mention you're dehydrated. Lie back down and I'll get you some water."

Josh vanished through the door nearby and I sat up again, investigating my surroundings. If my house was that close, I could get there and resupply. I still had to find Brody. I still had no idea if he'd even made it to his old house or if he'd found Carmen.

I scooched toward the far end of the bed and glanced out the window. There was no one out front watching the street. Heavy snow was collecting along the roads. If I could get out, traveling would be difficult. Sitting up made my chest catch fire. I wouldn't get far and my reasons for running would immediately be suspicious not to the trackers but to Josh. I had to bide my time before I could make a move.

Worst of all was the notion that I was totally safe if I stayed where I was. Without Brody there to distract me, I could pass as one of them, one of the Unaffected. It would mean I was with a stronger group, and wouldn't need to scavenge for scraps, or stay curled up under a tarp during the cold nights as my only cover. And I'd be with Josh. The reality of that thought hit me hard. There was no forgetting what we'd put each other through. How could we erase that?

And how could I give up on Brody like that?

Returning to my resting position, the door opened moments later and Josh reappeared with a cup of water and a small bowl. "Brought you some soup, too. Nothing too fancy I'm afraid. The kitchen was fresh out of, well, everything."

"You always made good soup," I said.

He set it down on the side table with a scoff. "Trust me; you won't like this. Unless hot water, thyme, and rice noodles are your thing."

"We'll call it minimalist."

There was a strange look in Josh's eyes now, one of suspicion that immediately put me on edge. "That guy you were with; Lennox. Did you know that he was an Affected?"

"You really think that this is some kind of virus?" I spoke. "You know what's out there, right? The Woods, the monsters…"

Josh closed his eyes. "What else could it be if it's not some kind of airborne toxin? It has to be something that's making us all hallucinate all of this."

"It's more than a hallucination, Josh. The Woods are a different realm! I've been in there. It's…terrifying."

Josh looked at me as though he knew more than he was saying. "No one's ever come out of them alive. That's what I've heard."

"And I've watched those wolves kill. They aren't a figment of our imaginations."

For the first time, he actually looked afraid. Josh adventured in some of the most dangerous parts of the world. He did it because it was his job and it had called on him to do so. I'd always admired him, and thought him reckless, for never showing his fear. I couldn't help but shiver now that he actually was.

"Some of the stuff I've seen since it happened…." He cleared his throat. "I *can't* believe. So yeah; when I say it's got to be a hallucination, I hope to God it is."

Josh was like me when it came to religion: he didn't talk about it. While he often explored cultures with profound religious attachment and was dutifully respectful of each one, Josh had rarely brought up the topic of God, of Heaven or Hell or anything remotely serious about them with me; only ever in jest. Even when we talked about the wedding, he was unusually nonchalant about the service and the venue. It went unspoken like a sunrise that's already happened before you've woken for the day.

Someone knocked on the door and it cracked open as Josh turned his head. Someone with a face too dark to make out whispered to him before disappearing.

"Try to get some more rest," Josh said, standing.

"Where are you going?"

He paused. "I have to take care of something really quick. Then I'll be back." He touched my arm.

I held his hand as he made to go. "Don't go out there."

Josh carefully detached my hand. A giant ice block sunk in my chest as he did. "I'll be fine." He left through the door without turning back.

A day I'd thought would be spent in agony was cut mercifully short. I'd somehow managed to escape the throbbing pain of my chest bruises and swam into unconsciousness. I dreamed of an altered version of my home that melded into Brody's and Carmen's with each passing second. I walked from my bedroom, down my stairs and into their living room. It was night. The curtains were closed and as I called to see if anyone was there, Carmen appeared. She was the bubbly, bright, and beautiful friend that I remembered, the one who had lived before all of the turmoil and lies. I turned my head for a second, and only that one. When I turned back, she was holding a knife and her smile was gone. "I knew it was you," she kept saying in a whisper. I'd wake as the knife came down at me.

After these on and off dreams, I woke to the door of my room opening and closing.

"Josh?" I asked in expectation, sitting up.

A woman was staring at me. She was at least ten years older than me though the directness of her gaze was electric. Her blond hair fell in wavy ringlets brushing her shoulders.

"You know, Josh never told me your name," she said, standing up from the bed. "He never actually mentioned that you lived here. But I knew there was a reason he made us hang around this shithole for so long."

I didn't say anything. I wasn't really sure what I could say. There was resentment in her voice and I had an inkling I knew where it came from.

"What did you do to him?" she sneered. "Leave him at the altar? Fuck his best friend?"

I glared. "Sounds like you've been neglected. I'd recognize that whiny tone anywhere."

Her eyebrows rose and she clicked her tongue as she made to leave. "I knew it was something bad. He wouldn't tell me either." She opened the door to Josh. His hand lingered on the knob as he took in her and then me.

"Get out of here," he said to her under his breath. She only rolled her eyes at him as she vanished through the open door.

I carefully swung my legs off the bed, cringing with the movement. "Who the hell was that?"

"Heidi: she runs things when I'm out."

I raised my eyebrows. "How long have you two been together?"

His posture straightened, uncomfortably so. "Who says we are?"

"She hates me."

He rubbed a hand over his beard. "It's been a long time since *we* were together, Liz."

The statement punctured me in a way I hadn't expected. Of

course, we had been separated for a while; which was a mutual decision. Then why did it seem like I shouldn't be here at all?

Instead of saying anything, I let my feet touch the floor and tried to stand up.

"What are you doing?" he asked.

The bullet wound in my leg raged and I burst into coughs at the effort.

As I huffed and puffed, Josh came to my side. "Stop," he said.

I was suddenly reminded of the time he took care of me while I had the flu. The warm memory melted as I cleared my throat. "I need to go," I said. "You've got things to do. I'll get in the way."

I crumpled toward the ground like bricks as I tried to take a step. Josh caught me, a hand awkwardly catching me under one arm, the other grazing my chest. He leaned me back onto the bed and said, "Liz, lay back down. You're not going anywhere like this."

He was right. But I was as stubborn. I tried to push myself back up to my feet and this time, he put a hand on my shoulder to hold me down. "Let me go," I said.

"You're not 'in the way'," he said and shook his head. "Is this about Heidi and me?"

I shook my head, maybe too quickly. "No.... Yes.... I have to find...Dana."

"I'm sure she's fine," Josh assured, glancing out the window. "I'm sure she and Michael and Mark evacuated with one of the big groups in December. They're probably in a community near Gideon."

They were probably fine. I had told myself that ever since we'd found their house empty days ago. I had to believe my sister had survived. After all, she was a lawyer. She was more than capable of caring for herself.

It was Brody that I wasn't sure about. I wasn't sure how long I'd been unconscious with Josh's group. Josh had said a "few hours". How long had Brody been gone searching for Carmen's body? Time seemed so fluid now and the sky always dark. What if those wolves had caught him again?

Josh gently pushed me back down onto the bed and I let him, exhaustion creeping into my body from the slightest movements. "I'll try to get through to anyone in Gideon, find out if they've been registered."

I nodded but I wasn't comforted by the attempt of placation. I needed to get out of here. If we were in the old Thai restaurant that used to be in town, we were less than five miles from Brody's house. If I could get through this window and down to the street, maybe I could—

"Liz?"

I glanced up at Josh's quizzical gaze. "Sorry."

"You don't need to explain," he said, "I'm going to let you get some more sleep." He turned and opened the door.

"Thanks," I said.

He stared at me for a moment and then without a word, left, closing the door behind him.

My gaze returned to the window. I reached out in my mind like I had in the Woods, sifting through my memories of Brody. I focused on the one of our night with Mexican food, dancing.... I wouldn't let myself think about what came after. I was determined to stay in the good of those few moments. "Brody?" I said quietly, hoping he could sense me. "I need you."

I opened my eyes to my own reflection in the window and the snow lighting on the frame outside. The pain in my stomach only grew deeper. I couldn't concentrate.

I lay back on the bed. I needed a breather, a moment to get my stamina back. Then, I'd try to make a break for it.

I didn't remember closing my eyes.

THEN

I dreamed of my first night back in my home after being released from the hospital. After days of doctors poking their heads in and out, nurses constantly asking me how I was doing, they'd let me go. My sister drove me and insisted on staying for the first night and thankfully, didn't call our mom. I still remember Dana's golden hair, highlighted by streetlights and the worried bags under her eyes when she smiled at me.

She led me into the house and helped me up the stairs even when I told her I could do it by myself. I paused in the doorway to my bedroom and stared. She continued past me.

"Everything is already made up for you. I'm sorry I told Mom where you lived and that she intruded. But she did give you clean sheets and a glass of water like when you were a kid," Dana said, with a small smile.

I swallowed hard. The last traces of Brody were stuffed in a box in the closet, a box that Dana knew nothing about. I pushed myself through the wretched ache and nodded. I sat down on my bed and the exhaustion hit me so hard, I could have fallen asleep sitting up. After spending days idly, wishing for movement and a reminder of normalcy, sleep was tempting and the oblivion I'd find in it blissful. I pulled back the sheets and slid beneath the covers. Dana said she'd be sleeping on the couch and shut off the light.

I hadn't expected to sleep a wink like all of those days in the hospital since it had happened, but I did. When I woke to rain and pale afternoon light, I didn't want to move. I didn't want to go outside. I didn't want to show my face. I wanted to stay in this room and remember Brody's and my last day together, like some sort of child refusing to believe it had happened.

I checked my phone. Nearly thirty missed calls, a combination of Vance, Mom, Josh, and a few numbers I couldn't immediately identify. Eventually, I recognized the last four numbers as belonging to one of the phones at the Flintland PD. It was probably Lennox trying to make an appointment for the IA statement. I set the phone back down on the table, face-side down and rolled back over.

I must be dreaming. Tell me I'm dreaming, I thought as I tossed and turned and let sleep take me again, hoping I would wake up, really wake up and turn over to find Brody there.

When darkness had fallen and the neighborhood was quiet, I emerged from my cocoon. I opened the closet and slid the cardboard box out. Inside were the only things that Brody had left behind as we'd quickly gotten ready for work that morning: his tie which he never wore two days in a row, his deodorant which he usually kept in his car, and his undershirt from the day before. I held it close and smelled it. A lingering scent of Brody's cologne was still there.

I left the box sitting in the middle of the floor and walked downstairs to the kitchen. There was a note on the counter from Dana; she'd run home to get a change of clothes and pick up some more groceries. She'd be back.

I made coffee, watching it dribble from the filter down into the glass carafe. I went days without it, not even wanting to settle for the crappy hospital coffee. I craved it. I cried and fought through headaches, wanting it, needing it. It reminded me of Brody, of our morning ritual. It was the intangible piece of him that I had, that I held dear. Something as stupid and as simple as savoring that cup of black coffee was the means to bring him to life again, if only for a little while.

The bowl of cherries sat in the middle of the table where Brody had left it. They were starting to shrivel up and mold.

I had three cups of coffee by the time Dana got back, each one tasting worse than the last. I offered her a mug but she declined.

Jittery for the next few hours, Dana suggested a walk. I didn't want to, still not ready to leave the confines of the house. She put in a movie and for an hour, I feigned interest in a young Tom Cruise flying through the skies in *Top Gun*. Then came the scene of Charlie chasing Maverick in her car, parking on the curb, her confession of having fallen for him. The kiss. I fought back the memory of Brody kissing me as he stepped through my door the other night. With pain thick in my chest, I retired back to the bedroom and the box.

I didn't sleep. I lie awake and held Brody's undershirt to me in bed and thought about how I would visit his body in the morgue in the morning. I thought about Carmen who came again to the hospital though we hadn't talked much at all and how she was more injured than I would ever be. I thought about Josh and his shell-shocked voice when briefly talked with him on the phone the day before. My thoughts kept turning end over end and I kept searching for a switch to turn it off but could never find it.

Finally, at close to two in the morning, I struggled into some clothes, my bullet-wound on fire the whole time, and slipped on my boots. I walked past my sleeping sister and out into the night to be amongst the dark, the stars, and the snow. It was there that I truly was alone, truly could get a breath of fresh air. I stared up at the sky with the understanding that I could break into thousands of tiny pieces at a moment's notice. I don't know why I hadn't already.

TWENTY-FIVE

NOW

"Liz."

My eyes sprung open. Brody's voice was so close, as though it had come from inside my own head. I sat up to a discord of painful fires in my chest. Brody sat in the corner of the room, his head bowed and arms crossed.

"You're okay," I said more to myself than to him.

"Am I?" There was a pause between the two words and as he lifted his head, I detected an emptiness in his eyes that sent a chill through me.

"You found Carmen."

He shook his head.

"No?"

"I got to the house," Brody said, his voice gravelly. "I got all the way there and I stood in front of it for the longest time trying to make myself go inside. But I couldn't. For some reason, I couldn't do it, knowing she was probably…lying there. All this time."

Before I could stop it, the image of Carmen's corpse dashed into my brain. Her body putrefying into the polished wooden floor, skin and muscles melting with decay, revealing only her bones. It made me want to scream, made me want to fling myself from the bed onto the ground, if only to distract myself from such disgusting imaginings.

"I abandoned her, Liz," he said, not looking at me. "When she needed me the most, I wasn't there. I still don't know *why*."

I swallowed.

Putting a hand to his forehead, he sighed. "But I shouldn't have left you. As soon as I heard you in my head, I realized that."

He *had* heard me. Tears pricked my eyes. "I'm okay."

"Clearly you're not." He got to his feet and stepped over to my bedside. "I saw him downstairs: Josh."

I nodded. "He runs this group. They were tracking me and because of that, they killed Lennox."

"What about Prisca and Tomiko?"

"I parted ways with them in Brummel. Lennox followed me, wanting to help. I never should have let him come."

Brody stared at my bloodstained shirt. "Thought I had the guy pegged for a coward. Guess I was wrong."

I sucked on my bottom lip. "Me, too."

Brody turned his head toward the door to my bedroom. "I was listening to Josh's group downstairs. They have a route they're traveling, though I'm not sure why they're heading north away from their base of operations."

"It sounds like the CDC has established a temporary field hospital here in Flintland. Josh called it Elon."

"Whatever it's called, I don't buy that they're out here searching for survivors, not with that arsenal. Plus, they kept mentioning this doctor, someone they needed to bring people back to."

"They're looking for Affected people: people like me."

"Then you're not safe here. We need to leave," Brody said, quietly. This voice was strange and distant.

I pushed against the bed to try and sit up and immediately regretted it. I fell back down. "I can't. Not like this."

Brody's gaze softened. "What the hell did they do to you? Did Josh do this?"

"No! Of—"

"Shh!"

"Of course not," I whispered.

Brody crouched down beside me, the earnestness in his gaze suddenly making me sick. "Listen, Lizzy, I know he was important to you but he's can't be trusted. I listened to some of the things that they've done," he said.

"What, Brody? What did he do?"

"They were talking about how that facility, Elon, is for quarantining those Affected. It sounds like something more than that. This Doctor they keep mentioning…Hruska? Sounds bad. Like Frankenstein bad. Granted, it doesn't sound like the majority of those people they meet along the way ever make it to him."

"Not anyone who puts up a fight, anyway."

"The ones that do though?" Brody's gaze was fierce. "Doc's a neurosurgeon. Isn't hard to guess what kind of experiments he might be running on people there."

The thought made me shiver.

"We need to get you out of here before you end up there or they do to you what they did to Lennox," he said.

I thought about Lennox and my last moments with Lynn in his body. "Something happened before Lennox was…" I couldn't even say *murdered.*

"What?"

"Lynn took hold of him." When Brody kept looking at me strangely, I clarified. "His ghost."

"Okay?"

"When I tried to get her to come with me, she kept saying that Lennox wasn't gone, that he was still there and that she didn't want to leave him alone."

"She was a disturbed girl, Liz."

I nodded.

"We don't know if she even knew what was going on."

Lynn had *seemed* lucid. But Brody had a point. Otherwise, why would she turn around and sacrifice herself like that? It didn't make sense.

"Why did you think of that now?" he bristled. *He's upset about Carmen. It's why he can't sit still.*

"I guess, I wanted some closure."

We sat in silence for a time before Brody got back to his feet and walked to the door. "I'm going to keep an eye on them, try to figure out what they're planning. When I say it's time, you need to be ready to move, Liz. We'll only get one shot of getting out of here without them noticing. In the meantime, get some rest and save your energy."

I nodded. As much as I'd envisioned us sneaking out of this place sooner rather than later, I knew it made more sense to stay where we were. There was no telling what we'd run into out there: more soldiers, wolves, desperate people trying to survive… We were safe here for now. I had to keep Brody's existence a secret. I had to make sure I didn't acknowledge him in front of anyone, especially Josh.

Brody vanished through the door and I closed my eyes to that bleak room once more.

THEN

Captain Vance arranged for an officer to pick me up at my house the next morning. Dana had helped me into fresh clothes which left me feeling like an invalid. I hated not being able to do things myself.

I wasn't expecting there to be news vans waiting when I got to the police station. Officer Jackman opened my door for me and once I was up out of the car, a woman in a black pencil suit and blown out hair marched over to me, shoving a microphone in my face. "Officer Raleigh, tell us your side of the shooting!"

My side? I had avoided the news the last few days though Vance had given me a small heads up that there were "concerned parties" wanting to know more about what happened the day Brody died. I had thought he was talking about Lennox and the city. I wasn't expecting this.

Jackman threw an arm out like a trained body guard, catching the reporter in the ribs as she pushed into my space. I swayed, trying to keep walking toward the doors to the police station and that's when I noticed more of them. A crowd had gathered there, flush with snapping camera flashes and cell phones at the ready to record anything I said.

I stared at the ground, forcing the exasperation down, down, deep down into the abyss where my brain had lingered these last couple days. I needed to not show anything. The media hungered for any speck of emotion, the faintest crumbles of sugar they could spin into vibrant cotton candy for their viewers and readers.

My name erupted from the mass as I stalked toward the doors. Jackman was somehow everywhere at once, suddenly in front of me with stern eyes and quick hands to block off each promising shot of me. Before I knew it, we were inside. A pair of officers were stationed at the doors to keep the reporters at bay. I silently thanked Vance for that foresight.

Jackman walked me up the winding hallway toward the main foyer and then down another hall toward booking and interrogation. I knew the way without being guided. Being heralded here made me feel like I was the criminal in question, the one being accused outright. In a sense, I knew that was the process of being cross-examined by IA.

Lennox was being paid by the city of Flintland and the Sherriff to ask the hard questions, to make sure that everything was done by the book in the case of the Dolan's, to make sure that we weren't at fault somehow for Brody's death. Knowing our history, I doubted he'd be sensitive to me. More or less, I knew what to expect when I walked into that room.

Jackman posted outside of interrogation room one and opened

the glass door. Inside was a nearly empty room, save for a smooth metal table in the middle with three chairs at it. Captain Vance and Lennox occupied two on one side of the table. The empty one on the opposite side was for me.

As soon as I stepped into the dim room and was awash in the familiar blue-green walls and tinted windows, a part of me stuttered. Even Vance's concerned gaze wasn't enough to bring me back. I'd pushed myself down into the void to try and ignore the reporters only to find myself struggling to breathe. I was drowning in here, in the silence, in the knowledge of the upcoming realization that I was about to relive the most horrible day of my life all over again. Lennox was waiting for me to fail, waiting for me to say something that would incriminate myself. And had I not been guilty of something, I could have brushed that aside. But I was guilty. I was at fault and he was going to sniff it out of me.

"Let's start," Lennox said, once I'd sat down. For the first time in a long time, I got the distinct impression that Jack Lennox wasn't impeccably preened for today's important inquiry. Nor had he gelled his hair or ironed his suit. His tie was disheveled, his eyes dull and his chin? God, was that actually stubble? Seeing him like this made me that much more uncomfortable, that much more unsettled for what was about to transpire.

"I want you to take me through the events of the day, Detective Raleigh. I'd like to get a good idea of where you were and how you were the day of the incident."

The incident.

It sounded so minor when it was put like that.

I cleared my throat. I hadn't taken anything for the pain this morning besides ibuprofen, wanting to keep my senses sharp. The bullet wound nipped at me as I faintly retraced my memories of the morning that Brody died. "I got up at six-thirty. Made coffee. Took a shower."

"How were you that morning?"

"Good. Considering…."

"Considering what?"

"My fiancé and I broke things off a few weeks ago. It's been hard. I've been lonely."

Lennox paused, a kind of sourness appearing on his face. "And that morning, you weren't lonely?"

"No."

"Was there someone there with you?"

My heart skipped a beat. "No."

"Then what was so different about that morning as opposed to all the others in the last few months, Detective Raleigh?"

I leaned in. "Have you ever had your heart broken, Lieutenant?"

"I'll ask the questions, Detective," he answered coolly.

Warmth spread across my chest. "My point was that there are some mornings that are better than others. Some mornings, I'm reminded of what I've lost, that there's an emptiness there. Other mornings, like that morning, I enjoy my own company. I have to."

Lennox seemed to accept the explanation, even as each lie made me filthier as it escaped my mouth. "What time did you get to work?"

"Brody and I began our shift around seven-thirty."

"You started at the same time?"

"We *arrived* at about the same time."

"Can you describe what kind of mood Detective Aritza was in that day?"

"He…um…," I fumbled and took a short breath, trying to not think too hard about Brody wrapping me in a towel before work, pouring me coffee, kissing my lips.

"It's okay," Captain Vance said, his voice placating. "That feels like a loaded question anyway, Lieutenant." He shot a glare at Lennox.

"I'm not asking her to recite everything Aritza said that day. I'm asking Detective Raleigh how her partner acted on duty. It could explain any kind of lapse in judgement or lack of reaction that happened."

"He seemed like himself," I said quickly. "Like everything was normal."

Lennox cleared his throat. "There are people you work with that had the impression that you and your partner's relationship was strained. Were the two of you arguing?"

I didn't know what to say. The emptiness that had followed after the convenience store robbery apparently hadn't only been visible to me. Others had pointed out that things weren't the same, enough to mention it to Lennox. The blanket was slipping off of my secret, and I was digging my nails into it trying to pull it back over.

"We were both kind of lost in ourselves, I think. Brody was separating from his wife and I had separated from Josh. There was a lot going on with both of us."

"But not that day, right?" Lennox said. "Everything was fine?"

"Yeah." There was a tremor in my voice that I couldn't quell.

Lennox asked a few more questions about our hours in the

morning, what we'd done at work up until the call came in to go to the Dolans. I told Lennox about the gist of Josh's phone call. I had already waded too deep into Lennox's summation that Brody and mine's relationship wasn't the same as it always had been.

"That phone call occurred before you went to the Dolans?" Lennox reflected. "That must have rattled you, huh?"

"Lieutenant," Vance snarled.

"Were you affected by the conversation, Detective? Did it distract you?" he rephrased.

"I was," I admitted. "I had thought things were over."

"Judging from your tone, you weren't happy about that."

"I wasn't."

Lennox frowned. "Why not? You gave me this speech about broken hearts and learning to love your own company. Yet, your ex-fiancé calls with the idea of maybe getting back together and you weren't glad?"

"It's more complicated than that," I said, exhaustion hampering my voice. My shoulder raged like someone was sticking a knife into my bullet wound, and prodding it around. It didn't help that every question made me stiffen in response as I tried to tip-toe away from the truth.

"Let's fast-forward to the Dolan's house," he said, flipping a page on his tablet. I didn't think he was done asking me about that conversation or Josh, but I was relieved to move on, even if it was only temporary.

Lennox's following questions were about our reasonable cause for entering the house, our history with the Dolan's, and what we found inside. I let my mind pull me through each vivid memory, describing what happened up to chasing the suspect from the back of his house to Apollo Way.

"My notes say that the Dolans had a registered handgun that they kept in the kitchen. This was the weapon that killed Detective Aritza and wounded you. Was Rafe Dolan in possession of that gun?"

Brody's head snapped back in my memory; his body crumpled. Adair Dolan's acidic stare as she ran toward me, fear glazing her bloodied face.

"Detective?"

I ground my teeth together. "No."

Lennox frowned. "You told dispatch that Mr. Dolan was armed?"

"He was, but not with their registered handgun. He was in

possession of a nine mil. We had disarmed him of that when Mrs. Dolan appeared."

"Did either you or Detective Aritza check for the registered handgun at the house when you were there?"

Everything from my shoulders up through my head burned. I managed to shake my head but only a little.

"I need you to speak, Detective."

"No," I croaked.

"Did you have any reason to suspect that Mrs. Dolan would use said gun to defend Mr. Dolan?"

"No! You can't take him!" Adair's screech rang through my head as I thought back to the chaos in the kitchen.

I nodded.

"Detective?" Lennox's censure was almost palpable.

"I never thought she'd use a gun. I never thought either of them would."

"But they did." Lennox closed the folder in front of him. "As a police officer, your job is to diagnose a situation quickly and make the best judgment. Clearly that wasn't the case that day."

"You weren't there," I struck back, my voice deadly.

"If I were, maybe your partner wouldn't be dead," he sneered.

Rage erupted through me like lava. I shoved my seat back as I stood up. Something tore in my shoulder and the immediate surge of pain was enough to buckle my knees.

"Jesus!" Vance leapt out of his chair and was around the table to catch me before I completely collapsed.

Lennox remained where he was, miff alighting in his eyes.

"Bastard," I growled as Vance helped me back to my feet. Blood oozed through the fabric of my shirt.

"Knock it off," The Captain whispered to me, helping me back in my chair. One look at my shoulder and he muttered under his breath. Vance quickly turned his wrath on Lennox. Somehow, he channeled it into a metered, "Any other questions?"

"One last one. An unidentified source mentioned that they saw Detective Aritza leave and enter your house the morning of the shooting before you stated you arrived at work 'at the same time'. Are you absolutely sure that there wasn't something going on between the two of you?"

Everything lost its color the moment the words left Lennox's mouth. Even the pain lessened in comparison to the stab of guilt that speared me. However, I didn't have a chance to say anything before Vance blew up.

"This interview is over," he growled, his arms open wide. "You got everything you need."

I didn't move. My eyes burned a hole through the sleek table between us as Lennox collected his papers and shut off the camera that had filmed the entire interview. He didn't say anything as he snapped his briefcase shut and hauled it and himself out of the room. Once the door was open, air rushed into the stale space. Pain and disbelief flooded back into me all in one. I gasped as a bead of blood trickled down my skin toward my stomach.

Vance was already telling Jackman to bring a car around to the lower-level back entrance. He was sending me back to the hospital and in secret, while the media was occupied with Lennox as he left.

After a moment, Vance returned to the room, a first-aid kit in his hand which he smacked down on the table. He rummaged around in the box for a few silent moments until he found gauze and shoved it into my hand. "Hold that on your wound," he said quietly.

I reached a hand up under my shirt and pressed the gauze into the blood, wincing.

"Is it true?"

Our gazes met. There was a despondency in Vance's honey-colored eyes and a sincerity that made me want to crawl under the table. I'd not only disappointed him but I'd hurt him, like I'd taken a knife to his chest and was holding it there now, twisting it.

When I didn't say anything, he got to his feet and shook his head. "For once, I wish you had...." His mouth stayed open as if he was trying to think of how to finish the sentence tactfully. When he looked at me again, his eyes were wet. In the darkness of the room, it was hard to be sure.

He left without saying another word.

NOW

The next day when I was well enough to sit up and not vomit my guts out, Josh brought me downstairs to the ground floor of the tea room and introduced me to some of his team members. Thankfully Brody made himself scarce for this.

There were five more people in the unit other than Josh, two support soldiers whose names I forgot as soon as Josh spoke them;

Clint, a rat-tailed good ole boy in charge of munitions; Gary, a quiet dark-haired medic with coke-bottle glasses, and Heidi, who offered nothing but the back of her head as she turned and walked into another room at my arrival.

Gary offered me a bowl of rice and as I shoveled it down, Josh caught me up on what their group's plan was going forward. They were heading north toward the towns of Kettering and Rockford. When I asked what their goal was, Heidi yelled from the kitchen, "It's none of your damned business."

"Wasn't talking to you," I answered.

Josh rolled his eyes. "This is a recovery mission, Liz. I told you that. We're looking for people, like you, who were left behind, caught in the cross-fire."

"How do you verify that they aren't Affected?" I asked.

Josh took a deep breath. "Most people are pretty obvious. Their behavior is erratic: they talk to themselves; they can't distinguish who is real and who isn't…"

"And you rescue them, too, right?"

I knew the question would put Josh on the spot in front of his unit, but I needed to see his reaction and theirs. It would determine exactly how easy it might be for me to get out of this mess.

Before Josh could say anything, Heidi answered, "With mercy." Her tone dripped with sarcasm. The sound of her knife chopping something got louder.

I turned my attention back to Josh. "Sounds like she's okay with murder. I wonder, was she the one who pulled the trigger on Lennox?"

The knife slammed down in the kitchen. Moments later, Heidi rounded the corner. "Murder? You dumb bitch."

I jumped up from my chair. "Takes one to know one."

Heidi stepped as close to me as she could, the tip of the knife waving in my face. "That fucking maniac killed one of ours first; Luke. A college kid studying to be a marine biologist. Killed him with a bat, a fucking bat to the head! He was barely recognizable when we found him."

"Back off," Josh said calmly, putting a hand around Heidi and trying to pull her away.

"Lennox killed him because he was about to murder me!" I yelled.

"And he had no reason not to!" Heidi spat. "You were a threat!"

"How?" I exclaimed. "You fired on us first! You had no way of knowing if we were Affected or not. There were people running scared and you made an assumption!"

"Liz, stop," Josh said through gritted teeth.

I got closer. "If anyone should be ashamed, it should be you."

Heidi's hand came up but I was ready for it, catching her wrist before her fist could punch my cheek. I wasn't ready for the knee she threw and found myself doubled over as she twisted out of my grip.

"Heidi, enough!" Josh shouted.

"Fuck you, Josh." Heidi wrestled herself away from him. "You're the one who made the call. You got Luke killed and you brought *her* back here when we should have taken her straight to Hruska. When are you going to make things right?"

Josh's eyes darkened.

A small glimmer of hope sink with Heidi's revelation.

"Outside, now!" he growled at her.

Heidi pushed him away and left the room, slamming the door to the entrance behind her.

"Seriously? What the hell is her problem?" I whispered, carefully standing back up.

He pointed at me. "Don't."

"Don't what? Hold you accountable for what you've been doing? Killing innocent people?"

"This is a different world. You can't make allowances for unpredictable behavior, for an enemy that hides in plain sight. Everyone is a suspect. Everyone is guilty before being proven innocent."

I held my stomach, groaning with the new pain. "Are you listening to yourself right now? These people aren't guilty of anything except having something inexplicable happen to them that they can't control! They aren't your enemy!"

"And how do you know?" he shouted.

I didn't say anything, knowing full-well not to walk into the trap.

After a moment, he lowered his voice and added, "Do you have any idea what's happened? Don't you know what they've done?"

"What do you mean?"

"Heidi's own sister saw her abusive ex, a piece of shit whose death was a godsend. Heidi tried to talk her out of it, tried to tell her she needed to go to a hospital. Her sister jumped off the roof because the ghost of her ex told her to. She's been at Gideon in a coma ever since."

I squinted. "And because of that, Heidi's taking out her pain on everyone else? Associating that one act with a whole group of people who are struggling to figure out what's happened to them? Not good enough!"

"We rescued a guy south of here that Lennox and his friends left for dead. Guy was beaten and nearly killed. Hruska was able to patch him up but...." Josh shook his head. "Guy is damaged goods. He was in the forest for a long time before he made it back out."

Clint chuckled. "Yeah, Astor's absolutely cuckoo now."

The name hit me. Astor: the one who had tried to kill Tamiko, the one who had managed to kill his own ghost. He'd survived and he was at Elon now.

"Astor isn't as innocent as you might think," I said under my breath.

Josh shook his head. "I don't have time for this right now, Liz. I need to go find Heidi and you need to stop standing up for these people before you get yourself killed." He stalked off toward the door Heidi had left through.

For the first time in days, I was unsure of everything again. I thought I'd had a good idea of where I stood.

I turned to Clint and Gary who had kept their heads down during the argument and rarely looked up. "What does he mean about what the Affected have done?"

Clint was the first to crack, scoffing at my question. "You've got to be joking."

I squinted. "I'm trying to understand."

Gary straightened his glasses. "You mean to tell me that you don't know any of the news reports? You been living under a rock or something?"

"Sorry if I didn't have the time to log online and catch up while I was fighting to stay alive."

Gary sauntered away from me into the kitchen. "It's a little ridiculous. It's international news."

"Then, give me something so I can put it in perspective."

Clint went into the other room and returned with a large scrapbook. "Read it and fucking weep for the world."

I slumped into one of the booths nearby, peeled open the thick cover and read.

There were printed articles of mothers neglecting their children because they didn't think they were real, wives killing husbands claiming they were "different people", kids being lured into streets, away from home because they thought they recognized a grandmother or grandfather no longer alive waving at them. There were stories of planes plummeting to the earth, busses full of people colliding with pedestrians, people leaping in front of subway trains and cars, stories of perfectly happy people, perfectly normal people up and leaving their homes, a lot choosing death over the idea of trying to live with this new way of life. There were stories of war. There were countless stories of loss. Stories of religions splintering into small sects and carrying out executions in the name of their creator. Racial killings masqueraded as justified trackers defending themselves. Stories of gatherings that became suicides.

They weren't only in our country: they were everywhere.

Splintered in between were stories of the grocery and stock scarcities, bodies being buried in mass graves, ships blocked from leaving countries because of borders closing and labor shortages. Worldwide stocks tanking. Fewer were the photos of the Woods growing across towns and cities, swallowing familiar landmarks in their swath of green. There were only a handful of aerial shots of wolves tearing across the countryside, sometimes alone, sometimes in packs as they hunted. The media had focused on the alarm inspired by Affected, and only Affected.

The craziest part about this was that all of the stories were dated to within a month of when this all began. One month and all of this had happened. When I asked Clint about it, he told me that they hadn't had access to the internet since the end of December. Cell reception had also tanked. Satellite phones and short-wave radios were the only way to connect with anyone now. That and word of mouth, which had only heightened the fear.

With every story, I realized the scale, how small I was in the enormity of everything. I knew how the media could spin these tales of terror, could make people believe that the entire world was ending. And who was I to say that it wasn't? When faced with the absolute behemoth of every single terrible story, how couldn't people crack? How couldn't they believe that Affected weren't dangerous? That I wasn't dangerous, too?

I don't know how long I sat there. Could have been twenty minutes. It could have been an hour. Eventually, I made myself put the scrapbook down on the table and stood up. I was woozy suddenly being on my feet, but I knew I couldn't stay there any longer.

I climbed the stairs back to my room and picked up my backpack from the corner. More than ever now, I knew where I needed to be. If

Dana had made it Gideon, I needed to get to her and make sure she was okay. I couldn't be certain that Dana hadn't been touched by this. What if she'd been taken by one of these awful tracking groups to be studied? What if she was already dead?

The whole world was operating on a hysteria fueled by horrible story after horrible story. There was no positivity in those Affected. We were people that needed to be studied or eliminated and nothing in between.

"Hey."

The sound was so close to my ears that I bolted from my spot like a frightened rabbit. Whirling around, I found Brody gazing at me as though I'd sprouted a second head.

"Hey, whoa, whoa, whoa." He put his hands up in front of him. "Shh, shh, shh. It's okay."

I let myself fall onto my butt and let go of my bag.

Brody took a couple steps toward me. "What's going on? What happened?"

I wanted to tell him. I wanted to offload the tens of hundreds of things that I'd grazed through, as if spreading the story would somehow make me forget all of it. Then I realized, maybe that's why so many people shared their stories. Because they couldn't digest what had happened to them alone. That's why the fear had spread into this monster that couldn't be quelled.

"Liz, I can't do anything unless you talk to me."

Forcing back tears, I looked at him and quietly said, "There's no way we can let them know, Brody. They'll kill me. We need to leave."

No sooner were those words out of my mouth before the door to the bedroom thundered open and I found myself staring down the barrel of a rifle.

TWENTY-SIX

"Ho-lee shit!" Clint said, his arms holding the rifle with a tremor. "I was comin' up to check on ya. Figured you'd read more than you could handle. But, fuck me. You're one of 'em, aren't ya?"

I raised my hands, my eyes locked on his. "Wait and listen…"

"Shut the fuck up," he said with a surprising amount of calmness. "They say it's listening to the Affected that gets you into trouble. We can't have that. Nuh-uh."

Brody was frozen. He had this look in his gaze, one of defeat. He knew there was nothing he could do to help me.

"I was talking to myself," I tried again. "I was talking—"

"SHUT YOUR FUCKING MOUTH!" The room practically shook from the boom of his voice.

Clint took in the room, then me again, then the sight of my discarded backpack. "Makin' a run for it? If you'd a kept your mouth closed, you coulda made it. Maybe. If Heidi hadn't been so darned suspicious of ya, I mighta let you walk out of here, too. That woman is always right, I tell ya."

The stairs creaked as someone ascended them. Soon enough, Josh appeared in the doorway behind Clint.

He looked between us before saying, "What the hell is going on here?"

Clint chuckled. "I caught her red-handed. She was talkin' to no one up here."

Josh eased into the room, slowly rounding his fellow soldier. "People do still talk to themselves sometimes, Clint."

"Nuh-uh! Heard her clear as fuckin' day. Said 'we can't let them know'. Said, 'We need to leave'."

Josh's eyes darted to mine. I noticed the twitch of his hand as he moved it closer to the gun in his holster. "Liz, why did you say that?"

All I could do was look into Josh's stare, his god damn

disillusioned stare and wish that this wasn't happening.

Brody had inched closer and was now right next to me. "I'm so sorry," he said under his breath.

"Liz?" Josh asked again.

"See? She can't deny it!" Clint chirped.

Josh whirled to him. "Shut up and put that damn gun away."

I watched Clint's grip only grow more solid on the rifle. "No, sir. Not after Luke. I'm not lettin' this one go. Can't let any more of 'em escape."

"We have no proof that she's even one of them!"

I finally found my words. "Please, Josh, I can explain everything."

"Yeah, okay," Clint interrupted. "Explain to 'im who Brody is, huh?"

All of the confusion drained from Josh's expression. "Brody?"

Brody stood suddenly. "Deny it, Liz. Come on."

Josh got closer to me, as though he was approaching a wounded wolf. "Do you see him, Liz?"

Brody shook his head. "Don't."

My breath left me as I answered, "I do."

"No," Brody moaned.

Josh straightened more, his hand now solidly on his holster.

"I knew it!" Clint whooped. "I fuckin' knew it!"

"Why?" Brody shook his head. "Why did you tell him?"

"Because I can't lie to him," I said.

My words made Josh take a step back. His eyes flicked between the air next to me where Brody crouched and me. I expected him to draw his gun, though all of my being hoped he wouldn't. If I were him, I would have without question. Now that I knew what they'd all been subjected to, what they'd all experienced in the last several months, I understood.

But he didn't draw the gun. Instead, he reached around Clint and pushed the bedroom door closed.

Clint momentarily glanced at him. "What the fuck are you doin'?"

Josh returned to his stance between Clint and me, his hand still poised over his holster. "I need proof, Liz."

I blinked. "Proof?"

"I need you to ask Brody about our phone call on New Year's Eve."

I frowned. Josh and I had split up by then. It would have been the day that Brody and I had gone to court, the day of the convenience store robbery. I had thought that Brody was tense about his and Carmen's interaction there. Maybe I had missed something.

I looked at Brody. "What's he talking about?"

Brody stared at the floor as though he was processing the information, his eyes intense, forehead straining. "I remember."

I couldn't figure out what was happening. He looked like he was in pain. "What?" I asked.

"Oh my god," he murmured. The look he gave me could have killed me. I wanted it to. It was the worst look I had ever seen him give me, worse than the one where I'd suggested he change partners, worse than the one in his apartment after he told me the reason for his and Carmen's breakup. The comprehension in them now was as venomous as the shame I felt from it. He remembered. He remembered everything.

"Knock off this bullshit. Let's end this crap," Clint shouted.

"Shut up, Clint!" Josh yelled as he turned back to me. "Liz, I need to know."

My voice cracked. "Brody, please." I wished I could reach for him but knowing that any sudden movements were a bad idea.

Brody closed his eyes. "I saw it happen. I saw us—"

"Brody, the conversation you had with Josh on the phone? What was it?"

He shook his head. "He was drunk. He kept asking about that night that I had dinner with you. The one where we danced. He knew something was going on before either of us really did."

The realization stung me. I looked at Josh. "You asked if Brody had feelings for me?"

Josh recoiled. It was only a moment but the look in his eyes was one of terror. He pulled the gun from his holster and aimed it at me.

The panic that had welled up inside of me had burst. Tears streamed from my eyes. "Please, Josh, don't."

He shook his head, tears in his eyes, too. "It's nothing personal."

I closed my eyes as he chambered the bullet, the sound echoing around in my skull.

The gunshot exploded through the room and made me shriek. But when no pain followed, I opened my eyes.

Josh had turned and shot Clint, who tumbled to the ground next to the door, dead.

"Get up, Liz. Get up," Brody urged.

My mind was frantic, trying to grasp what was happening as I snatched up my backpack and got to my feet.

Josh grabbed Clint's rifle and pushed his corpse out of the way of the door. He stood against the wall next to it and waved me to the side.

The gunshot still rang in my ears as shoes stamped on the floor downstairs.

"Josh! Clint!" Gary called as he neared the door. "Everything o—"

Josh yanked the door open mid-sentence and fired the rifle, the shot momentarily lighting up the darkened stairwell. The sound of Gary's body falling down the stairs followed soon after.

Josh put up a hand to keep me in place and descended the stairs alone. At the bottom, Josh said, "It's okay, it's me," before there were two more gunshots, a scream accompanying one. I assumed it was the two support soldiers in the kitchen. Heidi was the only one left.

I slinked forward into the hallway and slowly went down the stairs. Gary's mangled body was at the bottom, sprawled out and blood smeared across the laminate floor. I stepped around him and picked up his pistol from the ground nearby.

"Wait here, Liz. I'm going to find Heidi. Don't move," Brody said, and quickly darted off into one of the other rooms.

He was right. The stairwell was the safest place for the moment.

As soon as the thought occurred to me, Heidi stumbled into the kitchen, gun drawn. Her sights fell on Gary across the floor and then me, standing in the stairwell. She fired.

Gravity pulled me down against the stairs as the bullet cracked into the wall near where I'd stood. I cried out as my body crunched onto the edges of the steps. When I looked up, Heidi was only a few feet away, gun still drawn on me.

She scowled. "You meddling bitch." She aimed the gun at my head.

Gary's hand suddenly grabbed Heidi's leg. She jerked back in shock.

I raised my gun and fired.

Heidi collapsed with a scream.

I glanced down at Gary. He was as still as death again. Brody emerged from a wall nearby, winded.

"Thanks," I said, quickly getting to my feet.

Not missing an opportunity, I kicked Heidi's weapon away and trained my gun on her skull.

"What are you waiting for?" she yelled.

"Nothing," I said, starting to squeeze the trigger.

"Wait!" Josh shouted as he ran into the room. He barely looked at Heidi as he grabbed my arm. "Let's go."

"We can't have her following us," Brody said nearby.

I looked back and forth between him and Josh. I thought about all those countless news articles. I was going to vomit. I let Josh pull me along. He scraped Heidi's weapon off the floor as we ran outside into the wet cold. It was sleeting now, the road a slushy mess topped with snow. Josh shepherded me toward his Land Rover and we both climbed in. Brody appeared in the backseat as Josh hit the gas and we rocketed away from the tea house.

A sudden pop-pop and our side-view mirror shattered. I whirled around to look out the rear window. Heidi's form vanished into the mist the further away we drove.

Josh and I said nothing to one another for the entire car ride. After several hours, we stopped at a gas station on the highway. A cardboard sign over the pumps boasted NO GAS but that wasn't Josh's aim. After cutting the engine, he got out without a word and went inside. I stayed where I was. I didn't know how to react with him after everything that had happened. Thankful was the least of it. Josh had killed most of his crew to save my life. The carnage would only have been avoidable if he'd let them take me back to Elon. I'd half a mind to think that was his original plan, even if only for a few seconds.

After several minutes, Josh returned to the car with a bottle of whisky and tossed it into the backseat. It went through Brody, who watched its liquid slosh around inside of him. We were on the road in another few minutes.

"Where are we going?" I finally asked.

Josh looked in the rearview mirror. "We need to get some distance between us and the tea shop. I figured our next stop should be in Kettering. We can pick up some supplies from the discount stores there and then, keep heading north."

"Why head north?" I asked. "There's nothing up there."

"Exactly. We don't want to be found."

"We're going to hide?"

Josh took a deep breath and with it, the Land Rover picked up speed. "I slaughtered a bunch of people back there: people with a vested interest in helping the government get its hands on Affected people. They aren't going to forget this happened. They'll send more."

"I don't understand why," I said. "Chasing after one Affected person is a waste on their resources."

"Says who?" Josh spat. "The Elon facility is going to be the second largest in New England once they're done setting up. Soon, Flintland will have enough people and resources at its disposal that they can afford to send one very pissed-off woman and some willing soldiers into the depths of Northern Maine to hunt us down. When they do, they're going to obliterate the both of us. Anyone considered a threat is of no use to them anymore."

I realized what he meant. Heidi would follow us to the ends of the earth if it meant getting revenge for what had happened back there. What's worse was she had trusted Josh and he'd betrayed her.

"Even if she did let us live," Josh continued. "She'd take us to Elon to Dr. Hruska. From what everyone has been saying, that's worse than death."

The perpetual "boogeyman": Dr. Hruska. I never wanted to meet the guy in person.

"Maybe you shouldn't have killed them," I said.

"If I hadn't," he shouted, pointing in the direction we'd come from, "You'd have ended up in Elon anyway."

"Why didn't you let them take me? You made it pretty clear that you didn't trust anyone like me; that you couldn't."

Josh slammed on the brakes and the Land Rover skidded to a stop in the middle of the road. Putting the car in park, he unbuckled his seatbelt, reached into the backseat and grabbed the bottle of cheap whisky.

"Jesus, really?" Brody said as Josh's hand went through him.

Josh took a swig from the bottle. "Why do you think, Liz? You're not someone random. It's you."

He offered the bottle to me.

It took everything I had in me not to accept it. His departure was the reason I'd taken to drinking before. He'd broken my heart. I'd broken his in return. I shook my head. "We should go."

Josh shifted into gear and put his foot on the gas. We drove.

THEN

There was a knock on my door. I looked up from my empty tea mug. I hadn't opened the curtains. The February day was dark and rainy. I hadn't turned on many lights save for the one over my armchair in the living room. I'd been staring at an old magazine trying to distract myself, though I constantly vanished into my own what-ifs and could-have-beens. Photographers had set up shop outside the house for the last week, trying to get shots of me through any opening of doors or cracks in the blinds. I didn't want to make it easy for them and so the house and I remained in the dark.

I got to my feet and answered the door. It was rare for anyone to knock. Usually, it was Dana showing up to drop off groceries or offer to do my laundry. I hadn't done either in at least a week, not since the first news story broke, not since Vance had asked for my badge and my gun. I wasn't ready to confront people yet and I'd gotten into the habit of wearing my sweats all day and then sleeping in them. What was the point of getting dressed? To make myself feel better? To show some kind of decorum? I didn't care.

The door swung open and there he was. Josh hadn't been to Flintland in months. He looked the same and I wasn't expecting that. I didn't say anything before he reached in and hugged me. My fingers dug into the warmth of his sweater as I clung to him. The skin on my neck craved his hot breath. He smelled like scotch pine; of the woods that ringed Flintland.

I was the first to pull away. My shoulder still ached. I'd ripped the stitches during my IA meeting with Lennox and had to start the healing process all over again. I'd taken some pain meds for it earlier in the day but all they ever did was put me in a haze. I hated them. They were also the only things that made the ache go away.

Waving Josh inside, I closed out the darkness. Josh immediately turned on the lamp on the table beside the stairs and the light strayed into my shadowed dwelling. The first thing his eyes fell on were the empty photograph frames. I hadn't touched them since that day when Brody had found me drunk. All of that loneliness and emptiness came spilling back. When Josh finally looked at me, it was devoid of the warmth it'd had only seconds before.

"I shouldn't have come over like this unannounced," he said, swallowing. "I should have called."

"I wouldn't have answered. My phone is off. The press has been trying to get in touch with me all week. Surprised they didn't start firing off photos when you showed up."

"They did. I threatened to run over a few of them if they didn't stop."

"My hero."

The exchange didn't alter the tension in the air. Josh took a step back toward the door. "I'll come back another—"

I grabbed the sleeve of his sweater. "Don't go."

He glanced between me and the photos again and turned back around.

I led him into the kitchen and put the water on for more tea. He stood awkwardly next to the fridge as though the whole house had changed since he'd last been in it. "This might be more of a beer conversation," he said, with a humorless smile.

I shrugged and flinched. I wanted to say "Brody threw out my booze," but the thought of saying his name chilled me. Instead, I answered, "I don't drink anymore."

I motioned for Josh to sit at the table and he did, edging the seat out as though it might break from the simplest touch.

I carefully settled into a seat across from him and listened to the refrigerator kick on.

Josh nodded to me. "How's your shoulder?"

"I have to wear this sling for another three weeks, then PT."

"That's fun." Josh drummed his fingers on the table.

"How are things with the new job?" I asked. The last time we'd talked was the day I'd left the hospital. The day when I'd told him that Brody had died. I was sure he knew quite a deal more now.

The news was relentless. The story trended on social media for weeks. The hate messages I'd received far outweighed the compassionate ones. People were disgusted with my affair with Brody: people who knew nothing who felt justified to voice their opinions on my life. I'd deleted my accounts without much of an afterthought. It wasn't as if I used them much anyway.

Josh cleared his throat. "Well, it's not going great. We can call it creative differences but I'm going to settle for the fact that my boss is a raging asshole and isn't looking for anyone to give him any ideas."

"It's his magazine," I said blankly.

"It's borderline suicidal some of these places he wants me to go." Josh pulled out his phone and scrolled through a long text message conversation. "He wants me to go to Syria. I'm an adventure photographer; not a war correspondent."

"Say 'no'. He must have someone else that would be dying to

put themselves in the middle of a civil war."

He sighed. "It's not that easy, Liz."

What had opened as a normal conversation was starting to give me a headache. It reminded me of the fight we'd had before Josh had left. "Isn't that why you left in the first place? Because this was something you couldn't turn down?"

"Yes," he said. "It was a huge opportunity. But Hugh doesn't want adventure photographers. He wants multifaceted photo journalists who aren't afraid to delve into the cultures of all the places they visit. The exploits are more than just the fun parts: he wants a running dialogue with different domestic groups; a rich history to be discovered… If it means putting on a bullet-proof vest and carrying an AK-47 for protection, he thinks we should be capable."

"Is it what you want to do?" I asked.

"I don't know."

We sat in silence until the faintest whistle emanated from the tea kettle. I gingerly got up and removed the teapot with my better arm. As I pulled tea out of the cupboard, Josh spoke up again. "I talked to Carmen this afternoon."

The sentence was like stepping on a razorblade. It hung in the air like the steam from the tea kettle. I had tried to block Carmen from my thoughts over the last week. The news was brutal in its coverage, throwing both me and Brody to the wolves as our star-crossed affair was broadcast for all the world. The worst part about ignoring Carmen wasn't the guilt. It was my own selfishness; my own desire to remember Brody in *my* bed, holding onto *me* before he was taken away. They had separated. They weren't together. The news glazed over that fact every time.

When I didn't say anything, Josh continued. "She said they're not planning to have the funeral until the ground thaws. Probably April. She's been talking to Captain Vance about doing a memorial soon."

Every single word was like taking another scoop out of me. The more he talked, the emptier I became and the angrier I got at myself.

"She asked how you were doing."

I tore at a tea bag package bit by bit.

"Liz?"

I dropped the wrapper and looked at him. *That's bullshit. She doesn't care how I'm doing.* At least, that's what I should have said. I had opened my mouth in preparation to say it. Instead, I let the sentence dry up before even a sound was uttered. I didn't want to talk to her. Any apologies I offered meant nothing. I didn't want to leave my house. I knew I couldn't stay here forever. But most of me still wanted to try.

"You can't curl up here and assume the world is going to forget about you," Josh said. "Not after something like this."

"Can't I?" I poured the boiling water into our mugs and dropped the tea bags into them.

"No. You can't."

I turned and looked at him. "I don't want to be under a fucking microscope anymore. I don't want people judging me forever because I chose not to be lonely one night."

"Was that all it was?" Josh asked. The way he looked at me made my eyes sting.

The steam floated up from our mugs, twisted and vanished into the air. "We were both alone."

Josh's shoulders dropped, his head hanging. "How long did you feel that way about him?" His voice came out smooth but low and I recognized the defeat in it.

"I've always loved him as a friend, Josh. This was…new."

Josh released a breath. His shoulders were tense and he wouldn't make eye contact with me. "That's not true."

"Great," I muttered. "So, now you're going to tell me how I felt, too?"

"No, I'm saying it because I know how you felt about him, Liz. You chose him over me."

My temper crashed through me like beast. "*You* left *me*! Not the other way around. You didn't want to stay cooped up here because it wasn't enough for you. *I* wasn't enough."

Josh stood up abruptly. When he finally looked at me, it was the coldest expression I'd ever seen on his face. "You're not blameless in our break-up, Liz. You chose to stay with Brody over leaving with me. You could have left the job; you could have sold the house. This wasn't about choosing *things* as much as it was about choosing *people*. You chose Brody."

He turned and walked up the hallway to the door. As he opened the front door, he called back, "Now I know why."

He slammed the door behind him.

I locked eyes with his abandoned tea. I stared at it until the steam stopped rolling from it. The house became still once more.

TWENTY-SEVEN

NOW

Josh eventually pulled the Land Rover into the Kettering Discount Supply. Before all of this, it used to be a great place to pick up bargain-basement food and beer, products pulled from the shelves after the sell by date or because of non-harmful dents in cans or punctures in boxes. There were a few other cars in the lot, snow-covered. Still, we exited the car carefully, weapons poised for any surprises.

Josh pulled a crowbar from the trunk. No power meant no mechanically functioning doors. But as we neared the entrance, we noticed the doors had already been pried apart, enough space for a shopping cart to slip through. It wasn't a stretch to consider that people may have ransacked and looted the store in the months since the ghosts first appeared. We cautiously approached and one by one slipped through the opening.

I clicked on my flashlight as Josh turned on his headlamp. Both lights swiveled into the dim space. The entrance way looked like it had before, the carts in neat lines, bins full of toys and cheap candy on display. The corkboard was plastered with missing signs, several for children and a lot of them handmade. People had thought they could reach their community here, even while all of the carnage was happening.

I took the lead, keeping my flashlight and gun poised as I stepped through the next set of doors into the dark store. The empty register stood in front of us. To the left, the store opened up into a large warehouse with aisles of products and racks of clothing. It had never looked organized when everything was in operation either, but in the darkness, with our breaths clouding our vision, it appeared that much more destitute.

We swept the aisles, Josh taking the right side of the store while I did the other. We met in the back and quickly checked the offices. Not another human soul in sight. The majority of the stock was gone, only scattered bags of pasta, canned vegetables and fruit, and boxes of cookies, crackers and cereal left askew along various shelves.

Back at the front of the store, Josh pulled two carts free of the line and rolled one to me. "Fill it and be quick. We don't have much time."

I rolled the cart into the first aisle with the cans of soups and vegetables and dropped what I could scavenge in the cart.

"Why didn't you tell me?"

Brody's voice was suddenly right beside me and it made me jump. I exhaled a shaky breath and turned to him. He wasn't even looking at me, instead choosing to stare at the cans of cream of mushroom soup that I'd dropped into my cart.

"I couldn't," I said, pushing the cart further down the aisle.

"You could have, Lizzy." He walked with me. "You should have."

"Why?" I said, turning and pulling more canned goods down into the basket. "So that I could remember it all over again? So that I could rip off the Band-Aid? Besides, you wouldn't have believed me anyway."

"Are you shitting me?" Brody came around the other side of the cart. "After all of this has happened, you thought I wouldn't believe you?"

I shook my head. "Not with Carmen. Especially not after Carmen…."

Brody's lips cracked. "Did she know?"

The fire burned under my skin. I wanted to pretend I hadn't heard him, continue to pile things in my cart.

"Hey, don't ignore me! Did she know?" Brody shouted.

"Yeah."

"Did you tell her?"

"No. Lennox was investigating. It was his job."

"You told internal affairs?"

"No," I said through clenched teeth, finally turning to face him. "He guessed. The police department put out a truncated report, but the press got wind of it anyway."

That shut him up. Brody closed his eyes and took a few steps back. His form mingled with the shelves of canned goods, turning smoky.

I kept walking. "If I'd had it my way, she wouldn't have known at all."

Brody scoffed. "Why? Because you didn't think she could handle it?"

I spun around, my voice cracking. "Because telling a grieving widow that I slept with her husband the morning he died was a killing blow I didn't want to make. I may be a selfish person but I'm not cruel."

I moved down to the end of the aisle, my stomach swimming with the revelations of our conversation. Brody remained where he was for minutes, while I continued to scavenge the shelves. By the time I'd moved into the next aisle, he'd caught up to me again.

"Josh?"

I glanced across the store to where Josh was piling things in his cart. "I think he knew before I ever did."

"Was I the reason that you two broke up?"

The words stung. I paused and whispered, "Maybe."

He stared at the ceiling. "And then I had to go and die on you."

"Yeah."

I kept rolling the cart around each aisle, pulling boxes and bottles from the disorganized shelves while Brody followed behind me. Neither one of us said anything more. But the conversation continued to fester in my mind as I walked. By the time I reached the back of the store, and the cart was becoming heavier to push, my eyes had welled up with tears. I could barely tell where I was going to the point that I pushed the cart into the shelves. The loud screech echoed throughout the warehouse.

"Are you okay?" Josh's voice echoed from afar.

"Yeah. Fine," I answered shortly, hoping he couldn't detect the sob in my voice. I resumed topping off the cart.

Brody stepped in front of the cart. "I loved you for a long time."

I looked up at him, growing cold.

"It made me crazy. It made me hate myself. But I still couldn't help it. Remembering it now makes this…." He waved at himself, his hand going through the shopping cart. "…*this*…excruciating."

I reached out my hand to him, and he did the same. His fingertips flickered through mine.

"I can't believe you were mine and I couldn't remember it," he whispered.

I pulled my hand away. "Now you know why it hurts so much."

"We touched in that forest. We still can."

I frowned. "We can't go back there. Josh is with us now and we have to stick together."

"You said it yourself, Liz. You destroyed any chance of you two getting back together. We don't need him."

I swallowed. "What I need to do is survive. Josh saved me back there. He's put himself in danger for me. We stand a better chance with him than alone."

"I can't follow you around forever, Liz," Brody growled. "Sooner or later, we need to address what we're going to do. You can't pretend I'm not here around him. You can't do that to me."

It was true yet, I didn't know how to be nor wanted to be a bridge to connect the two of them. For now, there was a wall separating my past mistakes from each other. For the sanctity of my own mind, I needed them to stay that way.

"We'll find a way," I assured him, "but not now. Right now, we need to concentrate on getting out of here and find a safe place to spend the night."

Brody hesitantly nodded.

Pushing the cart toward where I'd last heard Josh, I found him sitting on the floor, back propped up against the shelves. His face was buried in the crook of one arm. I knew he was crying. An empty wine bottle lay on its side next to him.

I knelt down to him and put a hand on his knee. "Josh?"

"I didn't feel anything when I killed them," he said, sniffing. "I was so empty. I let it take over. Hell, we didn't even really know each other. We've only been together a couple months. But I can't…get their faces out of my head. Gary, Clint, Rich, Geena…. Their voices…."

I curled my fingers around his and pulled at his arm. "We have to go. We don't have time to dwell on this right now."

He yanked his hand free and let it flop against his leg. "Oh, but we have time for you and Brody to have a heart-to-heart?"

I closed my eyes. "You heard everything?"

"No." He shook his head. "I didn't eavesdrop. But I think you forgot we're in a big warehouse. Sound travels even if you don't want it to."

I sighed and stood up. "The three of us have a lot to talk about. But we can't do it here."

Josh slowly got up, using the shelves for support. They creaked under his large frame and he nearly fell, catching the cart for support. I noticed another empty bottle as it rolled out from under the rack.

"Two bottles in a half an hour? Impressive. Gimme the car keys."

He didn't fight me, handing them over.

"I'm going to go get the car and back it up to the entrance. That way, we can load the food right in. You stay here."

"Nope." He put a hand on my cart. "You're not going by yourself. Besides, it takes more than a couple bottles of wine to bring me down."

"I beg to differ." I removed his hand from my cart and walked toward the front. After a moment, he followed with his. The rattling of the carts filled the silence. "Remember Thanksgiving three years ago?"

"That, if I recall, was vintage port that my grandfather had kept since the thirties. My dad didn't tell me that before I started drinking."

"Didn't stop you once you found out either." I glanced over my shoulder at him and flashed him a weak smile.

"Are you calling me an alcoholic?"

"Nope; only a liar."

At the front of the store, we nudged our carts through the first opening into the entrance hall. I turned around and looked him in the eye, "Really. Stay here. Make sure nothing happens to the food. I'll bring the car around."

"Aye, aye." He saluted.

I squeezed through the doors into the bitter cold. The snow had turned back to sleet and it drenched my hair within a few minutes of being outside. Josh had parked around the corner to ensure we weren't visible from the road. I unlocked the car, opened the driver's side door, and slid in to the dry seat.

"You said inside that the three of us were going to have a discussion?" Brody said, somehow already in the passenger seat. "You still love him, don't you?"

I pushed the key into the ignition and turned the engine over. "What kind of a question is that, Brody?"

"I'm confused how you're going to try and make this work."

"I don't know." I put the car into gear and turned the wheel, backing out so I could turn the car around.

Brody narrowed his gaze. "How do you think we're all going to coexist?"

"I don't know," I snapped. "All I do know is that I'm not ready to lose either of you. Yes, I care about him. I care about you, too. Do not ask me to choose between you two. Not now."

Brody frowned. "Not *now*?"

"Not ever."

I drove around the building to the front doors. After backing the car up to the entrance, I popped the rear door and killed the engine. I got out, choosing not to look at Brody. When I was close enough to the mechanical doors, I looked up and stopped cold in my steps. Josh was gone, the two shopping carts abandoned where I'd left him.

"Brody?" I whispered.

He was beside me in an instant. After a moment, he moved to the entrance and peered inside. "He could be in the bathroom. That was a lot of wine."

I checked my holster. I'd left the gun inside; distracted by my conversation with Josh in the wine aisle. I could still picture it sitting on the shelf.

"We need to be sure," I said.

Brody moved ahead into the entrance, further past the second set of doors into the giant room. He stopped, his posture relaxing, and gestured to me. "He went back to the wine aisle."

Sighing, I shouldered through both sets of doors and passed Brody. Sure enough, glasses clinked from behind the shelf.

"I think we can both agree that you have alcoholic tendencies, Josh," I called toward the back of the store.

"That's your opinion."

Josh's voice was from behind me. I turned in time for him to emerge from the bathroom door as he zipped up his fly.

I turned back to the shelves and froze. The large inhuman silhouette was now visible against the back wall, the light from my remaining flashlight casting it in shadow. Not a moment later, the wolf's black face rounded the corner of the shelves.

Josh grabbed my arm and he hauled me toward him. "Go!" he yelled.

I practically tripped over myself as I raced for the car, the keys jingling wildly in my hand. Josh's boots clomped on the tiles behind me. Slithering through the gap between the front doors, I slipped and stumbled onto my hands and knees in the slush. Finding my footing, I rounded the car and climbed in the driver's seat, stabbing the keys in the ignition.

Brody was in the passenger seat, his head stuck out the window. "What the fuck is he doing?"

I leaned out my window. In the rearview, Josh stood at the mechanical doors, trying to force them closed.

The monster slammed through the first set of doors inside, not slowing down as it barreled toward Josh.

"Move!" I screamed, the car rumbling to life beneath me.

Suddenly, the doors were splintering into thousands of tiny shards, the scream of glass abrupt and earth-shattering. Josh was in the air, the sheer force landing him into the mush next to Brody's door.

I ripped my door open, and scrambled around the front grill of the Land Rover. "Josh!"

He looked up at me with dazed eyes, fresh blood dribbling down the side of his face into one of his eyes. I grabbed him under the arms and with his help, got him on his feet.

Glass shards framed the metal doors, too sharp for the creature to get through. It reared back and smashed itself against the metal handles in the middle, trying to force itself through the opening that Josh had left. With each smash, the gap widened.

I forced the back door open.

Josh dove into the back seat.

"Hurry up, Liz!" Brody yelled.

The tinkling of glass and crash of metal pushed me on. I returned to the driver's side door and climbed back in. With my foot fully on the gas pedal, I shifted into gear.

The car lurched forward, tires spinning on the ice and snow. I yanked the steering wheel to the right and the Land Rover screeched onto the road, rocketing away from the discount store.

"Brody, is it bad?" I said, trying to look over my shoulder.

Brody was now in the back seat, leaning over Josh, who was clenching his teeth. "He's got a nasty head wound."

"I'm okay," Josh groaned through the pain. "Keep driving."

"Josh, put pressure on your head. You're going to pass out."

"Lizzy, your scarf," Brody probed.

I ripped it over my head and threw it into the back seat. Glancing in the rearview mirror, I noticed that Josh had pushed the once white fabric against his face. It had already soaked up a fair amount of blood.

"Do you know where we're going?" Josh asked, his voice woozy.

"North." I hadn't even thought about which roads would take us north, only the fact that we needed to get as far away from the discount store as we could.

"You take the next left at the intersection of three and twenty-seventh," Brody said, locking eyes with me in the rearview mirror. "I'll navigate. In five hours, if we're lucky, we'll hit the Canadian border."

I nodded. "We'll have to stop somewhere before then. I need to look at Josh's head."

"There's a clinic in Collinstown. Brought a few battered women there after arresting the husbands. They should have what we need."

"Okay. Josh?"

I looked for him in the rearview mirror. He'd slid down below my line of vision. I glanced over my shoulder. He was slumped in the seat, passed out.

"Liz!" Brody yelled.

The force of a thousand tons of steel slammed into our car. The world spun out of control as my screams merged with the roar of twisting metal. I dropped into blackness before it was over. Brody's screams were the last sound I remembered.

TWENTY-EIGHT

THEN

The Purple Finch was a small grocery store and café at the other end of my block. I didn't shop there; could never afford it. It was known for its expensive wine selection, organic fruit and vegetables from local farms, choice cuts of meat, and daily pastries and sandwiches. I'd run into grab a coffee once and had walked out shaking my head at the hefty price tag on their daily blend. Kopi Luwac coffee: the coffee cherries partially digested by a palm civet, a nocturnal mammal from southern Asia.

I only went in because it was the closest store to home. I never travelled far from there anymore. Everywhere I went in town, I was recognized. At my favorite coffee shop, people stared at me with pity and revile. One of the last times I was there, someone spilled their tea on my table on purpose. The barista had kicked them out, but I never went back. I ordered most everything I needed online and had it delivered. I only went out at night; only for the exercise and fresh air.

That night, I needed something else.

The store smelled like fresh baked loaves of bread and batches of cookies, the rich smell of coffee permeating the air. It was a small space, with a picnic table set up in the corner, where an older couple sat enjoying hot bowls of soup and laughing about something quietly. I slunk into the wine section. I hadn't touched anything since the morning Brody had admonished me. Every time I thought about it, I got sick and thought about what he'd say if he could see me with it.

I couldn't do it anymore though. I *needed* a drink. I needed some kind of an escape from the here and now. It had been months since the shooting, months since the truth came out, since losing my job, since the memorial and then the funeral, since Josh had left again. Summer was waning. Cold nights were coming back. I wanted the warmth from a bottle of wine, a warmth I knew I could count on.

But as I rounded the corner, I recognized the silken dark hair and the army green jacket before she turned around. Carmen's eyes seared into me through my sunglasses; through my body.

Neither of us said anything for a full five seconds. Then I made the mistake of trying to go around her; of trying to act like she wasn't there.

Her gaze tracked me as I moved around the next aisle. "That's it?" she said. Her heels followed me. "You're going to pretend like I'm not here? Did that make it easier for you to sleep with Brody: knowing he and I had split up?"

My fingers scrabbled as I pulled my sunglasses off. "I don't want to have a confrontation with you here, Carmen," I said. "But I owe you so much more of an apology than I can ever give you."

"You think that's what I want from you? An apology?" Carmen chuckled humorlessly. "All I wanted was some acknowledgement from you, Elizabeth. I wanted you to understand what I was going through on my end when Brody and I separated. But you never even tried. Worse: you took it as an opportunity for yourself."

By now a few people in the shop were staring. I put the wine bottle I'd been staring at back on the shelf and headed for an exit. I couldn't do this. I didn't want to do this.

"That's right," Carmen's voice chased me as I rounded the corner toward the door. "Run away. Be a coward."

The words split me open. I gasped for the cold night air as I fled the store and when it hit me, it was like a spear shooting through me, like lightning striking—

NOW

Rattling in my ears. It made me sick to my stomach. I tried to open my eyes but the lights glared in. The floor was soft underneath me and shifted and swayed this way and that. I tried to move to keep everything from sloshing but found I couldn't. Something was tethering me down. I opened my eyes again. This time the light wasn't as painful. I tried to move my arms again. Something bit down into them and kept them at my sides. My feet were free but like gelatin.

Then, everything hurt. A gradual ache passed over me, as though I'd been treading water for days.

"Ah, she's finally awake."

What the hell? A voice: not one I knew.

The lights passed away and I was suddenly surrounded by shadow. Someone was standing in front of me. I couldn't tell who.

"It's okay, you'll come out of the clouds soon, dear."

The person got closer. Their eyes were round and glass like a large bug, viewing me without emotion. I strained to get further away, forgetting somehow that I was bolted into something. I looked down. A chair like the kind a dentist uses. There was even an operatory light with a magnifier on a swivel directly above.

"Where am I?" The words were marbles in my mouth.

"Where are my manners?" The eyes leaned away. "Welcome to Elon."

No. How? It didn't make sense. We were in the car, driving north....

The memories hit me: the discount store, the wolf, something hitting the car. "Where's Josh?"

"He's in medical. Ms. Summerfield's method of capture was a bit more destructive than is typically necessary with most of our subjects."

"Who?"

"You might know her better as Heidi."

I cringed. She'd caught up to us after all. My stomach did flips with the memory of our car collision.

I turned my attention back to the bug-eyed figure. "Who are you?"

"Romana Hruska." The person bowed.

Romana *Hruska.* Doctor Hruska, the feared neurosurgeon in charge of Elon's experiments, was a woman.

"I used to be one of the top neurosurgeons in Ostrava before moving to America. Second best in Boston as I later discovered. But that Patel character is *so* overrated. Well, he's Indian and a man, so I suppose that automatically makes him a genius to society." Hruska clicked her tongue. "But *we* know who the best is."

My vision had cleared enough to see who I was talking to. Dr. Hruska had a narrow nose, her blue eyes enlarged by a set of glasses. Brunette locks poked out from beneath a blue surgical cap. She smiled a row of perfect teeth. Someone might have mistaken her for a model once. But there was something murky about her, too. Her eyes were too excited, as though someone had presented a child with a new toy. Her scrubs were also too filthy. I wasn't in the hands of a doctor who actually cared about sanitation.

Leather straps held me into the chair. I focused on moving my legs again but they stayed there, ignoring my commands.

"Why can't I move my legs?"

"Just a little bit of localized anesthetic. We can't have you getting up and taking off; not while we have so much to do." Hruska leaned in again, her fingers gently widening the lids on my right eye.

I tried to pull away but found my head was also secured in place by two pads on each side.

"It's so curious," Hruska said, "the connection between what the brain perceives is a figment or a fact. This…disease, whatever it is, has somehow manipulated our minds into believing that we see the dead." She shined a light into my eye, trailing it left and right. "Among other things."

She switched to the left eye, following the same routine. "We still haven't discovered the source of the pathogen yet. Perhaps it's something that has been lying dormant in us for a long time, like a latent virus. Possibly hundreds of years old, judging by how widespread it is. It only makes sense that something in our environment activated it. The scale is still astronomical and the timing practically impossible."

Hruska clicked off the light and leaned over a pad of paper to take notes.

"You're overthinking the whole thing," I said, taking in my other surroundings. The room was small and unkempt. It reminded me of a janitor's closet, metal shelving with dozens of supplies lined up across from us. The rest of the room was surrounded by dingy, light-blocking curtains.

"You're telling me that I should accept this for what it appears to be? A religious coming? Revelations?" Hruska laughed. "If you wish to explain the irrational through faith, then that is your weakness. I cannot accept the impossible unless I've ruled out every other improbable option."

"Seems like they didn't have much faith in your scientific method if they stuck you here in Maine." I forced a chuckle. "Guess you're not really hot shit, are you?"

She finished scribbling and stood, crossing the room and opening a drawer. "Oh, no dear. I chose to run Elon. In Boston, I would have had so much more legislation clogging my efforts, restricting my studies. This facility, ramshackle as it is for the time being, allows me more freedom to do what I need to do. As a bonus, I'd never been to Maine before."

She closed the drawer and brought a rolled-up satchel back over to her medical cart. "There was a nice chiropractor's office in a gated community on top of Montroy Circle that we thought provided enough safety from the mutts out there. The potential is explosive." Her eyes glittered as she said the word.

"The mutts? You said it's all hallucinations. But you've seen the wolves. And the Woods?"

"We're all susceptible, dear. We all have the virus. Some of us have it worse than others. Your severity could unlock the key to what has happened to us all."

I watched Hruska unroll the leather satchel until silver tools sparkled under the lights. I tugged at my restraints again.

"Shhh. Not to worry. I'll make sure you don't feel a thing."

"You've must have enough people to test by now." The leather straps cut into my wrists the harder I tugged. "You haven't found anything, have you?"

"Well, there are so, so many variables to consider. Test groups have to be selected and observed for a period of time. Examinations need to be run and analyzed. This doesn't happen overnight. While there don't appear to be any genetic abnormalities between the Affected and Unaffected so far, it could still well be something we have not considered. It once took physicians fifteen years to diagnose someone with Lyme disease after testing the patient for a rash of other disorders first."

Hruska pulled a needle from her leather satchel. "Cancer has been a disease affecting humans since ancient Egypt. We've been studying it for thousands of years and in the last forty years, with actual funding, are still searching for a cure. And the coronavirus? Dare I say that was only a fraction of the complexity that this outbreak has. This, whatever it is, will not be solved by me, or by those I've trained. As time passes, it will evolve. We may never truly know what started this or how to fix it. But you'll be a stepping stone to the answer."

I watched Hruska fill the syringe from a tiny glass bottle and give it a few flicks.

I forced my mouth to keep moving. If I could keep distracting her, maybe I could get free. Even as the thought crossed my mind, my energy waned. Everything hurt. All I wanted was to escape back into the blackness. I had to stay awake. "So, you're going to practice on unwilling people, ignore the Hippocratic Oath in the name of science."

She chuckled. "I don't condone unnecessary suffering. But I am also limited in my resources as a doctor, especially with being a part of this smaller unit. I have to take what I can get." Hruska sat in her chair and wheeled up toward my head. "Now, this will sting for a moment, and then you'll be warm and relaxed, like you're in the bath."

I strained to move my head but the two stirrups keeping it in place wouldn't budge. As the needle pricked my neck, a scream echoed over the silence.

Hruska leaned back bringing the needle with her.

"Sounds like my next patient is awake a little sooner than expected. Be a dear and stay there for one moment while I give him some attention."

The doctor stood, leaving the needle on the medical cart and left the room, closing the door behind her.

Quickly, I focused on my legs again, trying to get them to move. If I could somehow get a scalpel into my hand, I might be able to cut myself free. Even then, I was in no shape to take on Hruska. I was about to crumble just lying here. I stared at my leg, begging for some kind of reaction. I watched my foot flop over as though it were dead weight. That was a start.

Come on. Come on.

Brody appeared from the shadows, his brows furrowed and mouth parted in surprise. "Liz! Thank God."

"Brody?" I groaned. "Hruska will be back soon."

"I've been getting the layout of this place, figuring out where the exit is so that I can get you out of here." He stared at the instruments next to me.

"I can't move. She's got me tied down to this thing." I struggled against the cuffs again.

"You've got to keep trying. That bitch is going to be back any minute."

I focused again on my legs, while trying to force the buckle on the cuffs to stretch. The straps were weathered. They had needed to improvise with their equipment. It was used, probably to hold other people down like me before.

Brody looked around. "Maybe I can get into someone here. There's bound to be someone injured nearby."

"Brody, don't," I refocused my efforts on the cuffs, straining against the nylon. The one on the left was looser than before. The material gave way slightly every time I jerked at it.

"There's nothing else I can do," he said desperately. "I can't let this happen to you."

The cuff was looser. Was it actually looser? *Come on. COME ON.*

Moments later, the door opened and Hruska entered.

I laid my arm back down on the chair, hoping she wouldn't notice my efforts.

Brody stared from his place near the door, his mouth agape.

"My apologies. Unfortunately, the rooms here aren't soundproof. I wouldn't have been able to concentrate with all of that screaming going on." Hruska sat back down and picked up the syringe again. "Now, round two." She placed her hand on my head and brought the syringe up to my neck once more.

I strained against the cuffs. They were still too tight. "Help!" I screamed.

The needle jabbed into my neck and a flood of heavy medication swept into me. I grimaced as she yanked the needle from me. In the seconds that followed, a thick cloud swept over my mind, lulling me into sleep, into tender, blissful submission. I stopped flexing against the cuffs, my gaze fixated on a water stain on a tile in the ceiling. It bloomed and reshaped the longer I stared at it.

"That's it. Be a good girl and go to sleep," Hruska cooed. There was a distant whir of something mechanical nearby. The sound slowly morphed into white noise, like waves rushing on the ocean, like the wind in the grass at my family's house in Middlehitch. I smiled.

Brody's eyes swam in my vision. "Trust me, Liz," he said.

Everything suddenly got quiet. I didn't remember closing my eyes, didn't remember moving from that chair. Regardless, I wasn't in that tiny, disgusting room anymore.

I was floating. Nothing around me but cold air and a damp chill; the same as when I came out of the river back in New Hampshire.

This time, I wasn't close to the ground. I was floating in a dark ether, surrounded by fog. Far below me were the Woods. The frosted tips of their trees poked through the cloud cover like the serrations on a knife. The mist cleared and I recognized more and more trees, prickling across the landscape like fur. The spaces in between each tree top called to me, begged for me to drop into their darkness. I vaguely wondered if they were soft, if they'd catch me when I fell.

Embrace the dark, it called. The wild, hungry, lonely dark.

Fear blushed through me, expanding from my head to my toes.

I didn't want to go.

I didn't want to die.

Even so, I glided closer to it, its heaviness kissing my skin like humidity, coating me like oil.

A hand slipped into mine and held me in place.

"I've got you," Brody's voice caressed me. "I'm not letting go."

I looked up, struggling to see through the blackness that had grown thick around me. "Brody?" I called.

"Hold onto me, Liz," he said. "Just a little longer."

I was slipping. The Woods drew me further in.

Brody's nails dug into mine.

Pain. Not ethereal. Real pain.

"I'm not letting you go."

I shot up back into my body, breath piercing my lungs. My skin was on fire, my fingers tingling, my eyes piercing with agony.

"Easy, easy," Brody said. I couldn't figure out where he was. His voice came from everywhere.

"What happened? Where are you?"

"I didn't know if it would work. I didn't think it would. But you're back," he rambled.

My vision cleared and I realized that I was leaning against the chair in that dark make-shift operating room. The floor thrummed up at me. My brain was firing at a million miles a minute, taking in every single little sound, every crease in the plastic that surrounded us.

"Take a deep breath."

I did.

"Now, another one."

I inhaled. The exhale lasted a long time, as I was realizing what had changed. Hruska was unconscious on the floor, a needle in her shoulder. One of the straps that had held me down had snapped. The cart of medical tools was upturned, each implement glistening up from the floor at me. My arms were singed with tire. "What happened?"

"I had to do something. She was going to lobotomize you."

I finally saw him, standing on the other side of the chair, a fire of excitement in his eyes.

"Did you possess me?"

"Like I said, I didn't think it would work."

I looked down at my other hand, still buckled to the table. I quickly freed myself and selected one of the scalpels on the floor. Everything rocked when I came back up, like the first time I'd gone kayaking: unsteady, nervous. "What did you do? What did we do?"

"The good doctor is down for the count for now."

My heartrate had picked up again. I took another long breath to calm it. "She drugged me though. I should be asleep."

"I found adrenaline in her cart. I didn't know what else to do to wake you up. It might not last."

For the first time, I noticed the surgical tube tied around my arm and the fresh syringe mark there. Thousands of tiny bugs crawled across my skin. As I picked at the tube with my fingers, my thoughts glazed back to that emptiness and Brody's hand in mine. "Every other time you've possessed someone and left, you left behind a corpse. What makes me so different?"

"I was *trying* to save you."

The look in his face should have put me more at ease. Disquiet gripped me though. All I could think of was his voice telling me that he wasn't letting go. "What do you mean? You weren't trying to save the others before?"

Brody stared at his feet uncomfortably. "We need to get you out of here," he said, changing the subject. "Eventually, Hruska will be missed. Someone will come looking." He gestured to the door. "Let's go."

I let go of the bed and swooned for a moment before my legs stabilized. I forced every muscle to cooperate and headed to the door. Brody phased through it and then after a moment gave me the all clear. I twisted the knob and pushed my full body weight against the door, nearly collapsing into the hall.

My vision swayed like water. The white hall was too wide and I felt exposed in it. It reminded me of a hospital, not a chiropractor's office. Every chiropractor's office I'd ever been to had the same 60's wood paneling, weird rooms that branched off each other in places that made no sense and doors never opened. What kind of chiropractor's office had Elon set up in?

"Liz!" Brody hissed at me.

I turned my attention toward the left hall. He was waiting by a different door. The daylight coming through the wall of windows behind him made my eyes sting and I shielded them.

"Hruska said that Josh was in the medical wing," I said, taking a small step. "We need to find him."

Brody sighed. "We don't have time, Liz. We have a small window to get out of here. Josh doesn't fit into that."

"I'm not leaving him behind."

"Yeah, I figured you'd say that." He waved at me. "Come on."

The fuzzy warmth in my legs was beginning to subside. I grunted as I made my way up the hall, trying to swallow back the sudden bout of nausea that mounted inside.

"There's a closet here," Brody said. "In it, you'll find some scrubs. That'll at least give you a disguise so you can get around without being obvious. Remember, this is a small unit. The minute they don't recognize you; they'll shoot you and ask questions later."

I opened the closet door and flicked on the light inside. I limped in, my entire body throbbing.

"I'm going back to guard the door and make sure no one discovers the good doctor. Come and get me when you're dressed."

I nodded and Brody retreated through the closed door.

With a shuddering breath, I approached one of the nearby cabinets and pulled open a drawer to some blue scrubs. As I stripped out of my torn t-shirt and pulled on a dark blue one, I paused. Bruises spotted my arms and torso, a large purple one settled over my right rib cage. Maybe that was why I was having trouble breathing. Cracked ribs would make it harder to get out of here by force.

I found a pair of pants large enough to slide over my own, shoved my boots back on and re-laced them. Lastly, I found a cap and mask for my face. My hair was slathered with mud and blood. If people looked too closely, they were going to notice, although judging from Hruska's attire, maybe I wouldn't look so out of place. I slid the scalpel I'd stolen from Hruska into my pants pocket. I didn't want to let go of it; holding it made the pain subside a little. When I was ready, I took as deep a breath as I could manage and left the room.

I returned to where we'd left Hruska asleep. Brody was nowhere in sight.

As those thoughts purged me, Brody slid through the door. "You still want to risk getting out for Josh?"

Brody was right. The adrenaline wasn't going to last long. Every second that ticked by was another one where exhaustion sank its teeth further into me. The right decision would have been to flee. They wouldn't kill Josh.

No. They *would* kill him. He'd exterminated a small team of *them*. He wasn't a valuable, ignorant soldier anymore. Probably the only reason he wasn't dead yet was because he had information about me. If I didn't talk, or went braindead under some terrifying procedure, he was their ancillary lab rat. Someone who had been in contact with an Affected. They'd probably get whatever they could out of him and then shoot him.

"Liz," Brody said.
The images faded away.
"Lead the way," I told Brody.

TWENTY-NINE

I followed Brody, staying as low and slow as I could. We reached a T-junction at the end of the corridor. Brody veered left and after a few moments of me waiting, he signaled with a whistle that the coast was clear. As we continued, I glanced out the long line of windows. We were on the third floor of an enormous building. The glass looked out over a parking lot of snow-covered cars. There were a number of covered trucks lining the front walkway down to a gate. No one guarded the entrance. Maybe they didn't have enough personnel yet. Maybe they were all out scouring the streets for more Affected.

"This used to be an old mental hospital back in the day. They converted it into a chiropractic center like five years ago," Brody said.

"Why the hell does Montroy Circle need a three-story chiropractic clinic?"

"I guess all the summer tourists didn't want to drive to Flintland Green for it. You know how uptight they are."

"Or were."

Brody nodded toward the trucks. "We need to find some keys to one of the trucks outside. It's the only way you're going to make it. It's a long way down into town without a ride."

Located at the top of one of the hills that surrounded Lake Grey, Montroy Circle was a twisted, winding six-mile descent back down toward Upper Vale. With me in bad shape and not knowing how mobile Josh would be, I knew Brody was right: we needed a vehicle.

Around the next corner, Brody waved me back. A voice down the hall to the right spoke followed by the static of a walkie-talkie. There were no footsteps. The guard was stationary.

Brody turned back to me. "He's got eyes on the other end of the hall. You'll need to get close and take him out with that scalpel before he can make a call on the walkie."

I had a fleeting thought about taking someone's life without them suspecting it was coming. It came and went as I reached into my pocket and retrieved the scalpel. Fuck this asshole. If Hruska and I heard that screaming of the other patient from my room, he would have, too. Hell, he'd heard mine, too. He didn't give a damn.

I rounded the corner, sticking close to the wall, but moving at a relaxed pace. I counted every step with trepidation, my heart thundering as I closed in on the oblivious security guard. When I was within a few feet of him, he turned.

My unarmed hand wrapped around his torso while the scalpel plunged toward his throat. A ribbon of blood stained my hand and the wall. The guard quivered and croaked as he collapsed to the ground, blood spurting from the wound in his neck. I grabbed the walkie from his limp hand and kept going, even as my body screamed at me in protest.

I didn't have time to hide the guard's body. I didn't want to finish him off. I needed to keep going. I didn't know how long I could ride the adrenaline rush.

We continued down the hall past another bank of windows, this one looking out on the forest behind the chiropractic center. There was a darkness in it that I recognized immediately, one that crawled up my throat toward my brain. The Woods were there. With them, there would be wolves.

"Hey, eyes on me," Brody said. He was walking backward a few paces ahead.

We passed a set of rooms with glass panels in the doors. Curiosity pulled me toward the nearest one and I immediately regretted it. There was a chair inside that looked like the one I'd been strapped to. A body was on it, not moving. The skin was pulled back over the face. Something grey and spongey stared back at me from inside the cranial cavity.

My stomach erupted and it took everything I had to swallow the bile back down. When I managed to get my bearings, I noticed a face in the window of the next door.

It was a Black man in his mid-forties with close cropped hair and a greying circle beard. His large studious brown eyes watched my every movement behind a pair of cracked thick framed glasses. "You," he said. "You're not a doctor, are you?"

I blinked. I was covered in blood. From the way Hruska had looked in that makeshift operation room, I *could* have been a doctor here.

But then, he looked to my left at Brody, someone he shouldn't have been able to see.

"You've got a ghost attached to you."

I frowned. "You can see him?"

"I can see all of them. You let me out of here and I'll help you escape."

It didn't make any sense. A person who could see every ghost? He must have been extremely valuable to Hruska. If I could get him out of here, he could maybe answer some of my questions, too.

"I don't trust him," Brody said, moving slightly to the right.

The man's eyes followed him.

I stepped up to the glass in the door. "Who are you?" I asked.

"My name is Astor. I had a ghost attached to me once, too. Not anymore though."

The name instantly inspired dread. Astor. He was the one that had once travelled with Prisca, Tamiko, and Lennox. He had somehow managed to kill his own ghost. And he'd plotted to kill Tamiko.

"He's a dangerous man, Liz," Brody growled, getting close to me. "We should leave him in there and keep moving. Josh is up this way."

I backed away from the glass.

"You're trying to get to Medical, right? Up ahead are some locked doors that can only be opened with a security pass," Astor said.

I stopped. "Brody?"

Brody moved ahead. A pair of glass doors stood ahead of us on a skybridge leading to the next wing of the building. He came up to the doors and glanced at a box mounted to one of the walls. "It's a card reader."

"No problem. We'll go back and grab the key from that guard I killed," I said, spinning to go back in the direction we'd come from.

"It's not just a card reader," Astor added. "There's a security camera on the other side. Unless they're disabled, you'll risk triggering the alarm."

I was lightheaded. "How are we going to get passed it then?" I asked, irritation staining my voice.

"I can manually shut them down from the security room. Before they realized how…special I was, they gave me a tour of the place. Figured I would want revenge on the people who left me to die in the Woods." He stared down at the floor. "I should be thanking them actually."

Getting closer to the door, I said, "If I open your door, what guarantee do I have that you won't kill me right here right now?"

He smiled. "What makes you think I'd want to kill you?" An ironic smile. A smile that I didn't understand the reason for.

"I learned about you from Prisca," I said.

His smile thinned.

"You were going to kill Tamiko using Prisca's son to do it."

"That wasn't what I was trying to do," he answered, his tone devoid of any joy.

"They found your journal," Brody added. "They uncovered your plan. Your insistence that we're not to be trusted? That's why those guys abandoned you, man."

Astor leaned in closer to the glass. "The ghosts *aren't* to be trusted. The thing in the Woods confirmed it."

I gaped. "What thing in the Woods?"

"The creature I talked to in one of those horrific buildings there. He told me that they were "corrupted" by the material earth. That they start to go crazy, wanting to return to their former selves. That's why they start possessing people. They can't get enough of what it's like to be alive again."

My eyes darted to Brody.

Either he hadn't heard or he was pretending he hadn't. He paced between the left and right walls. "We're wasting time here, Liz."

I glanced back at Astor. "So, you tried to kill one of your friends in order to convince the others that you were right? By having a boy possess a heartbroken widow?"

Astor wiped his brow. "Yes, at the time, my approach was barbaric. But I was doing it because I had run out of options. They weren't listening to me and they weren't going to unless something monumental happened. You can't tell me you haven't had to do things you weren't proud of?"

The flickers of Elden and Jake hit my conscience like shocks. We had destroyed the last remnants of that family, Brody and I. I knew how rooted Prisca was about the idea that her son couldn't have been a monster, couldn't have been capable of anything sinister. With the sheer volume of accounts I'd read about the things that attached people had done, I could only imagine how Astor's hand had been forced. Had his own ghost changed to the point where Astor had deemed it was dangerous?

I looked at Brody again.

Why hadn't Brody answered me when I asked him if he could have saved the souls he chose to inhabit the bodies of? Had he let them fall into the Woods' embrace?

"Hey, hey," Astor said suddenly.

I realized that my feet had gone numb and I'd slumped a bit. My adrenaline was wearing out. I grabbed the doorhandle for stability.

"I'm not going to hurt you," Astor assured.

Desperation made me open the door.

Brody was beside me in a second. "What are you doing?"

"We don't have time," I urged. We'd lingered in this hallway long enough. Someone could come along any moment.

Astor slipped out of his room and closed the door behind him. He was dressed in a torn brown suit, one that reminded me of a professor I'd had in college. It was thoroughly dirt-covered as were his shoes. He'd probably worn it since he'd been left in the Woods by Prisca's group.

"The security room is back this way." He motioned toward the hall we'd come from.

Brody put his hands up. "The hell is—"

"Stay here. At the first sign of trouble, let me know."

I followed Astor back up the hall until we reached the body of the guard I'd stabbed. He was laying there in a pool of red, his eyes locked on a floor vent about a foot in front of him. Sickness returned to me and I leaned against the wall for support.

"You saw a creature in those Woods? Something sentient?" I said, trying to distract myself.

Astor knelt next to the body and checked the pockets. "I don't know how to describe it. I stumbled upon a building not too long after waking up and took refuge in it. The thing seemed…ancient."

I took a deep breath. "This thing in the monolith told you exactly what you wanted to know?"

"Believe me, that isn't what I wanted. I wanted to be wrong. It said that in order to fix things, that I had to 'go to the center. That's where It starts'. Damned if I know what that means though."

I held my breath. The creature I'd spoken to in the monolith under the Woods had told me that there was no way to mend things. Astor's statement didn't make any sense. Was he lying? Or did that thing in the Woods lie to me first? Hell, was it even capable of lying?

"Ah, got it." Astor held up the keycard.

"I don't believe you," I said. "There's nothing that can change this."

He got back up and handed the card to me. As I took it, he put his hand on my arm.

I flinched, the idea of anyone touching me immediately making my skin crawl. Still, he held on. "You've seen them, too, haven't you?"

I flashed the blood-coated scalpel. "Back off."

Astor took a step back, putting his hands out in front of him. "You mentioned a monolith. I never said that's where I was."

I'd given myself away. "I only know it was that because Brody called it that. I found him attached to some kind of altar in the Woods. I managed to get him out, but I don't know what they were going to do to him there."

"It could have been important," Astor surmised. "I saw them, too, before I was chased out by the wolves: the monoliths and the altars. If only you had let them go on with their ritual."

I glared. "Excuse me if I'm not a cold prick like you. I saved my best friend from potentially having his soul sucked by a monster."

"Was that their intention or are you editorializing?" He didn't seem to have caught my tone.

I cleared my throat. "Does it matter?"

Astor blinked. "My apologies. I only meant that the altars have to be for some purpose we don't understand yet. It would have been beneficial if you'd discovered it."

I pocketed the keycard. "What do we do now?"

Astor looked to the hallway where I'd woken up. "I'm going to go to the security room alone. You should stay here and wait for my signal."

"What's that going to be?"

"When I've disabled the security cameras, you'll see a light blink off."

I nodded.

He began down the hall.

"Where should we meet?"

Astor hesitated. "If either of us get out of here alive, we'll see each other again in the Woods. I think you're as curious about how to prevent their spread as I am."

With that, he turned and fled up the hall. I watched him round the next corner and silently made my way back to Brody, turning over Astor's words in my head. I didn't want to go back into those Woods ever again. Not after what had happened when Brody had possessed me.

If anything, I now recognized their bottomless appetite and their insatiable desire to swallow everything and everyone. It was there all along. I'd been too distracted to notice it.

I couldn't go back, even if that was the only place where I could touch Brody again.

It didn't matter.

I wasn't even sure if Brody was Brody anymore.

As soon as he set eyes on me, Brody appeared beside me. "What the fuck was that about? Huh? He's going to get you killed!"

"He's going to disarm the security camera. Until then, we have to stay put."

Brody threw up his hands in the air. "This is exactly what he wants, Liz. He's going to tell them right where you are and send a team down here to pick you up and haul you back into one of these rooms to get your head chopped open. You're a sitting duck here."

He was right. Despite wanting to trust Astor, I knew nothing about him or his motives. Josh's buddies in his group had called him "cuckoo". What if his time in the Woods damaged his psyche? What if his only agenda was to bring down as many Affected people as he could?

Worse was that I was getting more and more tired by the minute. It was an effort to stay focused on the here and now and not want to slip into sleep to escape the pain.

"Scout ahead. I need to know what's on the other side of the bridge. I want to make sure that if we unlock this door and run, we have a place to run to," I decided.

Brody nodded and vanished through the double doors. I watched him cross the bridge and then vanish through the double wooden doors on the other side.

Seconds passed. I took a deep breath and pocketed the scalpel. I wagged my hands in the air, trying to keep blood circulating, trying to divert my attention from the time elapsing and the possibility that Astor was sending armed guards to my location at that moment.

Brody appeared back through the glass doors, his eyes dark and serious. "Hold up."

I stopped. "What?"

"You've got Heidi on the other side of the bridge. She's armed with a pistol. You're going to have to lure her out."

Fuck. That bitch had nearly killed me twice already. I didn't want to give her the best opportunity she'd had so far by walking through the doors and straight into her.

I flashed Brody a glare. "How am I going to do…" I stopped as the realization hit me. "Tell me what walkie channel she's on."

Brody disappeared and reappeared within another few moments. "Channel two."

I turned around and walked to the guard I'd stabbed. I turned with my back to the skybridge, kneeling over the still body of the security guard, and changed the channel on his walkie to two. Then, I did my best impression of Hruska into the speaker. "I need some help here, Ms. Summerfield!"

Heidi wouldn't know it was me. My hair was under a surgical cap. My face was masked. I looked like any other doctor in this place.

I tensed as the wooden doors at the end of the skybridge opened and footsteps jogged in my direction. A few seconds later, the secure glass door yawned open as Heidi's voice yelled to me. "What the fuck happened?"

Closer. I squeezed the scalpel.

Closer.

The footsteps stopped behind my right shoulder. Heidi leaned over me. "Jesus! Kenneth is—"

I spun, my arm uppercutting hard toward her face. The scalpel sliced straight up through Heidi's chin into her mouth. Her scream ruptured through the silence as she shoved me away. I lost my grip on the scalpel and it stayed in her as she fell on her side. I scraped myself up off the floor, blood smearing the linoleum, lungs burning, and darted for the skybridge. Heidi screamed incoherently behind me and her walkie-talkie chattered.

"Go!" Brody shouted from the end of the sky tunnel as I approached. I yanked the glass door open, sprinting for the wooden doors on the opposite end. A half a second later, a cacophony of noise blared from the speakers on either end of the hall. Two yellow revolving lights sprung to life and an air raid siren pulsed from somewhere far off.

The cameras hadn't been turned off. I didn't know if it was because Astor had indeed set me up or if I hadn't given him enough time. Either way, I'd made my choice.

My chest was on fire, struggling to breathe as I forced myself to keep going. I slammed through the wooden doors at the end of the bridge, my vision swiveling left and right. "Where do I go?"

Brody appeared next to me. "Josh is two doors down on your left."

I ran, my boots slapping against the tiles in the hall. I barely stopped in front of the chosen door and barreled through without a moment to spare.

Josh lay on a cot, his head bandaged and his arm handcuffed to one of the bed rails. He sat up when I entered, his eyes bugging. "Liz! God, how did you…" He trailed off when he took in the blood.

"Where's the key for the handcuffs?"

"Heidi has them."

"Fucking shit!" I hissed.

Josh yanked against his cuff and the metal clanged in response. "Liz, you need to get out of here. If they find you, they'll kill you."

"I'm not leaving you here with these monsters." I turned on my heel and pushed out the doors again.

"Don't worry about—" he yelled behind me, my footfalls and the closing door cutting him off.

I ran back to the skybridge door and squeaked it open. I couldn't see the other end of the hall where I'd attacked her. No telling if Heidi had reached backup via the walkie talkie or if she was still cowering in the fetal position on the floor. I had to get those keys though.

"Liz, you should listen to Josh and get out of here," Brody barked.

"No. Now, tell me if she's still there."

Unwittingly, Brody vanished like smoke. A few moments later, he reappeared a few steps ahead of me. "She's not. She must have gone for help."

There was no use. I couldn't go searching for Heidi now. I had to focus on getting out. My chest was thicker than ever before. I wasn't ready to say goodbye to Josh. Not after we had found each other again.

Metal crashed against the floor in Josh's room. I ran for it and pushed open the door. Josh was getting to his feet, the dislocated bed rail clutched in his handcuffed hand. "Easier than I thought," he said by way of explanation.

"Suppose we can thank the steroids and Lucky Charms for that," Brody said under his breath.

I ignored him and held open the door for Josh. "Can you run?" I asked.

"I'm willing to try," Josh answered, hefting the railing through.

"Let's move then." After I was out, I turned to Brody. "Which way now?"

"Go left. There should be a staircase we can take."

We edged down the corridor. The volume of the alarm made my

head want to cave in. No doubt everyone in this place was on high alert now and through radio coordination, would be coming to get us soon.

Brody merged through the stairwell door at the same time I opened it. Taking two stairs at a time, I stopped when he suddenly flung himself in my direction, his arm passing through the middle of my back. My vision went dark momentarily and after it passed, I found myself bent over on the stairs.

"Back! Go back!" he was yelling.

Gunfire ricocheted up the stairwell.

Josh's arm heaved up under my own as we barreled through the stairwell doors back into the hallway.

"Back to the skybridge!" Brody yelled.

Regaining my own momentum, I got to my feet and followed after him, Josh lugging the bed railing mere feet behind me.

We followed Brody back to the skybridge doors and out onto the track. As we passed through the glass doors, Brody stopped abruptly. "Brody?"

He stepped aside.

Heidi stood at the other end of the skybridge, pistol drawn, blood smearing her mouth, down her neck to her chest. "Stop!" she grunted, groaning as she held her jaw with the other hand.

Josh slowly stepped around me, putting himself firmly between the two of us. "Heidi, enough is enough. Let her go."

Heidi's rage morphed into disbelief. She closed the gap between us, keeping her gun drawn, her gaze fixated on Josh. "You're not him," she said, her tongue dragging with the words. "The real Josh wouldn't say that. He wouldn't even think that."

Josh took a calm step toward her, keeping his hands slightly raised, still holding the bed rail. "It's me, I swear to God. I swear on your sister's life that it's me. We were wrong. It's not a virus. It's real."

"How dare you mention her!" she squealed. "Here. Now. After everything you've done…"

"We might still be able to figure out how to stop this. We could save people like Jane; like Liz. We have to try."

"She's not my sister anymore!" Heidi screamed. Blood oozed from between her lips. "You've been duped, you fucking idiot! Just like all the other fucking idiots…." Her grip on the gun tensed.

"Fuck this," Brody grunted. He ran at her. This entire form thinned and hollowed, vanishing into the air even before he reached her.

Heidi's eyes changed, rolling back into her head.

That moment was all that Josh needed.

Josh swung the bed rail up into Heidi's gun and it went off, the shot cavernous in the glass space.

Brody was suddenly ejected from the mix, his form tumbling back as Heidi and Josh wrestled with the gun.

I dropped against the carpet, my hands instinctively going over my head.

The two forms swung from side to side, the gun misfiring here and there. The glass walls cracked with each missed gunshot.

"Fucking let go!" Heidi shrieked as she tackled Josh, throwing her full weight against him.

Josh fell backward, the bedrail dragging him off balance into the cracked crystal wall. The sound of shattering glass screeched through my ears.

Both their forms vanished over the edge.

I held my breath.

Or I forgot to breathe.

I wasn't sure which one.

All I knew was that I scrambled to get to the edge of the skybridge, to look over at what had happened. I didn't get there before I heard their bodies slam into the ground. Once I did, I stopped cold.

Whatever small, instinctual part of my brain that still worked nudged me into action. I leapt to my feet, boots pounding against the floor as I flung the glass doors open at the end of the skybridge and raced toward the stairwell. The commotion was somewhere behind me, people shouting and barking orders. The klaxon wailed on endlessly.

Shouldering through the door, I took steps two and three at a time, ignoring the snarling pain in my joints, the frenzy in my blood.

No.

No. It couldn't be. Josh had to be all right. He had to be.

At the ground level, I pushed out the emergency exit door, immediately accosted by icy winds. A storm was coming in. I hadn't noticed it while everything was going on. It was so hard to focus. I pivoted hard to round the structure, boots slipping in the slush until I was back on my feet.

"Josh!"

No one responded.

Skirting the edge of the building, the first thing I noticed was the blood, like a starburst on the snow. Heidi's limbs were drawn out in strange angles, her eyes fixed on me and her chest was crick-crackling as she drew sluggish breaths. Josh wasn't there.

I scanned left and right as I neared Heidi's body. "Josh!"

"Here."

I whipped around. Josh lay with both legs extended in the remains of the garden underneath the glass corridor. Running to him, I dropped to my knees beside him, my hand cradling his head.

He gasped. "I think she broke my fall." He drew a shaky breath. "Christ, I think I still broke my own fall."

In the building above us, dozens of footfalls rumbled over the skybridge.

We weren't getting out alive. There was no way.

"Can you move?"

"Probably shouldn't," he said, breathing shallowly. "Something's leaking."

I tried to get my arm around his back. Something wet stuck to my palm. I pulled my hand away and noticed immediately that his left hip was coated in blood. A gunshot.

Fuck.

Fuck. Fuck. Fuck.

Tears streaked my face as I searched blindly for something to press against the wound.

"Liz, it's over." Brody's voice was over my shoulder. "We need to leave now!"

"I can't!" It was true. Not because Josh had saved my life, not because I had loved him once, not because our histories were so entwined and knotted together. I was rooted to that spot. Even the tiniest fleck of relief over the idea of surrendering lightened me.

"Now, Liz!"

Josh's lips moved. I couldn't hear what he was saying.

I leaned in and listened.

Brody's hands plunged inside my body like twin swords of ice.

I screamed.

"Go! GO!" he raged.

I leapt to my feet even as the Woods trickled toward my soul. Somehow, I left Josh. Somehow, I forced my feet to lunge toward Heidi's still quaking body, make my fingers fish through her pockets for a set of car keys. I grabbed her gun from the ground.

The door to the stairwell broke open around the side of the building. Boots crunched on snow.

Somehow, I made myself run.

Behind me, bones crackled as Heidi's should-have-been corpse stood up, shards puncturing through ruined flesh as Brody puppeteered her into a standing position. Hers and his cries of pain struck me as he lurched her body toward the approaching army. I couldn't look.

As soon as the lot and the cars came into view, I primed the unlock button on Heidi's key fob. A silver pickup truck blinked its lights. I stumbled across the icy pavement toward it. Any moment, I expected people in police riot gear emerge.

I was at the driver's side door when the horrified yells escalated, when the pop-pop of gunfire echoed across the sky. I slithered up into the plush seat, a sob cracking through my lips, and slammed the door.

Jabbing the key into the ignition, I brought the truck to life and stomped on the gas pedal. The truck rocketed down the lot toward the front entrance, smashing through the small yellow gate there. I haphazardly wrangled a seatbelt on as I steered down the corkscrew road of Montroy Circle.

"Brody?" I questioned the air around me.

Nothing.

Maybe he was still inside of Heidi. Maybe they thought they could help her. Maybe he'd been pulled back into the Woods. Maybe he'd gone to try and find Astor.

Maybe that gunfire was the sound of them killing Josh.

The thought sat like lead in my chest, sobering, chasing away all desire for rest.

I wanted to let it go like a balloon, let it drift up into the cloud covered sky until it vanished. I didn't want to face the possibility that I was truly alone yet. Not until I was far away from this place.

THIRTY

The last twelve hours had been all but snow and white filmy sky. I'd begun to wonder if it was ever going to change, if I'd never see the sun again in my ruined future. I'd driven north toward the only place I knew that was safe: the camp site on Lake Storm where Josh and I had spent so many weekends relaxing, fishing, and enjoying nature's solitude.

Somewhere in between, I'd abandoned the truck from Elon, switched to a not-so-obvious Toyota. I hadn't gotten far in that. The adrenaline wore off. The dark embrace of sleep took me. I'd had enough sense to get off the main road, to park in someone's driveway and lean back my seat to hide.

I'd awoken in the dark, with the sounds of owls calling to each other across the road. It was freezing. My stomach was snarling with hunger. Everything hurt.

I was lucky the car had enough gas to get me to Lake Storm. I was lucky that Josh kept an emergency supply of food in the basement there. I was lucky that Hruska and the mercenaries at Elon hadn't found me while I was passed out.

I hooked up the propane stove on the back deck by lantern light. The lake was a glittering disc in the dark, reflecting the skies star-studded dome. I cooked a pouch of dehydrated chicken gumbo in a tiny pot, my breath releasing in gentle puffs against the frozen air every few moments.

I listened for the sounds of approaching cars, of footsteps in the snow, for Brody's voice. The last one I wasn't sure if I actually wanted. He'd made me leave Josh behind. He was keeping things from me.

I ate in the comfort of the cabin after I'd lit a fire and warmed the room. The beds weren't made and the sheets in the closet were motheaten. I'd left all of my supplies behind in the car accident. I used as many of the bed linens as I could and snuggled down inside of them until sleep found me once more and turned off the tide of thoughts.

The morning brought rain and a leak in the roof shy of my pillow. I cooked oatmeal and watched the front windows until I got sick of waiting for something to happen. I found a bucket in the bathroom to collect water from the leak and a mostly empty first-aid kit to mend what I could of the endless injuries that had battered my body.

I was searching the mouse-turd speckled cabinets when the rumble of an engine caught me by surprise. I snatched up the fire poker and knelt beneath the large windows in the front of the cabin to watch the empty dirt drive out front. The pines shielded my view for the longest time, but finally a truck appeared, one that I instantly recognized. It looked like the one I'd stolen from Elon, an unmarked grey Ford F-250, rocking unsteadily over the various potholes as it slowed and stopped out front.

Did Hruska know that Josh had a camp up here? Maybe he and some recruits had come here when they started their sweep in Maine? Maybe it was someone from a nearby camp who had noticed activity here? It was entirely possible that someone this far north wouldn't have followed CDC policy and stayed put.

I cautiously peered up over the window ledge. My stomach dropped when I noticed who climbed out of the driver's side door.

On my feet within seconds, I tore open the door and raced out onto the deck.

"Josh!" I called.

He lifted his head at his name. He was favoring his hip, still wearing the bloodied clothes from the clinic the previous day. He'd wrapped the wound with gauze but it had bled through.

A spark of relief lit up his eyes. "Thank God, Liz, you're all right," he said as he hobbled toward me.

"How did you…." I didn't finish before we were in each other's arms.

Josh held me to him, his breath puffing against my neck raggedly.

Tears flooded my eyes immediately. The sound of his voice, the smell of him, his breath on my neck were all things I never thought I'd experience again. I thought I'd lost him.

We separated. He clutched at his wound. "Gah, this…um…I need—"

"We've got to get this cleaned. We can't risk it getting infected,"

I said, wiping away my tears hurriedly. I gestured toward the splintered picnic table on the deck. "I'll grab something."

"Liz, wait—"

"Sit down. At least we have hand sanitizer."

I crashed back through the door into the house, my shoulders set, my mind burning with purpose.

I'm not alone.

I'm not alone.

I'm not alone.

When I came out of the bathroom, Josh was standing next to the fireplace. He had his hands up as though he was bracing himself against a potential attack.

"Why are you looking at me like that?" I asked, walking up to him.

"There isn't going to be any easy way to say this," he said. Slowly. Methodically. Totally unlike Josh.

"What?" The earth had dropped out beneath me.

"It's me, Lizzy."

Images sprung to my mind, things that I hadn't thought about in months, a life that seemed so utterly Elysian compared with the horror we faced day-to-day. I thought of the morning Josh put jam in his coffee instead of on his toast, the nights he'd stayed up late with me as I'd cried after fights with my mom. Of our random dance parties, of our Thanksgivings, of our fights and our reunions. I thought about running and pulling him into my arms at the airport, the touch of his worn and familiar clothes after he'd returned from a trip overseas. I thought about the taste of his mouth as we kissed.

My back stiffened and pain flooded through me as though a dam were breached. My mouth cracked as the sickening tide of realization came over me.

Josh's eyes looked far away and foreign. They were no longer his eyes.

"Y…you…." I couldn't bring myself to say what I knew had already happened. I recoiled a step from him.

He stayed put like I was the sea pulling away from his shore. "Nothing I say is going to make this easier on you, Liz."

Even his voice didn't sound like his. The inflection of laughter, of trust, of light wasn't there. Only disappointment.

I took a deep breath, though it came through stale and short. "Josh is gone?"

Brody nodded, not looking at me. "It was quick."

All of those memories I'd been recollecting were now drowning beneath a torrent of confusion. My once happy tears were already drying on my face, eclipsed by shock. "Why?"

He cocked his head. I knew without a shadow of a doubt that this wasn't a dream or a misunderstanding. "You can't survive out here on your own."

My skin itched and was cold. The longer I stood beside the bed, the more the humiliation overwhelmed me. I was a stranger in my own body. I wondered if that was how Brody felt now, if that was what he felt every time he possessed someone. How could he possibly like it?

"Did you try to save his soul like you tried to save mine?" I asked, unsure if I really wanted to know the answer.

"I couldn't hold him."

A shrill whine crept into my ears as the words left Josh's mouth. The more I looked at him, the less I saw of the man I had once wanted to marry. It was violently wrong hearing Brody in Josh's voice. They were not the same and they were never meant to occupy the same space.

"You hollowed him out to make space for yourself," I said, my teeth clenched.

Horror crept into the green eyes I'd once known. "Liz, he was dying."

My thoughts scrambled as I tried to imagine what Josh's last moments were like, if he'd cried as he was consumed by the Woods, if Brody had said anything to him. All I wanted was to be able to go back.

Brody leaned against the fireplace mantel, Josh's body like a dreadful trophy that he'd conquered. "This doesn't have to be all bad," he said.

I sniffled, wiping my nose. "What?"

"We can be together now."

I knew exactly what he meant. But I wanted to be wrong. "What does that mean?"

He took a hesitant step toward me, still clutching the gunshot. "We don't need to go back into the Woods to touch one another anymore. I can hold you now like this."

The words flared in my head. Brody was adamant about not wanting Josh to get between us ever since he remembered our triste. I now knew why Brody had taken Josh's body. And I was to blame.

I sighed, wiping my eyes. "You didn't even try to save him, did you?"

He set his jaw. "Liz, this is why I'm here. It has to be."

"It was a mistake." A renegade tear slid down the side of my nose. "We both made a mistake, Brody. You even told me that the morning after. That we needed to talk—"

"You don't think that," he said. "You've held onto me this entire time. You felt the same way."

I made eye contact with him. "What you're feeling, they aren't *your* feelings," I said, my tone edged with warning.

"I love you." He stroked my cheek. "I *know* that. I *remember* that."

My bottom lip trembled. "Don't you remember Carmen? Your guilt?"

"Carmen isn't here now," he said quickly. "We can't change what happened. We can only move forward. Together."

He reached out to hold me and I shrunk away. "You expect me to let you in after you let Josh go?" I scoffed. "This is too much."

"I can't let you go this alone anymore, not after everything you've already been through," Brody said, the desperation in his voice making me want to crawl inside of myself. For a moment, it had actually sounded like Josh. He reached forward again, pulled me toward him. I let myself be fooled again, savoring the last essences of Josh's smell, of him holding me, wishing it was him who was holding me. "I can protect you."

I pulled away, sitting on the bed, my hand resting at the edge of my pillow. "You can't promise me that, Brody."

"I can. I did." He knelt down in front of me. "Josh wanted me to take care of you. Let me."

All of the muscles in my neck and shoulders went rigid. "No, he didn't."

Brody frowned.

"Josh told me that our breakup was about choosing you over him. He was going to be my husband and I didn't support him because I was afraid of losing you. It's the same now as it was then. I have to make the right choice."

"Liz," Brody crouched in front of me. "Your relationship with Josh had faded. You chose to stay in a place you loved, with someone who made you feel good. You can't fault yourself for that decision."

The sentence made the hairs on my arms stand. "Do you want to know what the last thing Josh told me was? He told me he loved me. After everything I put him through. He still loved me." My hand slid under my pillow. "He didn't tell you to do anything. You did it because you can't stand the idea of not feeling anything for forever. He was an opportunity, a golden opportunity for you, and that's it."

Brody put Josh's hand on my knee. "That's not true. Josh would have wanted this. He would have wanted you safe."

"What happened to the Brody I used to know? The one who promised to always tell me the truth when it came to 'the stuff that matters'?"

Brody stared emptily at me.

My hand gripped the gun under my pillow. "The Brody I knew, the Brody I loved would never have done this."

I pulled the pistol out. All it took was those few moments of unpreparedness, a couple seconds where time sped up. The shot rang out in the tiny room and deafened me.

Brody fell back against the floor, cracking Josh's head against the wood. With dazed eyes, he watched me, bringing a quivering hand to his chest. The blood there oozed as I'd seen it do many times before from my old friend. But it was Josh's blood this time and it was Brody's consciousness that slipped away.

"Liz...," he whispered, disbelief clouding his gaze.

I knelt down next to him on the floor, my hand closing around his. The warm blood forced the tears from my eyes. "It's okay. You're going to be fine."

In a couple more seconds, his eyes lost their focus. The tremble in his hand was gone.

Brody was finally *gone*.

I stood, wiping my nose forgetting about the blood on my hands. I placed the gun on the side table next to the bed, pulled the sheets up around me on the mattress and wept.

I forced myself to drag Josh's body from the room three days after killing Brody, if only to ensure I didn't have to look at Josh's face any longer. The sorrow swallowed me whole. I spent those days with minimal food, curled next to a dwindling fire that I fed irregularly.

Sometimes the silence was unbearable. I'd try to sing all the songs I knew to have something to fill the void. "Intergalactic", "Enjoy the Silence", "I Think I'm Paranoid", "Harvest Moon" .... I got tired of listening to my own voice.

It was April now and the ground had thawed enough to allow a shovel blade into it. I finally buried Josh beneath one of the ash trees. It took hours to dig. I didn't do anything the rest of that day. I couldn't.

I'd run out of food and any attempt at making an impromptu fishing rod had failed. I'd stayed with the assumption that maybe Brody wasn't gone. Maybe he would come back. Maybe I had made the wrong choice after all.

Only when the pangs of hunger hit me did I realize I couldn't stay there lost in that darkness. I'd done it once. I couldn't do it again.

I managed to find gas for the Toyota before I decided to leave, siphoning from the truck that Brody had come in and from a motorboat at the neighboring camp.

The whole car ride south, all I had were my thoughts and my memories to keep me company and they were the worst companions yet. I forced myself to focus on the scenery as much as possible, focus on what I could forage from my surroundings. I needed to stay in the here and now. I didn't want to be lost to the past. If I did, I wasn't sure I'd resurface.

The days were long, each one longer than the last. I broke into houses to spend my nights. Most places had some kind of woodstove, supplies to scavenge, something to eat. A few didn't. In those I'd bury myself in the thickest of blankets and somehow find sleep. I dreamt of shadowy lands with hazy geographies, running toward something I couldn't identify in the distance. Sometimes, the memory of Josh's voice reached out to me like a whisper in my ear; sometimes Brody's.

These dreams never lasted long and I rarely slept for long periods of time. When I couldn't, I'd force myself to work out. I'd change my bandages. I'd force myself to eat one more stale Pop Tart.

Every time I found myself veering close to a forested area, I'd take a longer route to get around it. I knew there were answers inside waiting for me, something that would explain everything that was happening. Astor had said we should meet there. I still didn't know if what he'd told me was the truth. But I wasn't ready. I didn't have a reason to know now anyway. My reason was dead again.

It was another couple of weeks before I saw another person. I followed dirt backroads when I couldn't take paved ones, twisting my way through the Maine countryside until I finally crossed into New Hampshire. The White Mountains loomed ahead of me, their tranquility calling to me over what felt like an ocean. The signs of Cardend sent tremors through me, reminding me of my brush of death there.

I fully expected my path to be blocked by those woods. I knew I'd have to go through them eventually.

Middlehitch was my latest stop. Rain speckled my windshield as I drove through the ghost town and pulled into the general store. Gathering my empty gas cans and a cardboard box to gather food, I walked toward the doors. I was greeted with the soft poke of something in the small of my back.

I froze.

My own gun, the one that had once belonged to Heidi, was still in the car. A mistake; I usually wasn't so reckless.

"Put the boxes on the ground."

The voice was younger than I'd expected. I turned slightly and the weapon prodded into my back. "Don't make me shoot."

I bent over, letting the boxes and cans slide from my fingers down to the pavement. "Kid, I don't want any trouble."

"Keep your hands in the air."

I kept my hands up, my mind trying to scheme how I could disarm this little brat. She probably wasn't alone. It would be a risky move.

"All right, now turn around."

I did. My tension melted.

"Evie?"

She barely looked like the little girl I'd left behind on that bridge, cowering and hugging her knees. She was somehow taller, her long curls pulled back in a ponytail. She wasn't even holding a gun. Of course, she wasn't holding a gun. She had a stick.

"Liz!" she squealed. She looked over her shoulder toward a distant building. "Daddy! It's Liz! She's okay!"

Hank emerged from the darkened doorway of a restaurant. He was leaner than I remembered, hair mussed and a bit longer. His familiar scarred lip twitched in a smile the closer he came. "My god…" he said.

I let him come to me, grab hold of me, and my entire body gave into the hug. Where I normally would have the compulsion to cry being amongst other people again, people I knew, I was too tired to even comprehend what was happening. It was too good to be true.

"Are you real?" I whispered.

Hank nodded against me. "We are."

Evie had joined the hug, her laughter chasing up into the sky.

I'd finally become something more than myself, this lost creature in the wild world. I was part of a unit, something that filled in the holes I'd been traveling with since losing Brody. I finally wasn't alone.

Hank pulled away and I looked at our reflection in the store window. The three of us together. But there was something else there. Another figure.

I squinted.

In the truck window was another body, standing in the background watching from the shadows of the woods.

It didn't have a face.

Note From The Author

I hope you've enjoyed THE WILD DARK.

If you would be so kind, I'd love for you to share your review with others. Reviews are integral to indie authors. We rely on them so much. Thank you in advance.

ACKNOWLEDGEMENTS

The Wild Dark has been a labor of love. I started this book back in 2013 under the title "Cold Walls" with only a faint idea in mind: writing about a close friendship and love between two friends that defied death. It's taken a long time to bring this to fruition and I couldn't have done it without the help of a large support group of other writers, family, and friends.

Thank you to Brenna Davies for being stoked about this project and giving it a close eye with your developmental editing prowess. You were so instrumental in making this a reality.

Thank you to these lovely people for reading my book and providing their lovely early reviews: Morgan Sylvia, Cat Scully, John McIlveen, Renee DeCamilles, Janine Pipe, E.J. Fechenda, Wendy N. Wagner.

These folks also deserve some thanks: Bruce Coffin, Pan, Valerie, Emma J. Gibbon, Meg North, Heather Miller, and Heather (wonderfeather).

Thanks to my family and close friends for putting up with my reclusiveness and listening to me talk about the book non-stop. Thanks to my parents who don't quite understand my love of horror but support me nonetheless.

Thanks to my partner in crime, Colin, for letting me squirrel away in my office for hours on end. Thank you for liking and sharing my seemingly endless promotional material. Thanks for supplying me with coffee and dinner, treats, and necessary boosts in confidence as needed. You've been phenomenal. Thanks to Lemon Jelly, the cat, for not tearing the place down while I ignored you. Copious treats are coming your way.

STAY TUNED

FOR

THE WILD FALL

BOOK 2 OF THE WILD OBLIVION

COMING IN 2023

www.katherinesilvaauthor.com

ABOUT THE AUTHOR

Photo by Colin Borowske © 2021

Katherine Silva is a Maine author of dark fiction, a connoisseur of coffee, and victim of cat shenanigans. She is a two-time Maine Literary Award finalist for speculative fiction. Katherine is a member of the Horror Writers of Maine, the Maine Writers and Publishers Alliance, and New England Horror Writers Association. She is also founder of Strange Wilds Press and Dark Taiga Creative Writing Consultations. Find out more about Katherine at katherinesilvaauthor.com.